I0772222

RUNE TO RUIN

RUNE TO RUIN

SPEAR OF THE GODS
BOOK TWO

GREGORY AMATO

SED FERRO
PRESS

Published by Sed Ferro Press
Copyright © 2024

Cover design by James T. Egan of Bookfly Design
Illustration by Blane Bellerud
Edited by Sydney Taylor

Paperback ISBN: 979-8988061328
Hardcover ISBN: 979-8988061335

Published by Sed Ferro Press
3439 NE Sandy Blvd, #484
Portland, OR 97232

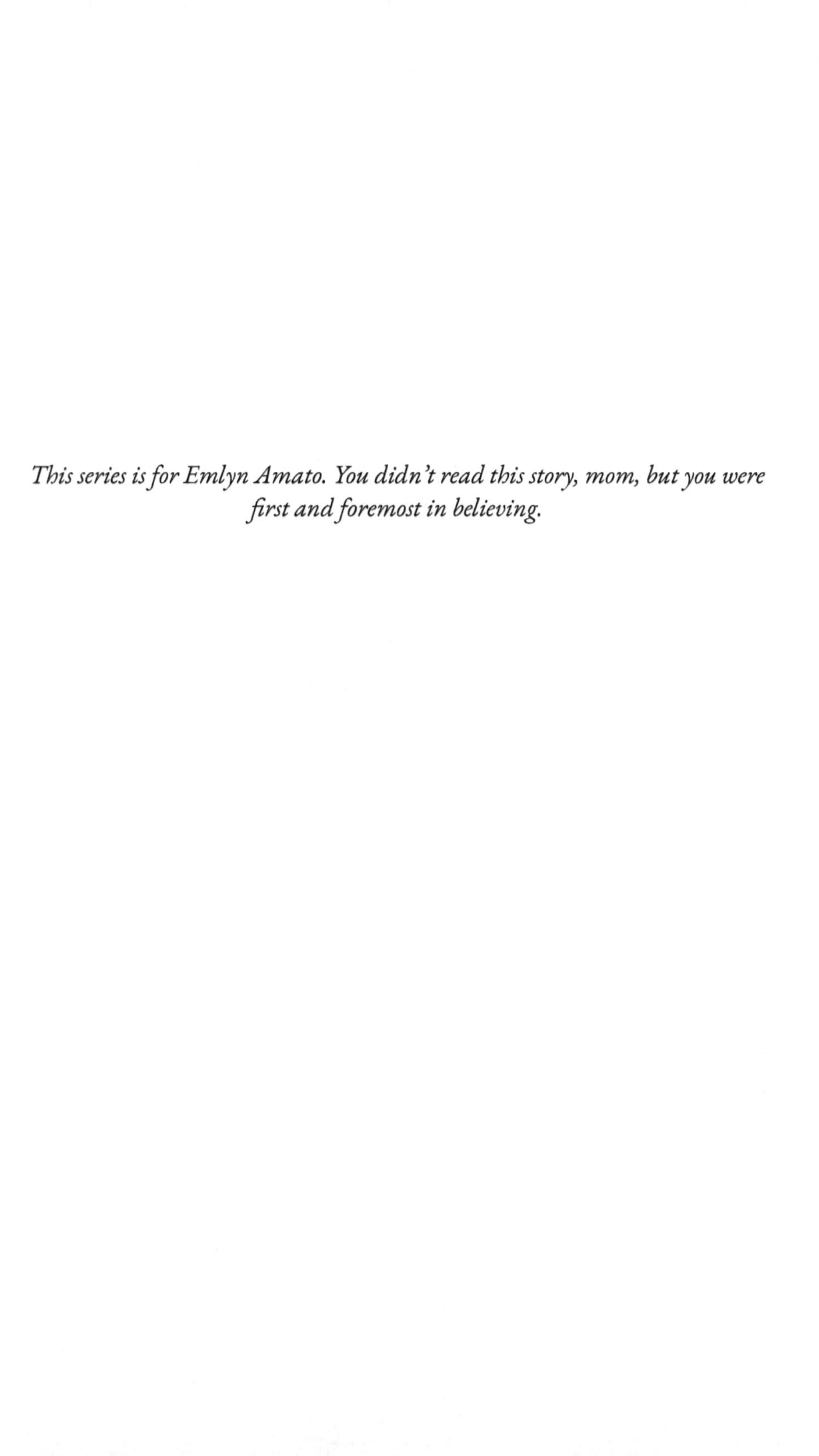

This series is for Emlyn Amato. You didn't read this story, mom, but you were first and foremost in believing.

Also By Gregory Amato

THE SPEAR OF THE GODS SAGA
Burden to Bear
Rune to Ruin
Fallen to Fury (forthcoming)

OTHER SPEAR OF THE GODS STORIES
Trollsbane
The Skald
The Sorcerer's Reward

STANDALONE STORIES
The Once and Future Sword

Contents

Author's Note		xi
Runes - The Elder Futhark (Pre-Viking Age Alphabet)		xv
The Story From Book One		xvii
1. On Rising at Night		1
2. The Dwarf's Errand		11
3. The Fylgja		19
4. Plans Without Plans		26
5. Rune		37
6. Scene of the Crime		49
7. The Stone Road		59
8. Down-Below		65
9. The Road to Myrkheim Is Not Paved		75
10. Dense Negotiations		81
11. Any Witch Way She Says		90
12. Sputum Democracy		97
13. Rewriting the Present		107
14. Getting a Head		114
15. A Wise Man's Heart Is Seldom Glad		120
16. Sun and Steel		130
17. A Song of Spring		139
18. Herding Cats		148
19. The Virtue of Revenge		155
20. Gifts and Repayment		165
21. The Dead Man's Pants		176
22. Mostly Harmless		183
23. Pawn Protection		188
24. That Roman Magic		195
25. Saxa Ex Machina		200
26. Blood Eagles Are Overrated		210
27. Harping On		220
28. The Queen in the Rock		231
29. The Courage to Look		238
30. No Fish Is an Island		247

31. A Short History of the End of the World   259

32. The Eternal Skald   263

33. Water Hazard   270

34. A Wise Man's Heart Seldom Glad, Again   278

35. The White Sea   283

36. Arrow-Odd's War   288

37. The Trouble With Peace and Quiet   299

38. A Troublesome Poet   311

39. Haldor's Story   316

40. The Solution to Idle Hands   323

41. Freely Offered   330

42. The Bridge to Hel   338

43. Ruin   341

44. The Man Who Would Be Prey   353

45. Upward Spiral   359

46. Brisingamen   365

47. The Wolf Inside the Door   372

48. Last Laugh   381

49. Heroes   395

50. Limited Hospitality   404

51. The White Sea, Stained Red   413

52. Not Again   421

53. The Raven-Haired Valkyrie   430

If you enjoyed this story   439

Coming Next in Spear of the Gods, Book Three: Fallen to Fury   440

About the Author   441

Acknowledgments   442

Major Characters   445

Glossary of Old Norse Words   449

Author's Note

Though Norse myths still predominate in *Rune to Ruin,* there are some Finnish myths involved in the story, too. Much as I've always loved the Norse myths, the stories that survive today don't include much adventuring by their chief skald, Bragi. It's the Finnish myths that have the more adventurous skald, even if they call Vainamoinen a bard instead.

The primary work of Finnish mythology I refer to is the *Kalevala,* or *Land of Heroes.* And sometimes, it is the work I take the most inspiration from as a writer. Why? Because *Kalevala* elevates the bard to the champion of mortals, the foremost hero, even the most powerful wizard.

Vainamoinen is not just the eternal bard of *Kalevala.* He's also its biggest badass. In today's world, where the idea of a bard is largely based on a weak Dungeons and Dragons character class, that might seem counterintuitive. It shouldn't be.

Recurring themes in the *Spear of the Gods Saga* include poetry and *drengskapr,* the Viking Age notion of being a bold person, or badass (*drengr*). In 2024, I think the notion of principled storyteller as hero is more important than ever. Today, the power of communication technology seems largely used to fight *against* unpleasant truths rather than to spread knowledge. It's easier to play to what an audience wants than to adhere to the true spirit of a thing that might be uncomfortable. And it gets more clicks, more views, more insipid updoots—all held up as measures of value, even if the message has none.

I think the skalds would shake their heads at that. Knowledge is more often painful than reassuring in the Norse myths. Just ask Odin about hanging on that tree. Real learning isn't easy or casual, or meant to validate beliefs already decided on.

I like Vainamoinen so much in part because he doesn't just tell stories about what he knows; he's willing to throw down over the truth of a thing. He doesn't preach about his ideals, he just lives them in the clearest possible ways, and that is part of his heroism. What is a person called who wanders, speaking the truth, telling stories, spreading wisdom, offering patience for the unknowing but wrath for those who spread denial and lies?

A bard. A skald. A *drengr*.

-Gregory Amato, 29 July 2024

NORSE
SWEDES
Uppsala
GOTLAND
Monastery
GEATS
JUTLAND
DANES
Roskilde
Lejre
SJAELLAND
FJON
BORNHOLM

FINNMARK
RISALAND
Island Tower
WHITE SEA
Arrow-Odd's Camp
SUOMI
LAKE AAINEN
KARELIA
LAKE LUADOGA
Lyngbakr
GULF OF SUOMI
Uppsala
EAST SEA
GARDARIKI
GOTLAND
Monastery

Runes - The Elder Futhark (Pre-Viking Age Alphabet)

Rune	Name	Ideographic Meaning
ᚠ	fehu	wealth; cattle
ᚢ	uruz	aurochs; strength
ᚦ	þurisaz	þurs, jǫtunn
ᚨ	ansuz	god
ᚱ	raiðo	ride, journey
ᚲ	kaunan	ulcer, blister, boil
ᚷ	gebo	gift
ᚹ	wunjo	joy
ᚺ	hagalaz	hail
ᚾ	nauðiz	need
ᛁ	isaz	ice
ᛃ	jera	harvest; good year
ᛈ	perðo	pear tree or game piece
ᛇ	eihaz	yew tree
ᛉ	algiz	moose or elk
ᛊ	sowilo	sun
ᛏ	tiwaz	the god Tyr
ᛒ	berkana	birch tree
ᛖ	ehwaz	horse
ᛗ	mannaz	human
ᛚ	laguz	water
ᛜ	ingwaz	the god Frey
ᛞ	dagaz	day
ᛟ	oþala	inheritance

The Story from Book One

Ansgar Styrgrimsson is a traveling poet and storyteller in the North—a skald.

Until about a year ago, his job was to deliver weapons for his foster-father. He knew how to pick his paths, how to run, ski, and climb faster and longer than others, and how to trade information with ravens and tell stories at mead halls to his benefit.

It was a simple job until one delivery went bad. Then Ansgar found himself needing more protection than expected, wishing he had more approval from his father than expected, and drinking more mead than he expected.

Blame it on the mead or not: He swore to join the crew of the *Sea Squirrel* that night.

The good news was he had found some excellent new friends in Haldor Skullsplitter and company. The bad news was they were a crew of monster hunters he had no business trying to prove himself with. Further bad news: Their last five skalds had all died horrible deaths soon after joining.

In the first few weeks of joining, Ansgar found out what seasickness was. Being pummeled, drugged, and even chased by the Midgard Serpent did not add to his confidence, and he felt like a burden to the crew.

But he also chanted for a powerful sorceress, traveled to Asgard to speak to the gods, and helped free a dwarf from bondage. That's enough to make a person bold.

He would need that boldness and a lot more as the crew traveled to aid the king of the Danes. Haldor's intent was to solve the king's troll problem right away, but the Danish court was a complicated place. Queen Alfhild was not so warm to the crew's presence. Also, she was a witch.

With the troll suspiciously hard to find, Ansgar did some wandering and made both friends and enemies. First among friends was the drunken wizard living in the forest nearby, who agreed to teach him the magic of the runes. Also a friend was the witch, Fanya, one of Alfhild's handmaidens. Maybe she could be more than a friend, he hoped.

Alfhild's mercenaries in the city: Definitely enemies. As for Alfhild herself, it was difficult to tell what she was up to. Especially after she tried to seduce Ansgar.

He never did figure that part out.

He did figure out the troll's location, though. Right in front of him, he realized, at a time he had no pants on. The troll gave chase, the skald was captured by Alfhild, and then things started to get weird.

Fanya, at least, helped him escape. Meanwhile Alfhild had the entire city of Lejre under attack. Trapped in a burning hall with his friends, Ansgar attempted what rune magic he knew to get them out. And failed.

Failed, but found himself turning into a giant polar bear. The Battle for Lejre was on, and it would take that giant bear, the turncoat witch, and the late appearance of a drunken wizard to stand against Alfhild's magic.

The dead rose to fight again, even Alfhild's dragon. Haldor's Heroes hacked them back down, but not without losing good friends in the process.

Ansgar barely survived. "Favored by Odin" they began to call him, and he earned his armring as one of Haldor's sworn men.

That's a lot of praise for one man, even if he still doubts himself now.

One thing he does not doubt: They will pursue Alfhild wherever she has fled to, and whatever the cost . . .

RUNE TO RUIN

Chapter 1

On Rising at Night

One night that winter in the Danish hills, I thought a witch had cast a spell to freeze my balls off. She hadn't. But in my defense, it was a reasonable belief at the time. I was feeling ill in body and mind before that happened, though, and those ill feelings are where I'll begin:

I sat bolt upright in the longhouse, sweat streaming down my face, thankful for the sounds of howling winds of the ice storm outside to mask my heavy breathing. The hearth fires crackled low, which made the place less smoky than usual but considerably less warm than my skinny bones preferred.

It was a sturdy hall, the kind that made you feel secure even when you were one wall away from icy death outside. Secure as those walls were, they were no defense against my own imagination.

Nightmares had come three times in a row. Had I cried out in my sleep this time? I hoped not and looked around to see if I'd woken anyone.

My crew slept undisturbed all around the longhouse on benches, under tables—wherever they could find space. They were more than a crew. Most of them were my Brothers now, all sworn to the same oaths and wearing the same armrings.

Haldor Skullsplitter lay resting against a wall, our leader on land leaving the rest of us space nearer to the hearth. His massive chest moved with each breath beneath a heavy wool blanket. His great axe, named Silence, lay propped against the wall beside him.

Kraki Bentleg, our leader at sea (good) and cook (terrible), never seemed to need a blanket. Or a shirt, for that matter. He sat in a corner, arms crossed, pale skin bright even in the low light of the hall. I did not worry about the old man. That sagging, pasty skin might not look like much, but I'd seen it shrug off blades and turn spears with little more than superficial wounds.

Svein, as big or bigger than Haldor, did not share the habit of sleeping in silence. He lay near the hearth fire, swaddled in wool, and snored like a boar in heat.

I hoped the noises from him and the wind had been enough to mask any sounds I might have made. And I thought it likely I'd made some unhappy sounds while asleep because I felt quite unwell. Indigestion accompanied the nightmares this time. I held one hand to my growling stomach. Sounds muttered back, not in my language yet unmistakable in their meaning.

I thought I heard a voice in my head whispering *go outside.* Soft, uncritical—a remnant of sleep, yet not of the nightmare, or else I might have been more hesitant to take the advice.

The land of the Danes was not some frozen Hel-scape. The winters here were usually mild compared to my mountainous home in the North-Way. The land of the Danes was mostly flat but for the hill the king's longhouse stood upon. This winter had been uncharacteristically harsh, though. Had I stayed inside that longhouse, my balls would have remained in a fully thawed state, if a bit chilly. But this night, the winds in my intestines competed with those outside for sheer ferocity.

The dead of such a winter gives a person two choices about where to take a shit: Inside, where it is cold, or outside, where it is teeth-shatteringly cold. I had some status that winter, having saved our crew during a heroic, if accidental, shape change. That shape was a giant polar bear—it was pure luck it hadn't been a marmot or a weasel or something else.

That change gave me the chance to charge through a flaming oak wall and save our crew, the sort of act that leaves an impression. That impression solidified when I tore half the enemy army's champions apart, eviscerated their giant boar demon, and broke their dragon's neck. I nearly killed our enemy, Queen Alfhild, too, but she'd disappeared at the last moment.

This was a better reputation to have than my previous one. As the ship's skald, I had been known for coming up with a good line of poetry or two, sure. When I wasn't vomiting over the side of our ship.

But I didn't have so much status that I had someone designated to deliver my defecations to the outdoors for me. And certainly not during this hour. *Only rise at night if you intend to spy on your enemies or relieve yourself,* went the wisdom of the time.

So I fastened my snow shoes and went outside to not spy on my enemies.

The ice storm I walked into gave me pause. I made my way not too far from the hall. Any farther, and the longhouse would have become invisible in the weather. Even holding the rope we used to ensured we could find our way back, I didn't want to stretch my luck. Keeping hold of a rope tethered to the longhouse while outside was one rule, as was not going beyond the rope to do your business.

I wasn't even at the end of the rope when I considered a hasty retreat, but that would mean yet another night of no sleep as my intestines played a long, slow song of lament until morning. I'd had enough of that and hoped some physical relief would give my mind a break. Those nightmares had been bothering me for weeks. Some nights were fine. Others, like the last few, showed me images I did not wish to relive.

Nightmares about seeing Fanya, the love of my life, holding her guts in with one hand while she held her spear high to cast a last spell. Nightmares of bringing a rock down on the head of a troll who called me "cousin" in his last moment. Whispers attacked me in my dreams. "Ansgar Kinslayer," they called me. The worst of the fear had subsided, but it still left me shaking.

I thought I heard the *go outside* voice again, but it was too soft for me to be sure. I was already outside, and I'd already concluded the voice was my own sleepy thoughts talking me through the thing I clearly needed to do: Go outside, do my business, come back inside, and hope for no more nightmares. That was my plan, a simple one under ordinary circumstances.

I held the rope tight as I squinted into the white darkness. The snow provided illumination, and at the same time, it shrouded everything behind it. How far I went out, I don't know—just far enough for good manners. It's important to angle your snowshoes out behind you at a time like that meanwhile hiking up some clothing and down other clothing. I like to think that winter improved my overall coordination. It also provided me a lesson in what being cold really was, a lesson that would serve me well later.

The wind picked up, and sky-shards pelted my privates. I soldiered on. In a moment of delicate balance, I held my cloak from billowing out around me and tried to perch in a position conducive to relief.

Fully relieved, I sidestepped and grabbed a handful of snow to clean myself. Relaxed and thinking I had finished the most difficult part, there was a sudden sensation like an icy hand rising through the snow and tugging on my sack.

Cold and fear shot through my body from the source up to my brain and leaked out of my ears. And I reached what seemed the only reasonable conclusion: Alfhild had reached through the ice storm with her magic, grabbed my balls, and literally frozen them off.

I flailed, looked down, and saw the snowball that had actually done the deed. Alfhild's evil hand still seemed a more likely explanation than anyone being out there and bulls-eyeing my manhood just for fun. And I still didn't see anyone who could have thrown the thing.

Shock and terror launched me into a defensive posture as I pivoted away from my attacker, wherever she was. Being knee-deep in snow isn't easy to do when you're wearing snowshoes, but the awkward steps I took in response to the attack put me in just such a position, my snowshoes sideways. I stood up in a whirl of windy powder, holding up my pants with one hand and drawing my seax with the other.

I saw nothing. No arm from the snow, no witch sneaking up behind me.

The wind flipped my cloak over my head. I stumbled and eventually fell. My pants were up at that point, at least. Once untangled, I managed to rise again.

Still nothing. Just cold and white and bleakness. In a panic that I had somehow been flanked during my ass-first trip down, I slashed behind me as I turned, ready to face the next deceptive attack.

The wind howled lower, like a sad wolf dying of ennui. The world was empty of all but ice and snow, as far as I knew. I felt an aloneness I had not felt before, as if most of Midgard had fallen away and just beyond the little bit I stood upon, there was nothing.

That thought was replaced by three others, all of which scared me far more: One, I could not see the hall anymore. Two, I could see none of my tracks in the snow. And three—and this one really made my skin crawl—I had lost the rope.

Had I died of testicular frostbite and was just confused? If so, this must be Hel. The Christians had their own version of this, but it was hot rather than cold for some reason and was meant for punishment rather than just being the realm of the dead. Christians were crazy, and this was definitely not their Hell. Was it Hel as I knew it?

Other than being cold, I knew a little of what to expect from the realm of the dead. Assuming I was dead, which seemed less and less likely. Where was the River Gjoll? Where was the bridge to cross it and the troll guarding said bridge? Maybe when you died, you had to *find* the River Gjoll and cross it.

My thoughts were interrupted by a woman's voice.

"You are standing on the rope."

The voice came from my right, and I whirled around. A lone figure stood there, just inside my ability to make it out and just outside my ability to discern any details. The air quieted and the temperature rose. The storm still raged—it was going around me, somehow. I could see the figure was a woman with a spear in one hand and a snowball in the other but little else.

"Fanya?" I asked.

The figure shook her head. No, not Fanya. Their spears were different—Fanya's was light enough to throw; this was a heavy war spear with wings under its point. The way she stood was different. Fanya had the posture of a hunter surviving in the forest. This woman stood taller, more regal in a form-fitting chain shirt, and with sleek, dark hair as opposed to Fanya's curly, fire-red hair.

I looked down, and I was indeed standing on the rope, the very end of it. It did not seem to me the rope would be part of the realm of the dead. I picked it up and held it tight, my last tether to safety. Maybe I would need a weapon to defend myself, but not yet. The woman with the spear could have killed me already had she wanted to. She pointed her spear, but not at me. She pointed away from the longhouse.

"Am I asleep then?" I said. "I don't understand."

"You have better eyes than that!" she said. "Use them!"

I squinted through the snow-blindness in her spear's direction and shrugged at first. Then I saw movement, a figure with a cape billowing in the wind. A sudden gust blew the hood from her head and whipped at her long hair. No one would choose to walk uphill in this storm to seek out the king's hall without great need. Mystery pulled me toward her, but any farther and I would lose my tether.

"So help her!" I shouted back to not-Fanya. "You stopped the weather here. Stop it out there."

She leaned on her spear and let her head fall in disappointment. "Oh, Ansgar," she said. "I cannot stop the weather. I only stopped your senses for a moment."

Cold wind struck my face like a hammer's blow, and ice threatened to freeze my eyes shut. I was freezing already and realized it only when the mysterious woman disappeared, robbing me of my false sense of comfort. Whoever she was, she had gotten my attention but had not made things any warmer.

Meanwhile, the storm had doubled its intensity. I stared ahead and picked out the wayward traveler. She trudged against the wind, making poor progress.

"Hey!" I yelled, one hand cupped to my mouth and one waving overhead. "Over here!"

She looked up and turned right, perhaps thinking to correct her course. But that would not correct her course. That would take her away from the longhouse, and she would be lost in the storm as it pounded her senseless. She slipped and broke a hard fall with her right arm while cradling something in her left. I could see her mouth move but heard nothing, and then I knew her.

That was Nanthild. And that meant she could not call back. I had heard her last scream from across the battlefield when her brother, Ulfberht, died in last summer's battle. She had not made a sound since. Nanthild the Frank earned a reputation for killing in that fight, but she was Nanthild the Silent in its aftermath.

The two young Franks had endured slavers and the harsh wilderness for years together until finding some shelter in the Danish king's hall. Ulfberht always said that Nanthild was the stronger of the two. Her brother's death had hardened her further, and in that hardening, there was no room for a voice anymore.

Tough as she might be, Nanthild would die in the cold if I stood around waiting. "Goat's breath and cat piss!" I yelled in the frustration of it all. I ran straight for her and hoped my decision wasn't about to doom us both. I went slowly to leave huge tracks for us to follow back. I would outwit the weather yet.

I was almost on top of her by the time she saw me. The storm was at the height of its fury by then, and I could hardly hear myself yell. The king's great hall in Lejre was known for its position perched high atop a hill in the center of the city. That made for a kingly impression, but it also left everything immediately around it without any windbreaks.

Why would Nanthild come up the hill instead of staying at the forge in the city below? Her usually hard eyes were soft when I found her, a combination of pain and fear and frustration. When I saw what she carried—who she carried—I understood.

Cradled in her left arm was a massive badger with black and silver stripes running down its face. Nanthild opened her cloak just enough for me to see. Her tunic bloomed red out from where she held the animal close to her body. The badger shut its eyes and swallowed hard. Blood dripped from the corner of its mouth.

Wordless as she was, Nanthild had told me enough. That was no badger —I knew the fur pattern on his face to match the beard of Finnr, the dwarf. He had done well in last summer's battle wearing this skin. Tonight, something had tried to gut him. Tried and maybe done it. No wonder the girl had raced up the hill in this weather. She needed a skilled healer, and one who knew dwarves.

No one but Huld would suffice. The old *vǫlva* knew a lot of mysterious lore. Maybe just as important, she was Finnr's friend. If Finnr could survive long enough for us to get him inside, Huld could see to him.

"We'll follow my tracks back to the hall." I damn near screamed that into her face and still barely heard it myself.

Nanthild nodded and closed her cloak around the injured dwarf-in-badger-form. I put my arm around Nanthild to guide her back the way I had come.

Only my tracks were gone. Again.

The wind had moved the snow and ice too fast for my feet to leave their mark. All my effort to kick divots heavy enough to follow backwards had been for nothing. And as simple as it should have been to turn around and go back in the direction I'd come from, the storm made it seem not so simple to choose that direction at all.

I turned back to Nanthild. She set her jaw and grasped my shoulder. I hoped she could not see the fear writ large on my face.

Nanthild urged me on, and on we staggered. A few steps forward, a pause, a few more steps, each one smaller than the one before. I guessed which way to go as best I could and cast about in the snow for that rope.

Then a gale came on so sudden and strong it blinded me and threw me back a step.

Only the Frank's free arm kept me from falling over. Nanthild the Silent was a lot stronger than she looked. The wind threw her back as well, strong as she was. The storm was getting fiercer as if it intended to deny us our destination. My hope was fleeing almost as fast as my tracks.

Guilt and fear of failure drove me forward. Fanya had died helping us win the battle. Died because she had decided to turn against Alfhild. To save me, but I had not been there for her. Now here were two more friends I would let down.

I kept going and lurched forward when the wind picked up. It prevented me taking a step back, but did not help much. We would not succeed against a storm this strong.

The voice of that armored woman cut through the wind. "There is more than weather against you," she said, her voice effortless against the screeching air.

"Where are you?" I shouted back just so I could hear myself. "Help us!"

"There is little I can do," she said. "Other than give good advice. Will you take it?"

"Yes!" Perhaps this was Alfhild in disguise, coming back to deceive me and freeze me to death. But I was already freezing, and I did not think Alfhild would have given me the opportunity to bring Nanthild and Finnr to safety. This woman's voice had a warmth the queen lacked. Contrarian as I was, I trusted her.

"Stop struggling in vain and speak a spell, then!"

When they say skalds compose poetry on the spot, the middle of a billowing ice storm is not the spot they mean. They mean a nice warm place near a rich jarl's central fire, surrounded by food and drink. And there may be some noise in the hall, but there is no deafening wind trying to kill the skald as he composes. But that was the spot I was in, and that was where I had to compose. Not in story verse, or the verse of proverbs, however. This was some powerful *seiðr* arrayed against us, and I would answer in *galdralag*, the meter of magical verse.

Difficult spots make for difficult composition, but one idea came to me, and then another for a counterspell. I thought of my friends who fell the night of that battle. Difficult composition is one thing, but anger can often find a verse quicker than calm. The verse came out like this, growling the first lines and with rising volume as it went:

> "Strange weather
>   whips the skald.
> Stumbling but steady he stays.
>
> Little poetry
>   provided to match
> A war of wits against the weary:
> A salvo the skald sings,
> A savior the skald sings,
> To Silence the skald sings!"

I knew I could not cut down Alfhild's *seiðr*. But I might cut *through* it. Maybe it would lessen the weather's power, or maybe it would reach Haldor himself, sleeping next to his axe, Silence.

For one clear moment, the weather's volume subsided. In that moment, I shouted Haldor's name with every bit of voice left in me.

Whatever controlled that wind did not like what I had done. Gusts assaulted me, alternating from both sides. With my left hand, I reached out to grab Nanthild's cloak as she grabbed mine, but my right was busy shielding my eyes from shards of ice.

I took a step and was thrown back over and over. The wind had redoubled against us. Flurries of ice and snow in the shape of wolves swirled and bit at our hands. A small gash appeared on my right hand where one nipped at me before dissolving back into white swirls.

Then we were being thrown back without even advancing anymore. We were overwhelmed. Hard as we pushed together, we would not make it many more steps, let alone enough to find the hall again. I grunted in effort and fell to one knee.

Nanthild's hand squeezed my shoulder. I took the gesture as her way of saying, "At least you tried." And I damn near started crying. Which, for a man of my people, would have been worse than dying. I bit my tongue to stave that off.

"Once more," I shouted. Better to die trying than to die not trying. I attempted again to rise against the wind. And I realized I couldn't.

I could not stand up because the behemoth Haldor Skullsplitter was standing over me, gathering Nanthild into his arms. He turned back into the gale, and I felt more than heard his rumbling voice. Meanwhile, I was tugged along by a presence just as welcome but with rather less warmth behind it.

"You can walk well enough, boy," barked Kraki. As gentle as Haldor was in cradling Nanthild and the injured Finnr, Kraki was not. Whatever *seiðr* had forced me down to my knees, the old man pulled me up and through it with a single yank on my cloak. That yank brought me upright, and I barely caught my forward momentum under my feet again. Then he was moving back to the hall, wisps of his white hair dancing in the light of the snow, dragging me through whatever resistance remained.

"The woman," I said, breathless as he pulled me. Perhaps thirty feet, a near infinite gap in that weather, was between us and the line of men stretching out from the longhouse door. Each one had a hand on the shoulder of the next one. The crew. Haldor's Brothers, of which I was one. Even the king and his champions had come out and lent their aid. The line could not extend to us all the way, though, so Haldor and Kraki had leaped into the white darkness to find us.

"Haldor has her," continued Kraki. "I did not notice her complaining about the cold." And he wouldn't because Nanthild was silent, which was exactly his joke. But he also wouldn't be listening to anyone complain about the cold. Like most other times, Kraki had come out to face the storm and whatever was in it without wearing a shirt.

"Not her," I stammered as Kraki marched on and I stumbled behind him past our crewmates. "The other. She helped. The . . . the valkyrie."

That turned a few heads. I had not meant to say it, but who was she? Not Alfhild, nothing malevolent. Perhaps a *dísir*, one of those spirits of dead women who walk at night. But her garb and her bearing indicated nothing of the sadness I would expect from such spirits. This woman was resplendent in her armor and held her spear as if it had been unbloodied too long. I didn't know what she was or if she was more than my imagination run wild. "Valkyrie" was the word that seemed most appropriate.

"Boy, I think the cold has gone to your head," said Kraki. "Get inside. Only two good reasons to go out on a night like this, and chasing women is not one of them."

CHAPTER 2

THE DWARF'S ERRAND

"WHAT WERE YOU DOING OUT THERE FOR SO LONG?" KRAKI asked once I was seated by the fire and clearly not dying of frostbite. "Licking some frost giant's balls?"

"Not at all," I replied through chattering teeth. "I didn't see your mother anywhere."

The warmth of the hall embraced me as I crossed the threshold. There was not so much fuel for fire that Hrolf could keep it toasty inside, but coming in from the ice and wind brought great relief. I stumbled in and fell to one of the benches nearest the hearth.

"Ha!" he laughed and slapped the side of my head. It was a decent hit and did me no favors, but this was as close as Kraki got to saying he liked you. That was one hard old man, if those words are even strong enough. "You are still delirious, boy."

Kraki grew up with Finnr's people, and Finnr was the only person I knew of who Kraki had called "friend." If the dwarf died, we would all take it badly, but none worse than Kraki. Hard as he was, I had no doubt yelling at me was a way of working off his own anxiety.

Further down the length of the hall, Haldor had, by himself, moved a heavy oak table next to the largest of the fires. Nanthild set Finnr down on the table. Huld was asking what had happened in a hushed tone, receiving only gestures toward the badger's wounds as responses.

My own anxiety returned with the warmth. I spread out numb fingers over the heat and remembered the gash on my right hand. Not wanting to bother anyone else, I asked for a bowl, water, and a clean bandage to bind the wound. I worked the bandage around my hand as the last of those who came to our aid returned.

King Hrolf was last in from the cold and held the door for my crewmate, Svein. It was not lost on me that the king would see himself in only after all others had taken shelter. That was the sort of man Hrolf was, seeing what needed to be done and doing it, regardless of how hard it was on him.

Svein waddled in with a smirk, as if the gesture meant his worth was as good as a king's or better. Being the biggest man on the crew of the *Sea Squirrel*, even bigger than Haldor, Svein seemed to think much of himself. I could not fault his fighting prowess, having seen the enemies he hewed with his axe or crushed under his boot. But Svein was lazy and fat, and so even though he was twenty years Haldor's junior, he did not have Haldor's agility or endurance.

"Lucky we were here to come and save you," said Svein.

"Yes, he is lucky, isn't he?" said King Hrolf. "Good to keep a lucky man around." The king strode back to his room behind the high seat.

The comment left Svein looking confused, but that was his normal expression.

Somewhere between the ice outside and the hearth fire in the center of the hall, I thought better of mentioning the woman again. I even questioned my memory of her. Maybe I had spied Nanthild because I have keen eyesight rather than because of some woman pointing with her spear. Perhaps the whole image was my mind creating the narrative for having seen Nanthild out there. Kraki's comment gave me leave to not mention her again.

Not all my crewmates were as apt as Kraki to knock me about in such a state. Most of them crowded around Nanthild and Huld. The *volva* waved her distaff over the injured badger in what appeared to be a gesture to ward off spirits seeking to enter him. That was my impression, at least, and the impression of the others. We were wrong.

"That means stop crowding here and clear out, fools!" shouted Huld. "You, short one," she said, pointing at Magnus as if she had forgotten his name. "You stay here and help. The rest of you, bugger off."

Dutifully buggering off, the brothers Innstein and Utstein held a quick council on what to do. Most others looked for some straw to sleep on or a comfortable corner. The excitement of the night was waning, and whatever Finnr's fate, it was best left in Huld's hands. The 'Steins never sat idle long, though, even at night. Soon, they were on to the next most exciting thing and sat on the bench next to me. Utstein had a bowl of hot stew in hand and Innstein a cup of ale.

"Lucky indeed you ran into Nanthild out there," said Utstein, handing me the bowl of stew.

"Incredible, in fact," added Innstein. "What are the odds one of us would be outside at the right time to see her?"

"Longer odds than I would take," said Utstein.

"You must be a lucky skald!" said Innstein, who took a drink, apparently forgetting who the ale was meant for. The silent judgment of his brother's shaking head reminded him, and Innstein stopped to wipe his beard before offering the cup to me.

I took it with a grin. The brothers were good-humored shipwrights and chronic gamblers. When Innstein mentioned odds, it meant he had actually calculated them and considered laying down a bet to see if anyone would take it. Their company comforted me as much as the stew and ale they offered. Much of the hall was quiet by then, and so we spoke in hushed voices while others wound down in their own ways. I needed little sleep to begin with and was still shaken, unlikely to fall asleep again that night.

Blood-stained Nanthild stood against a pillar, watching Huld weave her spells in between demands for herbs and unguents from Magnus. One assistant was enough; two would be a crowd, and Magnus was both fast and reliable. Nanthild was no more likely to sleep that night than I was, though.

Since the death of her brother Ulfberht, she had taken his place as Finnr's assistant at the forge. They had a small shelter right next to the forge, and both she and the dwarf preferred to stay there rather than the king's hall. It seemed the best thing for her, hammering out her pain into steel.

"There's no benefit to staying awake all night worrying," said Innstein. I thought he spoke to me, but I saw it was Nanthild he addressed.

"You'll just be tired in the morning and have the same problems," added Utstein.

Those two were much like the rest of the crew in being third or later sons, unlikely to inherit much. But unlike those other sons, they were considered accidental, unnecessary, or worse by their father. Most of the other crewmen had left to go seek their fame with at least some support.

Innstein and Utstein had barely survived their father's attention. They then survived in the wilderness by relying on each other in their early years. That probably explained how they finished each other's thoughts. I wondered how often they had gone to sleep with some mortal threat hanging over them —hunger, predators, slavers—because there was no point in worrying.

Nanthild glowered back at the two.

"We share your concern," said Innstein.

"Come share our company, and it will ease the burden," said Utstein.

"We'll share some ale as well. In fact, why are we sitting here with no drinks?" concluded Innstein. He checked my cup, saw it was empty, and snatched it away. "More where this came from." Both brothers rose and went to find three more cups.

With some hesitation, Nanthild detached her stiff back from the pillar and came to sit by me. She would not take any stew but nodded that she would share in the offered ale. Even brightened a bit. Among the morbid conventional wisdom of the time, they said the best way to overcome one tragedy was to suffer a worse one. It might be true, but sharing a cup of ale with friends seemed like a better salve to me.

There was one brief, quiet moment when Nanthild sat by the fire with me and I could speak with no one else hearing. I was uncertain about mentioning it, even to my silent friend. I was uncertain about what I'd seen. This seemed the best time to bring it up, and she was the safest person to ask. So I took the opportunity and whispered to her, "Did you see anyone else out there?"

Nanthild returned my gaze, her expression unchanged, but neither nodded nor shook her head. I took this as a bad sign. Had I really seen the woman, and had she pointed the way for me? Was she out there, some spirit showing me favor, or was she just in my head? Nanthild hadn't even been able to see me in that storm. Still, I did not want to ask around after seeing the look on Kraki's face when I mentioned a valkyrie.

If the woman was just my imagination, it would be better not to mention her again. With no answer from Nanthild, that was the course I decided on. I was even more thankful when the brothers returned with ale for us all.

"You see what did it?" Utstein asked Nanthild, a thumb hooked back in Finnr's direction.

Nanthild shook her head, and the brothers exchanged looks.

"Where was he?" asked Innstein.

Nanthild stared at the two, uncertain. I thought she meant to say she did not know, but then she pointed at the floor.

"He went Down-Below?" said Utstein.

Nanthild nodded. Somehow, those two could speak to the young woman as if she were speaking back to them.

"Back to Nidavellir?" I asked.

The Down-Below, or those realms beneath Midgard, were not places with definite locations. Not like a mountain you could find. They were sort of places, and, as you reached Niflheim, sort of states of being. All vaguely underground and inhabited by *vættir* and other things rarely seen in Midgard.

If humans were from the realm of Midgard, dwarves were from the realm of Nidavellir. Which was definitely under Midgard. Sort of. And not as far under as Niflheim. Sort of.

And definitely not as far down as the River Gjoll, beyond which was Hel, the realm of the dead. Maybe that part was just a story, though.

"What are you all on about?" demanded Kraki. The old man had been out of sight since just about the time he dragged me back into the hall. He reappeared out of nowhere, hand resting on the head of the bone club tucked into his belt.

"Wondering what Finnr was doing in the Down-Below," I said.

"Gathering intelligence," he replied, emotionless.

"How did you know—"

"Not all things happen with your knowledge, boy. Those things in the rafters last summer," he waved up at the ceiling, "those little shit trolls, we've fought them before, he and I. But why they would fight for Alfhild was a mystery. So he took the Stone Road and went down to find out what he could."

"Those little shit trolls" were short, with sharp teeth and crude but sharp stone weapons. When Kraki said "little shit trolls," the little part was literal, the shit part was there to indicate he had no respect for them even as enemies, and the trolls part as a recognition they were some sort of *vættir*.

He could have just called them "trolls," but he was Kraki, and he did as he liked.

Any supernatural, malevolent being was a troll. Just about anyone you didn't like was a troll, too, if you were using the term loosely. These were small, they were ugly, and their skin was a pale green. In your language, you would probably call them goblins. So goblins they will be.

"I thought that was where his people lived. Wouldn't he be safe there? How far down did he go? Is that where Alfhild went?"

Deep in the Down-Below is not a place humans go. But a very uppity dwarf, if he was known to wander far and wide, might travel to even the dangerous spots there. I could imagine Finnr walking right up to the bridge across the River Gjoll and asking its guardian if she had anything interesting to trade.

Maybe he had done that. And maybe she had knifed him.

"We both lived in Nidavellir, same as you live in Midgard right now. You safe here?" demanded Kraki.

Which was a fair point, all the monsters living Down-Below aside.

"I don't recall any goblins in the main battle," said Utstein.

"Thought they all fled after teeth and claws here had his skin change and stomped their master to death," added Innstein.

"I didn't really stomp her," I said, a little uncomfortable. "I just jumped. And I landed, and . . . it happened that I landed on Valborg's chest."

"Oh, that's not stomping at all, then," said Innstein.

"We stand corrected," added Utstein.

Nanthild pointed to the hearth fire, then to the walls around us and up to the ceiling.

"Exactly," said Innstein.

"What?" I asked, not as gifted with understanding her as the two brothers appeared to be.

"She was reminding you," said Utstein, "that Valborg set the old hall on fire. Tried to burn us all to death. I think she's implying: You did a good thing by stomping her to death, so don't sound sad about it."

Nanthild clinked her cup against those of both brothers and drank.

The memory of being the bear was choppy but not hazy. Maybe episodic was a better word. That initial breakout from the hall was the beginning. A bunch of little shit trolls—I mean goblins—broke in through the roof of the longhouse while the witch, Valborg, blocked our exit and set the place on fire from the outside. The goblins pelted us with poison-tipped weapons while we tried to break out of the place. I did break out, in bear form, and landed on the witch in the same leap.

She must have died quickly because I remember feeling her ribcage implode. We never did find her body, though.

"She stayed loyal to Alfhild, unlike Fanya," I said. "The goblins must have grabbed her body before they ran for some reason. Maybe she was in command of them. What do we care about them now for? Valborg is dead, she's not about to lead them here again."

"We don't," spat Kraki. "But come the spring thaw, we are going after Alfhild, and it will be better to know how she recruited them."

I stole a look at Huld. She had dismissed Magnus but was continuing her work. I couldn't tell if that was a good sign or a bad one for Finnr. It was one thing to be far from friends and one thing to take a bad wound. But that wound, far from anyone he knew, was enough to spill a man's life out.

I shuddered as that thought brought back the memory of Leif's final moments. Alfhild literally spilled his life out in front of us and used his sacrifice for her spells. Almost won that way, too. But she lost in the end. Leif was not yet a Brother, but he was a good crewmate. And to kill a crewmate in such a way—neither Kraki nor Haldor would forget it.

We would find her and kill her, even if it was the last voyage of the *Sea Squirrel.*

Now Finnr had crawled through who knew what just to find out more information. Maybe spending his life to do it. And it was for us, for the rest of us sleeping in the hall's warmth. So that we would not end up hanging upside-down with our throats slit, lifeblood draining down to power some witch's spell like Leif had.

My annoyance at being left out of the loop evaporated at the thought of my friend's boldness on our behalf. "To Finnr," I said. "That is one *drengr* of a dwarf."

We all drank deeply. There was little more to say, and soon the brothers reiterated their advice: No point in staying up all night worrying; go to sleep and rest up for the next day. Easier to seek vengeance when you're not so tired.

Nanthild was grudging about it but drained her cup and nodded her assent.

She found herself a spot alone by a pillar. Innstein and Utstein preferred to sleep under tables. I needed little sleep and so rarely found myself in the same spot two nights in a row, but even I was tired. I was looking for a suitable place myself when one more conversation demanded my attention.

"To Finnr," said Magnus from behind me, "and to Lucky Ansgar!" The fire-haired warrior was a head taller than me as long as I stayed sitting down. Despite his short stature, Magnus was among the most dangerous fighters on the crew. Not a year before, I had seen him kill eleven *berserkir* by himself, one after another. He was a gifted heckler of my poetry and a brilliant troublemaker, too.

"How is he?" I asked.

Magnus took a drink and shrugged. "His wounds are not too deep, but the bleeding was the thing," he said. "First step was to see if he could get back into his regular skin, which he did. Huld says she has handled worse. Last summer, in fact, when someone I know turned into a bear and let himself be stabbed, slashed, and bitten about a thousand times. Now that was a challenge."

I nodded and blushed a little, thankful for the low light. If not for Huld, I would certainly have died of my wounds last summer. When I woke up to all those broken bones, bruises, and gashes, part of me had wanted to die anyway, but there was nothing she could do about that. "No sense in waking up to greet him bleary-eyed and fatigued then," I said.

"Oh, but he might want to know more about that other detail," said Magnus, grinning from ear to ear. He dropped his voice even lower and whispered in a conspiratorial tone, "You know. The valkyrie."

I counted Magnus as my closest friend, but he could be a real fly in a forge sometimes. "All right. I can't keep anything from you, so I might as well tell you. But not here or now. Even I need to sleep." It was a brilliant delaying tactic, I thought. Even partly true as far as needing to sleep.

"Haha!" Magnus whispered. "Finnr went below looking for enemies, and here Lucky Ansgar has found a friend! I knew there was a reason we kept you around. Come the spring, that witch won't stand a chance."

CHAPTER 3

THE FYLGJA

IT WAS A SOBER MORNING BEFORE DAWN BROKE THE NEXT DAY, as if the weather had reached the end of its drunken revelry and finally passed out for a while. The wind no longer howled and ice did not pelt the long-house. When I woke early, it was to silence. Or relative silence. Svein's snoring continued as loud as ever.

The night's events were still a series of puzzles, so I lay still with my eyes open, turning things over in my mind. That got me nowhere, so I sat up and looked out over my crewmates and the king's other guests for a while before knowing what to do with myself. I watched, and seeing neither Magnus nor anyone else was awake, my eyes turned upward to the high walls and pillars.

Words are what I use to tell stories, but they are not the only way to tell them. Innstein and Utstein were not just expert shipwrights but also great woodcarvers, and they had decorated the place fit for King Hrolf with their own mode of telling a story. I stared at their carvings, transfixed.

They had carved into crossbeams and along the walls to tell the story of the Battle of Lejre. Looping creatures with giant heads wove their way around the building. They gave way to a ship full of warriors under a bright sun. Men fought amongst one another until the moon rose, bringing more beasts than the carving began with. Dozens of them lashed out with tendrils towards a high hall surrounded by flames.

There, the carvings broke off on the wall I had crashed through. Flames were carved there before the next series of images. On the other side of the flames, the depiction continued.

A giant bear and a giant man holding an axe. A horseman with a great spear. A long-bearded king holding a heavy sword. The monsters fell back out of sight. Then the heroes were depicted again, only with tendrils coming up from beneath them, growing and growing, until it showed a bowman with a beard down to his knees. Behind him, a lone figure with long braids held her spear high, its tip touching lightning strikes that shot down the entire height of the wall.

Tall and powerful was how I remembered Fanya. That and being one of very few people who could successfully sneak up on me. She could cast a mean spell—calling the wind was one thing I saw her do—but her last spell was to call the lightning. Nothing so dramatic as to strike down our enemies, as I'm not sure any sorcerer could do that. But she brought a storm to light the sky, and the sky lit the way to Alfhild.

Those brothers knew how to make a memorial. Fanya would have liked this depiction. But she would not have liked to see me sitting around the hall moping. The weather was clear, and I would not be missed—for a little while, at least. So I decided to go and sit out for a while.

Fanya had called it *útiseta*, sitting out. My foster mother, Taika, said it could be done to summon spirits, but Fanya showed me how to use it to quiet my mind. And in quieting my mind, I could see and hear even farther than before. Not just sights and sounds; it was a way to notice things, a way to see deeper.

As I made my way out of the hall, I came close to Innstein and Utstein. They were under a table each, still as stones and barely breathing to my eye. Light sleepers, but I snuck by them.

By the door was Beigadh, one of Hrolf's champions. Beigadh the Bold, they called him now, and with good reason. He slept sitting against the wall, shield resting on his legs and covering him up to his mouth. The only sign of sleep I could see was the occasional flicker of a few mustache whiskers.

On I crept, thinking of the door's heavy latch and the sound it might make as I lifted it. But there was not a sound. I lifted the thing and palmed the door just to test it.

Then I nearly jumped out of my skin.

Beigadh's eyes were open wide and staring at me. He made no move to turn his head or move his shield. Only his eyes tracked me.

"Hmmmmm," he growled, lower than a whisper, louder than a shout.

I put one finger to my lips and gestured at the sleeping men and women in the longhouse as if he should be more careful not to wake them. His eyes never left me, but he grinned at that and let me go about my business.

Out I went into the cold and dark of early morning. The sun had only just begun to color the sky. The white of the snow and ice covering everything magnified the tiny amount of light. I would not go far from the hall this time. It was enough to be outside and see the sky. As long as I was alone.

The privacy would be important, so I made my way around to the other side of the longhouse. I wiped away the snow from one of the splitting stumps under the eaves and sat down.

There was not much to sitting out. Be outside. Sit down. Shut up. Try to keep from going insane when your imagination blooms a garden of fear and paranoia. Hope the thoughts it leaves you with by the end are worthwhile. That is what I did the last time, the way Fanya showed me. The goal had been worth the journey. For all my crazy imaginings, I had come around to some sort of brief peace. I had already been enamored of that woman, but that had been the first time I felt I could trust her.

I sat out for a few minutes and focused on my breathing again. Trust. Who else did I trust? My Brothers. Or most of them. Not all to the same extent. Magnus, most of all. He was my opposite in many ways, the best possible bad influence on me. But he was cheery and appreciative despite all the differences, and I knew I could rely on him. Those thoughts cheered me. Magnus was inside, though, and the questions I had, he could not help me answer.

"How did I become the bear?" I whispered. "Why couldn't I do that in the storm?" I shook my head, unsure who I was asking other than myself. An unfocused idea, not likely to get me anywhere. "Fanya, I need your wisdom," I whispered, imagining her with my eyes closed. Deep breath in, deep breath out. "Perhaps I could speak to you even if you cannot speak back."

"You could use Nanthild for that," said the woman.

Her voice was the same as it had been in the snowstorm. I opened my eyes, and her outline was the same as well. I could see her clearly this time. It was much the same regal impression—the way she stood with one hand on her hip, the way she held her spear, the way she smiled in full battle garb. That woman wore heavier mail than Gudbrand Shirtless, and I think he never wore less than a full mail shirt, even when bathing. Bright gray eyes glinted diamond-like from within a socketed helm. Her hair was raven black, the blue sheen showing and disappearing as she moved through the very beginnings of morning light.

"Are you in my head?" I asked.

"If I was not in your head, how would I be standing right here?"

Some answer, that.

"I have had enough excitement and worry for some time," I countered. "Clarity would be more welcome. Are you a valkyrie? Or some *dísir* from ancient times, a spirit attached to this land?"

"I could be a *hamingja*, your luck personified."

"I don't think my luck would carry a spear."

"I think I know something about the luck you need, and it definitely needs a spear!" she laughed. "Maybe some friends with axes, too."

"I have those already."

"And yet you still just about got yourself killed last summer. I am not a luck-spirit, though, nothing so flighty."

"What then?"

She shook her head in a matronly manner, as if observing a child misbehaving, but instantly forgiving me for making her laugh. "Call me Svipul. You are lucky, and luckier still that I am here to follow you."

"Follow me? Oh shit, am I about to die?!" And for a brief moment, I really thought I might. Her tone had been reassuring, but her statement had not.

A *follower*? A man might have a *fylgja*, his follower guardian spirit, and never see it—until the end of his life, when seeing it would be a sign of impending death. I had both heard of them and told tales of them but never took that idea too seriously. After all, I wasn't trying to see mine.

"Someday," she said. "But if I were a portent of death, would you have survived the storm? You forget your own lore! A dying person may see their *fylgja*, but it will more likely be in animal form. Do you know what animal you might see? Because I am a woman, not an animal. And you should believe that I am here trying to help you not die so soon."

This was a lot to take in. Even if I accepted her statements at face value, I still did not know the implications. "Is it likely I will die soon without your help?" I asked, unsure where else to go with the conversation.

"Very much so."

I waited for more, but none came. "You are rather morbid and cryptic for a *fylgja*."

"Not that you would know, but I will not deny either point. And you are welcome."

"Thanks . . . um . . . yes. Thank you for helping me find Nanthild. Will you keep helping me? I mean, will you be here or somewhere else?"

"I will be with you. But you will not always see or hear me."

"And others?"

"Will not see, will not hear."

"A man experiencing such might think he has lost his sanity rather than gained a *fylgja*."

"Some men might. Some men might spend their mornings obsessing over how others view them. Perhaps about whether someone has made a comment that might be considered an insult and how to avenge every small thing that is said without sufficient respect. Are you such a man?"

"I think I spent this morning being sad and wondering how I turned into a bear."

"I have known sadness of the like. It is part of living fully. A burden all but the most timid bear."

"Is Fanya one of the *dísir* now?"

"People die. And dying, they end."

"What are the *dísir* then, and what are the gods? What are the *landvættir* and *draugar*? Are ravens really the spirits of dead skalds? It seems to me there's not such an end as you say, at least sometimes."

"It is not so simple. But you should know how a person lives on after death—you remember them. You make new memories of those who are no longer here and spread their stories. You create images in the minds of the living. What are the gods if not those memories melded together?"

"I don't know, but I wouldn't trust them. And I think ideas are lovely, but I don't think they inhabit the forests or threaten to sneak into me through an open orifice as Huld warned me they might."

"Well," she said, shouldering her spear. "You know it is complicated, then, don't you? As to changing your skin last summer—you cut open your hand to let it in."

My hand. I had tried to cast a spell and failed, bleeding onto the wrong side of the wooden disc. The cut—that was the opening the spirit used.

Huld had warned me once to pucker up my asshole because "they have ways of getting in." I was not expecting that.

"That explains the way in but not the spell. The spell was a failure."

"Your carving was a failure. You cast a different spell. A powerful one. Turned your every fiber toward it with no other thought. That is how it found you and why you were still there, the skald still able to whisper ideas to the bear."

I stared at her and blinked, wondering what she was talking about, if not the carving. "I spoke no verse."

She shrugged. "There is power in verse form, but sometimes a single word can have power. As long as the will is focused on nothing else, not even on living. You said '*No*' with your will behind it. Something heard you, something bent on your same will, and it entered you."

"Was that spirit you?"

She laughed at that. "That may have been when I heard your call."

That was one furious spirit then, despite her lighthearted manner now.

"But a spirit riding you never stays for very long. Even with your *vǫlva*. Who is a strong one, by the way."

"She reveals very little. Can you tell me anything else about her?"

"Such questions are better left to her, and I think you've learned enough for one morning." She turned then, toward the dawning sun, and walked into the light.

I blinked, and then she was gone. No more evidence of her than of a light breeze. I sprang up to look where she had stood. No tracks.

The rays of sunlight shone through the tree line from the southeast, lighting the white-covered landscape in a soft orange glow. Mist from my breath made long clouds in the air that disappeared as readily as my *fylgja* had, if that was who she was. If anything was as simple as it seemed.

"Goat's breath and cat piss!" I shouted.

From atop the hill, there was no echo. I was staring down at the city below and beyond it to frosted fields and snowcapped forests. I woke up some sleepy residents, perhaps, but I cared little at that point. Dawn meant time to rise, especially for those of us in the king's hall. There was plenty of work to do in the winter. Perhaps I would find some and throw myself into it before I brooded overmuch on recent events.

The slow crunch of snow and ice drew my attention. The pace was that of a man trying to make it seem he was walking quietly even though he knew full well he was not. He was actually trying to walk with some noise so as to avoid surprising the person he came upon, which could be awkward for both of them.

Magnus poked his head around the corner of the longhouse, his wavy red locks lit even brighter by the morning sun. He shuffled toward me, gazing out at the landscape as he did.

"That's what Fanya said," said Magnus. "'Goat's breath and cat piss.' A good expression for modern times."

I stared at him for a good, long, awkward while, not knowing what to say. "Is that everything you heard?" I asked.

"Was there something else to hear?" He was not humoring me. He had heard nothing.

"You didn't see a mail-clad woman carrying a spear? Hear a woman's voice telling about how I changed my skin into a bear's?"

Magnus squinted at me in disbelief. Then he changed his expression as if to indicate recognition. "I see women holding my spear often, don't you? As for the bear, I thought you were favored by Odin. Of course, that would be unlucky, and you are a lucky skald. So maybe not?"

I sighed and shook my head. "Come over here and sit down," I said. "It is complicated."

CHAPTER 4

PLANS WITHOUT PLANS

AN HOUR OF QUESTIONS, EXPLANATIONS, AND WISECRACKS later, it seemed my burden was somewhat lighter for having shared it. Only when conversation on the subject appeared completely exhausted did we head back into the longhouse.

"I was wondering about the bear thing," said Magnus as we walked. "We all were. Not happening again? Innstein won't be happy about losing his wager."

"He bet I would turn into a bear again?"

"Of course he did! He likes the long odds as you should well know by now. I think he had his brother up to something like five hundred to one that you would do it again by next winter. They both came to me for my opinion. I told Utstein he should give whatever odds Innstein wanted because it was unlikely to happen. And that if it did, we would all probably die this time, so he wouldn't have to pay. I told Innstein he should pump the odds as much as he could because if you turned into a bear again, it would only be to save us all from disaster, and then, as Utstein would just be glad to still be alive, he'd happily pay."

"Wait, I can guess the rest: You offered both of them this advice but said you wanted a percentage of the win."

"Only one in ten pieces!" said Magnus, taken aback. "That's a bargain for such good advice!"

I shook my head but could not stop smiling. Incorrigible as Magnus was, it raised my spirits to be around him.

Beigadh greeted us and held the door as we approached. The main entrance was his home as of late, and finally the weather permitted him to be outside again. A dozen weapons or more were already piled under the cover of the hall's long eaves, but we would not add to them. Leaving weapons at the entrance was protocol for other visitors, and clearly, more than a few had made their way up to see the king while Magnus and I talked.

"It seems to be a great exaggeration," Beigadh said as we passed.

"What does?" Magnus asked.

"The situation your friend describes," Beigadh continued. "I could hear him even with the door closed. I think if there had been people carried off or eaten, I would have heard of it. All I heard of was barley stores being lower than they ought to be."

"Food disappearing is a serious issue," I said. "But what is this about people carried off?"

Beigadh shrugged and pointed further into the hall. "Listen for yourself. Your friend mentioned it. The one who likes to talk."

Normally, that would be me or Magnus. Being he did not mean me or Magnus, there was only one among our crew I thought it might be. That was Ulf, the crew's *þulr*, our main diplomat and negotiator.

Visitors and strange news were both interesting. I thanked Beigadh for holding the door, recalling Svein's lack of manners with the king and trying to somehow compensate for them.

Beigadh grinned as the door shut behind us. I looked ahead to a throng of people crowded farther down the hall. Servants moved around merchants and farmers, freeholders and would-be warriors. They worked quickly to stir pots for porridge and the day's stew, feed the fire, and keep the place clean.

Those servants were thralls no longer. When King Hrolf had offered rewards, Kraki just shook his head and told him he didn't like men who kept thralls, however good he claimed to treat them. Hrolf, as a sane man, didn't want to have conflict with Kraki. But a king couldn't be seen as taking orders, and so he made no response.

But I noticed that Hrolf had made a point of ordering the thralls to Roskilde to do a lot of fishing. He had to know that this would take them right by the *Sea Squirrel*, which was beached nearby. He equally had to know that Kraki considered anyone who boarded the ship to be no longer a thrall, regardless of anyone else's opinion on the matter.

So it happened that Kraki led all the thralls to his ship, had them lay hands on its hull (which I suppose was good enough), and pronounced them all free.

When Kraki came back to Lejre to tell Hrolf this had happened, the king acted very surprised. "Well, it seems I've been outwitted then," he lied, as just about everyone around understood. Then he told the freed men and women they could stay or go as they pleased. He added that he needed workers and servants, and offered a wage for any who stayed to help rebuild his longhouse and his city.

Most stayed, as Hrolf had been well-liked for some time. The wage was a low one, but it was a wage. In that way, Hrolf kept the crazy old captain satisfied, got what he needed, and did it all looking like he'd respected an oath rather than bowed to a demand.

Now, King Hrolf sat hunched forward on his high seat, elbows on his knees, a look of distinct dissatisfaction on his face. If only the rest of his problems as king were as easy to fix as offering some silver for labor, he would have perhaps looked happier.

The king's other champion, Hromund, stood just behind the king in silence. The kind of silence you get not so much from a mountain as from a mountain that might have an avalanche at any moment. There was no immediate cause for concern about the king's safety, but Beigadh the Bold had a thing about entrances now and Hromund the Hard had a thing about not letting the king out of his sight.

Those two champions did not have their names by chance. As a consequence, those near the door or the king had polite manners indeed.

Ulf did not lack manners. He was quite the skilled charmer, in fact, and knew how to speak and act to get things done. Ulf had a way with words and so did I, but those ways did not have much in common. He was the ship's translator before my time on the *Sea Squirrel* and might be the most important man on the crew after Kraki and Haldor. He might still translate for us, but I knew more languages and knew them better than he did. He offered more advice now as Haldor's closest advisor, Kari Swifthand, had fallen in last year's battle.

I started to hear what Beigadh meant as I approached the semicircle gathered in front of the king's seat.

"We must act now!" Ulf implored. "Was not enough blood spilled last summer? Now we endure the enemy breaching our walls at will. We must seek these things out and destroy them. If not for our safety, then for the safety of the city folk below us."

Ulf was in his element, using words to bend men to his purposes, and I think he had disliked sharing that ability with a young, halfway-competent (in his mind) skald. We were a proud people, and even then I understood how Ulf would resist being replaced or having his importance as the previous translator lessened. Even so, it was an absurd fear. Though we were both translators and speakers, his art and mine were nothing alike.

There is a magic in the poetic meters, even those not specific to casting spells. And that is where I ply my trade. But there is other magic to be used with words, if only you know your words very well and perhaps your audience. Ulf knew persuasion, even if (especially if) it involved making up reasons men should be persuaded. It was different from my art of describing, chronicling, entertaining.

"Murderers! Monsters!"

And despite being the entertainer, it seemed to me Ulf had the more dramatic art between us.

"Hemming, tell what you found!"

"Goblins," said Hemming.

(Well, you know what I mean.)

The crew of the *Sea Squirrel* was comprised entirely of stout fighters and tough men, but for two exceptions. I was one. Our tracker, Hemming, was the other. Gaunt as Kraki was, Hemming was so bone-skinny he made the old man look well-fed by comparison. The man was brilliant at woodcraft, though, even better at hiding than me. If you needed to hunt something, Hemming was your man.

He was not the most popular at the banquet table, however. Smelled like cat piss most of the time. A patchy beard did not help his looks, and he looked as if he would vomit or cry out at any moment when the press of people was too great. Hemming did not like cities and slept indoors only when necessary.

"And some of those in the city have disappeared?" I asked. "Who is gone? I heard only some grain had gone missing."

A plain man in plain clothing stepped forward. Ingolf's looks belied his even temper, and this would be no exception. "It's true some grain was stolen from our stores," he said. And he would know since he had calculated and apportioned out food in limited supply. Hrolf wanted as much as could be distributed safely to the others in Lejre, as they had suffered no less than the inhabitants of his hall. Ingolf was the man he trusted to do that. "About a week's worth for those of us staying here, by my estimate. We have more than enough for the rest of winter. For now."

"Perhaps for now," said Ulf. "But how much more can we afford to lose?"

"It seems Ingolf knows the answers to such questions," I said.

"Ansgar, it is good to see you healthy!" said Ulf, opening his hands wide to emphasize my first nickname. I was Healthy Ansgar just for throwing up over the side of the *Sea Squirrel* a few times and thought I had shaken it. "I was not aware you had recovered. Perhaps you might prepare some of that good luck you have in such quantity."

There were some chuckles at that—few from our crew but some from the less familiar warriors who had flocked to the king's new hall. After word got out that the Lejre's troll was no more, people had come back to the city. I knew better than most since it was I who told every raven I could find to get that word out.

Got a few good stories out of those trades, too. Mostly about trouble brewing between Arrow-Odd and Ogmund Tussock again. Far to the north, though, nowhere near here. Those stories were not about to help me in this case. Ulf had the momentum of the occasion.

The king had made it his unspoken policy to allow arguments to play out without his intervention. Only when he was done listening would he speak. He eyed me with some curiosity then. What would I do? Respond to the mild chiding in kind or slink back and let others decide what to do?

Asking questions out loud is an act of heresy when a speaker spouts nonsense.

"It sounds like Hemming needs the luck most," I said, "since he hasn't described how goblins breached our walls."

"Oh, they didn't get in!" said Hemming. "I picked up their tracks outside. They came nearby, though, and I tracked them back to the fens. There, the trail ended."

Having taken back the momentum, I grinned. "Maybe instead of luck, we could rely on some wood. Unless, Ulf, you don't have any wood to spare."

Ha! That got me the greater chuckle. But I had raised the stakes, poking at Ulf that way in front of the other men.

Hromund's lip curled up in amusement at my comment. He was an old hand at sniffing out aurochs-shit, but kept his mouth shut about it. I think that lip curl meant I was giving voice to the man's otherwise unspoken thoughts.

Ulf's smile remained unbroken, a mask of protection against showing his real thoughts. "Jokes by the jester are no surprise," he said. "I think we can expect little worth hearing from him, however."

We had entered a battle of wits. It had not been my intent to start one, but Ulf had told me to go away, and since when had I ever followed that sort of command?

So I spoke the following verse:

> "Great skill
>   grain counting
> but knows not the names of the taken.

> Did those disappeared
>   declare it so,
> or is drama the diplomat's domain?"

It allowed Ulf a wide range for his counter, and I was wide open to losing if anyone really was missing. But for the first concern, I was a better poet and not worried about clever counters. As for the second concern, Beigadh's name was not Beigadh the Ignorant. That man had his ear to the ground for threats to Lejre, and I had seen what he did to those threats. If people really were missing, he would have known long before Ulf.

Ulf's response was predictable but bit me deep all the same:

> "Healthy Ansgar
>   always has questions,
> as if his words were weapons.

> That left his witch
>   wanting for lifeblood.
> Hope his luck lasts longer this time."

I had not spent much time thinking about Ulf, but I realized with that stanza the extent of my hate. It was not a sudden thing and had I paid more attention to previous incidents, I would have known to avoid him altogether. There was no ambiguity about twisting the metaphorical knife in my guts over Fanya's death. It was doubly insulting, given every one of our crewmates knew what was going on. A potent verse.

But mention of Fanya surfaced another memory in me of the previous summer. I saw that shit rag Ulf pleasuring himself while spying on three bathing witches, though I had never called him out on it. He still did not know that I knew. Neutral-ish as my first stanza had been, my next was as cutting as possible without allowing him to legally kill me:

> "Far wandering in that
>   forest where witches bathed,
> I saw Ulf's weapon-washing as well.

> Words of a *drengr*,
>   he wet the weeds without blood;
> that spy polished his spear in secret."

A few hand gestures helped on that last line. I played fast and loose with the alliterative stresses in the verse. Or, in other words, I cheated a little. And exactly none of the men cared when they roared in laughter at Ulf's expense. Hromund grinned even wider, looking part proud and part predatory.

The orange firelight was not sufficient to show how flushed Ulf's face became, the kind only fear for one's pride can produce. It was there, I am certain. Ulf shouted and shoved men aside to regain attention and make a second verse.

The 'Steins would not let him. They were ostensibly occupied with a more important matter.

"I win ten pieces of hacksilver," shouted Innstein. "That's six fights Ansgar has started and you bet it would only be five before we set sail."

"Thor's sweaty balls, brother; you can't claim this one!" Utstein responded. "It was Ulf who started the fight, not Ansgar."

And knowing full well what they were doing, the brothers took the stage. They went back and forth, ignoring Ulf as he implored them for silence enough to respond well. But they continued as only those two could until Kraki made his way, wordless, into the middle of it all.

"What do you say, Kraki?" asked Innstein.

"Who started the fight?" asked Utstein.

The mad elderly cook stepped forward and shouldered his bone club. "Me," he said.

Silence.

Nobody was stupid enough to say anything in the wake of that implication. Even the king would have been a brave man to be the next to speak.

"I hear a lot of nothing," whispered Kraki, the low volume of his voice more frightening than a shout. "Finnr rests now, but he had things worth saying. Now, you all who he risked his life for, you listen: This is no natural winter weather. We are vulnerable as the city is rebuilt, and something from Down-Below knows it." He paused and looked at Haldor and King Hrolf.

"So Alfhild sends her *seiðr* our way even still," said Ulf.

"Finnr says no," continued Kraki. "Alfhild made allies in the Down-Below, those little shit trolls we fought last summer. But she abandoned them. Finnr had to fight his way through them to escape, but he thinks they are the source of the ill winds blowing our way."

There seemed to me nothing to do about the problem but sit around and wait.

King Hrolf scratched at his beard. "Then I have a proposal," he said.

"We are not at sea," said Kraki and stepped away.

Now if I were the author of any of the other sagas, I would give you that line and leave it at that. And like any reasonable person, you would be wondering, "What did he mean by that?" What he meant was that his authority extended only to where the *Sea Squirrel* went. He could tell the king was about to hire the crew to go after these goblins, which were not at sea. That was Haldor's domain since he led on land. It was an agreement Haldor and Kraki had come to years before, and the key to sharing that kind of authority is to make sure you never, ever overstep.

So what Kraki meant by "We are not at sea" was really *You need to talk to Haldor because I have no say in this matter.*

Which was interesting because there was a snowball's chance in Muspelheim we would be able to follow those goblins without Kraki. They would not be in the cave so much as under it in the Down-Below. Kraki had spent most of his life in the Down-Below. How old he was and how many battles he had fought were anyone's guess, as many of those battles were fought for the dwarves beneath Midgard. The rest of us wouldn't even know how to find a way in.

Haldor had said nothing during the conversation but stepped forward at that comment to hear what the king would say.

"Grain is not my greatest concern at the moment," said Hrolf. "A starving man doesn't stop for lunch if he sees an army approaching. I have rich rewards in store if you lead a group to the Down-Below. These trolls are on Danish land, even if they are under it, and therefore subject to my rule. I will know the source of this ill weather and end it. We will take our message and take our weapons and find out which they prefer."

Haldor folded his arms in contemplation. "That's not a request I would deny," he said after some thought. "But I defer judgment where judgment is better." Translation: *It's my responsibility, but I need to give it over to Kraki as long as he accepts.*

"If I need to choose, I won't hear any second-guessing," said Kraki. Translation: *I'm going to make some unpopular decisions.*

"That's a reasonable thing," replied Haldor. Translation: *I accept your unpopular decisions.*

"A small group is better than a big one for such a task. I will take five others."

Svein stepped forward, as did Haldor. Most of the crew did, as well as some of those I did not know. The king rose and let one hand fall to the pommel of his sword.

"All five must be no larger than I am," said Kraki.

Haldor grunted and curled his lip. Translation: *I don't like this unpopular decision.*

"Your shoulders are too wide, and the king is too tall," said Kraki. "There will be tight passages even for me." Translation: *No takesie-backsies.*

Haldor stepped back. Eyes went to Svein's confused expression. He did a strange thing then and turned toward Ulf for a moment. Seeing no response, Svein stepped back as well.

"Step forward, any man who has fought underground," said Kraki.

Many exchanged looks. Only Nanthild stepped forward.

"Or woman," corrected Kraki.

Low comments and laughter had the hall humming with disdain. Looks were exchanged, shoulders were shoved. Some of the would-be warriors who had come only when Lejre's troll was safely dispatched could not believe a woman, especially one of slight frame, had fought in such a battle.

Where were they when the danger was at its greatest? I had not bothered to talk much with them. My attention had been spent speaking to others of the crew, learning their pasts, their stories, as much for my own interest as at Haldor's command. Some of the seekers of Hrolf's hall were interesting in their own rights, but they were secondary to me. They had not fought with us. They had not seen Nanthild the Silent go about her work. Yet.

None who fought last summer laughed along with them.

The spotted history I knew of Nanthild and her brother included no time when they would have been underground. Perhaps the fighting she meant to reference was in caves as they made their way through the wilderness. Maybe there was a story of them going Down-Below during that time.

"Nanthild is one," said Kraki. "Magnus and Ingolf as well. Hemming." That was four, so only one more to choose. Kraki's eyes surveyed the hall, going over each possibility. It was an important decision, one that could mean survival or death in the Down-Below. I wondered if he would choose Huld in case they needed a spell or three. Perhaps one of the untested men if he'd sized one up as a good recruit.

"Where is Gudbrand?" I asked. The king's staller had the job of keeping horses fed and sheltered. Technically. In truth, he was the king's problem solver and, in an emergency, his surrogate in command. When the previous king was nowhere to be found and the city was under attack, Gudbrand Shirtless mustered Lejre's defenses. A mounted warrior wearing heavy mail and wielding an atgeir was the kind of imposing presence Lejre's people needed at the time. "A Danish guide for traveling over Danish land seems important."

"Dispatched on another errand," said King Hrolf. "He carries the war arrow to the Danes to muster what ships and crews he can find. We do not know where Alfhild has fled to. For all we know, she may return with her allies on a fleet trying to burn this city anew."

Gudbrand was probably being overfed by some jarl eager to get the king's favor. Or holed up in a farmhouse and being treated like visiting royalty. That man had lived more stories than I had yet heard, including fighting his way out of certain death with my father. If anyone could recruit fighting men to come to Lejre once it was spring, it was him.

King Hrolf seemed deep in thought until he yelled for Beigadh. All eyes pivoted from one side to another as a crowd watching a ballgame would do. Quickly but quietly, Beigadh the Bold entered and strode forward through a parting sea of would-be warriors.

"A raiding party assembles under Kraki's command. You are relieved of your duties to me during that time. Do you agree to join them?"

"He can guide us, but I will still choose one more to go Down-Below," said Kraki.

"I agree," said Beigadh, eyes darting from Hrolf to Kraki. "Perhaps someone will watch the door in my place."

"One of the king's men joins us," said Haldor. "That means one of us will take Beigadh's place until he returns."

Not so many men stepped forward for this job. Svein was noticeably absent as a volunteer, though Ulf stepped forward.

"I volunteer," I said. "It was I who caused everyone to go outside last night. Let me watch the door for a time."

Nods and murmurs of assent indicated this seemed a reasonable thing. Murmurs, which I hated beyond any reasonable measure, were on my side for once.

Kraki cut those murmurs down in an instant. The old man never did much I expected him to do, and this was no exception. "Ansgar the Skald cannot stand by the door because he is coming with us to the Down-Below. He is lucky. And he has that magic sword."

Oh, did I not mention I had a magic sword? You didn't miss anything. That was the first I was hearing of it, too.

CHAPTER 5

RUNE

"I NEED TO GIVE YOU THAT MAGIC SWORD," SAID FINNR. HE lay on the same table, unmoved from when Huld did her work. Whatever that was, herb lore or calling spirits, it had worked well enough. The dwarf was able to sit up and prop himself on his elbows. He could face us but was not able to sit up yet. "Probably should have given it to you already. Time didn't seem right."

Most of the crew gathered around the table, which had been moved to the end of the hall opposite the king's high seat. Still near a hearth fire but well away from the main throng demanding Hrolf's attention. Interested onlookers more curious about a wounded dwarf than a king's daily responsibilities were put off well enough by Kraki's glare or Haldor's voice.

"Sworn men here only," boomed the behemoth. "So swear, or move on." This was Brotherhood business, and all but a few of us gathered around.

Hemming hated the indoors and so was not present. Ulf acted as *þulr* for the king, help he needed in dealing with all the demands of a city coming back to life, so he was back with Hrolf. Svein was close enough to listen but was supposed to be watching the door with Beigadh, having been the man selected to replace him for a time.

Finnr tried to sit up further but fell back with a low groan. "Nanthild," he said, to the Frank's immediate attention, "down at the forge. I'm in no shape to retrieve it."

Nanthild took off as soon as she heard this, apparently knowing exactly which sword to fetch. I wondered how many other people knew I had a magic sword before I did.

"And now is the right time?" I asked.

"Well, of course," coughed Finnr. "What if you die in the Down-Below? Then I would have never given it to you."

It was a gift I wanted to refuse, but Huld was standing right next to me. You try saying *No thank you* with a staff-wielding sorceress breathing down your neck, and you see how that goes.

Maybe you think magic swords are wonderful gifts, like fine woolen capes or fitted boots. All benefit and no downside, sure to provide an advantage. They are not. I've never heard of one endowing a benefit where it didn't take more than it provided. Besides, what did I need a new weapon for? I was a skald, and a sword would not help me sing or tell stories.

Magic swords are like horses. People who only know horses from their imaginations have idealized versions of what owning one is like. Prancing happily around, running for ages, coming when whistled to. The reality is that horses eat a lot, I am convinced they somehow shit more than they eat, and they bite and kick and never stop smelling. People who own them know they are at best a necessary evil, and at worst . . . well, at worst, they end up killing people you didn't intend to kill. Often their owners.

Like magic swords.

"Are you going to tell us what happened or just wave your sword around?" demanded Magnus.

The dwarf smiled and stymied a laugh, but his potbelly twitched anyway beneath a rough blanket. "Went to the Down-Below," he said. "Thought I had more friends there than I did. And you know me. Sticking swords where they aren't always wanted. Didn't bring this one, though, it's not for me. Was for Haldor, but turned out it was for the skald."

"In that case, you've had this sword finished for some time now," I said. "And yes, I recall it being made for Haldor. Why give it to me at all?"

"Haldor could not swing it," said Finnr.

"What makes you think I can lift anything too heavy for Haldor?"

"I can lift it," said Haldor. "Can't swing it."

I'd been leading a strange life for the better part of a year, but the last twelve hours had been just about the strangest so far. Now I was a man chosen out of many to go on a raid, and the straightforward Haldor Skull-splitter was speaking in riddles.

"Must be confusing," said Finnr. "You're in good company. I forged the thing, and even I couldn't understand what was going on until the wizard gave me an idea."

"The wizard" was Ketill. Chanter, painter, carver of runes, and my some-times teacher of the same. Friend of ravens. Exploder of dead things. Decent archer. And right up until the end of last summer's battle, a constant drunk. We lay recuperating from the battle under the same tent. I was there for my injuries and he was there to stop the feverish shaking that followed his deci-sion to quit ale and mead forever. Since that time, he had come and gone from his hut in the woods a few times but never stayed long.

"What idea was th—?" I tried to ask.

"That's enough," Huld said to me. Turning toward Finnr, she added, "You need to rest. *Seiðr* is powerful. I could use it to weave spells that would see things from across the world, lock your limbs, or heal your wounds. But *seiðr* isn't so powerful it can keep men from doing stupid things. Stop aggra-vating those stitches."

Finnr laughed at that. "No force in the world!" he said and leaned back to rest.

"The rest of you, back away," Huld continued. It was not a suggestion. "Stop crowding him. The skald can speak to him, but I won't have him mobbed."

Haldor nodded and stepped back first as an example. The semi-circle of crewmen dissolved onto benches nearby, close enough to hear conversation but far enough that the conversation would be only me and the dwarf. I turned to give the dwarf space and noticed the crew staring at us. At me.

"Off with you, all of you," said Haldor, hooking a thumb towards the high seat. "Get over there and make sure these new would-be lords don't get unruly."

The men shuffled off, some grumbling. The 'Steins took up seats further away and pulled out their *hnefatafl* board. Everyone left but Haldor.

"What did you expect?" whispered Huld in mock surprise. "You turned into a bear, and now you have a magic sword. 'Favored by Odin' is what they say."

Haldor gave a great *hmph!* at that. He had little time for gods.

"I would rather just be a lucky skald," I whispered back. Odin was no god to have on your side unless you wanted an early end. He would just as soon kill you in battle as help you, and I hoped I was lucky enough to avoid his attention.

"Lucky or not, attention is on you. If not Odin's attention, then the attention of the crew."

"I think their attention will be on this supposedly magic sword," I said. "Why does Finnr think it is for me, anyway? It was forged for Haldor."

"It was *conceived* of for Haldor," said Huld. "In the grove, Alfhild spoke a prophecy, and the sword was to be the thing that would kill the troll."

"He didn't need it," I said, recalling the troll in Alfhild's cave. She had been behind the thing the entire time. The troll was her son, Olgram, and Haldor had ripped off one of his arms, a mortal wound. Olgram's final moments were spent asking me to kill him and then, in the most bizarre experience of my life, calling me "cousin." Killing a troll was rather more complicated than I had thought it would be. "And why would Alfhild speak that prophecy, anyway? It was about killing her son, and surely she would not do anything to increase the chance of that happening."

"Your tutoring with the wizard was not very complete if you're asking such a question," said Huld. "Or were you even paying attention on that rooftop when I called that spirit and bent it to my will?"

"That episode is clear as fog to me. And from Ketill, I learned will and intellect and the old runic alphabet." Nearly all my belongings—my lyre, my sling, my clothes—had burned in the fire. All but my beaver skin pouch and carving knife. The tools of magic I had been taught by Ketill hung on my belt, failure as I had been to use them correctly.

The old *vǫlva* shook her head. "I will part the fog, then: Prophecy is not spoken by the *vǫlva*. It is spoken by the spirit inhabiting her for that brief time. Did you not see Alfhild breathe it in just before she spoke? She could not tell it what to say, only be its conduit. That is how prophecy works."

That was more or less how I understood *seiðr*. The spirit riding the person, at least. I suppressed a shudder at the thought, at the reminder that had been me for a time. "And then what? She breathed it out?"

"Exactly."

I shook my head. "And when she cast those spells against us, was the spirit speaking for her then, too?"

"That was not prophecy," snapped Huld. "That was a trap! A trap with a very big lure. Sacrifice can do that, and it was an ill deed to draw ill spirits. They did her bidding willingly."

The next shudder I could not suppress. I was used to spirits in many ways. The *landvættir* had always been good to me during my travels. But they were spirits of the land, and in the land was where they belonged rather than in me. I did not want to be ridden by a spirit again, and I especially did not want it *known* that I'd been ridden by a spirit. What can I say? To describe gender roles back then as rather strict would have been the understatement of the millennium.

Huld grasped my shoulder as if to comfort me but changed her tone to the sort that might address a small child. "Worry not, young skald, I will protect you from the spirits! They are not so frightening as you think." Her tone changed again, and now it was deadly serious. "They may even help you when they appear."

I stared at Huld, wondering what I was looking at. Did this woman know what I had seen? Could she hear my thoughts?

Your vǫlva is a strong one, by the way, my *fylgja* had said. How far did Huld's wisdom go?

She smiled back with nothing but innocence. I did not know the story behind her look, but I knew the innocence in that look was a lie.

"I think someone is at the door," she said. Cupping my chin in one bony hand, she twisted it so that my face was pointed at the door near us where Svein and Beigadh stood. That woman knew how to change a subject.

Svein would be the champion's stand-in while we were gone. He pantomimed attacks with his axe and tried to hand it to Beigadh, who kept his arms crossed and ignored him. I could hear bits through the din of other conversations in the hall. Svein was trying to impress the champion with the heft of his weapon: My axe is heavier than your sword, therefore I am stronger, therefore I am better.

The knocking came twice, and Svein either ignored it or did not notice it.

The gray in Beigadh's beard bristled outward. Seconds later, I saw him step away and mouth one clear statement: "Get the door."

Svein took his time putting his axe away, just enough defiance to show he would do the thing in his own time. Then, perhaps realizing he had no idea what was on the other side of the door, he took it out of his belt ring and hefted it onto his shoulder. With his other hand, he unlatched the door and held it open just a bit.

"What is the password?" he demanded.

Nanthild shouldered into the entrance, throwing the door wide and knocking Svein's huge frame away with it. She did not acknowledge the hulking form as she brushed past. Password indeed.

Svein laughed as the young, svelte Frank drove through and then past his bulk, but he moved more than I had expected him to. Nanthild was quick and sure-footed in battle, but she had to weigh less than half what Svein did. I was still clueless as to how she'd gotten so strong.

There was no time for that thought to meander any further. Svein reached forward to pull the door closed, eyes on Nanthild's ass as she hurried on with her parcel. Svein was still chuckling when he realized he could not shut the door. The butt of a spear blocked it at its base. On the other side, a growl spoke the guest's wordless introduction.

"I would let him in if I were you," said Beigadh.

Svein snarled as he turned toward the champion. "Who comes?" he demanded through the door.

"Your trollwife mother, if she finds a big enough tree stump to sit on," snapped the voice on the other side. "But on this side of the door is Ketill if you would bother to check before slamming it into the face of a guest!"

Oh, to hear Svein's thoughts for just a few moments. He could respond to that insult with his own, or even with a fight. But Ketill was a wizard. A *galdramaðr*, and though they knew his name and what he was, our crew knew little about him. What they did know was this: He had arrived at last summer's battle when things had looked hopeless, and he started exploding our enemies into chunky giblets.

Svein let him pass, and I was glad of it. A man that big would get the entire hall dirty if he exploded.

In strode my teacher of runes. He was clad in a heavy gray cloak and pulled back his deep, drooping hood. He carried a spear, his longbow apparently left behind in favor of a weapon that could better double as a walking stick. Both eyes looked healthy where one had been milky and clouded before. They were sharp now—so sharp it was like having two spears pointed at me whenever his gaze came my way. His characteristic stumbling gait was gone without the constant drunkenness. Sober for months now, the lack of alcohol had initially been a serious shock to his system. Now fully recovered, there was a hint of madness in almost every interaction.

"Is this how the new king treats guests in the winter?"

This was no exception.

Beigadh, a man who could convey much by saying little, simply shook his head and grinned.

The wizard shook off the dust of snow that still remained on his cloak. "Some hospitality," he growled as if his breath were fire.

I meant to stay clear of him. At least for the moment, as staying clear of angry wizards is excellent life advice. But there was nowhere to go, no reason I could think of to excuse myself.

"*Skald!*" came the sudden shout as that spearpoint gaze trained on me.

"Are we preparing for battle with such shouts?" I asked.

"We are ever preparing for battle or preparing our graves, and I prefer the former," said Ketill. "Did you not notice that was more than a blizzard last night? I could feel it all the way through the forest." This was no grandfatherly figure coming to see if we were hale and hearty. He had come for intelligence. "What happened here?" he demanded, pointing at my bandaged hand.

"A wolf bit me," I said. "But not a real wolf, a wolf made out of the storm. I was outside and saw Nanthild carrying Finnr, only he was a badger and he was wounded. I couldn't see the hall, and the weather tried to kill us, so I spoke a verse and then the weather turned into a wolf."

"And it bit you?" he said with one eyebrow raised.

"Yes."

Ketill drew a deep breath, mitigating his ever-present exasperation. "And then?"

I shrugged. "And then the crew was there. They had formed a line out from the end of the rope and brought us back in. They heard my yell."

"No yell would pierce a spell like that," said Ketill. His tone was dismissive, but only to get to the heart of what he wanted faster. "What was the verse you spoke?"

I told him. It seemed not so powerful spoken outside the need for it.

He leaned back and thumped his spear once. "That was well spoken, a good counter," said the wizard.

At first, I thought I had misheard him. Over months of tutoring, Ketill had never told me I had done well. The closest he had come was *Perhaps you are not as stupid as most people. Or some, at least.* This new compliment was out of character and out of sorts. I struggled to keep my composure through the elated confusion that followed.

"Your runes still need work if our last conversation tells me anything," he continued. "But you grasp the subtleties of *galdralag*. The double meanings, the repetition. 'To Silence the skald sings.' That spell must have made his axe ring loud enough to hear in Roskilde. Why were you outside at night in the first place, though?"

I thought about how to answer that for a moment. "I was busy not spying on my enemies," I said.

The wizard understood. He even got a chuckle out of that. The madness subsided for that moment. I considered there might be magic in humor as much as in poetic forms.

Things were going very well, I thought. And yet, when Nanthild laid the canvas-wrapped parcel she'd been carrying on the table at Finnr's feet, I knew it was time to receive that gift I would rather not receive.

"Ah, the sword," said Ketill. "About time."

Huld propped Finnr's head up with a pillow. Haldor and Ketill kept close at hand. Every eye among them was on me, and probably more than that from afar. You'd think a skald would be used to that sort of attention, but this was the wrong context for it.

Then the dwarf nodded at Haldor, who pulled back the material to reveal the etched hilt of a sword. A simple thing at a glance, two or three pounds of forged steel. The crossguard and pommel were decorated but not bejeweled because jewels on a sword are stupid. This was a killing instrument and not a decoration, even if Finnr had added a great deal of artistry to it.

"Haldor," said Finnr, "go ahead."

Haldor Skullsplitter, the giant of a man who carried entire trees by himself, threw back the rest of the canvas, took a strong grip of the handle in one hand and its sheath in the other, and drew. The drawing of it was slow—dramatically slow as if Haldor had taken to silly mummery in his spare time. Seconds passed, the sword was only halfway out of its sheath, and Haldor's breathing became labored.

When fully drawn, the sword tipped downward like a falling boulder, and he only kept the weapon off the ground with two hands on the grip.

"It's very pretty," said Haldor through clenched teeth, "but I think the balance is a bit forward." With a final effort, he laid the sword down on the table. "Anyone else?" he asked, sweat dripping from his forehead.

This sword was for me? Anything too heavy for Haldor was too heavy for me and eleven of my friends.

Svein stepped forward, smiling. He was even bigger and stronger than Haldor and licked his lips at the thought of outperforming our leader.

"Good luck!" Finnr hummed in a mocking tone.

Where Haldor had been able to lift the sword by its grip but not raise its point, Svein came not even halfway. The handle came up off the table only a few inches. He regripped with both hands, set his feet, and lifted. The sword came no farther off the table. Then down it slammed as if to sound a rejection.

Svein huffed and cursed, his smile gone. Before he could try a third time, I decided to speak up.

"Now, see that," I waved my hands around in a confused gesture, "that does not make any sense. Is that how uncursed swords act? What are the rules?"

Every magic sword has rules. Take Tyrfing, for example. The sword was dwarf-made and, upon its theft, dwarf-cursed. The dwarves who made Tyrfing made it very clear what the curse consisted of, but every idiot warrior from the North still wanted the sword. Cuts from the thing were always lethal, no matter how minor—its curse and its power at the same time. And that was too much power not to use. Tyrfing has a rich history of killing people, but you mostly need to know this other rule: You draw that sword, it needs to take a life. Which sounds like a simple rule to work around until you try it.

Anrngrim the *Berserkr* got it from the king of the Rus. How Arngrim "got it" was a story of some debate. Some tellings described how he killed the king and took it. Others said he befriended the king and inherited it.

A minor inconsistency.

Arngrim seemed to do just fine with the sword, but it failed his son Angantyr as he was slain in battle.

Angantyr's daughter, Hervor, snatched the sword from her father's burial mound. Hervor used it to raid all over the world and later gave it to her son, Heidrek. Heidrek's brother, Angantyr the Second, asked to see his brother's sword. Having unsheathed it without thinking and having nobody else around to kill, Heidrek had to kill his brother. Angantyr the Second was therefore Angantyr the Short-Lived. That sword collected tragic deaths like a horse's ass collected flies.

Some gift. Still want your own magic sword? I had less cause to be wary of mine than that death machine, Tyrfing, sure. Finnr had laid no curse on it.

That did not make me any less suspicious, given the impossible weight of the thing.

"Try it and find out," said Finnr.

"Haldor couldn't—" but I was cut off by a less friendly voice.

"Pick it up," growled Ketill. The ancient *galdramaðr* had mastered the runes and their magic long before I was born, and the impatience of age was naked in his raspy voice.

How could I pick it up? I was tall but skinny. Strong? Only in my ability to compose poetry. I was a simple traveling skald before joining Haldor's crew and not the kind of heroic warrior-poet of most other skalds. But I had to try, even if failure was certain and murmurs of the entire hall indicated a lack of confidence.

And, I had noticed, everyone in the hall had stopped their business and was now staring at me.

I shook my head and drew.

The sword was light in my hand. The collective intake of breath was so sudden it sounded as though the longhouse itself had gasped. Nothing shuts up a room full of hypermasculine braggarts faster than the chance to gawk at a magic weapon.

It was not light as a feather. It had some heft, but the balance of weight made it easy to move, and I know my swords. My foster father made the best weapons in Midgard and had schooled me in their crafting. I might not wield a sword very well in battle, but I knew a good one when I held it. This was excellent and nowhere near as heavy as Haldor and Svein had made it out to be.

It wasn't just comfortable in my hands. It hummed a contented tone, so low I wondered if only I could hear it.

"Aha!" yelled Ketill, wisps of silver hair dancing across his face in his excitement. "You see? Because he killed the lindworm! He is connected to the blood."

"What's this about dragon blood?" I asked. "And what's this about me killing it? Haldor killed it first."

Near the end of last summer's battle, Alfhild's lindworm had almost squeezed the life out of me and was only stopped by Kari Swifthand. That intervention had cost him his life. Haldor finished Kari's work and avenged him, though, grabbing hold of that wormy dragon's neck and burying his axe into its brain.

The trouble with killing monsters during that battle was that Alfhild was a powerful sorceress, and one of her spells raised her minions after they fell. So, on my second encounter with the lindworm, I drove its neck backwards until I felt it crack and crunch under the pressure. Then I tore its jaws open and left the corpse slack-jawed and staring at its own ass. That was not my usual way of doing things; I was a bear at the time.

"Did you idiots explain nothing?" said Huld. "Just handed him a magic sword to see what would happen! He doesn't even know why he's got it yet."

Haldor shrugged. Handing out weapons just to see what would happen was standard Norse education.

"It was meant for Haldor," Finnr explained. "But he killed the troll before I had even finished my work. And then we had a perfectly good and dead lindworm to work with. So we harvested what we could, and I finished the sword. At the end, I tempered the blade in its blood."

Who knew what "harvested what we could" actually meant? Knowing Huld, she probably now had several dried lindworm organs and more than a few teeth and claws in her stores.

"I am just a master smith, though. The rest was these two," said Finnr, gesturing towards Ketill and Huld.

"I drained the monster dry, and quenching the blade in its blood seemed the best use," said Huld. "The wizard chanted some *galdr* and acted confused."

Ketill shook his head and sucked his teeth. "You can never tell with these things." This from a wizard with hundreds of years of knowledge to draw upon. "But you killed the lindworm the second time. After Haldor put it down and Alfhild raised it. That gives you the stronger connection. It must be why the sword is heavy for him, and even more so for Svein, but you can use it. Who knew it would be so choosy?"

"Can I give it back to Haldor then?" I asked aloud. The sword's hum increased. The tone did not change, but the message was unmistakable.

The sword was angry.

"Nevermind," I said, hoping my fear did not come through in my voice. The hum subsided to a low growl.

"Wait, what's that?" Eyes wide, one bony finger pointing, Ketill drew our attention back to the blade.

A rune glowed along the fuller. Not a consistent glow, it pulsed in an uneven rhythm. Invisible, then bright with the colors of the northern lights.

Why not glow and stay that way? And as I thought that, I felt the connection. It was pulsing in rhythm with my heart.

"*Nauðiz,*" murmured Ketill. "Need."

That was when I recognized the hum.

The rune, *nauðiz,* was like any other rune in the old Futhark alphabet. Those letters were used only for sorcery by my time in Midgard and only by those with extensive training in that esoteric lore. Amateurs sometimes tried their hands at it, but a fool carving his own runes was likely to carve his demise in them. Ketill's first priority for me had been to feel the essence of each letter.

Consider your own letters, or maybe the letters of the alphabet used just before the one you use now. What is the letter's name? What are its sounds? What is its essence?

I imagined the essence of *nauðiz* and heard the sword hum with its tone. That rune touched me deep inside.

"And you think it needs me?" I asked. More confused than ever, I looked at the weapon, then at Finnr to see if the thing's maker had any ideas.

"No idea!" Finnr replied to my unspoken question. "It is not just the magic of my craft in that thing anymore. Dragon blood is unpredictable. But it seems to me it wants you and that it recognizes intent. Otherwise, Nanthild could not have brought it here from the forge."

Huld nodded. Ketill shrugged.

"Try something," said Ketill.

"Try something like what?" I asked.

"Try using it," he said, never taking his eyes off the sword. "Try *needing* it."

"I don't know what I need this magic sword for," I said. "I am recovered enough to be hungry. The only thing I need right now is a bit of dried meat to slice."

Ketill grinned. It was a toothy, dangerous look and one I had once thought impossible. But he was doing it, and that bothered me. I followed his gaze back to the weapon.

There was no more sword. It had become a seax. An excellent size for slicing some dried meat. It was lighter than the sword had been, but again, the balance of weight was perfect.

"Ha!" said Ketill, stamping his foot in excitement.

The rest I figured out by trial and error. Mostly the latter.

Chapter 6

Scene of the Crime

Little shards of ice that lay about from the storm whipped up and slashed at my cheeks after we set out for the Down-Below. Wind without new snow or sleet was an improvement in the weather, but it was still bitterly cold. No matter which way we turned, the wind pushed back at us, and so it was slow going. Still, no one complained—out loud, at least. Inside, I could not help but ask why it was so cold and if I really needed to be out there.

Beigadh had so many furs covering his shoulders that he looked like a shambling mound of animal parts. The layering was effective, though, and he knew best where we were going. At least initially. The fens, where Alfhild had kept her troll son hidden, was the most likely place for us to find a way down. We followed in Beigadh's footsteps, a cheery lot but for me.

Hemming was out of doors and, therefore, happy. Ingolf was a stoic's stoic, and Nanthild was a strong and literally silent type. Magnus was fine as long as he could laugh at my discomfort, even though we picked him to drag the sled with our supplies. Those would be useful in case we had to make camp or were caught in a storm. Ketill came with us, an escort as far as Beigadh would go.

Then there was Kraki, who was never bothered by anything other than complaining. For Kraki, trudging through the bitter cold was as good as any spring morning, and setting off to kill things would have been preferable to any picnic. If we had picnics back then, which we did not.

"How do we get to the Down-Below?" I asked, hoping the conversation would distract from the discomfort.

"The Stone Road," said Kraki, his gaze remaining straight ahead as we shoed our way through uneven snow and ice.

"How do we get to the Stone Road?"

Kraki eyed me with half surprise and half annoyance. "You're a skald and you don't know how to get to the Down-Below? Have you never told tales of trolls disappearing as quick as they appear?"

"Something like that. Farm stories, mostly. Like when trolls from the Down-Below come around to make mischief. But those aren't trolls like Lejre's troll. More like the kind that upset livestock or pull on children's feet for fun."

Kraki nodded. "And what happens to them?"

"The trolls run," I said. "Or rather, they retreat. 'Take the Lower Passage,' they say, back into the Down-Below."

"So you do know it."

"The Lower Passage?" I said. "That's the Stone Road?"

"More or less," said Kraki. "The same way sorcerers may disappear into the ground. Just like fish can breathe underwater and we can breathe above it. Dwarves can't breathe underwater, but they can travel through earth and stone with ease. We cannot do it the same way as Finnr. A man is not a fish, but he still may swim if he tries hard enough."

"How do they swim through stone?" I asked.

"Oh," said Kraki, as if hearing me for the first time. He shrugged. "Magic?"

I shook my head, no better off than I had been before. "But we don't need Finnr to take us down like that?"

"You would not want to be dragged down by the dwarf," Kraki continued. "It is not pleasant being pulled into the earth."

That description kindled a memory from the previous summer. "What about being pulled underwater?" I asked.

"Sounds like drowning," said Kraki.

"Not drowning," I said, already struggling to describe the experience. "Or dying. I mean pulled downward and . . . through something." The old man eyed me with some suspicion. "Last summer, that was how Alfhild captured me. I was running from her troll and jumped into the river. Thought I had gotten away. But then I was pulled down at some impossible speed and dragged through spaces that seemed too small even as I moved through them. I assumed I had blacked out when I came to in a cave."

"Something like that," said Kraki. "As little freedom to move as you had underwater, you will have less as you pass through earth and stone. The spirits still need to accept you, to take the Stone Road at least. And you need a gate. When we say the Lower Passage, there is no acceptance asked for and no existing gate. A rougher trip, that, but it can be done at will and without the niceties the Stone Road requires."

"That's how she got away, then," I said.

Nanthild pulled on my cloak at that. She looked confused and made a gesture I could only interpret as *Say more.*

"I mean, that must be how Alfhild disappeared at the end of the battle," I said. "She was about to cast some kind of spell at Gudbrand, but then the cat was on her, tearing up her face. I had about a dozen of her minions crawling all over me and I couldn't get to her in time. The cat pounced on her when Gudbrand and I could not get there. I shook off my attackers, but once I had thrown enough of them off, she was gone. I think she disappeared into the earth. Took the Lower Passage. Otherwise, Gudbrand would have cut her down, or I would have mauled her."

"Everyone has a plan until a cat tears your face open," said Magnus. "Maybe we should have brought the cat."

"I never saw that cat again," I said. "Pity. Named her Rota."

"The Tearer?" asked Magnus. "Good name."

Uncommunicative as he was, I detected a slight nod of approval from Beigadh. That was about as effusive as he got.

"We are not sorcerers or dwarves," said Hemming. "Do we force them to let us on the Stone Road?"

"There are ways for forcing it, and that is taking the Lower Passage," said Kraki. "I would not suggest it. Better to be accepted willingly than to coerce such spirits."

"The forest always treated me well," I said. "Why not go there and ask a boon? Maybe in the Sacred Grove?"

Nanthild winced at the mention of the grove. It was a peaceful enclosure, well cared for and used only for occasions of great importance. I had the feeling the *landvættir* were a little closer there, and I liked the place. It was also where Alfhild had tried to murder Nanthild and her brother, so I could understand her distaste for it.

"Different *landvættir*," Kraki continued. "Stone takes a longer view of the world than anything that grows green in the light of the sun. It's slow to warm to people."

"They do not like us?" asked Beigadh. "What did we do to them?"

"Nothing," said Kraki. "That is the point. It is a matter of familiarity, and you lot aren't familiar. They know me from my folk and my folk from thousands of years. They lived with those spirits and each took care of the other. Or used to . . . " He trailed off in his last sentence, which was both quieter and tinged with bitterness.

"Is that why Finnr has stayed in Midgard so long?" I asked.

"Hmph!" snorted Kraki. "You ask a lot of questions, skald, none of which help us get Down-Below."

It seemed to me being silent was not about to help us get to the Down-Below either. Aside from how the *Sea Squirrel* got its name, I knew none of the stories of Kraki's life.

"Where are we going then?" demanded Magnus. "Are we jumping in the nearest hole?"

"I'll escort you to the fens," said Beigadh. "That was the idea, as I was told." He looked at Kraki.

"The skald will guide us from there."

"How will I do that?" I thought about my trips to Ketill's hut in the forest. The *landvættir* would give me signs, subtle ones, and I would follow them. I was never entirely clear on whether that hut sat in a fixed location or if the deeper parts of the forest shifted it from one place to another. The fens, however, were not a place I was familiar with navigating.

"You came out from Alfhild's cave, you can find it again."

I wasn't quite as confident of Kraki's statement of fact as he was. I nodded and said something generic and racked my brain to think of how to find my way back there.

In the midst of that racking, Hemming gave a loud sigh. "Ansgar the Skald knows everything. We've heard this all before."

Well, that was a telling statement for at least three different reasons. The turning of virtue into vice, the casual criticism, and the extrapolation from "I" into "we" all made me consider punching the tracker in the jaw. It was the only fight with any crewmate I might win, Hemming being both slight and short. I had not seen him fight at the battle last summer and wondered where he had got to. He was a useful man to have around sometimes but not one of much renown given who we sailed with.

No fighting amongst the crew, though. Haldor might not be around to enforce such a rule, but his presence loomed large regardless.

"The skald has been there one time," said Ketill. "He might find the way, but I have investigated it more than once. I will point the way once we reach the fens."

"You've visited the cave?" I asked. "Did you find any sign of Aldis?"

"If there was any sign of Aldis, it was gone by the time of my investigations." The wizard looked away from me as he spoke, his tone absent the terseness I might usually expect. Something was on his mind he would not give voice to.

"I thought you killed her," said Hemming. "Should have, at least."

"Fanya cracked her over the head and she did not pursue us," I said, recalling the episode. I had been more concerned about where I could find some pants than whether a witch with a serious head injury needed finishing off. "That was when Fanya warned me what was about to happen. We ran for the hall as fast as we could after that."

"Hmph," said Hemming.

"Don't worry, Hemming," said Magnus. "If anything weak and injured needs to be put down, we all know who to call on."

Hemming kept his mouth shut for a while after that.

I had little confidence in finding the cave a second time. I didn't know the fens, wasn't sure if the *landvættir* would guide me as they did when I walked to Ketill's house, and wouldn't even know where to start looking.

Beigadh brought us to the edge of the fens, a bit past where a lone linden tree grew. It was not a landmark to help me find my way, but the memory of it helped awaken some others. Perhaps the fens would be familiar enough, and if not, Ketill could guide us.

"I expect you came this way," Beigadh said to me. "Is it familiar?"

I nodded. "The linden tree looks a lot better than the last time I saw it."

"No matter," said Ketill. "I know the way."

I thought about recounting why I remembered the tree but decided a blow-by-blow account of my explosive bowels was not timely. It had begun there, the unraveling of everything in Lejre. I had shat myself unconscious under that tree and woken up face-to-face with Lejre's troll. Then it had been a footrace, jumping into the river, and, just when I thought I had escaped, Alfhild grabbed me and pulled me through water and rock into her cave.

Not always easy for me to do, but I kept my mouth shut and let the wizard lead on. Soon, I saw the wisdom of doing so.

Mist hung over the fens, obscuring our view beyond about a hundred feet. Alfhild's magic had kept us out of here completely last year, but she and her magic were gone from there. Even the smell of it was gone, and that rotting iron scent always followed her spells. Despite the absence of that malevolent *seiðr*, it was still a mysterious place. Nothing like an invisible wall, but there were clearly boundaries here, and I could feel us pushing on them.

"Keep closer!" said Ketill. "This is a strange place and not one for having a casual walk."

"Is this a Myrkwood?" I asked. The realms were places, and there were places in between the realms. Myrkwoods were the in-between places. More subtle than crossing a threshold—you might not even know you had entered one. I was fairly certain I'd traveled through one once, on a trip through a forest. Almost got eviscerated by a witch. Almost lost a bet to a sorcerer. But the boundaries of the Myrkwood, if I was right about that place, had been nothing but some dense fog.

"It is the edge," said Ketill. "And it is not a place to become distracted. Follow me."

Kraki waved us all by to take up the rear position. It was his natural place, watching everyone's backs. It also gave him a chance to make certain everyone stayed focused.

In-between or not, the snow we crunched over was the same as any other. It was a meandering route to avoid some of the trees and taller plants, but we soon reached the mouth of the cave.

I had never looked back as I came out of it, but I still knew it was the right one. No sight or scent, just a feeling that this was more than the entrance to a cave.

Ketill struck flint to light a torch and entered first. He ordered me to help Magnus with our sled full of supplies, then shooed Hemming in to go ahead of us all.

Foxfire glowed along the walls here and there. Ketill's torch added to the light, and the impossible maze of Alfhild's lair now seemed to be only a single tunnel down to the main area. I pushed the sled to help Magnus pull it and nearly tripped on the slick rock, which now seemed the most dangerous thing about the place. Well, maybe second most dangerous.

"What is that stench?" demanded Beigadh, holding a forearm up to his nose.

"Goblins," said Kraki. "They piss all over the place. Worse than cats."

"Is this where they live now?" I asked.

Kraki shook his head. "We're close to a gate here, but this is not their home. Just a familiar place for them to piss."

We brought the sled through the tunnel and I found myself in a familiar area after only a few dozen steps. It had seemed like a long way to run, getting out of there at the time, but no longer. While Magnus unloaded some of the sled's supplies and Hemming prepared a small fire, I looked around the cave. It all seemed so much smaller and less mysterious than when I'd been a prisoner waiting for Alfhild to carve off parts of me for her spells. There were more rooms than I remembered, one for each of Alfhild's handmaidens I supposed, plus another.

It was that other room I wandered into. The stone slab before the great boar statue. The place where I had ended Olgram's life.

The slab was still there. Olgram's body had been recovered and burned, or I assumed it had been burned. Broken pieces of the boar statue lay strewn across the ground. I wondered if Ketill had ordered that after investigating this place or if it had come apart when that boar demon met its end.

More interesting was the stone behind the statue. The rest of the room looked as if it had been carved out by dwarves, but there at the back, two seams of rock came together as if closing something off.

"Here is the gate," Kraki announced, jolting me from my concentration.

I looked at the old man and back to the seam. "Are you sure?"

"Did you expect a wooden door with hinges?" He walked in closer and put a hand to the seam. "This is a gate to the Down-Below."

"It just looks like stone. In fact, why is this all granite and not limestone?"

Kraki shook his head. "Did you listen to the wizard? We are on the edge of an in-between place."

"What now, then?"

Kraki looked down to examine the destroyed statue. He kicked a piece of the snout and grunted.

"The statue of Alfhild's god," I said. "I saw it when it was whole. It would have blocked that seam."

"Blocked as they wanted it to," said Kraki. "It would have stood sentinel. Now, it is rubble, and the way is clear. Tell the story of the boar's death." He turned to go.

I started to follow, but he turned back abruptly and pointed to the seam in the granite. "I know the story already. Don't tell me, tell the deep *landvættir* here. Unless they are a bad sort, they will quite favor those who had a hand in the destruction of that thing. They don't know you yet, but that story will tell them who you are." He waved his hand at the statue pieces on the ground and left.

I was alone in the room again, trying to avoid looking at the slab I'd killed Olgram on. I wondered if the *landvættir* saw that and disapproved. If they did, I could be endangering our entire mission.

"Since when do *landvættir* not like a good story?" said Svipul. I heard her before she stepped around the entrance to show herself. Ten feet beyond her, Magnus pulled something off the sled. He plainly couldn't see or hear her.

I kept my voice low. "My presence here may complicate things."

"Oh, well! Better to just not try, then. Maybe you can even go home."

That stung. Stung in a way that made me want to lash back out rather than shrink away. I snarled and turned from the *fylgja*, kneeling to face the seam. And I told the story of last summer's battle.

I started with turning into a giant polar bear. I told them of rushing down the hillside and of my encounters with the demon boar. Told them of how I eviscerated the thing under the moon but how Alfhild had raised it. I was not that monster's bane—that was Ketill. A rune-carved arrow ended that thing's existence in a thousand bloody chunks across the battlefield.

And I told them how Fanya had lit the sky for me to find my way to Alfhild.

I was so deep in concentration, Ketill's hand on my shoulder was a shock when I felt it. The wizard's face was all intensity. He spoke a confirmation of my story and more details of what he'd carved onto his arrows. Spoke a spell in *galdralag*. The air in the little room became thick with humidity and the stone around us seemed to subtly breathe in.

He finished his verse, and I felt the stone breathe back out.

"*Is fire supposed to be blue down here?!*" Magnus shouted.

"The deep *landvættir* have heard us," said Ketill and gestured for me to follow him to the rest of the group.

"Good," said Kraki. "That's a good sign. They don't always do it, but when they do, it's a good sign. Now take a torch each."

Magnus shoved a torch into my hand. My look that darted to Ketill was answered before I could ask the question.

"He stays here with Beigadh," said Kraki. "An anchor to this place in case we need one. And two is much better than one in case something unexpected comes through that door." He pointed, and I heard what had begun in the room with the broken statue.

There was a low grinding of stone on stone. Somehow, the two rocks that came together were folding further inward against one another. Strands of stone unwove and unlocked, shaking the ground beneath our feet and vibrating the very air. These *landvættir* were slow indeed, which only heightened my sense of fear about what unknown land we were about to travel through.

Kraki was already headed for the seam. He even almost smiled, transfixed by the rock's movements. It must have seemed something like returning home—more welcome than a sunrise.

There was no great door, no gaping hole. The seam had become a gap in the rock about the height of a man, with no space to squeeze through. Just a crack I could barely put a hand through.

"Keep the torches close," said Kraki.

For what purpose? I wondered. We could not fit into that crack.

"Magnus and Ansgar together. Ingolf and Nanthild together. Hemming with me." And with that, he snatched the hesitant trapper by the collar and strode toward that impassable gap.

In a few steps, he was gone. The sound of grinding stone began again and swallowed the two of them without difficulty. Well, some difficulty, given Hemming was yelping and trying to claw himself out. Soon he also disappeared into the rock.

Ingolf swallowed hard. This was not something any of the rest of us would attempt had we not just seen it done. "You said you had fought underground before?" he asked of Nanthild.

The Frank gave him a blank stare. Then she grinned, seeming to remember Kraki's question about taking volunteers back at the longhouse. She shrugged and charged into the stone.

If I had to bet a piece of hacksilver, I would bet that Nanthild had never fought underground, and that she'd simply refused to admit it. It's not as if Kraki could have asked her.

Ingolf seemed to reach the same conclusion, shaking his head as he followed.

It was impossible, I told myself. There was clearly not enough room to fit. "Come on, skald!" encouraged Magnus. "It's only difficult if you make it so!"

I muttered something under my breath about that being entirely untrue as he pushed me forward.

CHAPTER 7

THE STONE ROAD

IT WAS A TIGHT FIT AND NOT A FAST PROCESS. I THOUGHT I would panic twice, but I mastered myself to avoid embarrassment. I did, in fact, panic after I realized no one had said anything about how we would return to Midgard.

But then, no one could guarantee we would live to walk the Stone Road for a return trip.

The grinding of the stone felt like it would crush me. The sensation was hard to take, but there was never more than mild discomfort. The stone was pushing me forward. Forward and *down*.

Down until the Stone Road spit me out into a tunnel. I stumbled, knew I could not catch myself, and rolled on the solid rock below me as I lost my torch.

We were no longer underground in Midgard. We were *beneath* Midgard. In Nidavellir? That seemed a reasonable assumption about where we were headed, but this still had the feel of an in-between place. The air was thin, like high on a mountain, despite being underground. What sounds I made thudded dead rather than echoed in the narrow corridor. The incongruence made me suspect we had stepped into the threshold but not fully across it. If I had to guess, we were still on the Stone Road.

The tunnel was hard and wet, not unlike those in Alfhild's cave. Not a limestone tunnel worn smooth under the slow trickle of water, but a thing that was engineered, if crudely. I stopped rolling and stood up, nothing too bruised or battered. My torch was there, still lit as it had avoided the puddles lining the ground. I wasn't sure what was next.

Much of my early life consisted of being told what to do next and then doing the opposite of that, or at least taking the directions sideways. Don't pretend I'm alone in that sort of infantile rebellion. It is juvenile, or they wouldn't call young people juveniles. But there comes a time when a young contrarian faces a situation that either enshrines this behavior as virtuous or murders it and hides the body of the immaturity that once existed.

There was no one to tell me what to do for my own safety and for the safety of my friends. The only person responsible for my next actions was me, and I had nothing but uncertainty to base my choices on.

I panicked a second time as I held that torch and looked down the tunnel, seeing nothing but darkness.

"What are you doing over there?" asked Magnus.

I whirled on him before I could contain my surprise and smacked my head into a low outcropping of rock.

"Well, that's not helping," Magnus continued. "Hold the torch up so I can see. I lost mine on the way in."

Magnus had come through the crack with me, I had just been blinded by the torch's light and not seen him. I was not alone after all. My breathing came under control by degrees.

"No sign of the others?" He dusted off his cloak and peered down the same way I had.

I shook my head. "I haven't heard anything either."

"And no goblin sign?"

"If you mean small piles of skin and hair and bones picked clean, no. Just rock." I moved the torch up higher and turned. "And it's not smoothed out, it's all jagged edges."

"Aye," smiled Magnus as he shifted in his cloak and hiked his belt up. "Not a bad idea."

"What is not a bad idea? Jagged edges for a ceiling?"

"It's a great idea," he continued in a whisper. "We aren't supposed to be here. Nothing particularly tall is supposed to be here, so better to make it uncomfortable for any unwelcome guests. Then they make mistakes, make noise, get their weapons caught on a bit of stone when trying to strike."

"If no one is supposed to make much noise, how will we find the others?"

Magnus shrugged. His lack of worry about being lost in the wrong realm did not buoy my spirits. "Better pick a direction then."

I held the torch as high as I could and lowered my head so the flame would not dim my sight. Visibility was poor and the mechanism for it unwieldy.

I did not want to be responsible for making the wrong decision, but looking cowardly in front of my friend seemed even worse. So I picked a direction, and we walked. Slowly, quietly.

Being much shorter, Magnus did not need to duck down under some of the ceiling's dips as I did. We went under a few of these, and minutes later, my vigilance began to relax.

Relaxing was nearly the death of me.

The lightest of light sensations brushed my skin. Maybe I didn't even feel it, just noticed how the light flickered, indicating the movement of air. Encouraged by this sensation, I took a few steps in that direction to get a better look. With my left hand on the torch, I dropped my right to the sword I'd named Need. It was an absent-minded recognition that I might need a weapon at some point. I hoped Need would know what sort of weapon when the time came.

Whatever inclination we had towards silence ended with Magnus shouting my name.

I had assumed the ceiling to be short and craggy throughout but fairly consistent. That assumption was proved wrong when I saw the yellow eyes and pale skin gleaming over my head. A niche above me had been carved out. A good place to wait and ambush the unwary.

For once, my awkward physicality was a boon. Magnus' shout caused me to hold my torch up even higher as I turned. So when that pallid, bat-like thing came down on me, I inadvertently shoved the fire right into its face.

The fraction of a second when I turned back showed me something else: We had been flanked, as two somethings bigger than goblins bore down on Magnus. I got out the words "Behind you!" before I crashed to the ground from the thing's awkward fall. I dropped the torch on the way down, and the impact knocked the fire out of it.

On instinct, I struggled to get away from my assailant, but he caught me by my pant leg and pulled me closer. Yellow eyes glowed above needle-like teeth just white enough for me to see them in the darkness. Fetid breath blew rotten spittle through those teeth and onto my face. I had to stay away from those fangs at any cost.

My assailant and I struggled in the awkward desperation only two people terrible at wrestling could approximate. Still, it drained me early on, the fear preventing me from breathing and having any sense of graceful movement.

That's the problem with overcompensation in fighting. You can't make every single movement the fastest or strongest or else you tire out too quickly. My heart pounded in my ears as I flailed and kicked. My assailant hissed and spat as he pulled me closer, wasting energy trying to pull me in despite my stiff-armed resistance against slick, leathery skin.

Unable to stand or crawl, I was caught on the bottom of a hold by my long-armed opponent. I knew enough about wrestling to know two things: One was that being on the bottom was a disadvantage, and the other was that I was terrible at wrestling.

Magnus and I fought for our lives in the darkness against foes we could neither name nor see well. No glorious sounds of steel on steel or the brave banging of shields were there to embolden our spirits. Our death struggles were silent save for grunts and gasps and the vicious hissing of our enemies.

"Can't see a damn thing but their eyes!" said Magnus. A crunching sound like a broken nose followed. "Where is your torch?" His voice the same, the broken nose must have been a gift given rather than received.

With teeth that close to my throat, my torch was very much not the priority. There was no thinking my way out of yet another fight. Some fights have to be fought to their brutal, bloody ends. A sense of urgency came upon me, and I remembered one last thing I knew about wrestling.

When grappling from a disadvantageous position, the best thing to do is pull a knife and stab your enemy until he retreats or stops moving forever.

Need hummed for my attention while I was locked in a grip with the bat-thing. Not knowing what I reached for, but only that the weapon had changed its shape again, I held my attacker's jaws at bay with one hand. I reached for Need with the other to find a short knife. I stopped pushing, and the bat-thing lunged at my throat only to find the point of my blade in its eye.

It reeled away in pain and clutched its injured face. I pulled the thing back to me in the sort of frenzy that only a fight's sudden reversal can produce. And I stabbed it in the face again. And again. And again.

My assailant's defenses shredded, the knife grew in size with every stab until it was a large seax I was plunging into its throat and chest. The iron smell of blood overwhelmed the thin air of the tunnel, but to my nostrils, it was a scent of victory. My heart threatened to leap from my chest, and a giddy, inadvertent laugh escaped my throat. I felt my attacker slump, too much of his life spilled out onto that cold, unyielding stone to rise again.

Dizziness came upon me as I realized I wanted to keep stabbing, but a snort from only feet away checked that response.

Fighting the one creature that was on top of me had been difficult enough going mostly by feel. I could even see. Not much, but my eyes had adjusted well. And it was plain from Magnus' blind slashing that his vision had not adjusted as quickly. I briefly considered intervening but imagined Magnus striking me by mistake. He would do better with light to fight by than with me coming directly to his aid.

I ran my hands over slick stone as my eyes scanned the shadows. The smell of iron and bile paired with what I felt on the ground, but I had no time to be sick.

Magnus grunted in pain, and that was something to hear. Acknowledging pain or discomfort, ever, was not Norse. It was especially not Magnus-like. The gasp turned into an angry roar as whatever teeth had bitten him marked a target for the warrior. A squealing, shrieking sound followed. Magnus' counterattack had found its mark.

"Left," said Svipul.

There are times when there is no time for consideration, even if what you need to consider is the phantom voice of a woman in your head. So I searched to my left and did not pause for questions.

The torch was there.

How would I light it?

"Oh, did you need a light?"

Part of the tunnel wall jutted out where I had picked up the torch. Out of necessity, I made a huge assumption. Need changed as I brought it down with all the force desperation would allow and banged on a rock. Sparks flew, illuminating the tiny crystals around them, though not near enough to the head of the torch. I tried again and again—not enough sparks this time, wrong position another time.

"You trollwife's thrall!" I screamed. "Get it done!"

Need came down one more time with an ear-splitting clang that shocked my ears. Sparks flew, making three yellow eyes glow bright in the darkness where four might have been. Magnus had taken one as payment for that bite.

In the brief illumination of the sparks, he leveled a kick at the same creature and sent it crashing against the opposite wall.

The torch caught fire. Only a little at first, and I had to wait for it to fully catch. I bit my tongue while waiting those precious seconds and hoped I would not be too late when I heard a crunch and a rock falling. But with light, I saw Magnus had made his own way. The one-eyed creature lay twitching on the ground, a fist-sized rock near its head. Magnus had lost his seax in the fray and stood now unarmed against the last one. He was bleeding but grinning all the same.

The thing hunched and hissed as if cursing us as I held the torch high. The element of surprise gone, the light returned, and its allies dead or dying, I expected the thing to retreat into the bowels of whatever place it had come from.

But that was my way of thinking. The creature concluded something else. Perhaps the others were its kin and it wanted vengeance. Perhaps it could not abide intruders into its realm. Perhaps it still thought it could win when it charged Magnus, even as he grabbed it by the lower jaw, lifted it into the air, and slammed its skull repeatedly into the wall of solid rock.

Perhaps a lot of things.

What do we do now? My mind was right back to where it had been before I realized I was not alone. I had no better answers, only more uncertainty tinged with fading rage and a lot of blood on my hands and clothes. This was why Haldor and his Heroes offered no sacrifices to the gods, relying only on one another. Might and main indeed. There would be no Norns responsible for their fates, no White Christ to beg boons of. They would not call to anything outside themselves to keep them safe. But a Brother would look after his Brothers.

Infantile rebellion could not survive in a Brother who'd taken that oath seriously. That, or the Brother would not survive long.

Somewhere in that tunnel, my contrarianism died. I left its corpse there, without ceremony, in a dark corner below the world I knew. Perhaps its ghost still walks those dank halls, but I did not hear its footsteps. I think it knew better than to follow me.

CHAPTER 8

DOWN-BELOW

I'M CERTAIN I HAD BEGUN TO ANNOY MAGNUS. HE WANTED TO keep moving, and I kept turning to talk at him. My blood was still up, and I had to relate with him over what had just happened. The elation of a close victory is much greater than that of a victory easily won. Maybe his blood was up too, but Magnus had more practice at fighting and then getting on with things.

Soon I realized the greater the elation after victory, the greater the drop after it. Without a further threat for the rage to focus on, it turns into detached tiredness. Magnus knew about that, too, and kept us moving when I might have stopped to rest.

It was probably just a few minutes that we walked. We continued along the same tunnel as it curved around and led gently downward. Eventually, we heard Kraki's voice and called out to him. He came to meet us in the tunnel.

"About time," said Kraki, looking me up and down. "Skald, your britches are tighter than Kari's before a fight."

"We met a few who turned out to be bad hosts," said Magnus. "Just the two of us."

"Stone must have spit you out in a different spot. If you squirm too much, it makes the trip difficult."

"I'll try to relax more the next time I drown in solid rock," I said. "Where are we? Is this Nidavellir?"

"Close enough if it isn't. You won't find a sign posted that says 'Here ends Midgard.' We set down in a forest. This way."

We turned from that narrow tunnel into the wider one Kraki had come through. The way was mercifully straightforward, leading to an antechamber that gave me a gratuitous ten to twelve inches above my head. Just outside the antechamber, we could see torches. It was brighter there, lit by more than torches. Boulders jutted up, seemingly at random. On those, small crystals shot out and glowed dimly, adding their light to the chamber.

If the others were confused and concerned, they didn't show it. It would be unseemly. Magnus was excited to relay our exploits. Three kills between us and none for the others yet. The reception was a warm one by Norse standards. Even Nanthild smiled a little.

"The skald is finally blooded," said Magnus. "Well, while he was in his own skin."

"Perhaps he should have turned into a bear and saved your arm," growled Kraki.

"Maybe a small one, otherwise I might have been walking down the tunnel ass-first to get myself out."

Dark humor for dark tunnels, and it got a laugh even from Ingolf. Reassurance surrounded me like heat around an icicle and melted my fear away, drip by drip. I had found a place for myself among the crew and even as a Brother, but that had been by going off and doing strange or ill-advised things on my own. This was the first time I had been among them as one of them, having participated like one of them. Belonging is a powerful thing.

The life-and-death struggle I had just survived seemed a lifetime ago. Magnus's arm still bled, though, so Kraki demanded Hemming have a look at it.

"You crawled down a hallway that smacked of telling you to be on guard," said Hemming, "and you were still surprised?"

"I was looking the other direction at the time," said Magnus. "If I wasn't keen on embracing the unexpected, I wouldn't have a torturer of animals tend to my arm."

The irony of Hemming as a healer was not lost on anyone else, and he shrugged to admit the fair point.

"Are we not in danger of being attacked here? What about the forest you mentioned?" I asked.

The canopy of that area was high—higher than I could see, as if, underground, there was a sky wholly separate from the one above. There was no sun or moon, but crystals glowed in the distance like stars of many colors. The area I could see, which was less a room and more the subterranean equivalent of a huge grove, was full of rocks.

"This is the forest," said Kraki. "Mostly untouched, to my eye."

"It's a bunch of rocks," said Hemming, apparently not enjoying the scenery.

"There are rocks, and there is ore running above and beneath us," said Kraki, now a bit less patient in his tone. "If Finnr were here, he could feel those veins running through the stone same as you could follow a scent Up-Above. But Finnr isn't here, so be grateful for the crystals that grow here. They grow on their own, some of them, but others have been tended to. Like trees above ground. Dwarves keep and tend places like these." The old warrior shouldered his bone club and knelt down low to look at a green crystal sprouting on the ground, its light gentle but its color distinct.

The shrub equivalent Kraki had gently examined was one of too many examples to catalog. Great crystals jutted out like dull quartz, painting the area in a faint, misty sheen. Lights of the many colors glinted off metallic surfaces. Upon closer inspection, I sniffed and recognized the scents. One was iron, another copper.

The air was cleaner here than in the tunnels. And some of the smaller crystals seemed like the equivalent of tree saplings. Kraki's description of a forest began to make sense.

"Some forest," said Hemming, his voice cutting my attention like a rusty knife. "There's nothing for us to eat down here."

"You mean nothing to kill," said Magnus, still squirming as he sat under Hemming's ministrations. "We won't be staying long, I think."

"Not 'we' yet," said Hemming. "The wound is cleaned but needs a poultice to prevent infection."

"I've had worse," said Magnus, standing up from the rock he was seated on.

Hemming looked to Ingolf, then to Kraki. He knew what needed doing, but he was used to being told what to do. And he was also used to just a bit of scorn from almost everyone, being the smallest and least warrior-like of us. Magnus was short, but we all knew what a monster he was with a weapon in his hand. Hemming was not about to contradict him despite the bad decision.

"Less bleeding now," said Kraki through gritted teeth. "More fighting later."

Magnus looked at the old man, and their eyes conversed in a silent argument. At the end of this argument, Magnus sat down and waited for Hemming's poultice.

"One guard to keep an eye out," said Kraki. "Ingolf, you will stay here while we scout the area. Ansgar is with me, shoulder to shoulder. Nanthild, you will follow us but keep back. Stay unseen and unheard. If we are attacked and we can win, come to our aid. If we are attacked and it's hopeless, get back to these two and warn them." That was grim, even for Kraki. A bony hand fell on my shoulder and gave me a great shove in one direction as the cook wasted no time. "If you see something that looks like a dwarf, point it out. If you see something that doesn't look like a dwarf, kill it."

With the most direction I had ever gotten from the old cook, we set off looking for signs of signs of something. I still was not sure what. Kraki knew, though. Soon, so would I.

We headed off into the darkness with torches held high. The bright crystalline glow of the underground forest lasted a hundred steps. It was much darker at two hundred. At three hundred, the torchlight did not illuminate anything much other than smooth stone and shadows.

Leave a person in the dark long enough, and it will have an effect. My mind conjured all manner of ill things lurking just beyond what we could see. Even an experienced wanderer can only take so much darkness and fear before starting to see things that aren't there. I had experienced enough of that in my travels alone to be used to it. Still, this was different.

Nothing makes you appreciate the open sky as much as the lack of it.

I had lost count of the steps when I saw the first tracks. They were partial tracks, to be sure, and really just faint prints on the ground. Whether foot or paw or claw or hoof, who could say? I knew we might find goblins, but what else might we run into in the Down-Below?

"What could have made this?" I asked. "And what did we even fight in that tunnel? I have no name for them."

"Elves," said Kraki, his nose crinkling an inch from the print I had pointed out.

"I thought elves lived with the *Æsir* and *Vanir*. Beautiful and bright and—"

"Lots of different kinds of elves," he said, not explaining further for some time. "These are probably the troll kind," he continued after a long pause. "Not too unlike dwarves, some. Not too unlike what you fought in the tunnel, some. I have encountered that kind before."

"What kind were those?"

"Dead."

Something in his tone stilled my tongue. There is a point at which dark humor becomes a black hole around which nothing is terrible or wholly unpleasant because all violence has melded into a sort of grim gleefulness— humor and violence fused together to never again be parted. That was what I heard in his voice.

Kraki was not looking for lost grain or for weather-manipulating goblins. Kraki was looking for a fight.

"Everything dies," he continued, more somber now. "Enemies die. Kinsmen die, even if you never knew them. Friends die unless you can't make any, in which case you die much earlier than expected. You will die. If you have friends, maybe you can survive in the memories of the living."

How many such memories did the old man carry with him? And yet, it seemed that they would die when he died because he would say little of his past.

"One torch lights another," I said. "But the fire dies if a man does not share it."

Kraki sneered without looking at me. He took my meaning, which was a request to hear more of his past. But I took his, which was to shut my mouth. Which was easier than normal to do because I suddenly wanted to hold my breath.

Something stank. Like a weasel had rolled around a pit of cat piss and distilled the new musk into a concentrated perfume.

We crossed a trickle of water across the floor. It was difficult to see it was even moving at first. I motioned with the torch in the direction it had come from. Kraki nodded, understanding my intent to investigate the source behind a large boulder, but put up a hand for me to wait.

The bone club came off his shoulder, and that aged body went from relaxed to the springy tension of a fighter readying for battle. He threw his torch over the boulder and bounded forward. What he expected to find, I had no idea. It was just a natural trickle of water, after all.

Shadows shuffled in the darkness. I heard a low-pitched thud like a glancing blow and the shriek of something human-like, but much bigger. A series of heavy footsteps told me that large something was headed in my direction.

I saw the troll about five long strides away. Its eyes were opened wide with terror, lanky hair overhanging both of them. Its maw gaped open but not as a threat. The terrified troll held its leg, and gulping air as it pivoted awkwardly away from me.

It saw me and must have taken the fire I held to be a danger. Or perhaps Kraki had instilled a universal fear of humans with his introduction. The troll thought it was going one way, then tried to go another. Pivoting on its hurt leg, I could see the thing's realization it had made a mistake as it buckled and went down face-first. The thing howled in an unknown yet universally understandable language of pain and terror.

In that fraction of a second, Kraki reappeared. The old man was on it in a moment, crawling up its back, his club raised in both hands.

"Wait!" I said.

I was more surprised by this than either Kraki or the troll.

Kraki gave a disgusted grimace and brought his club down with renewed vigor. The rock next to the troll's head exploded into shards and powder.

The old bone club was not a pretty weapon. Too big to have come from a man's skeleton, the full length of the bone as it had been used by its owner was unknown. It was cut, or chopped, or broken in some way, the handle sharpened into a spike. A tight leather wrap worked its way up the handle as a grip. The bulbous head resembled part of an upper leg bone, only more than twice the expected size. Part hammer, part makeshift hook when he wanted it to be, I had seen it crush the bones of mail-protected warriors and splinter shields while Kraki was in a frenzy.

"Wait for what, stripling?" I had heard this tone from the old man before. It meant he was halfway to attacking me right after finishing the monster that shuddered beneath his feet.

The troll said something in a language I did not understand, its voice pitched high in constriction. A plea for mercy? It did not seem to be a shout for help that might be nearby.

Whatever it said earned a retort in that same tongue from Kraki, a kick, and further shouting. The troll covered its head with long, lanky hands as it buried its face in the stone floor. Kraki spat on its back in disgust. With a final tirade, he used a word I recognized, though pronounced as through the monster's language.

"*Orikr!*" Weak. His voice echoed off the stone beneath us and carried farther than the harsh whisper meant to. The languages of Down-Below were connected to those Up-Above, after all.

"If he's weak, what harm will it do to question him?" I asked.

The old warrior's chest heaved in frustration. His eyes two deep wells drained dry of mercy long ago, he had no words.

I drew Need and, not actually knowing what I needed, flicked the weapon downward and out of my own sight. When I drew it up to the torchlight, it was unchanged from the long seax it had been at the end of my last fight. Unchanged in shape, at least. The blade's rune glowed with a faint blue sheen.

"What's that, then?" barked Kraki.

The troll looked up to see for himself and recoiled at the sight of the blade. A fresh set of shivers ran up and down its huge body while eyes tight shut tried to deny the weapon's existence.

"Hey, you," I demanded of the troll, kicking his shoulder over to expose his face. "I have questions."

The guttural ramblings I got in response contained no words I recognized. "Translation?" I said.

"Irony of ironies, the skald needs a translator. It said: *Message to deliver is all. Was trying to be quiet but got scared and took a piss. Do not strike.*"

It was a moment before I took the meaning of that statement. I looked again at the trickling stream. I had gotten both feet wet in it when I had shuffled back to avoid the troll's charge. But the stream no longer trickled because it was never water.

Well. Once upon a time, it was water. Now it was an aromatic on my boots.

"You troll-cursed . . . *þurs!*" I almost said 'troll-cursed troll' before realizing that was bad form. It's important to make sure insults are sufficiently articulate. *Þurs* was almost as generic as *troll* and usually meant something similar, maybe a little more monstrous. Not my best line, but better than the total failure that 'troll-cursed troll' would have been.

Actually I had seen something like the troll's people before. In a different forest, on a different delivery attempt. They'd been roasting a man's ribcage and spoke my language, but the there was much of the same dull, lanky look in common. In your language, you would probably call them ogres.

"Also asked to put away weapons," added Kraki. "Used the informal rather than formal form of address, though. I've killed men for that."

"There's troll piss all over my feet!" I hissed.

"Don't stop your questions on my account," the old man mocked. "There is a strong flow to this interrogation."

"Just ask about the message. And why it did not attack in the first place."

To my surprise, the troll answered before Kraki could. It was still gibberish to me, but I noted the understanding of my speech. I looked once again to the old man for translation.

"The message is for you," he said. "And a request to halt the invasion."

"What invasion?"

"The invasion that is you and me standing right here. Was that not clear? We are from Midgard, and we did not come here to make polite requests. When you got here, you killed the first thing you met."

"Only because it tried to kill me!"

"Only because you invaded its realm, brandishing steel and fire," said Kraki. Then, with a shrug, "And because it was a hungry, bloodthirsty simpleton that would kill anything it came across. But still. Parley requested. In their shit city of Myrkheim. With you."

"With me?"

"Is there an echo that rephrases sentences here?" Kraki looked over one shoulder and then another as if genuinely uncertain.

The troll added a series of high-pitched whines that sounded like begging.

"That was begging," said Kraki.

"I know that!" I said.

"Well, then! We have finished the interrogation. Cut its throat and be done with it so we can find those gob—"

"I want to parley." The words hung in the stale air like a fart at a wedding.

"Boy, there has been enough of your stubbornness."

"I am not–well, I am stubborn, but so are you!"

"I don't make a game of it. No refusals just to be difficult."

"I am not—" but it was going to be the same thing back and forth, I could see. Unless I found a way around. I could argue with Kraki all I wanted, but the logic would not pierce him. Not logic then, but loyalty. "I help crew your ship. I wear Haldor Skullspltter's armring. I know I am not the crewman you would choose or the best man to wear this, but I wear it the same as you. I ask you to trust me when I say: I do not agree to the parley to be difficult. It is to learn. And I cannot do that if you kill him."

I was not just trying to be difficult. I could feel it in my bones that this wasn't a contradiction but a thing I had to explore.

Kraki took a long and deep breath. "My armring is my own." That part was true, and I had misspoken. Haldor's version was two axe heads coming together, but Kraki needed to swear no oath to him. It was his ship, and he merely let Haldor and his crew be a part of it. The design on Kraki's arm, an eagle of some sort, was not in a style I was familiar with. Only he wore that design.

Mercy was out, and logic would always boil down to the fact that enemies were less dangerous dead than alive. But when I called on loyalty and honor, Kraki halted. He might consider me a fool and my reasoning absurd, even make me the butt of jokes later, but he would not stop me from making my own decision. That was a line he would not cross.

"Going your own way is foolish here," he said. "You endanger the group by doing this." I was not the only one who could call on honor and loyalty.

"I will parley if this one can give a guarantee of safety during the parley. For me and for the others."

What good was the word of a troll? Better than nothing was my facile reasoning. But I didn't get through all my adventures by making a series of good decisions, as you well know.

"So you think you know what you're doing in the Down-Below, do you? Even if they lead you to the gates of Niflheim and down to the River Gjoll?"

"This parley could prove beneficial!" I began. Then, on a moment's consideration, asked, "Where exactly is Myrkheim?" hoping very much it was nowhere near those lower reaches of the Down-Below.

The old man sneered. "They call every city 'Myrkheim' to outsiders. It will be dark there."

"Is it still in Nidavellir or further down in Niflheim?"

"Having second thoughts?" Kraki harumphed and shook his head. "No, it won't be another realm away. And it is not nearly so cold as Niflheim. Neither will it be a good place to visit."

The troll mumbled something and Kraki turned his head. He sneered as he spoke, but translated anyway. "Says the group will be left alone during the parley. I say talking benefits us little, but I won't stop you making your own choice. Are you certain of this choice?"

"Yes, if his word is binding."

Kraki nodded. "Then I will tell you one thing so that you do not keep making the same mistake: Your first assumption here was wrong."

"What was that?"

"That this is a he," he said. "Congratulations on saving a trollwife, skald. Now she owes you a life debt. You probably need to marry her."

Starry-eyed lashless eyelids fluttered at me as the trollwife smiled.

CHAPTER 9

THE ROAD TO MYRKHEIM IS NOT PAVED

HER NAME WAS GLUMRA. I DIDN'T UNDERSTAND MUCH OTHER than her name and that I was supposed to follow her.

She led me down an invisible path I knew I could not retrace through the cavernous stone forest. With those long legs, she strode ahead of me despite her hurt leg. The light of the torch showed me her back but little else. How she could navigate in such a place, I did not know, and asking would only get me more troll-speak.

We walked. For ten minutes or an hour, I could not tell in that place.

I had not brought my sling or bullets, thinking this would all be very close-quarters. But I had brought my beaver skin bag full of wooden discs for carving spells. So I hatched a plan in case I needed to find my way back at speed: I excused myself to behind a rock to pee, which seemed only appropriate, and carved rough arrows into the discs. After that, it was a matter of discretely dropping those discs as Glumra strode on ahead of me.

I hoped that would be enough if I needed it. More than that, I hoped I wouldn't need it.

I had dropped nearly all my discs when we came to the archway—not a small one for goblins or even a human-sized one. This was a great archway through which three trollwives could walk abreast, yet I could see nothing on the other side of it.

Glumra beckoned and stepped aside, gesturing me in. It was the kind of entrance that made me want to look behind me. I could see nothing to the rear other than rocks and a few dead gems with their luster gone. Something moved to my side, but it was not trollwife-sized. It was smaller, smaller than I was. After a moment, I was unsure if it had just been the fire flickering shadows into movement.

No way but forward, I reasoned, so I entered and the trollwife followed. This room (room? dungeon?) was not marked by the stale air of the tunnels or the welcome glow of the forest. This was something else, as if the dulled crystals outside indicated a forest that was dead and decaying. Cold mist hung heavy in the air, and I suppressed a shudder.

"Welcome to Myrkheim," said the voice. Female, familiar, but not my *fylgja*. The voice billowed out at me like smoke from a dragon's nostrils. How did I know that voice?

Hel's dragon, I thought, as soon as a hint of recognition hit me.

"Valborg," I said, drawing Need as a sword.

Nidavellir was not the realm of the dead, but here was a dead woman's voice. In life, she had been one of Alfhild's handmaidens. Had she really died, though? Surely, she could not have survived the injuries I gave her.

"Ansgar Styrgrimsson," said the voice full of false welcome. I still saw no source for it and wondered if it was really her. "Ansgar the Skald. Ansgar the Healthy. Ansgar Bearshirt. Ansgar the Lucky, if I hear rightly as of late."

The trollwife's expression changed. Whatever fawning adoration had been channeled into that ugly visage melted into quiet neutrality in the presence of Valborg's voice. She strode ahead of me into the mist, and I did not follow. Perhaps Kraki had been right to suggest killing her and being on our way, but I clung to a belief that a parley agreement was a bond, and that *vættir*, even trolls, could not break their word.

Also, I was carrying a scary weapon that would make anything in the dark mist reconsider attacking me.

"You aren't the first dead woman I've heard from today," I said with too much bravado to be convincing. "And I have an agreement to parley in safety in case you wanted to try burning me to death again."

"Oh, skald!" she said, chiding me. "You really do not understand women!" No dispute on that count. "We never wanted *you* to burn to death."

"It just happened that I was in a hall you set on fire intending to kill all my friends?"

"Exactly. So let us forget about such unimportant things."

Like how I caved in your ribcage and left you to die?

"Such unimportant things," she repeated, almost cooing.

"I killed you."

"You are forgiven!"

"I wasn't asking for forgiveness and wish for none, witch," I said, hardening my voice. Valborg pitched her tone for comfort, and that made me uncomfortable. Better to prod her for information than to relax. "I was remarking on an unexpected thing. Pity Alfhild's magic raised you after that kind of death. Kinder to leave you in peace—or pieces, I would say."

Being alone was never something I had felt uncomfortable with. Preferred it, in fact, at least most of the time. But not like this. Being alone in the wide world Up-Above had a feeling of boundless freedom, a lightness that gave spring to the step and speed to my skis. Here, I was surrounded by emptiness rather than openness, the kind that meant hostile intent just at the edge of what I could see or hear.

Perhaps it was no different above or below. But below, I was not a hunter. I was prey.

Footsteps answered my impetuous comment. They were Glumra's, or something just as big, and they were headed my way. And something else. Many somethings else, smaller but no less of a threat.

"You assume so much," said Valborg, panting the last two words as if disappointed more than insulted.

"I did assume you wanted to go on talking," I said, swinging the torch up and noting all the tiny yellow eyes glinting in its light. "But I can arrange your silence." I was surrounded. I probably could not arrange anything at that point, but I figured it was not a bad final sentence for a man's life. Pity no one Up-Above would be able to tell the tale if it went that way.

Whirling to find the source of those thudding footsteps, I saw the glowing pairs of eyes part. I readied for a coming attack, but Glumra took careful steps as if delivering a crown rather than raising a weapon. Beside her, a smaller frame, about half my height, hopped in giddy excitement. Three legs, no—two legs and a staff. An old goblin with a scar running from one eyebrow through his mouth and down to his chin. I was so focused on him, I did not notice what Glumra carried at first.

"It was not Alfhild's magic that made me this way," said Valborg's head. The trollwife cradled the talking head in her arms, careful to support it from below but also to give freedom of movement to the chin. "But I didn't want to arrange for silence as much as more conversation. With you, in particular."

"I expected less dripping during this parley," I said.

"Please excuse that," Valborg grinned. "I am wet with anticipation."

The trollwife grimaced, but that was not much different from her smile. I wondered if there was a trollhusband, shuddered at the thought that Kraki might be right about me needing to marry her, and reminded myself to stop thinking so much.

The old goblin shouted something in the language Glumra had used. A necklace of roughly hewn amber beads around his neck bounced with his angry gyrations. Every finger had a ring, some more than one, and what I at first thought were gnarled pearls on some of those rings were actually teeth. He caught me staring and gestured at me with his skull-crowned staff to say something more pointed. Again, something about the language was familiar without being understandable.

"Be at ease, Harbard," said Valborg. "There was no offense meant. His people are merely here to talk. Remember, we have invited this one specifically."

This set off a round of yelling from the goblin. He went on so long it must have been a story rather than a string of threats, and he used his hands and feet to punctuate whatever he was saying. There was almost a dance-like quality to it, though not for fun. I could hear an odd harmony in the words, an intent augmented by his movements. It created a poetry that was alien to me and indeed grating to my ears. But it had a logic and rhythm that increased the potency of the message.

I didn't know the specifics, but I know poetry when I hear it, even if it is in a meter of Myrkheim. Was the goblin a wizard?

"Yes, we know you sank your shaft into heroes and virgins," said Valborg, a hint of exasperation in her voice. "But please, only you know the *galdr*, only you can—"

He pointed at me and in an unclear but understandable voice, spoke what sounded like "*Argr*." Which, if I was right, meant he had just thrown the ultimate insult at me, accusing me of being unmanly and sexually perverted. Maybe even an open-mouth chewer.

There was no hesitation before Glumra's meat hammer of a hand wrapped around his throat and lifted him off the ground. He struggled in vain to pry the fist loose, but it only squeezed harder. His feet looked for ground but found none. Desperate for air, he could not even make a croaking sound. The pressure exerted threatened to pop the one remaining eye out of his head.

"Enough," said Valborg.

The trollwife obeyed Valborg's command and set the goblin down, releasing her grip on his throat.

"Choose then. Continue to delay us and see me hold control over both tribes. Or bring us to the temple and find yourself in charge once again. We want the same thing, but we will need the skald's help."

Harbard muttered something. Context, gestures, and Valborg's responses were helping me to understand the language. I needed Harbard to say more, though.

"Because he is lucky!" returned Valborg's cheery voice. It was in no way a convincing tone and in no way meant to be taken as such. "And because he knows languages. He may be able to read what we cannot."

Harbard spat. I thought this meant he had refused as he turned around, but then he gestured for us to follow. I walked forward. The many eyes glowing in the dark tracked me but did not come close enough to show me their owners.

The other goblins, or whatever manner of *vættir* they were, watched in silence as the three of us walked away. Four of us, I suppose, since Valborg was carried. Three and a half, if you want to be technical about it, given that witch was done walking. Step-step-CLACK went the walk of Harbard, his staff striking the hard surface with more emphasis than necessary.

Glumra had trouble slowing her pace to match the goblin. He was half my height, after all, and she was my height and half again. We walked for a while in silence. I followed by torchlight at an easy pace. Harbard clacked his way quickly across the floor as he tried to keep up with Glumra. The troll-wife paused after each dainty step so as to not outpace him too badly.

It was the kind of silence that sucks away the ability to converse. I was fine with that since it gave me time to think. And what I was thinking was this: Of my three guides, I trusted none. But neither did they trust each other. Whatever happened, my best way forward was to rely on them putting themselves ahead of one another.

We strode across a great, open stone floor. It was smooth like a limestone cave but level like a jarl's hall. This led to a narrow path over a great chasm, one I did not relish crossing. Dull lights burned far across the chasm. I could only guess at their sources. My eyes had adjusted to the darkness well enough to see many other paths—some winding, others straight, and a few so thin I doubted they would bear my weight. All led to different stone plateaus among the dulled lights.

My torch burned out midway across that path. With no other use for it, I tossed it over the side and waited for a sound. I never heard one.

Goat's breath and cat piss.

The plateau on the other side of the path was a rocky mess, just about nothing notable at its top as far as I could see. One large pile sat next to a set of stairs down, which was where we headed. I gathered from the stairs that our destination was just beneath us. From that side of the plateau, we stepped (carefully) down, the steps made for smaller feet than mine. Now it was Glumra's turn to go slowly.

The steps ended, and we entered a series of halls or tunnels, depending on how charitably you wanted to describe them. A maze or just a way to take me via a circuitous route, I could not tell.

Archway to bridge to plateau to stairs to tunnels is what I would have to reverse. Even if I was being guided out, better to remember the right way back in case I was peacefully led down an unfamiliar path. One thing was at least in my favor: My sight had adjusted to the darkness quickly and I could see well enough to make my way without a torch.

The archway we came to was smaller than the boundary to Myrkheim. I walked up to it and recoiled. It smelled like rot. Rotting wood, rotting fungus, rotting meat. I sniffed and held my nose for a moment, hoping the stench would lessen.

"Try not to insult Harbard's temple," said Valborg. "And please don't remind him of the dripping. He has enough to complain about."

Chapter 10

Dense Negotiations

Inside the temple was a ring of yellow stones. No, not gold. Yellow. Puke yellow, slowly pulsing a dull light. Stone benches sat inside the ring. The strange temple I could accept, if not fully understand, but Valborg's last comment was a strange one. I had many questions.

All my questions were cut short when Harbard turned round, walked up to me, put up his hands and staff, and bade me stop. Glumra also stopped at the edge of the ring, then bowed and entered. Harbard grabbed my wrist, motioned me to ape his movements, and also bowed.

He stayed in his bent-over position, looking at me while I remained standing straight. The goblin holding me by the wrist was disconcerting enough, but bowing meant something in my world, and it had all to do with submission.

Then I remembered Valborg's words, and that I was very much not in my world anymore. This was a sacred place to the goblins and perhaps to others. In this case, bowing meant the mere recognition of it as a place of respect. To not bow might be akin to spitting on the goblin. Or maybe something more minor, but now was not the time to test boundaries. So I bowed and stepped into the ring, Harbard matching my step exactly.

There were no horns or shouts as we entered, no warning that we'd crossed an important threshold. But a dragon's roar would have hit me with less fear than the sudden silence. The entire world outside those stones was closed out, at least what I could hear of it.

There were *landvættir* down here. Not the same as Up-Above; not even the same ones that had allowed us on the Stone Road. These were darker, angrier, and more suspicious if that was possible. The air around us stilled as if the whole cavern we stood in held its breath in anticipation.

Harbard walked the perimeter of the ring, holding his staff above his head. He chanted a *galdr*, alternating high and low pitches. It took me a moment to recognize it, but it was for the rune *opala*, as expressed in Harbard's tongue. Even in the goblin's voice, the sound was recognizable.

Opala. Inheritance.

Valborg bade me sit at one of the four benches facing one another. Glumra took one next to me and laid a small wool blanket down on the bench to her left, upon which she placed Valborg's head. Harbard sat across from Glumra. All four benches faced the very center of the ring, and that was when I saw the skull. Small, like the head of a child, but malformed and with small, sharp teeth running along the jaws. It was the skull of a goblin, no doubt, little different from the one on Harbard's staff.

"Thank you, Glumra," said Valborg. "I suppose you have questions, skald. This is a holy place and where we come to discuss matters of controversy. The father's father watches us, and as such, agreements here are binding. This circle is of our community, but you are not of our community. Thus, you entered only with Harbard."

"Can I exit only with Harbard?" I asked in a higher pitch than I intended.

Valborg smiled. Nothing quite like a severed head smiling at you. It was a clean job, whoever had done it. The eyes were perhaps a little sunken, and there was that pallor indicative of being near death, but it was not quite as pale as a corpse. There was some kind of rune magic there mixed in with herb lore, at least if you could assume it was the same stuff Odin had used to preserve the head of his advisor, Mimir. A bit of drippage, sure, but if the smell of death was on her, it was masked by the air all around us.

Harbard said something and chuckled. His comment was meant at my expense, but I remained still. Could he really think I was unable to understand him entirely? His words were masked, but his meaning was readable through tone and mannerism, and . . .

And I realized his words were not so masked after all. Many of the words were recognizable once I allowed for goblin fondness for hard consonants. As I heard more from him, I began to understand. His inflection was also heavy with deep sounds, like he was spitting from the back of his throat. The language Down-Below was not a variant of East or West Norse, but close enough that I thought I could puzzle it out with enough examples.

"This can't be Harbard's temple," I said, looking from Valborg to Harbard. One raised eyebrow told me he was about to take the bait. "Look at all the heads around! Valborg, this has to be *your* temple and these skulls your peers. Harbard must be an underling here."

The goblin exploded in a litany of curses: "Shit" and "brains" in combination, something something "mare," and a long-winded combination that I thought could loosely translate as "churner of a goat's ass."

I made a note of that one for future use.

The net effect was as I had anticipated. A few more patterns of change emerged in three tirades, each one after the goblin had sat down and seemingly finished the previous rant. Realizing that sound-for-sound replacement had occurred helped me understand far more clearly, though. The Norse "f" was swapped for the Down-Below "p." The soft "th" sound the Norse "þ" made was replaced by a hard "t" in the language of Down-Below. There were others as well, and soon I had a feel for those replacements.

It wasn't always that simple, though.

The vowels changed, but sometimes it wasn't a one-for-one change. This part was not at all clear. Vowels changed *and* his words were longer. Was there a rule to bridge the two languages?

Heads were mentioned, or skulls, and something about fathers.

I thought I had things handled well until Valborg winked at me while Glumra's attention was on the goblin. She continued staring at me as if we were two conspirators.

What could that wink mean?

Before Harbard could erupt again, Valborg interrupted with an answer to my earlier question. "You are protected under a parley, skald. There will be no breaking of oaths here. There are principles unfamiliar to you involved, but that is the truth."

"In other words, I am trapped."

"*Trapped yourself!*" barked Harbard in his clearest statement yet. He followed with an explanation of the many ways in which I was inadequate.

And then I had the last of what I needed. Vowel changes depended on other vowels in the same word. A vowel change often also meant a dropped syllable in the corresponding Norse word.

I could understand almost everything he said at that point. But none knew my game thus far, and I was not about to let anyone know that yet.

"What he means," said Valborg, "is that your principles dictate the parley keeps you safe. This is an Up-Above idea. But as we are bound to that idea from Up-Above because you demanded it, you are bound to the protocols of Down-Below. That means you must leave with Harbard, and no one leaves the circle until the issue is resolved."

"What if resolution involves someone dying?"

"That is the most frequent solution, yes."

I felt much less clever after that.

"But first, I must make some points of clarification. First, it is Harbard's temple and his circle, and he rues the day he raised me. Yes, it was he who did it, not Alfhild, in the wake of the battle last summer. Since that time, I've led both Glumra's clan and Harbard's. It is his staff and his circle by ancient rites. The skull of his grandfather in the circle, the skull of his father on his staff, his family guiding the clan's decisions."

"His family guided the clan's decision to follow Alfhild's call?"

"*One acorn grows to crowd out the others,*" said Harbard. The statement was clear, though I was uncertain of the meaning behind it.

Valborg explained once more: "He says he knew it was a risk, but he took it for his clan. All tribes thrive by dominating their neighbors, no different from Midgard. Alfhild offered power, as she did for me. As she did for my sisters. For a price. Harbard consulted with his ancestors before making that decision. I was Alfhild's emissary to the Down-Below."

"Is that why he, um—" I struggled for the right words. "Why he preserved your head" sounded doltish since the head was talking to me. "Why he saved your life" was clearly not correct.

"Why Harbard called me back," she said.

What a genteel description!

Glumra nodded her agreement with a smile at Valborg's head. The troll-wife appeared more pleased with the situation than Valborg did.

"I suppose you are going to tell me you also aren't behind the weather that has hit us lately," I said, reflexively holding up my bandaged hand. "And that you don't know where Alfhild is now."

"No, that was me! I sent scouts to the city, but they thought better of asking for an audience. I had to get your attention somehow. As for Alfhild, I believe she has abandoned us. None know of her whereabouts."

I wasn't sure I believed that last part. "Well, you have my attention, though that's a bizarre way of attracting it. Why me if you're so eager to forgive me for killing you?"

"To please Harbard."

Harbard spat. I got the feeling nothing in the world would please the goblin.

"You may have gleaned something of the situation from our initial conversation, but let me make it plain: Harbard preserved me in this form because he thought to keep himself in Alfhild's good graces. He only found out she had been routed later, and no one knew where she had escaped to. But Glumra and her tribe like me quite a lot. Isn't that right, Glumra?"

Glumra made low-pitched cooing noises that could have put Svein off his evening meal and batted those lashless lids at Valborg.

"In the wake of Alfhild's absence, Glumra's tribe and Harbard's chose me to lead them both through this difficult time. Harbard, of course, is less than pleased about this."

"*Leave!*" Harbard hissed at Valborg, earning an equally dangerous growl from Glumra.

Valborg's face froze for a moment while only I was looking at her. She went from detachedly happy to scowling, and she winked at me again. "Harbard would like to see me gone," she interpreted, her detached grin returning. "But he has forgotten an important thing for us!"

I puzzled over Valborg's expression as Harbard grumbled wordlessly. As much as was being said, something unsaid was afoot.

"I thought you might help us, skald. And, of course, we would leave you all alone, even pay you if you did. Glumra, show him how he can help us."

Glumra spoke up but fumbled for the right word. *Skin-poem?* I concentrated hard on that and realized I was only supposed to look confused. I was well-practiced at looking confused, and it worked. Glumra reached into a sack hanging at her side and produced a treasure I had seen only one time before.

A codex. Pages of parchment flapped as Glumra waved the thing in the air and repeated herself. "*No sense, no sense!*"

Every hair on every part of my body stood ramrod-straight. My people carved runes on stone and wood, but our writing was limited to that. A codex, its characters painted on animal skins rather than carved onto wood, was worth an incalculable amount. Insert your idiom here: Worth a king's ransom, your weight in gold, a dragon's bed. I had seen one brought back from Miklagard by my grandfather, and he had to limit my use of it. Left to my own devices, I would have worn those pages out. Who knew what forgotten knowledge was contained in there?

"What is this?" I demanded, now working very hard to act confused.

"Alfhild entrusted me with this codex containing ancient Roman magic. Neither of us could read it, and I thought one from Down-Below might. Frothi puzzled out some of those secrets to create his crossbow. But that was from the drawings only, and Frothi was not keen on sharing what he had puzzled out before he died."

"Not my doing," I said, trying to keep my hands from shaking as I took the codex. "Gudbrand skewered him with his atgeir."

"So touchy, skald! It was not an accusation."

"Also, he deserved it."

"*Deserve to peel your toes!*" spat Harbard. The goblin kept talking, and his language kept getting clearer to me.

"Oh, Harbard, the meandering stream never reaches the sea! Let us stay focused on what is important." Valborg switched to address me. "Harbard sent for a cousin who we were confident could read the codex, but he was killed in the battle. And so, we are back to puzzling over drawings only. Unless a man like you, who knows many languages, might be able to read it and share the lore. Good for you, good for Harbard and his people."

"Give me a moment to examine this," I said, opening to a page somewhere in the middle.

I knew right away I could not read it. The runes were not of my language, despite a few (very few) similarities. They were not Latin or Greek —I knew those letters well. But what would this be other than Latin or Greek if it was Roman lore?

No wonder Harbard and his people had been frustrated with the thing. Powerful lore at their very fingertips, but it might as well have been in another realm entirely.

"*Does not understand,*" said Harbard. "*Useless.*"

"This is not much," I lied, deciding I needed to wipe the goblin's smirk off his face. "Perhaps I can find someone who can read it. It won't have value until then. But it might satisfy King Hrolf, assuming he believes you don't know Alfhild's whereabouts."

Harbard exploded in phony laughter so hard he fell off his seat.

"They say I am a lucky skald. But I think it is Harbard's clan that is lucky. Lucky we don't just kill them all and take their treasure as weregild for those who died last summer."

Harbard straightened and approached his response with something approaching sober fury. "*What is 'weregild'?*" he asked of Valborg.

She explained it was blood money. Compensation for a killing or for some other transgression.

Harbard snarled at me. "*Come collect death instead.*"

"Harbard says it will go badly for you if you stay here."

I managed a look of surprise. "Is that how it happened last summer?" I asked, speaking directly to Harbard. "You had us penned up in a burning building. We still killed your most valuable asset, and then you fled."

Gesturing, gesticulating, and fragmentary statements were Harbard's response. He pointed at Glumra, indicating her tribe would not be so easy to fight. Glumra pointed back and made it clear she did not want to fight if she didn't have to.

The arguing continued without much direction. Harbard was distracted by his anger at every statement I made, which tickled me but did not help give me an idea about how to resolve things with that codex in my hand. Glumra listened but was more interested in her mistress, Valborg. And that left Valborg, or what was left of her, who was most interested in me for reasons I still did not understand.

"*Take your skins for food unless you leave,*" Harbard snapped at me.

"Harbard reiterates that you and your friends can leave with their skins," said Valborg.

"And what about your skin?" I asked. "Most of it is gone. What is left stays down in this hole to dispense wisdom. Is that what you want, to live down here in the dark?" Hel's dragon, I didn't know what she wanted. I just wanted to get her talking and see if I could figure out that wink.

Harbard was in high spirits at my question, making a gesture with his hands that Valborg should shoo, go away, return to the Up-Above. "*Take what Alfhild brought on us and leave with skins!*" he exclaimed.

Glumra gasped, interpreting 'What Alfhild brought on us' as Valborg. The trollwife let out a terrified wail and spoke one word over and over: No.

The thought of losing her mistress was bad enough, but now Harbard and I might come to an agreement on the subject. Soon, she was shouting at Harbard and he shouting insults back while he shook his staff.

In the midst of that back and forth, Valborg made her move. Ever so slightly, she mouthed something to me. Once, and I raised an eyebrow to convey my continued confusion. Twice, and I still didn't get it. But the third time, it was clear as a summer day, and I cursed myself for taking so long to figure it out.

Help me, she was trying to say.

Setting Glumra against Harbard seemed a good idea. I had thought the two fighting each other meant they would not fight me. Instead, it forced them to find a compromise. And the compromise was this: Glumra would accept Valborg was an advisor only, leaving Harbard the chief of his clan once again.

Thinking I could not understand, Harbard said Glumra could place Valborg's head down in the center of the negotiating area, next to the skull of his grandfather, a position of utmost respect. And that would be her new home.

That was good for Glumra and Harbard. It left me with nothing and Valborg a prisoner. The head grinned at me in a forced smile that broke like a tragic wave falling short of the shoreline. Harbard was about to get what he wanted from Glumra, so his next offer to me would be less favorable. But he hadn't yet rescinded his first offer to me.

Which meant I could find my way clear of this with one statement.

"I accept Harbard's offer," I said and snapped the codex shut. He had just said, '*Take what Alfhild brought on us,*' and Glumra had interpreted that as Valborg. But he had also said, '*and leave with skins.*' I interpreted that to be the codex, its pages all animal skin, but also as letting me and my friends leave with our skins intact.

So, I accepted and hoped the circle allowed for ambiguity. I knew Glumra was slow on the uptake and that I might need to make a run for it once it became clear what had happened. Assuming my interpretation was going to work.

Valborg translated literally. So literally that it might seem I was taking the codex and leaving. Her voice cracked, doubtless with the uncertainty as to how I was about to interpret what I had just accepted.

I gave her a wink back.

As the mist around the circle faded and the surrounding area came back into view, I got the feeling the circle had seen things my way. We had an agreement. But could I get out safely? It had to be with the goblin or risk . . . well, I wasn't sure what it might risk.

Harbard's eyes darted from Glumra to me. He was hinting, suggesting, that I knew more than I had let on. *"Not to control what others do,"* said Harbard, or some approximation.

He had promised we could leave with our skins, but Glumra hadn't. She'd only promised a safe parley, and now the parley was done. Harbard was being subtle with someone who did not understand subtlety, though.

Of the four people in that circle, Glumra was, lucky for me, the slowest on the uptake.

Valborg was the fastest of all of us, having already calculated what would be of greatest advantage from each of our positions. Her analysis led her to one conclusive act, and she shouted, "I KNOW THE WAY OUT!"

I sprang forward and grabbed the witch's head by the hair, to no great thanks from her. Pure instinct, for whatever my instincts were worth. I tucked the codex under that same arm. Then I grabbed Harbard by the collar of his robes and dragged him back with me, bounding back toward the way we'd come. Even if we had an agreement, I couldn't leave without him.

Harbard shouted. I took a deep breath and hoped I hadn't been wrong about the circle. The goblin squirmed but could not get his footing. I had to drag him close and hug him to me before I felt safe crossing the barrier as an outsider.

Clearing the circle with no issue, I dropped the goblin and laughed out loud. Practically back in Midgard!

All I had to do was trust in the reanimated head of a witch who'd tried to kill me and all my friends.

Chapter 11

Any Witch Way She Says

"Hel's dragon, woman, you are more difficult dead than you were alive!"

Running away I could do, but running away with a severed head for a navigator I had less practice at.

"I am trying to guide us out of here. You are the one being difficult by not letting me see!"

"Here, see?" I was shouting at that point, heedless of how that might draw yet more attention to us. We were past the archway and into the maze of halls and tunnels I was relying on Valborg to guide me through. Perhaps I'd skipped a step in not letting her see clearly.

I untucked her from under my arm, where she had not appreciated the view. What followed was a scene involving me holding her straight out in front of me with both arms while my legs did all the work. Try it sometime. You would be surprised how much you run with your arms, and mine would either keep us alive or provide comedy for any would-be observers.

Thump . . . thump . . . thump . . .

Glumra's footfalls were slow but steady. I had a head start, given her initial shock, but her cry was loud enough to alert her allies. I was less concerned with how many were after me than how close the closest one was. I did not look back to check.

"Left!" said Valborg at the exact moment I saw no viable path to my left.

"There's nothing there!"

"You have to crawl through the opening in the floor."

"And that gets us away?"

"Not quite, but Glumra is too big to follow."

The opening in the ground would indeed be too small to accommodate the trollwife. It might be too small for me, too. Suddenly, I realized Kraki's wisdom in taking none of the bigger men on this raid.

"Hurry!"

As if I needed encouragement.

I hit the ground harder than intended and at an awkward angle. There was dirt here rather than just solid rock, but it was cold and packed so dense that it wasn't much softer. I felt a jolt up through my head when the bottom of my chin hit. I would feel it more later, I had come to realize. Injuries in the course of fighting or fleeing hurt little when they happened, but the aftereffects were brutal. So I forgot the fall, kept my grip on Valborg, and pushed her through the opening.

"Some of the smaller folk dug this out," she explained while I squirmed. "The dirt around the rock is soft, and so they go under the wall as a shortcut."

I rolled onto my back and dipped my head into the crevice, searching for a handhold on the other side. "I am not one of the smaller folk."

"You are skinny, though."

Skinny or not, I had a hard time shimmying forward, and the other side was just out of reach. There was little horizontal space for my elbows. Panic like I had felt traveling through the stone to get here seized me as I had a vision of having my legs wishboned by an angry trollwife.

Thump … thump … thump …

The slow rhythm of Glumra's footfalls was like terrible music to accompany my absurd position.

"MMMPHHHH!" said Valborg. I had pushed her through to the beyond, only the beyond curved upward a little earlier than I expected. That was good news for me since it meant the other side was reachable. It was bad news for Valborg, who ate a mouthful of dirt while I made that discovery.

There was nothing to do but stretch out and make steady but slow progress to the other side. Panic would not help me, I knew, but it was a fight to keep control and continue my rhythm of movement. My progress was slow, and the slowness was agonizing in anticipation of what would come next.

Thump . . . thump . . . thump . . .

And then I was stuck.

Arms out beyond my head, I could grab the other side of the wall and pull, but it did no good. Something had caught, and I could no longer reach down to free myself. I might have to shimmy the other way enough to free it, then hope I could keep the thing off the rock outcropping on my next attempt.

It would be too late by then.

Was this really my end? My last thoughts would be of how I should have listened to Kraki.

I squirmed and the pressure suddenly let off. I was not stuck anymore. I could move, could pull my way to the other side, the ogres too big to follow. I would live, after all.

Live to tell Kraki he could eat Surt's flaming ballsack!

As I rose, I realized what had happened: Need, the sword, had caught fast on some of the rock. That was what had me stuck. It had shrunk itself to a small carving knife to get me unstuck.

It was darker in this new tunnel, but I had little trouble with that and did not miss my torch. I could see the mouth of the entrance, now my exit. In the drunken adulation of surviving what had seemed like certain death, I may have stepped on Valborg. By the gods, I swear I did not mean to. I was too giddy to stand straight and stumbled a little as I murmured something about never second-guessing Need again.

Valborg, on the other hand, was very much second-guessing me. I wiped the mess from her face and asked if she was alright.

Eating a face full of cold, hard dirt she could endure. Being stepped on, she could endure that, too. But being awkwardly comforted by the man who had killed her—well, that was too much even for the witch, and she cried.

I tried even more to comfort her. That was a mistake, as most things men do to comfort women are mistakes. Otherwise, the women would not need so much comforting. That is a paradox I never did solve.

Luckily, her desire to get out of the Down-Below was greater than her hatred for me. Blinking back tears, she confirmed I was headed the right way. We came to the great cavern with dull-glowing crystals. Back up the too-small steps carved into the side of the rock face. Across the plateau to the bridge.

I knew two things about the bridge. One was that the width of the bridge varied and got down to about only three feet at its narrowest. The other was that there was no bottom beneath me.

"Faster!" said Valborg.

"Nothing as fast as catching the edge and falling," I replied. "How is there no bottom down there? We're already so far down there should be nowhere to go."

"It doesn't work the same as you would expect in Midgard. Below is nothing, as in a literal nothing. A vestige of *ginnungagap*, according to Harbard and his tribe."

So it wasn't just a long fall after all. It was a void I had dropped my torch into. The primeval void out of which sprang the first of everything if Harbard was to be believed. I knew varying creation stories about the world, but they all began with the ice of Niflheim on one side and the fire of Muspelheim on the other. I wasn't sure if I believed I was crossing the primeval void, but I believed quite strongly in not falling into it.

Sweat soaked through my shirt, not just from the exertion. Shouts from behind sped me on despite my fear. My eyes were quick to adjust to the darkness, so on I ran. I leaped the last few feet from the path onto the broader area and breathed easier. Then I sprinted as fast as my feet would carry me as Valborg guided me back to the entrance to Myrkheim.

"Are we safe once we find the archway?" I asked.

"Would Harbard be safe from your people if he stood a few paces from Lejre's gate?"

This was not comforting. I recalled how many dozens of pairs of glowing eyes I had seen just inside the archway. I might need to fight my way out of Myrkheim and then fight through more after that.

Skittering noises echoed off the walls and high ceilings as I ran, but I saw no movement or glowing eyes. Even as I entered the great archway of Myrkheim, there were no trolls of any type. I slowed then, expecting a trap. My wary pace had me swiveling my head side to side while I turned Valborg's always the opposite way.

"What are you doing?" she demanded.

"Looking in as many directions as I can. Tell me if you see something."

"I see you are not moving fast enough!"

For the second time during that escape, I pressed on faster than I wanted to, but even as I saw the archway, there was still no sign of resistance—not even the skittering noises that had set my teeth on edge. I crossed the boundary and breathed another sigh of relief.

I was trying to adjust my hold on Valborg when a giant hand seized my throat from behind.

"Ack!" I said, or something similar. I grabbed at my assailant with my free hand. My outstretched fingers got just about halfway around his forearm as he turned me in his fist. That he (it looked like a he) had not crushed my windpipe outright was a great stroke of luck.

Confusion was writ into pale folds of flesh surrounding two sunken eyes with no lashes. The ogre wasn't sure if he should kill me. Yet.

My free hand hung onto that arm like it was a beam of wood hanging over a crevasse. It did little to alleviate the choking. His skin felt like hardened leather wrapped around stone. Instead of going for my weapon, I kept hold of Valborg's head with my other hand and brought her around to face this ogre. Maybe she could say something to him to get my neck released.

"*Stop this right now,*" said Valborg.

"*Where is Glumra?*" muttered the ogre, keener than I had hoped.

"*This man is under a parley,*" shouted Valborg. "*Release him!*"

The ogre snarled. He could smell something wrong. Lips curled on the side of his mouth to show huge, crushing molars the size of my sling bullets. That he hadn't killed me yet was only because it was taking him time to puzzle things out and decide what to do.

He squeezed harder. I gasped but saw movement out of the corner of my eye. Even as just a shadow in the dark, I knew that figure, and so I kept my eyes locked on the ogre. Valborg kept talking. The ogre responded with incredulous looks. And that way, we held its attention for just a few more moments.

That was more than Nanthild needed to drive her forearm-length seax into his leg. Big, strong, tough skin, whatever. He still had hamstrings.

Well, just one after that.

The wound sent him over sideways, myself and Valborg with him. He released his grip on me and swung an awkward backhand at Nanthild. I grabbed Valborg's hair and dove into a roll to avoid his inevitable fall. Even that quick move narrowly avoided the ogre's massive arm reaching out for us.

"Arooooooooo!" whined the ogre as he propped himself on an elbow, his other arm ready for a counterattack. "*Parley!*"

Nanthild had already danced well out of his range, every inch of her blade coated in gore. Now it was her turn to snarl. She was much stronger than she looked and every bit as quick as you might expect. The ogre would not have had an easy time with her in the first place, but he had no chance after that crippling wound. She advanced and circled, considering her best line of attack.

I wanted to see her kill him. Not because it was still difficult to breathe. Because he had ignored the rules of parley when it suited him, then tried to tug on its lever once the benefit was reversed. In your language, you would call that kind of monster a 'lawyer.'

"We don't have time for this," said Valborg.

Nanthild shot a look at me rather than the head. Yes, there was a talking head in my hands, but Nanthild was more interested in what I had to say.

"She's right," I agreed. "We are pursued. We need to get back to the group and get out of here."

Nanthild wiped her blade and sheathed it. Then she pointed and beckoned me to follow.

I was about to ask how she had been there for us. Then I remembered the movement out of the corner of my eye before I passed through the gates. It had to have been Nanthild.

"When I left with Glumra, you followed me rather than Kraki," I said.

Nanthild nodded without turning back to me.

"But you didn't follow beyond the gates?"

This time, Nanthild turned toward me and put two fingers to her eyes.

"Of course," I said. "Too many eyes beyond there to follow unseen, so you waited."

Unlike me, Nanthild knew the way back to the forest where the rest of our group was. She pointed at each of the wooden discs as we passed them. She had seen me drop them and taken note. And she had waited, out of sight, for the moment I might need her.

"Nanthild, you are some good Brother."

Only the slightest nod in response.

"Does she not speak?" Valborg asked as we wound our way through black caverns and dark plains.

"Not since last summer," I said. I considered adding details but thought better of it. Details like that can be used against you, and I was not interested in giving Valborg an edge of any type. I trusted her to see us to Midgard, as that was in her interest, but I did not trust her beyond that.

The witch was quiet the rest of the way to the forest.

Chapter 12

Sputum Democracy

No one was quiet when the three of us (two and a half?) found the rest of our raiding party in that forest of crystals. The soft glow of them shone bright as sunlight now that my eyes had adjusted, and I saw more of the place more clearly. Many of the rocks themselves were deadened crystals, once much larger than those now growing. Decay and dust had settled over everything, and the forest was only growing anew in the form of the smaller crystals.

Magnus strode out to meet us first, but he had other things on his mind than the history of our surroundings.

"Best to keep a good head on your shoulders," he said. "I never heard advice about keeping an extra one in a bag, though."

"No bags!" gasped Valborg, in a tone sounding like she had seen the inside of one already and did not wish to repeat the experience. "I can help you. I already did. No bags."

All the smooth confidence of her introduction had melted away in a rising sea of panic. Valborg could smell the Up-Above. So close to being free of her keepers, so close to seeing sunlight again, yet so much at our mercy. The myths described Mimir's head as Odin's trusted advisor, implying he was somewhat content in that role. Now I imagined Mimir as rather less happy and the myths about him as inadequate.

"Another mouth to feed?" growled Kraki. "We were supposed to come back with the heads of our enemies, but not the ones we killed last summer. Did you negotiate for this prisoner and give something away, or is taking her with us a favor for the goblins?"

"I stole her." Five pairs of eyebrows shot up at once, all surprised but very much in approval. "Well, it is complicated." The eyebrows fell and the grim expressions I was so familiar with returned. "It might take a while to explain. In fact, I will let Valborg explain since she was the one calling that weather against us."

"It's true, I did that," she said. "I said it was to draw the skald down here for his skills. It was my plausible explanation. I meant for you to kill me."

"What?" said everyone, including me.

"You said you knew the way out," I said. "You wanted me to take you with me."

"And I would see you clear of this place! I do not want to end down here! What lore I know is yours, as much as you want to ask, if only you will take me back to Midgard first and end me there. You don't know what it is to be such a prisoner, unable to even move."

"This is not a rescue mission," said Kraki. "Where is Alfhild?"

"I don't know. After they brought me back, I heard she fled the field, but I don't know where she would have gone."

"Then what use are you?" demanded Ingolf.

"She helped me find my way out of the place we parlayed," I said. "And because of her, I have this." I produced the codex, expecting impressed reactions and getting none. "It's a codex!"

"What does it do?" asked Hemming.

"It contains lore. Lore of ancient Romans and their sorcery!"

"There is more I can tell you," said Valborg. "Only I can't tell it right now. The crossover—it allowed me to see things, to know things I couldn't know. That was the greatest value I had to Harbard. But a ritual is required for me to speak such things. I will do this, but we must get out of here!"

"Some deal," said Ingolf. "An already slain enemy, letters we can't read, and a promise. This is not what we came for."

"He made as good a deal as anyone might have," said Valborg. "He made a deal that the goblins must let you all leave with your skins, which is more than they intended to offer. He tricked them, but he was never going to have an offer from Glumra and her troll kin."

"Trickery and fighting?" said Magnus. "I don't know what you're on about, Ingolf, but this seems to me it's going quite well. I'd say he's even gotten ahead of himself!"

All eyes pivoted toward Magnus as the joke fell flat. Nanthild crossed her arms and shook her head.

"So the goblins gave up Valborg and safe passage for nothing in exchange?" said Ingolf, shaking his head. "And they gave you this codex as well? I don't understand how they benefit."

"Their chief made a mistake when he spoke," said Valborg. "It's Glumra and her tribe who want me back. Harbard has no reason to send anyone back up now that he is back in charge. His rival is gone, and he lost a useless item. Aside from injured pride, he has only gained from your incursion."

"So we are doing goblins a favor after all," said Ingolf.

"We take advice from dead enemies now?" asked Hemming.

"Silence!" The bellowing came from Kraki, louder and starker than anything I had heard the old man shout before. His voice reverberated among the stone around us and made Hemming wince. It was his longtime home, after all, and this place was strong with unseen spirits—like the forest where Ketill lived, but I had come to at least some understanding with the spirits there. Down here, I knew nothing other than to listen when Kraki spoke, especially when his tone hummed with violence.

Kraki put his club in his belt and approached me to take Valborg's head, examining all sides of it. Gently, he placed it on a waist-high rock before addressing it. "I know you," he said after a long moment. "You burned our hall and set the goblins on us. We killed you."

"That is all true," replied Valborg.

"And yet here you are. You have crossed the threshold between life and death and returned. What do you intend with us, witch? To vex us like Gullveig or give us dire prophecy?" Kraki shook his head and turned to the others. "Alfhild would see our end. How do we know this is not still her creature?"

"What have you to say in defense, skald?" demanded Hemming. "You brought her to us. Why?"

I had no idea why. It seemed right at the time. But this could not be an answer I gave lightly. A capricious thought would earn me scorn and shame, heavy burdens to carry trudging back in the snow. A profound insight or clever twist of reason was needed for justification. And not only my honor rode on the winds of my answer, but Valborg's fate. A foolish jibe might put her in the center of that circle with nothing but darkness and the occasional troll demanding answers. Or worse.

"She was in need. She asked for help."

Blank stares met me. I met them with silence.

"Soft," said Kraki.

"And you are so hard? Who would you help, then?" The words were out of my mouth before I realized I was speaking. Or realized I had stepped forward to shout them straight into the old man's face. "Is anyone in need of aid unworthy of it, or do you think they should kiss your feet first?" The next words came freely in verse form, and I cared little if I was heard by ogre or goblin alike:

> "Calculated courage
>   is a cold sort of honor,
> those without chains leaving the helpless to chance.

> I stared down evil
>   and stood not idle—
> what say you when you recognize a wrong?"

The old man's fists clenched and his jaw locked shut. He breathed in so deep I thought he would take in all the air in Nidavellir. Kraki's eyes were wide like I had only seen them twice before, and those were in times of battle.

If it came to blows, it would certainly be quick. I had angered a *berserkr* —a real *berserkr*, not one of those oversized fools trying to compensate for poor fighting skills with big weapons and casual cruelty. Kraki was old, walked with a limp, and looked to be mostly skin and bones. He had also run down and killed seven men in my defense one time and could have taken on many more at that.

"Freedom cannot be given," he said through gritted teeth. One of his eyes twitched. "It can only be taken." His body shook in spasms while spit foamed at the corners of his mouth.

I could see the *berserksgangr* welling up in him and prepared to draw Need. I would need a small army to defend myself and was unlikely to find one, so I decided it was better to die armed than not. Dying unarmed seemed just about like dying with your pants around your ankles. It's not how you'd want anyone to remember you.

But Kraki's arms pointed down and remained ramrod straight. Was he holding back? Since when had Kraki ever held back? Something was wrong, something unexpected. His eyes were clamped shut now, and I looked to the others for some sign of understanding.

Magnus' gaze found mine. "Just let it pass. He has control. I've seen it."

Kraki stood there shaking with rage but refusing to lift a finger against the man who had just insulted him. It was like being separated from an angry polar bear by an invisible wall—so close to danger, and yet not.

"There is nothing more for us down here," said Magnus.

"We have yet to level a warning against future incursions," said Ingolf. He paced away from the head and sat on a rock, wary of the witch's gaze.

Hemming moved that direction as well, and it seemed to me this might be a difficult argument without Kraki at his full senses. Magnus was of my mind, but Ingolf and Hemming were not. I was uncertain if Nanthild would agree with me and want to return to Midgard or if she felt she had not yet spilled enough blood.

"We've taken two valuable things," I said. "And Nanthild hamstrung one of them. If you won't take Valborg's word, consider the message already sent: Six of us can come down, do as we will, and leave no worse off for it. They have no good reason to risk our wrath again."

"I heard that, and I heard Kraki," said Ingolf, eyeing the old man still fighting to keep control of himself. "He is right to be suspicious. I want to hear from the head itself."

"So I am an 'it' now?" demanded Valborg.

"You are a head, I see nothing more," reiterated Ingolf, an uncharacteristic anger creeping into his voice. "When you had a body, you aided Alfhild in murdering Leif. What do you have to say for yourself that we should believe anything you say?"

A reasonable question, even if an impossible one. What had come between us in the past was still a gulf where no trust could reside. This woman tried to kill us all, burn us alive for her master. What could she say that would convince us she was a friend or ally? What could we ask that would help us determine that?

It was a cold calculus most of the time, indeed. Maybe not cynicism, but wariness was standard, and here I had delivered this thing to my Brothers and expected immediate acceptance and agreement. I was coming to see how naive that had been but not how to resolve anything.

"Behind you!" Valborg said.

Ingolf grabbed Hemming by the collar and dove forward, pushing off his seat with those long legs. The man knew when it was time to change direction.

A massive stone axe whooshed past them and struck the rock they had been sitting on with an ear-splitting clang. Huge figures appeared out of the dark corners of the forest and from behind the larger rocks.

"Circle!" Ingolf called to the rest of us as he scrambled forward with Hemming.

The sounds of battle woke Kraki from his painful reverie. Eyes wide as shield-bosses, he turned to find himself facing two ogres. He leaped at them, howling, and disappeared behind a large boulder. He would have done us little good in a fixed formation, anyway. The remaining five of us formed up with our backs to each other, Hemming to my left and Magnus to my right.

The gods help us if they attack on my left, I thought. Hemming and I were the weakest links there, but there was no time to reposition. We stood with weapons drawn, our eyes scanning the darkness for any hint of where the attack would come from.

Screaming and banging from the other side of the boulder reached us. Whether frothy-mouthed Kraki was giving or receiving the best of it was difficult to tell.

Soon, we saw the gleaming eyes coming toward us. Eight, nine, ten feet up they were. Headed straight for my left side.

"Straight line on me, shoulder to shoulder," said Magnus. A serious tone, a business tone. There was no desperation in it, only recognition of a job to do. And our job would be to kill a line of six ogres. Or five ogres and one ogress. Glumra belched a command in her language as she pointed at me and directed the group to halt.

I drew Need, its form the original sword Finnr had forged. Two wicked edges gleamed in the forest light. Along the fuller, I could see its rune come into view with a steady glow.

"Hemming, protect our rear," said Magnus, no doubt expecting an attack from where our attention was not. "Why have they stopped?"

"They want me," said Valborg. "They want to make me a thrall to their circle, forever giving them advice."

"Magnus . . ." said Hemming, drawing out the name.

"Stand fast," replied the red champion. "They don't yet have our measure." Whatever that meant. Hel's dragon! He was smiling for some damned reason.

It was clear we were overmatched, but just as clear they would take losses if they came straight on. Four of us held a line in front of Valborg's head, Hemming watching our back and sides. In the open ground of Midgard and with long spears, we might fight to a draw, big as these things were. But in the Down-Below, with only long knives and axes and my sword, we would not come out well.

Glumra shouted and gestured again when there was no response.

"Glumra says you can still live," said Valborg, her voice breaking in fear. "If you hand me over."

The trollwife nodded vigorously, adding that it was a good deal.

"If Kraki is gone, perhaps we should vote," said Ingolf.

It was a fair suggestion in a life-and-death situation. Magnus was the most experienced warrior of us, but Ingolf was the most strategic. Neither had been chosen as a second.

"I take it you would give up the witch," said Magnus.

"That does seem reasonable," came the high pitch of Hemming's voice.

"I'm inclined to agree with the Skald. He stole her fair and square." Magnus paused. "Two and two. Nanthild, what's your opinion on the subject?"

To my left, I saw Nanthild lower her seax and step forward. Anger and helplessness pulled at my insides. If Nanthild put up her hands, it would be three to two in favor of giving up Valborg. Even without a rule about such things, Magnus and I would have little argument against the rest of the group.

The young Frank drew back her head and then shot it forward, the projectile of spit flying impossibly far. Glumra had to be thirty feet away, and it struck her between the eyes. Nanthild stepped back into the line.

"Well spoken," said Magnus.

My hand ached, and I realized I had been clenching Need as if to squeeze something out of it. I loosened my grip and let the tension subside, ready to come back the moment I would strike. This was no tunnel fight. There was room to swing, and I was anchoring our left flank. *Might as well see what happens*, I reasoned, and I flicked the weapon down out of my sight.

When I brought it up, the steely glint of Gudbrand's atgeir pointed at my enemies like Odin's spear.

"Head," said Magnus, "Offer them their lives if they leave quickly."

I thought the atgeir was impressive, but it wasn't *that* impressive.

The ogres chuckled in a grinding sort of laughter. One slapped another in the chest, perhaps surprised. Glumra's eyes narrowed in on me.

"They understand Norse well enough," said Valborg. "They heard you. Stay wary. They will rush you without warning if your guard goes down."

Our guard remained up. It was a long moment of staring, and we realized all other sounds had quieted. Time seemed to stop, as if a great chasm had opened between now and the immediate future. I could see us falling in battle, but we had to wait out these painful moments first. Just as I thought Glumra would egg them on again, Magnus broke the silence.

"They don't know the crew of the *Sea Squirrel* but I wonder if they know its captain," said Magnus, nodding in the direction Kraki had disappeared. "Do they know his name from before his time in Midgard when he dwelt in the Down-Below?"

Valborg translated the responses of the ogres: Broken or Marrow-Meat. Weakling or Skinny Bones. Their friends, Brok and Grom, would have some fun with him.

"I don't know what you mean to accomplish here," said Valborg.

"I just know his old name is all," shrugged Magnus. "He told me a story about it once. Not much. But he told me his name was only Kraki in Midgard." Magnus paused. "Ask them if they know Fundinn Shinsplinter."

There was a short but sharp intake of breath from our enemies. Then a pale form took shape to the left of the largest of the ogres, its eyes gleaming like embers in the dim light. I recognized the bone club more easily than the man-turned-demon.

His crooked gait was gone, and the flesh sagging around his skinny arms pulled taut as he prepared to strike. Kraki wound up for a massive swing, his hips twisting back and then forward as he stepped. The club looked light as air in his hands. Then it struck the troll like twenty pounds of steel, destroying its knee and buckling the joint backwards.

That ogre came down like a screaming avalanche, one arm reaching out to break his fall while his friends scattered. Kraki was out of the way of both body and arm faster than I could see. Down the ogre went. He raised his head only to make the collision with Kraki's bone club come sooner. The strike came down like a clap of thunder, cratering the ogre's skull and driving it down into the hard ground. The ogre's body slumped and remained unmoving while a pair of amber eyes and crooked teeth loomed over the body, ready to swing again.

Our enemies had fled by then. I almost wanted to flee myself. The slavering form of the man I knew as Kraki looked about for the next to kill but found nothing. Blood spattered his weapon and torso. Red rivulets ran down his face. I did not bother to ask whether any was his. He did not look angry so much as hungry. Starving, perhaps, with violence the only sustenance possible.

Kraki's breathing went from great, heaving gulps of air to ragged breaths. He was slowing down, allowing himself to tire, accepting the fight was over.

"We're not done yet," said Magnus, halting Kraki from slowing down so much we would need to carry him. "Hemming, bring the head. We will go back the way we came."

"Not the same way," said Kraki. "The Stone Road is not like roads in Midgard."

"Can't we just walk through the rock and trust the *landvættir*?" asked Magnus.

"I might," said Kraki. "The Stone Road spit us out in different places, and that is not a good sign. For you, it would be walking a forest with no path unless we find a gate."

"I saw no gates anywhere in this place," I said. "Other than to Myrkheim."

"Different sort of gate." It was Valborg, speaking softly as if fearing contradiction. "I know where to find one."

"We're back to trusting the witch," spat Hemming.

"She saved my life," said Ingolf. "And probably yours."

"Shut up!" said Kraki. Each voice appeared to take a toll on him, as if he had the worst headache in the world. He shook it off after a moment and looked to Magnus.

"Still with us, old man?"

Kraki nodded, mouth open, still working to control his breathing. "Follow the witch," he said. "They will attack from behind if they can. The skald and I will guard the rear."

We passed the bodies of two more slain ogres as we followed Valborg's directions. Both heads were bashed in, their blood splattering the boulder Kraki had disappeared behind. It seemed Brok and Grom had not had as much fun as they'd expected.

Standing near Kraki was the scariest and most dangerous place to be, but for that very reason, it was also the safest. The old man read me right if he read confusion and at least a little fear.

"Fundinn Shinsplinter, eh?" I said, hoping to relieve some of the tension.

"Another time," rasped Kraki.

CHAPTER 13

REWRITING THE PRESENT

Among my people, or at least the very rich among my people who could afford expensive dyes for expensive clothes, blue was the best color to wear for battle. Perhaps that makes little sense when you can wear colors to blend into your environment, a more practical idea. Why bother wearing your good clothes if they were about to be hacked, slashed, and stained with mud and blood?

Because you could afford to do that, of course.

I was not rich, and I did not wear blue. Not that you would have seen it well in the dim light of cavernous Nidavellir, but the illumination from Need was telling me something. The rune burned bright blue when battle was upon us. Imagine my surprise when that light faded.

Valborg's gate was far enough down corridors and open chambers with multiple paths that I thought we might lose our pursuers. We came to a small side chamber off of a cavernous but rocky area, and there was the runestone.

A serpent hewn into the stone carried roughly cut letters to tell the story. Or about the story, the biggest elements being the pictures carved from bottom to top.

"What does it say?" Hemming asked Valborg. We were out of torches. Letting our eyes adjust to the dark was better than using fire in some cases. Torches will night-blind you as easily as not, and they are excellent for revealing your position to your enemies. But eyes can only adjust so much, and reading that runestone's inscription was not easy with no torch available.

"It says 'this way to the Up-Above.' Or something to that effect," replied Valborg.

"You don't know?" demanded Hemming, shaking the animated head angrily and turning to the rest of us. "I knew it! She planned all along to trap us!"

"The runestone is the gate," said Valborg. "This is a memorial chamber for a dead clan."

"How do you know this?" demanded Ingolf.

"I made Glumra take me around on many walks. Especially in this border area. I was looking for a way out if I ever got a chance!"

So Valborg had devised a plan for escape. Meanwhile, I wondered what Kraki's plan had been for us to return. Or if he'd ever had one. It was not the time for such questions, though.

"Skald!" said Kraki. "Read the stone and tell us what it says. What happened to that glowing blade of yours?"

"It is . . . not glowing."

Kraki fixed me with a hard stare but had time for little else.

Distant footfalls echoed from outside. We had not lost our pursuers after all, and their fear of Kraki would not last if they had increased their numbers.

I shook Need and saw a faint glow on one side of the blade. It was just enough for me to make out what was carved. The runes cut into the stone looked more like slashes on a mutilated corpse than letters chiseled with care and artful form. Still, I could read them. They outlined a scene of pictures on the front of the stone almost fully my own height.

The panels told a story I was dimly familiar with. Dragon ships approached the land, and a great king set forth onto the shore. As he and his men camped and drank, a fox skulked its way about.

Then, at night, all the men asleep, the fox reared up in all its trollishness and revealed that it was a *brunnmigi*, a well-pisser. He urinated into the men's drinking supply and disappeared into a nearby rock, laughing. In the last panel, the king was shown vomiting in extreme fashion, having drunk deep of the water soiled by the *brunnmigi*.

"It's rough," I said, considering the elder runes and how they formed the words of the language Down-Below. The elder runes? Yes, the same ones

Ketill had taught me. Not used for sorcery, here, but for the language itself. Perhaps the Down-Below language was just the older version of Norse.

"I think they say, 'Our great ancestor–Vatnillr?–made King . . . Hjorleif? drink . . . his mighty pee. Never forget.'" Looks of disbelief greeted me. "That is what it says!"

"No surprise," growled Kraki. "These little shits venerate any troll doing trollish things. Probably didn't even happen."

"Ymir's bones!" a voice boomed around us.

The walls awoke with life, if you could call it life. Dozens of skulls lining the walls came into view as Need's glow increased. Small and sharp-toothed, these were goblin skulls or something like them. One such skull set high above the others moved, its lower jaw moving up and down in a comic pantomime of speaking. "You invade our house with your manling smell and dare insult our relic! Seducers of sheep, eaters of grain, we will suck the marrow from your bones and pile them high!"

"HA!" laughed Kraki, already untying his pants. "Suck on this bone marrow, you beardless bastard."

"Wait!" I shouted.

"Wait for what?" asked Magnus. "Should we be smashing the skulls on the wall instead of peeing on them?"

"No one pee," said Ingolf evenly. In this context, it was a serious and weighty command. "Let the skald explain."

"Explain fast," said Hemming with his ear to the ground. "They are close now. Bigger group than before."

Kraki pointed to Magnus and Ingolf. "With me," he said, waving his club toward the room's entrance. "We fight three abreast, backs to the entrance."

Nanthild stepped forward, clearly unhappy she would not be in the front line.

"Kill anything that comes between or behind us," Kraki told her. "Take the place of the first man to fall if it comes to it." He nodded belatedly at Hemming as well, though we all knew if he had to take up part of that formation, we were as good as dead.

I noticed he did not give me a command, which meant one was implied. Also implied but not said: Ansgar is a terrible fighter and only good for waving a big glowing weapon around. Fair enough, I had some semblance of a plan. Two, in fact, although peeing all over the goblin runestone would have negated the first. "Valborg, who are we speaking with here?"

"The first elder of a dead clan. Or at least the oldest elder whose skull they still had when this was made," she said. "They are sometimes smashed by rival clans."

"Good idea," added Magnus.

"Curse you, sun-dweller!" screeched the voice. "Curse your families!"

I had more questions for Valborg and could have gone on for hours had there been time enough. Emergencies are sometimes good cutoff points for those of us who like to prepare but hesitate to act. And it was clearly time to act, one way or another. Addressing the skull, I intoned in my most respectful voice.

"Oh, Wise One, we beseech you and apologize for our rude entrance," I said, hearing Magnus hold Kraki back from demanding I retract our collective apology. "But hear me: Your people agreed to parley and also agreed to safe passage back for all of us. Now they go back on their word. To break that truce is bad luck. It would be far better luck to honor the agreement and allow us safe passage. You know this, I am sure."

I wasn't sure of any such thing, but I thought it was a good guess. Valborg blinked at me in the sort of way I took to mean she would have nodded if only she still had enough of a neck. "Get his consent," she mouthed and winked at me.

The skull took its time considering a response. Or just delaying.

"They are out there," said Hemming. "Just beyond the shadows."

"Soon they will be in here!" crowed the skull. "These walls hear much, Ansgar the Skald. You may *leave* with your skins, but I will squeeze your insides out of you on the Stone Road!"

"That would have been good to know before we followed the head here," said Ingolf.

"Agreements are not my doing," Valborg shouted back.

I doubted Ingolf could hear her retort as he and Nanthild dove for cover. A loud crash of rock signaled that Glumra and her ilk had begun a tentative attack. Stone shards exploded on the edge of the tunnel entrance and I was grateful it was not a path straight on through. I did not fancy having a head-sized rock come flying at me. I could not see Magnus or Kraki, but I could hear the fighting, which Nanthild quickly joined. The front line had turned into a wild melee.

"But I might take payment instead," added the skull. "There was an agreement after all, and you can keep wearing those delicious skins. If you give me the head."

The skull was cannier than I had anticipated, and the demand was valid on its face. As much as I had interpreted Harbard's words in my favor, now the skull was twisting them back around toward its own purposes.

The polite words were only my tentative idea, though. With that failed, I had a backup. There was likely fighting to be done, but not by me. I would be busy defiling an ancient monument.

"The witch is mine as a spoil," I said, stepping towards the runestone. "I killed her, and I will have no negotiation for her now."

"Fancy yourself a trickster?" said the skull. "No more parley, then. Fundinn cannot fight forever. He is *old*."

A monstrous roar split the air, followed by a cry from Ingolf. There were more rocks crashing and more screams that I thankfully did not recognize.

"Hurry," said Hemming, as if I did not know time was running out for us.

"An old thing is at the heart of the issue," I said. "I understand how important the memory of an ancestor is." I thought of my mother or my imaginary version of her since she had died of illness when I was too young to remember. "And I know the runes you have on this stone. They read, 'Never forget.'"

"Ha! You know our story! We get you in the end!"

I spun Need around my wrist and caught the weapon as it changed form. It was a pick, the precise tool I required.

"Does he understand?" I asked, addressing Valborg. "I think there might be a misunderstanding."

"What?" the skull cut in. "You think you can fight them all?"

"Not at all," I said. "But I know how careful one should be when carving runes. There could be a problem if, say," and I held up my pick, "someone was to chip away all the stone containing the word 'Never.' Then your runestone would be a powerful spell for forgetting this scene ever happened."

If stone could gasp, that is what I felt in the room at that moment. Dead silence outside, a stalemate for the time being. If the skull had a stomach, it would have dropped, and that was where I wanted it.

"Let us take the Stone Road from here in safety and you lose nothing more. All you have to do is consent. You can overwhelm the Shinsplinter and the rest of us eventually, but not before I destroy every memory of your ancestor. Or was that you? Hard to tell, and soon not even your people will ask such a question. Your choice. Will you finally die when the world forgets you, or just live on wondering who you are?"

There was a long pause, long enough to warrant consideration of both angles and the imagination for a third way. And then there was some more pause, either to make us sweat or to give the impression of defiance, or both.

"You will also retract that curse on our families," I added, grateful I remembered that line. Need came to life, blazing bright blue and humming the tone of *nauðiz*.

"I retract. Take the Stone Road then," said the skull. "I consent. Never return here."

"Consent has been given," shouted Valborg.

Hemming's shout to the four fighting outside came immediately. "It is time for us to return!"

They were not far afield, and to great relief, I saw four figures return. Nanthild carried Ingolf as well as she could. Having the strength was one thing, but Ingolf was nearly a foot taller than she. Whatever injury he had taken, he was at least still alive.

The skull winced, or as much as a skull can wince, sighed, and was silent. Consent was given, but I was suspicious. What unseen thing might happen if we left this way? What of Ingolf's injury during the journey?

"You have no conditions to levy," I told the skull. "We will return if we see fit. But I will offer a service to you in Midgard if you see us all safely back to the seam we entered. There is a wizard chanting there, if you need to find it. Any injury, anything I deem suspicious or unjust through the Road, and there will be no deal."

"There is little for me in Midgard," said the skull.

"There are people who have not heard your story," I said and let the implications sink in. The skull could have new life in the memories of many —of anyone listening to me tell the story. Even in his own realm, his existence lasted only by means of a carved rock in a dark corner. But to have that story on the lips of a skald would be greater fame than he could have hoped for. Even if Glumra and her ogres smashed every skull in the room in retribution for helping us get away.

"Agreed! Go now, quickly!" shouted the skull.

The runestone ground its way open like a puzzle coming apart. In went

Hemming, who needed no encouragement. Nanthild dragged an injured Ingolf behind her and held the man tight as she backed into the stone. Kraki commanded Magnus in next. When the way was clear, the old man grabbed me by the collar, his grin a toothy yellow, and in we went with Valborg tucked under my arm.

The trip was uncomfortable but by then was a slightly more familiar version of uncomfortable. It was as cold as the wrong side of Hel's bed and probably a lot less soft. We were always moving forward and up, always with the sensation of being buried in solid rock.

The sensation of being buried, but I kept breathing. And as I breathed, and the air went from dank to dry and clean.

I didn't even panic this time. I even shouted with joy when I heard the faint sounds of Ketill's chanting.

We spilled out into the room in Alfhild's cave, all piled up atop the hard stone. A small sled sat half-unpacked just outside the room. A scowling Beigadh sat by a small fire, his head turning as we grunted.

Behind us, the seam in the rock that was the gate rumbled until it was nothing more than a crack.

Ketill stepped into the small room and took notice of Valborg straight-away. "You were supposed to bring back the heads of our enemies, the kind that are no longer living."

I slipped off the top of the pile, the least uncomfortable of the bunch. Hemming groaned at the bottom, his eagerness to be the first through paying off with bruised ribs. Nanthild shoved all others away to help Ingolf out of the pile.

Beigadh pushed by the wizard to better see what he meant. "That is the witch who nearly burned us all alive," he growled. Then, turning his gaze to me, "Are you not the lucky one, the *galdramaðr's* apprentice in lore and wisdom?"

Ketill's bushy eyebrows came together as one as he looked on. "Wisdom and folly often fall within one another's shadow."

Chapter 14

Getting a Head

The hike back to Lejre's hall was cold and dark. Ingolf tried to insist on walking himself. He took about three steps on his own before falling against the nearest wall, unable to continue, blood dribbling out the corner of his mouth.

We strapped him to the sled and pulled him as fast as we could. The tracks slid over the ice-packed snow easily, but the return trip seemed to take twice as long as it had coming out.

Cheers greeted us as we entered the hall, but we did not return them. Kraki sneered and stalked off to his own corner, lying down without explanation. The rage was draining, and he'd had no time to rest on the way back. I think he was asleep before the rest of us were even inside the hall.

We pulled the sled right through the main door. Ingolf was coughing up more blood rather than less by then. Huld saw to him right away.

Cheers became muted when guests saw the injured man and that we were not celebrating. The cheering died utterly when the guests saw Valborg's still-living head. Night had fallen, but everyone— visiting freemen, would-be champions, and especially our crew—was too excited to hear details to sleep.

Servants poured ale for the guests. It seemed to me the darkness of night had crept in to fight the flickering light of the low hearth fires. What had happened, and what was even happening now? The guests were uncertain and had to mutter their uncertainty to one another in a feeble attempt to reduce it. Murmurs threatened to envelop all other sounds in the hall at one point, but King Hrolf gestured to Hromund and Hromund to Haldor.

"Shut your mouths!" Haldor bellowed, shaking the very walls.

Hromund stepped past the king, locking eyes with every guest who would dare look up. There was no more murmuring. King Hrolf bade us step forward and tell what had happened.

I even told the *brunnmigi*'s story, just as promised. It got laughs all around but from the king. Then I told our story as I knew it while I cradled Valborg in one arm. In the middle of my bumbling explanation for why I had taken Valborg with me, Hrolf interrupted.

"I think I have part of this story," mused the king as he stroked his beard in mock thoughtfulness. "But I am missing the whole." Hrolf sat in his high seat, gazing upward and gesturing as if trying to puzzle out a riddle. The gallows humor would continue for some time, but no one was fooled about his mood.

That was one angry king.

"Good thing the current king does not take half-measures," shouted Huld from across the hall.

Hrolf eyed the *vǫlva*. It was a quiet place where she attended to Ingolf but well away from the high seat where most attention was focused.

A low fire mewed rather than roared down the center of the longhouse, the minimum required to keep a bed of hot coals for the night. The king demanded more fuel for the fire. When it came, he directed the servants not to the main hearth fire heating the hall. Instead, he had it sent to the quiet corner brazier where Huld tended to Ingolf. There would be little heat coming for most of us, and the hall was even chillier for King Hrolf's sour mood.

Innstein and Utstein did not look up from their game of *hnefatafl* at a table near our discussion. Out of the corner of my eye, I could see them both smirk. If the king was angry, at least it was clear who he was angry at.

Hromund stood to the king's side as if to interdict a sudden spell cast by the head. The champion was loath to leave Hrolf's side in the best of times, and this was not the best of times. He was no more warm to my retrieval of Valborg's head than Beigadh had been.

"Skald!" snapped the king, about one octave too high and three notches too loud. His shout brought me out of my reverie. "I am confused about why we would free an enemy," he continued, now sounding more reason-able. "Perhaps I cut you off. Got only bits and pieces. Severed your narrative. Have you more to say that would stitch things into a completer picture?"

Not loud, not dramatic. The king's voice was even, conveying his utter displeasure only with words. The restraint in his tone was the most unset-tling part. Like a soft hiss before an explosion.

"We went down to find Alfhild, but she was not there," I said. "No one knows where she is, but we all still want to know. Here is a way to find out something more."

"This would be a welcome thing indeed. The very thing you were sent to bring back, in fact. So out with it."

"Alfhild's location is not something Valborg herself knows. She is in a position to learn something more, however, as she's crossed over between life and death. It requires a ritual, but I'm confident—"

"A ritual such as my hall burning down would be as unwelcome as the last time," retorted the king. "Or any other such trollishness as this witch may bring with her. How long did she work with Alfhild, whispering poison into my uncle's ear? How many lies did she help weave to turn good people against me—against you?"

A thick cloud of smug rolled over Hromund's expression as he nodded ever so slightly. Others were not so pleased at seeing King Hrolf that angry. Freemen shuffled wordlessly. Servants froze or scurried away. Even the flames seemed to whisper as they ate the firewood.

Haldor stepped forward to stand with me. "He made an interesting deci-sion. Now we need only decide what to do next."

"Perhaps burying the dead should be next," growled Hrolf to an audible gasp from Valborg.

Huld snarled loud enough to be heard all the way across the hall.

"I have had enough of burying from last summer," Haldor replied. "And as much as we appreciate your hospitality, we intend to leave you come the warmer weather. But where to sail to find Alfhild? We don't know that, and here is an opportunity to find out."

Hrolf drummed his fingers on the arm of his chair, and there seemed to be nothing else in the entire hall willing to make a sound as he considered his response.

Innstein picked up a *tafl* piece in two fingers, pinky out like a dainty lady taking up a sweet. Slow and careful, he placed it back down on the board and winced as the placement made the tiniest sound. Both brothers looked to the king to see if he had noticed.

The king shook his head in disapproval, and the brothers went quickly back to staring at the board in silence.

No one dared make another sound while I struggled for a response. Haldor would speak up for any of his Brothers, but I had to speak for myself as well. By then, I knew the smell of a situation where anything I said to calm things would simply inflame them, and that smell was strong. So I took a breath, closed my eyes, and spoke a verse, hoping Hrolf was less of a poet than he was a warrior:

> "Greater the host
>   who gives the guest
> a chance to tell her own tale.
>
> No hall of fury
>   finds its heroes
> too filled with fright to listen."

The hall remained still and silent after I spoke. I could hear the 'Steins staring and holding their breath to see what came next. They were not the only ones.

And then someone laughed.

Not the chuckle of general amusement. It was a laugh I knew, and it was never at anything so humorous as another man's misfortune. That wheezing, hacking laugh cracked the air, punctuated by a slow thump every two steps.

Ketill struck the ground a final time with his spear and halted within arm's reach of Valborg's head. He faced the king as if shoulder to not-shoulder with the decapitated witch. His wool cloak and hood were draped in casual disarray. Burn marks and tears in his clothing spoke of long use and hard wear. Stains hinted at seasoning that could have been blood or soup or vomit—or all three. But none of the *galdramaðr's* haggard clothes hinted at half the gnarled look of his face.

"They say a wise man's heart is seldom glad. Is that what the king wishes to avoid? Too much wisdom that will weigh heavy on his heart?"

The king leaned forward, his chair creaking. "Wizard, I do not fear you or any wisdom you might threaten me with. I will not flee new knowledge any more than I did fire and iron. Neither do I appreciate fire being invited into my home as a casual guest, regardless of imagined benefit."

"It is less imagined than you think," continued Ketill. "She will know more than she ever could have before. But it is not for just anyone to get the deep lore from her by asking questions as we are now. Her *hamr* holds on, barely, her skin reduced to her head. Her *hugr* has a foot each in this realm and the realm of the dead. The power of that journey back and forth cannot be denied. The part of her that walks in Hel can answer things this part cannot. And I know a ritual that will allow the asking."

"And let that be my last day."

All eyes turned toward Valborg, most confused.

"I will tell the skald all I know," she clarified. "But not to be propped on a table forever."

"Uh, why me—"

Hrolf knit his brows and interrupted me. "Question what you like, but the burner of the previous hall will not linger in this one. Do not stretch my hospitality over-thin, or there will be none left."

How many times had I seen that look of sad desperation on Valborg's face in only a few hours? It had to be a most miserable thing to have no means of avoiding ill will. If we could not stay, I had no good ideas about where to go. Ketill's house was a far walk, even in daylight. The Grove occurred to me if I could find it in the dark of night. Even if I could, there could be no fire to warm us without risking the wrath of the spirits there.

Nanthild pulled at my arm to get my attention. She tapped Need with one hand. As I did not understand, she took a step back and huffed. Trying a new idea, she made a fist and pumped it up and down.

"I still don't understand," I said.

Innstein's fist came down so hard on the table that it knocked half the game pieces out of position and the other half over. "Surt's flaming ballsack, man!" he shouted. "She's telling you to go to the forge."

"You know, where your sword was made," explained an exasperated Utstein. He pantomimed Nanthild's movement with his own fist. "With a hammer?"

Utstein turned back to his brother and murmured something I could not hear. It had an immediate and obvious effect.

"*You were not winning!*" bellowed Innstein. He stood up, knocking over the bench he'd been sitting on, and stormed out of the hall.

Two other bench-riders jumped up quick enough that they did not fall over. Both had the good judgment to laugh about it rather than complain.

Utstein shrugged. "He gets that way sometimes."

King Hrolf stared at the remaining 'Stein. "Two things," he said, reclaiming the attention in the hall. "One: Nanthild's idea is a fine one. You can stay in the forge overnight for shelter. No fires. I won't see my city burned any more than my hall."

"Is that the second thing?" I asked.

"No," said the king, bending forward and locking eyes with me. He lowered and slowed his voice. "The second thing is that Innstein had that game won in four moves." He stared through me with a cold glare, a young man looking and sounding at once more like Kraki or Ketill in their moments of fury. "How easily one can claim a thing will happen when it is the opposite that should be expected."

I gulped, tried to stop myself so that I would not show any reaction, and nearly threw up. Hrolf was as canny a man as I'd ever known. He'd known what was going on in the 'Steins' game even with his attention focused elsewhere. And his last comment was a warning to me. A warning that he expected something ill of Valborg's presence, and I was being naive to not expect the same.

Which, from a man who seemed to see everything, sounded like ill fortune indeed.

"We will . . . ahh . . . we will be off then," I said. "Off to the forge. Until morning."

It would have been an unceremonious exit even without carrying a severed head.

CHAPTER 15

A WISE MAN'S HEART IS
SELDOM GLAD

KETILL CONFERRED WITH HULD BEFORE HE WAS READY TO COME with me to the forge for this ritual. The *vǫlva* wrapped up some of her things and handed them over. A vial and herbs of some sort. Apparently, the wizard had the knowledge required but not all the necessary materials.

"Hope she's worth it," wheezed Ingolf as I left.

We were out the door with Nanthild. A few moments later, we passed Innstein, the Inside-Stein who was, ironically, outside. He was screwing up his face and pulling on his beard.

"About time," he said as we passed by. "What's next?"

"A ritual not for the faint-hearted," said Ketill.

"Why does it need me, though?" I asked. "Shouldn't you do the asking since you will conduct the ritual? I can look for extra blankets so we might stay warm without a fire."

The wizard shook his head.

"A gift always looks to be repaid," he continued. "You've saved her from a bad fate when you had no responsibility to. If I were to question her, it would be a demand, a coercion. But for you, it is a balancing of things and more likely to go well."

"Hmmm," said Innstein, pulling on his beard even more.

"Is that true?" I asked Valborg.

"It's true," added Valborg. "But why is *he* coming with us?" She moved her eyes toward Innstein.

"Ha!" laughed Innstein. "I am a useful person to have around. Someone who did not even hear the king's last few statements. Someone he can't be angry at for making a fire."

I shot Innstein a look. Had he really done that whole act in order to get out of the hall? "How could you possibly have known what was coming next?" I asked.

He shrugged. "My brother and I anticipate a great deal. We knew you were headed to the forge, so we just asked, 'What's next?' And you know, it doesn't take much to know there will be a fire in a forge. Nor much more than that to conclude the king might not like that idea. So off I went."

I hoped one day I would be half as wise as the 'Steins were.

Nanthild put a hand on my shoulder and smiled. Whatever the complexities of her thoughts on taking Valborg back with us, there was nothing ambiguous about her support. I was grateful for it as we walked down the hill to the city below. Maybe even more grateful for the fact that support did not need to be spoken.

We arrived at the forge, which was where Nanthild spent most of her time. Unlike the rest of the crew, she did not care to stay in the king's longhouse. What had been a dump of broken and neglected tools a year before had been quickly transformed under Finnr's direction. Much of the work that turned the place into a dwarf-worthy workshop had been done by Nanthild's brother Ulfberht.

Attached to the forge was a simple hut, Nanthild and Finnr's house now. A room for the two to sleep in was about all it amounted to, but it was theirs. The forge itself was a wider open work area with an empty table in its center. Buckets of sand filled with misbegotten knives and other tools lined the floor alongside the table. Nanthild had been working more than I had guessed. A closer look revealed straighter and smoother blades as I went from bucket to bucket. She was learning. Perhaps the dwarf had found more contentment in teaching an apprentice than in making the items himself.

Innstein started a fire in the forge itself, and Ketill began to set up, spreading out his tools on a table.

"You should sleep," Ketill told Nanthild. "There is no accompaniment on this journey. We will be here in the forge. A fitting place for such a ritual."

"So, is this a journey or a ritual?" I asked. "And why now?"

"I am a woman apart," said Valborg. "And if haste for my sake does not move you, consider that your king will be happier once I am no longer here."

Though the wizard reiterated she should go to her quarters, Nanthild stayed with us in the forge, waving her hands in a gesture I did not understand.

"She can't get to sleep with this going on," said Innstein. "I mean, who would?"

Ketill shook his head. "Very well, but both of you: You do what I say when I say to do it! This is not a stew where if you throw the herbs in too early, the only consequence is it bitters. The stakes of this ritual are high. You will stand back and listen if you insist on remaining awake."

Innstein and Nanthild nodded, far too interested in what would happen next to do anything but go along.

"Stakes like . . . " I said, hoping the wizard would finish my sentence.

"Like leaving your mind a blasted waste of what it once was."

And then I regretted letting him finish my sentence.

"It will not go that way," said Valborg, seeming to sense my lack of enthusiasm. "And it will be over soon."

Ketill directed me to lay a blanket down on the floor and placed Valborg's head opposite my seat. Then he laid out small, stoppered vessels on one of the worktables. "The *volva* is well-provisioned," he said. "I did not bring herbs or oils with me, but she has provided us some. They will help."

Whatever the combination was, it was savory herbs you might cook with and also something you certainly would not cook with. The freshness mingled with the old and musty into a pungence that made me cough.

"Rub this onto her forehead and then your own," Ketill said.

I did as I was told, though it made little sense to me.

"Why my head? Shouldn't it just be hers, as in Odin's spells?" I asked. There was some precedent for smearing a severed head with oil and herbs. Odin alluded to it in his runesong, bragging about the spells he knew. He could speak to the dead this way, though details of how he did that were never forthcoming. Certainly, he never mentioned anointing himself to cast his spell.

"This is not the same as speaking to a dead person," said Ketill. "She died and returned, but only in part. And no, it is not the same idea as Odin described because that is far simpler than what we are doing. What we are doing is closer to hearing a prophecy, only you are going to the spirit instead of the spirit coming to you. You must cross the boundary with her, speak to her as a whole."

"Are you telling me," I asked, suspecting and dreading the answer, "that this ritual will send us both to Hel?"

"The realm of the dead is where the rest of her is," said Ketill. "So, yes. The scent of the oil will help connect you. I will chant and ground you here in this realm. But you must do the crossing, and you must do the listening."

"What if I hear or see things better left unheard and unseen?"

"Nothing hides as many secrets as death. Many of them too terrible to acknowledge in life."

Valborg had been silent for a long while, which perplexed me. "Do you have nothing to add?" I asked. "Can you not tell us what you know now and avoid this . . . trip?"

"We can avoid it entirely if you kill me now," said Valborg. "That weapon of yours would do it. Perhaps something more mundane would end my life as well, but I saw what your sword did. That is a powerful weapon."

"If I kill you now, we won't learn anything about Alfhild," I said.

"You will not have me pass without extracting what knowledge you can. Oh, don't be offended. It is a reasonable thing to expect. You saved me from a worse fate, after all. The wizard is right that this balances things. Had I remained there, it would have been many such journeys instead of one. And in between, they would have left me to the darkness and silence. At best."

I thought about some of the other things that Harbard and his folk might have done to Valborg in the darkness. The shudder came even though I tried to suppress it.

Part of me felt Valborg deserved no favors from us, and perhaps I should have left her to that fate. Something was wrong with it, though. Not that she would have endured pain, even torture, but that she would have endured it with no end in sight and without the ability to raise even a hand in her own defense. That, I could not abide.

"Let's get it done, then," I said, sitting down and readying myself for what would be Valborg's final ritual.

"A favor," she said.

"The skald has done you a favor already," said Ketill.

"We could negotiate, but you need me and I need you. And it is a small thing."

"You can ask, but I won't decide on it until we're finished," I said.

"Let me see the open sky again," said Valborg. "I would see it once more before I die. Perhaps a view of the sunrise."

"The sun setting might be more appropriate for a fire witch," said Ketill.

"I won't complain either way. But I prefer the morning now."

I did not understand that but nodded. It was indeed a small thing.

"I see," said Ketill. "Ready yourself then."

Something kindled a memory, dim and from the previous summer. The raven, Humor, did mention something about trusting some elements more than others, but only a hint. I was too furious at him to listen at the time. Valborg, the fire witch. If that held for the others, Alfhild was associated with water. No wonder she had been able to snatch me out of a flowing river to drag me down and into the caves beneath the fens.

That would leave earth and air, Aldis and Fanya. Fanya had been hidden in the forest when she wanted to be, sneaking out from behind a tree in total silence. But she was not of the earth—her last gasps called the lightning that lit the battlefield and showed me where Alfhild hid. She was air. That left Aldis to be earth. That was where we left her, under the earth in those caves, after Fanya cracked her over the head. Maybe the earth had taken her back, then.

I felt enlightened and stupid at the same time. How had this never occurred to me before?

"Speak your consent," said Ketill, and again, I was confused.

"Wizard, you know more than you let on," said Valborg, her voice softening with every statement. She turned her eyes to me. "I consent to the skald receiving what wisdom I have at the last. Only you who snatched me away from the Down-Below. I would have gone mad there—I was half-mad with fear of it already. As Ansgar the Lucky intends, so will I go and find what knowledge I can."

I looked at Valborg and Ketill blankly.

"This ritual does not involve coercion," said the wizard. "But it does involve risk. It will be uncomfortable at best. Just speak what you consent to. Be specific about what you are willing to see."

"I, um, also consent," I said, trying to sound thoughtful and mask my terror as Ketill began his chant. I was responsible. "Consent to receiving this wisdom. Whatever it is."

Everyone believes they want to learn the deep lore before they learn it. It drives some of them mad. I had no idea what I was saying at the time, much like the words I spoke to join the crew of the *Sea Squirrel*. I would soon find out, though.

Strange but familiar fumes wafted over me. Was the forge not well ventilated? No, it did not smell like wood smoke. The mist snaked through my nostrils, searching out every sensory organ as it crawled through my insides.

That was the last image I recall before the world was filled with fog, leaving only me and Valborg's head. Tendrils wisped up and outward, slowly spinning amongst one another. I stared at this dance for long enough to lose my sense of time. At some point, the world came back into view.

It was frozen as if in ice, but without the cold. Ketill's mouth was open, stilled in the middle of a chant. When I turned to Valborg, she was whole again, standing up, her dark hair shining in the low light. Like me, she was aware and moving. And not alone.

"Now ask your questions," said Svipul.

"Why are you in—"

"Shhhhhh," she said, soft as buttercup petals on warm water. "Not questions about me! Your former enemy is now a friend and owes you a great deal. She has crossed the threshold of life and death. Ask her about Alfhild, about your real enemies; ask for a prophecy. But do not delve too deep."

"Right," I said.

Valborg smiled and stretched, her body full of color and life but all blurred in a haze. A moment to be herself again. "Alfhild knows you live," she said. "All of you. And she is plotting, planning, scheming for your blood. She will have it, and then Hrolf's, if you do not take care. Would you know more than that?"

Dream-like, her words came to me and seemed the wisest I had ever heard, despite carrying little more than the obvious. I had to be more specific, let my will focus on questions more precisely. And I had to ask in *galdralag*.

But when would I have another chance to answer unanswerable questions? Here was an opportunity I would not find again. And so I asked what needed asking and also what was on my own mind.

> "Things we know,
>   known by all,
> not the knowledge I seek here.

I will find secrets,
    unfathomed otherwise,
unless you're unable to answer:
Where the witch has wandered to,
why I'm called cousin by a troll,
and nether truths yet unknown to ask."

Svipul's eyes flashed with fear as she disappeared into the mist.

Valborg closed her eyes, and her neck relaxed backwards, as if in pleasant sleep while she remained standing. A few deep breaths later, she was back. Or something was. Valborg opened her eyes, and they glowed pale blue above a lazy smile. Strands of her hair floated weightless around her. When she spoke, it was her voice and another woven around hers.

At the same time, images formed out of the mist between us. A tower, tall and black against a bleak sky, set on a craggy mountain of an island. Across the sea from the island, the weather cleared. A man in a red cape with a bright golden headband sat at a long table. To his left was an old man with a long beard, his features otherwise obscured. To his right was an enormous man who I supposed had to be half giant.

Others sitting at that table were less notable. Clad like lords and champions, though I did not know their names. Except for one. My father, Styrgrim the Bear, was there. Over this scene, Valborg spoke her first verses.

"The Arrow points
    ever at your enemy,
his great host
    hastening northward.
Grasping at revenge,
    more regret he'll earn,
a yield to share
    with his yeomen.

The Wolf of Bees'
    weave wavers.
Sacrifice required
    to sail on.
The cost of loyalty

lays many low
  one way or another.
    Know you enough, then?"

Valborg's smile turned straight and taut, her eyes paler. I got the sense I could stop then, one question answered. But I did not want to stop. I wanted answers to all my questions. And so I felt us descending together, going deeper to answer the next question. Deeper where? Not just beneath Midgard. It was as if we were floating down through a spiritual abyss.

The voices she spoke in were less happy now.

"I see a winter,
  but not of snow,
when hospitality
  turns hostile
and ancient lore is
  likened as useless.
Inspired fables
  are fully forgotten.

A spear of the gods
  they spoke of, preparing
better fortunes
  before they fade.
A few with the sight
  see a long way,
But few know that much.
  Know you enough, then?"

Again, the same last line. A challenge more than an offer. We were very deep now, and yet I thought the fear was not so bad.

No sweetness was left in her voice, not in tone or pitch. Her visage darkened even as flame outlined her form. Eyes drained of color stared at me, less woman and more *draugr*, grim and hungry.

A hand in my periphery waved, familiar and comforting. A way out if I just took it. Not yet, though, not yet. There was more to learn. The need to know what was next held me fast; the mystery of what the next stanza would be was an intoxicant like no other. The next words came in rasping corpse-breath, the witch sounding very much like the dead thing she was.

> "A hidden wolf
>   waits and watches,
> biding time
>   to break cover.
> The raven banner
>   buried a truth as well.
> Here is more to know
>   than a man might want:
>
> One witch
>   went to her death,
> hewed down
>   by a Hero's hand.
> That history
>   is a hard one to face.
> You seek such knowledge?
>   Not enough do you know!"

An implicit accusation I had caused Fanya's death? Fear gripped me and left me gasping for air. Not fear of violence or death, but an existential dread. Fear that I would face something so horrible I could not stand to see it but that I no longer had any choice.

The images changed. We were no longer in the present looking at the man in red or my father, nor at Alfhild or her shadowy tower. I saw the past through a girl's eyes and heard with her ears.

She stood in the middle of a longhouse, richly decorated but empty of people. Sigils hung from the walls, a golden cow on a bright red field. Long tables ran down the hall, all set with stews and breads and roast meats.

It was a welcome scene, yet fear flooded my senses. She turned suddenly, looking for danger. So did I, as we were merged, Valborg's young self and I. No one appeared despite the feast laid out, and yet the fear only increased.

The roof shook and came away, ripped off by the hand of a giant. He reached in and laughed as she ran. One enormous hand grabbed her and kept her pinioned from shoulder to knee.

She cried out for him to stop, and I cried out with her. I could smell the rancid mead on his breath, feel her helplessness as it was my own. He lifted us up through what had been the roof and into the mist beyond.

And, like in many dreams, we were in a different place for no reason. This time in a bedchamber off of the main hall. The man was a giant no longer, but it did not matter. He towered over us, one hand crushing our wrists together. A rough shove turned us around and bent us over onto a bed of straw, our face driven so deep it was difficult to breathe. We fought but could not move as our dress was lifted from behind.

That was fear and pain as I had never known. It threatened to grind what was left of my sanity into nothing. Death had buried this secret, a nether truth I had not been meant to find.

"Stop!" came Svipul's voice, a clarion call like a war horn.

The word released my mind from its paralysis. I freed an arm. The *fylgja* stretched out to me, urgent, and I to her, wide-eyed in terror as I was. I grasped her hand.

Screaming, I fell back from that place.

CHAPTER 16

SUN AND STEEL

"Skald!"

The word rattled around my head in semi-recognition. Did the person shouting refer to me? Yes, of course. That was me: Ansgar the Skald.

The name came belatedly as I blinked through a haze separating my senses from the world. The shouted word reverberated as if I were underwater. The source of the shouting was a gray blur standing a few paces away. Another blur, smaller and brighter, took a step closer to me.

Nanthild reached out for me as Ketill spoke again, clearer this time.

A memory of being reached out for reared up and seized me—my hands pinioned, my face shoved down into straw, straining but unable to move. I knew what came next, and I crawled backwards in a panic. In seconds, I was gasping for air and shuddering.

Seconds later, I saw there was no straw, and my arms were free. I was in the forge. But the fear did not leave me. I checked behind me and to my sides, pulling my cloak tighter and looking for a way out.

Nanthild's eyes went wide. She had no idea what was happening. How could she? I was in a different place for a long moment, not really present.

"What's wrong with him?" asked Innstein.

The voice fell on my ears like a hammer blow, the fear in me rising with each word. Nanthild took another step forward, and I started at the movement. I backed into a corner, trying to go further and bury myself in the dark. If I could just hide, I would be safe.

"Hold," said the wizard. It wasn't a shout or a raised voice at all. But that voice stilled the room and shook my bones with the force behind it. If a word could stop time itself, that was it. "You two, out."

Neither Nanthild nor Innstein argued though they left with confused looks.

I had more space then. Maybe enough space. Ketill and Valborg were in the same spots I remembered them being in. My eyes flickered from one to the other, looking, appraising.

Valborg opened her eyes. "You are safe," she said, her voice choked with emotion.

Tension ran out of my shoulders. The hyper-alertness began to fade. I breathed out, realizing I had forgotten to breathe in for some time. There was no straw bed, no hall with its roof being torn off. Here was Finnr's forge, Ketill's materials laid upon the work table, Valborg's head propped on a stool. I was not in danger. I was safe.

"What happened?" said Ketill.

"Don't," said Valborg, cutting him off. "Not now. He went deep with me, deeper than I have gone myself. There was more than prophecy. I did not mean to show—" She stopped then and shut her eyes tight. "You are safe."

Why would that simple phrase have such an effect? What had happened to me? I could barely recall.

"What is happening to me?" I demanded.

"You were with me in a memory," said Valborg. "A memory from long ago. It was me; all of it was me. But I am partly dead. You were so eager to know more. And the dead part wanted to show you something better left alone."

"Show me what?!" I shouted as I rose, the memory of that torture refreshing itself.

"My father."

I stood there for a long time, just breathing in and out. Batter-brained as I was, I was beginning to understand. I felt that rape as if it were my own. The pain had been quite bad. The fear, though—that had been beyond imagination. Even with all my skills as a skald, I did not think I could describe it adequately. And I understood more than that. I saw the unseen parts of her story implicitly. The confusion, the helplessness, the fear when she finally ran conflicting with her fear of staying.

And I felt her desire to burn.

I took a tentative step forward with one hand on the table next to me. Good, stable. No panicking again. I caught Valborg's look.

"Alfhild said that to you," I said. "'*You are safe.*'"

"It was the first time I felt so." The right words spoken at the right time are their own spell, regardless of verse form. Alfhild hadn't needed any esoteric poetry to gain a loyal servant for life. She just knew what Valborg needed to hear. "I did not mean to show you the why of it."

There was more in her voice than just regret. There was fear. She had been powerless then and was even more in a man's power now. It would have been easy to leave her, forget her. Let Ketill deal with her if he would. Send her back to Glumra if I was angry about what she had inflicted on me. All those thoughts crossed my mind as I stepped forward, still chilled and exhausted in body and spirit.

"You are also safe," I said. "You'll have your end. And a last sunrise."

Ketill approached me, one tentative step after another. He reached out with a wizened hand to grasp my shoulder. "Come and sit where it is warmer. Speak in your own time."

The fire Innstein had lit was more than welcoming warmth. I moved a bench toward the heat of the forge and placed Valborg's head on it next to me.

"The memory of it will fade," said Valborg. She was trying to comfort me.

I did not want to test that idea by replaying it in my mind, so I thought backwards from there. "Memory of the prophecy," I said. "Will that fade as well?"

"Perhaps, but I know it in my bones. The ones I still have, at least."

Svipul had been there. She had warned me. She had winced at my question. *Nether truths yet unknown to ask* left me open to anything that spirit might dredge up. And I'd had a chance to stop even then, but my will sent me plunging onward. The mysteries hinted at were too great. I was too curious to keep from looking at them.

"I chose to go that deep," I said. "Not knowing what it meant, but I chose it all the same. You are not at fault." I stroked her hair and gave an inadvertent laugh. "Wizard, this must be among the strangest things you've ever seen."

"Do not underestimate my experience with strangeness," said Ketill, sitting down beside Valborg. "There is no deep lore without it. The normal man lives a normal life. Only the very strange push on any boundaries, and they are, therefore, the only ones worth knowing."

We sat and talked for a while. Valborg told Ketill the prophecy, each part of it. Her voice remained the same throughout the telling, to my great relief. I still shuddered at the last two verses.

"There was more than the verses," I added. "I could see images. Not very well, but I saw a few things. A man in a red cloak and gold headband. Others sitting with him were a giant and a man whose features I could not see. And my father. I did not understand any of that. A mountainous island loomed, dark and mist-shrouded, a tower at its top."

Ketill nodded. "The man in the red cloak and golden headband sounds like Arrow-Odd. The prophecy indicates he is at odds with our enemy. Your father is with him, the others I don't know. Yet it does not bode well for them, so we should take care."

"Why could I not see Alfhild?"

"I think that prophecy showed you exactly where Alfhild is. The tower on that island—that wasn't revealed to you by chance. But often enough, a sorcerer can obscure his or her exact whereabouts. That is as good as could be expected."

I nodded. "I wanted to get closer. Know more. Always more." It was my fault.

"I could feel myself being pulled down after that," said Valborg. "Always down. I tried to shout a warning, but it was as if I were split, and the other part—the part that wanted to show—was the stronger."

"And that is where your father was?"

"Yes."

"That's a hard thing to endure," said the wizard, his voice heavy with implication.

I knew at once he had gone that deep before. Who knew when or why, or what he saw? I was in no mood to ask about it. I was chewing on another curiosity. One closer to my mind and more practical as far as knowledge, though I wasn't certain if I should ask it. Soon, I was grinding my teeth at the thought, and I had to give that question voice.

"Valborg, who is your father?"

"Why know his name? He is better forgotten."

"He'll be forgotten after I kill him." There was a logical reaction to what I had seen and heard and felt, and that was revenge.

"Do you wish to do this on my behalf or yours?"

I turned to her. "What does that matter?"

"It matters to me. You helped me freely when you did not need to—when it made others angry. I don't wish to leave a burden behind on your shoulders when I leave this world. I want peace."

It was nine long breaths and much self-searching before I answered. "I don't know. The two motivations are twisted up together like your *hugr* and mine were. I cannot honestly separate them. But I know this for certain: If he still lives, I will kill him, or I will have no peace myself."

She stared back, taking her own time to answer. "Varg Tiorvi of Gotland."

"Varg the Charmer?" said Ketill. "The sorcerer with the cow?"

"The same," she answered.

I'd heard generally of this cow being a potent weapon. Few details, though. I had thought it was just made up. How would a cow be a weapon?

Addressing me again, she continued, "You have sworn no blood-oath over this. He is a dangerous man surrounded by other dangerous men. If you can find your peace without ever seeing him, that is what you should do."

To Hel with that, I thought but nodded.

"The sun will rise soon," said Ketill. "Consider her words. Not the prophecy. I mean the seeking of peace. It is a fair thing to desire."

It was a reminder I had a job to do, a responsibility for another person only I could fulfill. And the best I could do for her was to end her time in Midgard.

Maybe it was good advice to forget Varg the Charmer. As she said, I'd sworn no oath. I might even take my leave of the crew and run back to Dafvik, where fewer things would try to kill me.

I sat with those thoughts for a long moment. They were attractive thoughts. Comfortable and comforting. I could end my silly quest to find my father and prove myself to him. Who knows how many head injuries I could avoid by heading home instead of moving forward into the stormy seas ahead? I would head home with tales to tell, the likes of which few men would ever live even if I left right now.

Valborg must have sensed my inclination as I picked up her head. "What story will you tell after I am gone?" she asked.

"What would you have me tell?" I asked as I left the forge.

"Not the sad story from before, when I ran. There is nothing I ran from worth telling."

I headed back up the hill toward the longhouse as I considered her question. *She tried to burn me in a hall* would not be the best introduction to her story. Hmmm. *She faced death a second time and with an open heart.* That I could tell about.

"Hati chases the moon now almost past the horizon," she said. "Has Skoll chased the sun into view? I would see as much if you can steady yourself." Referencing wolves that chased the sun and moon around the sky meant she was waxing poetic. I suppose that's only appropriate as one prepares to die.

I threw my cloak over my back and made sure I held her so that she could have a better view of the sky as I walked. It was still dark, and only part of the sky hinted at the sun's coming arrival.

The sun and moon ran, but they would be devoured by those wolves when *Ragnarǫk* came. No peace for them as they tried to avoid confrontation. The witch may have told me to find my own peace, but her reference told me something different.

Something itched at that thought. Not metaphorically—I mean my arm itched, and it was not satisfied with a scratch from above my clothing. I reached inside my cloak and inside my shirt down to the source above my left elbow.

Haldor's armring was hot to the touch.

Death would find me in the end, even if spears spared me. Valborg had faced life's spears and to an early end. But so what? That was when she really lived.

"Your story will not be about running," I said. "Your story will be about fighting." Just like every other story worth knowing.

I thought I could feel her smile tucked up under my arm. Snow glinted a soft blue in the early morning air. The earliest stage of twilight was underway, so I still had time to find a suitable vantage point for Valborg's last view. Hrolf had said Valborg was not welcome in the hall, but he said nothing of setting up a short distance from it on the same hill.

"I am surprised you never asked why Alfhild was so interested in you,"

Valborg said, unprompted. "But that's a question needing no ritual to answer, in case you want to know."

"Was I so interesting? She pulled me out of the water as an opportunistic thing, I thought."

"You were separated from the others and in her realm, yes, but you had more value to her than just as a sacrifice."

That was true, I just hadn't thought about it in a long time. Alfhild had glamoured herself during the summer and tried to seduce me in Fanya's form. Why would she do that? I had never gotten an answer, never really looked for one. The witch queen's motivations seemed unknowable to me.

"As a lesson to Fanya? The culmination of a spell of control over me? Something else?"

"You don't know, do you? I think the wizard knows or knows something. You should ask him."

"Ask him what?"

Valborg was quiet for a while as we ascended the hill, and I did not rush her. She started to speak a few times and stopped, looking for the right words. "I've revealed too much already and don't wish to make the same mistake again. If you want to seek more knowledge later, ask the wizard."

I felt like it might be a long time before I could do that.

From the top of the hill, I could see the stark forests had not yet come back to life. Steady pines that remained green throughout the winter stood by them. I found a splitting stump to set Valborg on so she could face the coming sunrise.

The more questions I thought of to ask her, the more I silenced them. I would not spoil the view, for one. And for another, my brain was addled enough by what I had seen. I did not care to delve into any new knowledge just then. So I stood, I watched, and I waited.

Sun painted the snow-capped Danish forests in a warm orange. The light hinted nothing of how the sun fled the wolf but rather promised that spring would come again. Against a blue background, I saw Humor gliding away from the sun's last rays. The moon decorated the sky even yet and seemed to be the bird's destination. Perhaps the moon threatened to conspire with the sun against those wolves, their messages carried by Odin's carrion birds. The thought of such a conspiracy comforted me.

I drew Need quietly. The weapon had become an axe with a prominent toe, a bit like Haldor's axe, Silence. The rune glowed a dull blue as if to express solidarity with the sadness of the coming stroke without denying its necessity.

A soft crunch of snow spoke of someone creeping up behind me. Magnus had come out early, alert despite looking every bit a man who'd not had enough sleep. He looked from me to Valborg and back, gesturing in silence. I did not understand him at first. Then he pointed at himself, drew his axe, and made a motion as if he was volunteering to finish Valborg for me.

Unknown to him, Svipul stood just behind him with an approving look.

I shook my head. *It has to be me*, I mouthed.

With no explanation, he somehow understood. I thought he would leave then, but he just put his axe back into his belt and stood with me.

We were quiet for a long while as the sun took its slow road across the sky.

"This is the first time," whispered Valborg, drifting off without finishing.

"The first time for what?" I asked, wondering if another prophecy was in order and hoping it was not.

"The first time anyone has done for me as I wished. With me in mind. Not part of a bargain. Not an attempt to gain. Just for what I wanted."

I had no words for that. The dark colors of early twilight gave way to warmer hues as the sun came closer to the horizon. No dying light of a sunset for Valborg. No waiting for the last rays to call down the executioner's axe. She wanted to see one more beginning, to watch the clouds announce the sun's arrival before it showed over the treetops. To marvel at how the day bloomed by the second, making every moment brighter than the last. That is how she would die. Not waiting for time to run out, but in wonderment of what is and what is about to be.

"Thank you."

The axe fell true and bit deep. Her face was unmarred except for a trickle of blood coming from the top of her hairline, where the blade's toe had bitten. Valborg died smiling.

Twice then, I had killed out of mercy. It was less awkward the second time but just as draining, violence enacted on someone I had no wish to be violent to.

"Pyre or burial?" asked Magnus.

"Pyre, no question."

Magnus did not ask if he could help before he started helping. We laid a base and split logs for kindling together. Having my friend there felt good.

Moving felt good. Not moving carried the fear of too much brooding, and I felt the fire witch should be laid to rest with no small testament.

Others had woken by the time we set the pyre alight. They understood enough to leave us be. I stood with the fire as I watched Valborg disappear into a sea of flames. There was no trace of a skull by the end. Was the disappearance particular to the rites of the witch, or did the *fylgja* have a hand in it? I had so many questions but decided that one did not matter.

Magnus did not speak. I think he knew I had no desire to talk and no need for counsel. He even waited with me as the last flames flickered out. Only when I turned away from the ashes did he turn back with me. I heard warriors stirring in the hall as we approached. And I knew that, like Magnus, they were my Brothers.

And that was where I belonged.

We would face those spears life pointed at us. Face them with plenty of our own.

CHAPTER 17

A SONG OF SPRING

I walked into the hall bone tired but with the feeling I'd at least accomplished something important. Valborg's prophecy would be valuable, a thing to stop the naysayers still suspicious of my decision to bring her back. That was not the reception that greeted me.

Ingolf was feverish and had a hard road if he was to survive. As I heard the news from Huld, too many eyes were on me for comfort. The looks had redoubled in suspicion, bringing back the sudden, paralyzing fear. I could hear what those eyes did not say: The skald lent his luck to an enemy rather than a friend.

"He has the eyes of a thief," some of them whispered. And I supposed my wide-eyed, darting glances might have given that impression. I wondered how many with the "eyes of a thief" I had run into before had no thieving in their pasts but only some terrible experiences.

I crawled to a corner and waited for the panic to abate. Few bothered me since I had been up all night. Almost none knew the nature of my distress. I got slightly better over the course of a few days, but nights remained difficult.

Ingolf did not die but was bedridden and bitter about it. "A straw life," he called it, unable to move much while his ribs healed. There was much muttering about luck and sidelong glances full of suspicion directed at me. The hall seemed chillier than ever.

Grim weeks went by and the weather remained normal—normal still being very cold and icy, all but confining us inside for a time. The vicious winds Valborg had called up were gone, but the snowfall was heavy. I wished for something to do, anything, and threw myself into trying to decipher the Roman codex. It was a pointless endeavor.

Whatever those runes were in the codex, even Ketill did not recognize them. I brought it round to every merchant visiting the hall, and none recognized it. In a fit of what I assumed to be genius, I brought it to Stanislav, one of the few surviving Rus we had fought against last summer. He had been badly wounded but recovered, and Hrolf had spared him. I was certain he would recognize the script and tell me its secrets, but no, he just shook his head. Even drew some of his own letters for me in the snow. They were nothing like these.

A Roman codex. Yet not written in Roman letters, which I knew. Was it truly Roman then, or something else?

The few drawings were the only parts we could understand. Alfhild's champion, Frothi, must have found those sufficient to make his crossbow, but I could not figure out even that much.

Ingolf puzzled over the codex for hours at a time. The letters were a mystery—vaguely similar shapes to our runes but nothing that could be pieced together. He spent more time staring at the drawings with an ever-serious expression plastered on his face.

Soon, I was caught up in wondering what my position with the crew was. Again. And here I had intended to march up to Kraki and tell him I was going after Varg Tiorvi, whether on the *Sea Squirrel* or not. I would come close to mentioning it, Kraki would glare, and I would take those glares as indications that he was not in the mood for conversation.

Nanthild was not even a silent comfort. She spent her time back at the forge rather than the king's hall, and soon Finnr was well enough to join her there. The mood of the king's champions had soured ever since I came out of the Down-Below with Valborg's head. They seemed to laugh only at Ulf's jokes, most of which were at my expense. I could not very well express my distress to any of the men, even Magnus. Saying anything to Ketill was at once logically obvious and emotionally unthinkable.

I wondered if it would have been different had Kari still been with us. But the lindworm broke his neck in last summer's battle, and so there would be no speaking to him at this point. Nor repaying him for saving my life . . . three separate times.

When he was still alive, he'd told me it was the waiting that was always the worst part. When it was time to fight, you just fought. Nothing wrong with that. But the anticipation—the time when you were ready to act but could do nothing but wait—that was the worst. Kari had been a wise man. I wished I had asked him how to deal with that mind paralysis.

And while the panic did not threaten me the same way it had when I went too deep with Valborg, it assailed me at night. The darkness would set my mind to racing and prevent sleep. Or I would sleep, and the panic would find me. Dreams were varied, but the feeling of helplessness was the same.

Then there were the other thoughts. The ones that crept in, always announced by a single word: "Cousin." I recalled Olgram's last word with a mixture of curiosity and fear of that curiosity. I considered asking Ketill about Alfhild's interest in me, on Valborg's advice, but stopped myself every time. Secret knowledge seemed a lot more dangerous than it had before.

I told no stories, composed no poetry, played no songs. The beautiful lyre King Hrolf had gifted me fell out of tune. I ate sparse portions at the morning and evening meals. I chewed on the answers I had gotten from Valborg's ritual over and over, but they brought mostly new questions. All I knew was I wanted to kill a man, and I was stuck doing nothing but waiting until the weather was good enough for sailing.

Being stuck in that great hall among great warriors was one thing, but being stuck with their disapproval gnawed at me. So I did not speak much, despite being a skald. No one commented on my reticence. Other than my *fylgja*, who only I could hear. I did repeat the prophecy many times at Haldor's request, but just the words. I could not convey the chill that the ritual had given me and did not try. My only counsel there might have been Ketill, and he saw only a puzzle to solve.

"The first two stanzas tell us where to go," said the wizard. "Find Arrow-Odd, we will find Alfhild. Though why he would be interested in her is unknown. I don't like this bit about the cost of loyalty. And what is this about the 'wolf of bees'?"

That question was the single thing I had an answer for. "That's Haldor. Humor named him as such last year."

"Named him the wolf of bees? Ah, the bear. Because of his size."

"Actually, it was because he was using so much honey in his porridge."

The wizard hesitated and then, seeing I was serious, laughed.

Ketill had less interest in the second two stanzas, which most puzzled me.

I brooded on those by myself. And the last two frightened me to even think about. My instinct screamed that the answers to these stanzas contained more wisdom I would rather do without.

"You were deep with her when she spoke those lines," Ketill said. "Hidden truths, secrets perhaps better left secret. What do you think of when you think of them?"

I shuddered and did not know why.

"The hidden wolf, I don't understand. Maybe to do with Kraki's dream last year. He wanted an interpretation of a masturbating wolf."

"That is . . . strange."

"Strange, yes. But soon after, we had a visit from Halfdan the Toothless, whose symbol is the jaws of the wolf. He asked us if we were headed north to see what Ogmund would pay. I wonder if he went north himself or if maybe we will see him again as this hidden wolf."

Ketill sighed and pulled on his beard.

"They may be unconnected," I continued, "but I don't know what else to connect this hidden wolf to. The raven banner is different—that is my father, Styrgrim's, banner. So there is some secret he's kept. The last part—I think that was Valborg's dead half getting even with me for killing her. Rubbing it in my face a bit."

Ketill nodded uncertainly, his bushy eyebrows coming together as one. He said little more about the prophecy, but it was plainly on his mind.

Meanwhile, I was waking up in the middle of the night in a cold sweat much of the time and playing it off as indigestion. Most of the men found this annoying but went right back to sleep. Only Kraki seemed to keep a wary eye on me.

I could not speak of what I had experienced. So how would I convince Kraki to take the ship to Gotland to kill Varg Tiorvi? The more unease I felt, the more isolated I became, leading to more unease. Time was the enemy of all, but so were the nightmares. Not every night, just enough nights to leave me weary in so many ways.

Weeks passed, and whatever defiant energy I'd had leftover from Valborg's end had long since burned away. It was well and good to feel resolute in the moment, but carrying it through for two more months was something altogether different. Conversation became forced and awkward, as in more forced and awkward than usual. Magnus could tell something was wrong but left me to myself.

The 'Steins were ever playing *hnefatafl* and would do so near me, daring me to challenge one of them to a game.

One day, they got an unexpected result.

"I think today is the day," said Utstein.

"You said that yesterday," replied Innstein, "and yet it was not."

Whether they were talking about the game, or their betting, or me was unclear.

"Oooohhhhh, here are those beautiful brothers," Svipul cooed as they sat conspicuously near me while conspicuously not acknowledging me. "Are you going to say anything?"

I wanted to do something—anything—after Valborg's prophecy. The desire to act ran up against the inability to do anything and fell flat. I was like a climber at a sheer wall of ice. That feeling was bad, and it made me brood on unhappy thoughts, which was worse. The cold of winter can sap a person of energy that way. I was still a skald but not acting like one, so I said nothing.

"They cannot talk to you. It would seem too much like propping you up. I will talk to you and give you advice! You should say something. Something cheerful!"

My *fylgja* would not shut her face.

"They like you! Or at least they do not think you are cursed, and that is something. See how they sit nearby? That is what passes for affection among men, is it not?"

She was irritating both for being too cheerful and for her astute observations. As an astute observer myself, this raised a number of questions about how I was still alive. At the same time, it answered several more about why irritated people had previously tried to kill me.

I wanted to tell her this but was the only one who could see or hear her. Talking to yourself, whether people thought you had a *fylgja* around or not, was not a mark of sanity.

"You need to talk first! Ask them about their game, perhaps. They have already met you halfway."

The brothers laid out the familiar eleven-by-eleven board with the black attackers on each edge, a group of white defenders protecting their king in the center. Utstein moved first, attacking this time. I knew the game well enough to understand the mechanics but never had much interest in playing.

To say nothing seemed more cowardly than quiet. The two brothers were friendlier to me than most. I had to take the *fylgja's* advice.

I left the table to the confused looks of the two brothers but returned immediately with my lyre.

"I will play while you two play," I said.

"Do you know any good *hnefatafl* songs?" asked Innstein.

"Or sad songs for my brother's dead king, maybe?" said Utstein.

I plucked the strings of the lyre over and over as I brought them into tune. Satisfied the gut strings played the notes I needed, I pointed back at both of them. "Not for a moment will I consider betting on your game."

The two were taken aback. Eyes wide, hands in the air, mouths open. What an insult!

All an act.

"I know your minds, you two," I said as I tested the strings a final time. "You will have to be content with a tune to inspire spring."

So I played while they played, all of us engaged in our own mock subterfuge. The brothers were there to encourage me to stop wallowing. It was not enough, but it was enough to prod me into getting my lyre. With that, I was committed. My *fylgja* settled in with a smirk.

Slow and sad, I strummed the first theme, knowing nothing of where I was going with the song. Slow and sad for winter because there is no spring without winter. Improvisation was something my foster father had praised. Demanding as he had been in my studies, he always encouraged experimentation. He locked me out in a blizzard for being too lazy with my Latin once but never punished me for trying something new.

After the day's work is done and the evening meal taken in, we would pass the time with music and stories. My previous lyre had bettered many a cold evening by providing more warmth than the fires inside could muster.

An audience formed, not that I wanted one. Spring would have been a happier time to look forward to if the previous summer had not been so full of death. The song's tempo increased while I thought of the winter winds buffeting me months before. I looked at my *fylgja*, who had snuck up on me in that weather. Whatever she was, she had said an impromptu "Hello" by introducing my manhood to a ball of snow. I trusted her, but I did not trust her sense of humor.

I was in a great hall among great men, but I was as trapped as they were. More so, as they had the patience to wait out the season while I stewed. The former queen was out there somewhere. It was she who called in those things from the Ironwood we fought. She who hired those Rus who turned on us. She who was responsible for Fanya's death.

The tempo further increased, but the tone changed from sad to angry in the second theme. Bring the winter, bring the ice, I thought. We had taken the Stone Road, the path to the Down-Below, where dwarves and trolls of all kinds dwelt. And we had come out with the animated head of a dead *volva* to tell us dark wisdom and secrets. The ritual I had used to ask her those secrets wrapped my mind in a spider's web. One I was still trying to emerge from.

Secrets are most often hidden or buried. But sometimes, they are sitting right in front of you, only remaining secret due to a failure of observation. It was at that moment in the music that I recognized one such secret right in front of me, though I had seen it before.

Utstein had lost many of his attackers, the remainder of which were spread out across the board. He could no longer swarm his brother's king as Innstein methodically opened a hole for his king to escape. The king's exit to the edge of the board seemed soon at hand.

And yet just as Innstein's king came out from behind its wall of defenders, one of Utstein's pieces that had been out of position discovered a clear line of attack. Innstein defended, but that opened another line of attack. I had seen that smaller force drive into the heart of enemy territory before. Not just the tactics involved but the same moves.

The *exact* moves. The game was rehearsed.

The theme halted on a series of discordant chords, ending on an off-note as if to ask a question. Here, I recalled Valborg's end, an end she had requested so as to not linger in Midgard. I recalled building her pyre with a rising harmonious chord progression.

The tempo was slow, but this was neither sad nor angry. There was pain in it, not forgetting what had come before. But there was hope as well, like a sprouting seed that had taken the worst of winter's onslaught only to rise from the earth stronger for the experience. The theme grew in complexity with each interval, slow and then medium, but never hurried.

Some of the crew were beating a rhythm on the seats or the walls. I thought I might match it, but there was no consistent cadence, only gentle thrumming. I raised the pitch by an octave and speeded the tempo up, picking quicker notes that blended into the theme in a pitter-patter arrangement. My lyre showered the music in warm tones among the hall's gruff inhabitants.

I could feel the song finishing as I picked notes higher and slower, letting the music fall through the air to land gently at our feet. Then I realized the men were stock-still and staring at the ceiling and that no one had been beating a rhythm at all.

It was raining.

Murmurings began. All different, but all ultimately saying the same thing: Lucky skald.

"Perhaps the witch was not the only one who could affect the weather," said Innstein.

It was some feat to distract those in the hall, an even greater one to see most of them bolting for the door. But I understood. The winter had been long and hard and with much gloominess to brood on. Did any of them have a plan other than to get wet out there? Probably not. And the rain would be quite cold. But it was our rain, our first rain of the season, and it was the most welcome sound any of us had heard in a long time.

"We can finish the game later," said Utstein. "Let's go join them."

"You are the Outside-Stein," said his brother and shrugged.

"Hold," I demanded. "Neither of you are going anywhere."

"Ha!" said Innstein. "In all our lives, I think no one has succeeded in telling us such a thing!"

"You're not going anywhere unless you want me to begin speaking very loudly," I whispered. "Very loud indeed. About how you aren't really playing *hnefatafl*, you're just going through the motions of a memorized game."

"Ha!" guffawed my *fylgja*. "What a reversal!"

"The why of something is always more important than the what," I said. "So tell me why while our friends are distracted outside, and I will keep quiet about it."

The 'Steins stared at me with the silence of men who are so badly caught in the act they don't know what to do. They said nothing, then eyed each other in the conversant silence only they could conjure. Innstein spoke first.

"Easier to listen if we are running through a memorized game."

"And more likely that others nearby will speak freely as we appear to be paying attention to nothing but the game."

My eyes widened. "You can't be serious. You use it to spy on people?"

"Of course not," said Innstein. "We are just listening while other people speak freely."

The 'Steins were lazy unless they had ship repairs to do. Or that was what I'd thought. They spent so much time just sitting, playing their game, that this seemed the obvious conclusion. Only they were not playing at all, but listening. All the while, people around them assumed they would be enmeshed in the competition. So they wagged their tongues in perceived safety.

Meanwhile, the 'Steins were listening to every word. No wonder they always seemed to be a step ahead.

"We can finish the game later," repeated Utstein, louder than the rest of our conversation.

The 'Steins rose and headed for the door. Even Innstein, whose name I had to imagine, indicated he did not want to be out in the rain.

They left me alone on the bench, blinking as if doing so would let me see even more of what was right in front of me. It was not so great a discovery, I suppose—not like a hoard of treasure or seeing someone's true nature while they hid it well. It was just the realization that so much of what I thought I understood might be a misunderstanding.

"You should play the lyre more often," suggested my *fylgja*.

CHAPTER 18

HERDING CATS

OVERCOMING BOREDOM AND BROODING WAS ONE THING, BUT the weather clearing up led to something even worse: Work.

Nor were there sunny days, so it was work in the rain and mud: Repairs to the hall's roof, the chopping of wood, and carrying of water went on endlessly, and digging a pit for a closer outhouse soon came up. Though I wanted to see that project completed, it was not a process I wanted to be part of. Therefore, that is what I was assigned. Soon, I was silently cursing my cold, wet feet and wishing to be back indoors.

Svein and I were literally in the muck, surrounded by five-foot walls of earth. About six feet wide and more than twice that in length, it was a closer proximity to the big man than I preferred to spend my time. I also hated digging, especially digging while wet and cold. The weather may have warmed past snowing, but not by much.

At some point in that process, chunks of wet dirt collided with the side of my face. Some of that volley ended up in my mouth. I would have turned suddenly to face my assailant, but it was a small space in that pit, and I knew who was responsible.

"Stop sighing!" said Svein. Half annoyed with me, half amused with himself, the big man at least did not shovel any more dirt in my direction.

After a pause to think and consider my position, I continued digging. "Interesting thought," I said, still spitting out dirt.

"What's 'interesting' about it?" demanded Svein.

I did not answer.

"Well?"

"Hold on a moment, it's complicated."

Svein could smell a lie as long as it was obvious enough. "No, it's not!"

"You're right, it's not," I said and went back to digging. Just before Svein was ready to demand an answer again, I continued. "It's just that I need to figure out a way to explain it using concepts simple enough and words small enough that you would understand."

It took him a full heartbeat to recognize the insult, and then he was after me. I was already up and over the lip of the pit. I rolled out of arm's reach and then stood looking down at the angry behemoth.

The hole was too deep for him to amble up. I had no trouble hiking my legs up, but he did. Despite being taller than I was, weight was not on Svein's side. Neither were his legs limber enough to make the same move I had. He hopped angrily as he tried to hold the lip and get one foot up at the same time, then slipped down and started over again. A few failed attempts later, he settled for a straight-on approach, hoisting himself onto his midsection and slowly dragging himself forward.

But it was still raining, and the mud was slippery. Soon, Svein was sliding backwards, all his brute strength availing him nothing other than to leave claw marks in the ground. For some reason, he forgot to leave his feet under him, and then he was on his ass in the mud pit.

I addressed the prone warrior in short words and simple concepts.

"This pit is just about done. One of two things can happen now. One is that you finish up and go tell Haldor you let the skinny skald go early because you are so much more useful than he is. Then Haldor thanks you, and you get a snack. The other is that you come after me in any way, and then I start composing poetry about how you attacked me but I bested you because you are a terrible fighter. One who will never be as good as Haldor. And you know what will happen then? Lots of poetry reminding you about that. Every. Single. Day.

"So: Snacks or poetry?"

I left Svein huffing himself red in the face. I thought about wiping my face off, then thought better of it. If I wasn't going to do any more work, at least I would look like I had done my fair share. Maybe attract less attention that way. I had nothing in particular in mind next, I only knew that I was not in any mood to deal with Svein's idiocy. I decided to go back to the hall and warm my fingers by the fire.

The raven got my attention before I had taken my second step. Humor swooped down and landed a few strides in front of me.

"I don't have any eyeballs for you," I said.

"No wonder you can't see what's going on, then!" responded Humor. "So many errands the wizard asks these days. Fly to Roskilde, take messages, bring messages back. It's like he thinks I work for free!"

"Didn't you get not one, but two great feasts for ravens last year?" I asked. "I think you've had the first pick of several good meals from your time here. But if you're hungry, we won't begrudge you something."

The raven made a sound like a burp. "I ate already."

"So you just came to complain?"

"Complain? Not at all. I came to remind the wizard what a good job I've been doing for him despite his meager compensation."

I nodded, grinning. "No news from Roskilde then?"

"Of course there is news from Roskilde, but I don't want to tell it twice."

The port town of Roskilde was where the 'Steins did their work. The *Sea Squirrel* needed cleaning and probably some repairs after that winter, and their sole purpose was to ensure the ship's seaworthiness. If there was news from Roskilde, it was likely news about when we might set sail.

I gulped, realizing I had still not made my intentions clear. And time might be short.

"Ketill is probably in the hall," I said. "I'll come hear this news with you."

"And tell them I need some eyeballs!"

Humor flapped up to my arm, and we entered the hall together. Someone had added wood that was not quite as dry to the hearth fires, increasing the smokiness inside. It was warmer there but less easy to breathe. I took it as Hrolf's subtle suggestion that people should not be lazing about the hall while there was work to do. I had no doubt he was busy himself as I spied his empty high seat. Most of those inside the hall were moving to one place or another, with few seated on the benches. Except for three.

Ketill, Haldor, and Kraki sat on a bench and spoke in low tones. A serious conversation, then. I looked around for Huld and did not see her. Maybe on one of her errands or maybe disappeared for a time. I could never tell which. The king and his champions were out, but some of his guests remained in the hall. A few had come in to avoid the rain, but most had been lying about regardless of the weather.

"A message has come in," I said, raising my arm to let Humor kick off and flap his way to the table. "Though it might be more than just information."

"Hmph! I'll speak honeyed words, and then this wolf of bees will lap them up." An outstretched wing indicated the comment had been directed at Haldor.

"Troll-cursed, daft birds," muttered Kraki.

"He is useful sometimes. A good reminder, just now," said Ketill, which was about as cheery as Ketill ever got. "Probably misses having High Pants to talk to."

"Where is High Pants?" I asked. King Hrolf's hawk was not a talker, at least to me. To ravens, maybe. To most, he was a bloody maniac of a bird.

"The king sent him to accompany Gudbrand," said Haldor. "They're not likely to return until he's brought the war arrow around to all the Danish lands calling for ships and warriors."

"A boring job," said Humor. "But not as boring as mine. Probably with better compensation."

The three men eyed me as if I'd done something wrong.

"He told me he wasn't here to complain at all," I said. Which was true, sort of.

Ketill shook his head. I got the feeling I had walked into an argument in progress, which was quickly becoming an argument about other things.

"Svein did not care for my company. He is finishing the pit now. I thought I might be useful some other way."

"Tell us what your witch's prophecy means, then," barked Kraki. "Then these two can be done with arguing over it. An end to endless discussion would be welcome."

Haldor sat up straight and folded his arms. "Ketill thinks the prophecy indicates a trap. You heard the prophecy directly. What do you say about it?'

"You mean the indication we should go north and find Arrow-Odd?" I asked. "There is a big risk for certain. *Grasping at revenge, more regret he'll earn.*' But if his army is pointed at Alfhild in the first place, I don't know how we would go after her and ignore Odd in the process."

"It is not that part," said Ketill. "I mean the second stanza. *Sacrifice required to sail on.'* That word is not there by accident for a crew with a rule against sacrifice."

"A warning," I said. "If the word choice is no accident, it is a warning against Haldor specifically."

Ketill thumped the table and nodded.

"I will die no matter what," huffed Haldor. "So will you. So will we all, at some point. I won't spend my life cowering from its end."

"So you see, skald, there is little argument about what the prophecy means," growled Ketill. "It is only what to do about it that is in question." So that was the disagreement. Ketill finally had a way to interpret that part, and thus interpreted, it would be ignored as irrelevant.

"Sometimes a prophecy can go more than one way if it is contingent on a choice," said Haldor. "I won't sacrifice as the seeress mentioned. And Kraki must decide whether this means he won't sail north."

There was no point in playing to Haldor's preference. His mind was made up, and I was not surprised. Haldor was a hero, like one from the sagas. And in the sagas, heroes often received prophetic warnings. In every single case, they ignored them.

"I am going to Gotland," I said. I couldn't think of a soft way in, and the tension of making myself plain had gotten the better of me. "There is a man I need to kill."

The wizard stopped dead at that and looked up, eyes bright. "The skald has spoken."

"King Hrolf pays us for killing the witch," said Haldor. "Which we would have done for no payment at all. Who is this man you want to kill in the meantime?"

"Varg Tiorvi."

"That is some statement, skald," said Haldor. "Many people have tried to take Varg's lands and life. Entire armies, in fact. They have all failed to do so. Do you intend on this even if the crew sails elsewhere, leaving you to attack him all by yourself?"

"One man might find a crack that an army cannot."

Kraki screwed his face up looking at me, trying to discern something. "That is a task to get yourself killed."

"Or not," countered Haldor. "Luck has found him when he needed it. As it does many a person whose courage holds."

"I would welcome the help and call that my luck," I said, "and I would prefer to then continue pursuing Alfhild. But I must do this thing first."

"Why not go after him later?" asked Haldor.

I shook my head. "I know where he is. I will not put it off."

Humor hopped around and cocked his head at me. "Nobody seems to be where they're expected right now. He could be off raiding or trading!"

"Varg the Charmer stays in his hall, and with good reason," said Ketill. "That's for one thing. For another, what is it you mean by 'nobody seems to be where they're expected'? Are you telling us there is unexpected news from Roskilde?"

"Hrolf wants to talk to Huld, but she is . . . " the raven trailed off and eyed me. "She is not around at the moment. Finnr and Nanthild are off in the woods. Innstein and Utstein are down by the docks in Roskilde, looking at pictures."

"Looking at *pictures?!*" roared Kraki. Rounding on me, he continued. "They are supposed to be repairing the ship, and they are looking at *pictures?*"

"They could be looking at images on a runestone they found," I said. "It isn't necessarily—"

"No runestone," interrupted Humor. "They had this thing made of skin. Lots of skins! And they flipped one skin over and there was another one. And another one. And another—"

"So they are looking at the codex," I said. "They probably found something useful for the ship."

"Useful, nothing!" Kraki was standing and shouting every word by then. "There is something in those pages turning their minds to mush. Where is that damned king? Maybe he knows a shipwright we can hire."

"I am sure they will do a fine job," I said.

Haldor bit back a grin, and I realized my every utterance was only adding whale oil to the fire.

"A fine job is one thing," Haldor cut in. "But this is no time for experimentation. We need the ship seaworthy. Skald, you will go to Roskilde and deliver that message. You will then take the codex and bring it back here. They are not to see it again until we set sail."

"I am going with him," said Kraki. "I want to see the state of my ship. Something is wrong, I am certain of it. Those brothers take too many liberties!"

"What about sending Humor to deliver the message?" I said. "He can fly much faster than I can run. And certainly much faster than—" and I realized I had talked myself into a corner.

"Faster than the Bentleg can hobble?" growled Kraki. "I seem to remember moving plenty fast enough to keep your skin-bag intact when it was Rus mercenaries or trolls Down-Below. Now *move*."

The old man dragged me out of the hall faster than I could carry myself.

CHAPTER 19

THE VIRTUE OF REVENGE

THOUGH THE WALK TO ROSKILDE WAS ONLY A FEW MILES, IT seemed like it would be a very long trip indeed. Kraki was furious at the idea the *Sea Squirrel* was not being taken care of. And as that fury had neither of the 'Steins to channel it at the moment, it was all focused on me.

The shouting turned a few heads as we made our way through the city.

"What is a skald's use when labor is needed?" he bellowed. "If we left it to you, there would be a thousand verses about getting revenge without ever getting it!"

At least it wasn't raining anymore.

"I have no verses about revenge yet," I countered, tiring of the captain's constant disapproval. "Any such verses will be a long time coming if I have to find my own way to Gotland. What do you have to say about that, then?"

He bared his teeth and growled as a response. I don't know what might have come next without a distraction.

"Oy!" shouted Inga. The brewer caught our attention as she waved her giant spoon just outside her hut. She held a pack full of juniper berries under her other arm. "Are you two done? I have something for you."

Kraki's face went in many directions at once. He wasn't one to go from aggravated to pleasant quickly. In fact, I wasn't sure if he ever quite got to pleasant. But he wasn't about to turn down a gift from a *drengr*.

And Inga was a *drengr*—not a warrior by choice, but she picked up a spear last summer when it was needed. Inga was not the only brewer in the city, but she was the king's brewer. Some of her graying hair had escaped her headband and hung loose.

"You've got dirt on your face," she said as we approached.

"I am hard at work," I said, hoping it would make actual steam shoot out of Kraki's ears. I think it came close. "You have something for us?"

"For you in particular. If you can hold the work and hold the shouting for a moment, I'll fetch it." She darted inside.

"Do you need any help in there?" I may have an aversion to labor, but I was a smart young man. Smart enough to know that if you help a brewer, the brewer may pour you something very tasty.

"We already have an errand," Kraki said through his teeth.

"It is good you are here," Inga said from inside. "I think you may find this useful."

"I know how to use ale," I said. "Perhaps overmuch sometimes."

"This is different. Your friend, the dwarf, is not the only one with great skill in his craft."

As much as hearing hammer strikes could lead a man to Finnr's forge, the smell of heated barley would tell you in an instant where to find Inga. That was some great aroma lingering from her latest work.

She emerged holding an aurochs horn, its wide end stopped up with wax. At its other opening was a cork. A simple braid of leather was wrapped around the length of it and fastened to a carrying strap. Here was a drink, but for later.

And here was Inga, her face drawn tight as it held back emotion.

"You know, I always thought the troll killed Lambi," she said, speaking of her slain husband. "Crushed to death. What would do that other than a troll?" She shook her head. "But then I saw you fight the lindworm, saw it wrap around you. And then I knew."

"It was really Haldor who killed it," I said, less comfortable by the second. "The first time, at least."

She nodded. "And Alfhild raised it. And then you put it down forever. Do not be modest—I saw the corpse, saw its mangled jaws. That was vengeance for my husband, and I never gave thanks. A brewer can't make unpierceable armor or a sword that cuts through stone. But I know my craft, so take this and use it well. It is Memory Ale."

She handed me the horn, and I nodded. Maybe I thanked her, I don't know. I was too overwhelmed. Parts of the battle came back as she described them. Thinking of her husband dying made me think of losing Fanya. And forward-thinker as I was, I was still a young male Norseman, uncomfortable with feelings.

Some semblance of rational thought returned after a few moments. "I know this from some of the myths," I said. "But I never tried it myself. How do I best use it?"

She waved a hand and shook her head. "Drink this, and whatever you hear and see for a time, you will remember it all perfectly."

"How long a time?"

She shrugged. "You can never tell with these things."

"Sounds a bit like *galdr*," I said, noting the eerie conjuration of Ketill. All cooks, but especially brewers, are wizards of a sort.

"Perhaps. Who knows if you will need this? But it is what I can offer. Make what use of it you can."

Then I did thank her, and we took our leave, again heading to Roskilde. There was no more shouting as we walked.

There was also no more talking at all for a good while past the north gate. For a time, I savored that silence along the path out from the city and into the forest beyond. Soon, the silence became tedious, though.

"Can Finnr brew Memory Ale?" It seemed like an important question.

Kraki shook his head. "Finnr is a smith."

"Any idea how long this stuff lasts once drunk?"

"Varies."

"It would be helpful to know more about it before I decide when to use it."

"Doesn't matter."

Something was going on in Kraki's brain, and I could not fathom it. But I reasoned we would soon be in Roskilde, and so if he did find himself in a shouting mood again, he would likely be shouting at the 'Steins. I decided to keep prying.

"It seems like it matters a great deal."

"What you use it for should be clear enough if the need arises," he said with only a hint of snappishness. "That is not what matters."

"What matters then?"

He rounded on me. "That's a gift for revenge taken. Think that's not a sign?"

"I, uh," I stammered, not understanding what he was getting at or why he sounded like he was about to strangle me.

"Tell me why you want to kill Varg Tiorvi."

That was a long answer I had little interest in giving, so I settled on the short version. "Revenge."

"Have you ever met the man?"

"No."

"Revenge for what, then? Make it plain, or you can swim to Gotland."

I swallowed and considered how to word this. "What I saw when I heard Valborg's prophecy—I saw something from her past. She did not intend for me to see it, but I saw it all the same. I will not tell it, as it does not deserve to be told, but neither will I let it pass. Varg needs to die."

Kraki nodded and continued walking. "You cry out in your sleep."

My face went red and my jaw locked shut. I quickened my pace, hoping to arrive at Roskilde as soon as possible.

"Magnus tells the others you have bad digestion. It goes with your story from when you went out into a blizzard to take a shit. But I know stomach pains from other pains and am not fooled. You gave Inga revenge for her husband, now you seek revenge for a dead woman. A dead woman can't repay you with a gift like Memory Ale."

"I am not interested in a gift later. It is something that needs doing for itself."

The old man quickened his stuttering gait to match my speed and faced me. "I know of a monastery on Gotland near the coast. The abbot is Candidus, a decent man for one of those White Christ followers. We can land there without difficulty. There will be plenty of difficulty as we approach Varg, though. He is set up in the center of the island, all the better to make use of his cow. That cow will be a hard thing to defeat."

A weight lifted from my shoulders. I hadn't noticed it there until it was gone. Whatever magic this battle cow had, I was sure we could overcome it.

"We will have one other errand today," he continued. "But first, I will see to my ship."

There was little more to say before we reached Roskilde, and I became increasingly wary of saying anything at all. Kraki was doubtless turning over the lack of work in his mind again. I could hear him huffing at each thought. It was near time to get out of his way.

The small fishing village had expanded since we'd landed there nearly a year before. A few dozen buildings huddled close together, almost as if they would share hearth fires. The docks had plenty of ship berths. More had been added last autumn after the battle. Word spread of Hrolf's victory, and that brought more trade with more ships. More ships meant more people, and more people meant the need for more fishing boats. That all meant more materials and supports for ship repairs.

The 'Steins were working on the *Sea Squirrel*, situated atop one such set of supports. Or at least they were looking at the ship. They might have been scraping the keel or tarring the hull, testing for weak areas, or cleaning it top to bottom. They were not engaged in any of those things.

Innstein held the codex while Utstein gestured at the area going from hull to prow. Innstein nodded at something and turned a page.

"That would add to the ballast, if it's right," he said. "Maybe not a bad thing. Complicated, though."

"I don't understand how we'd fasten it," said Utstein as he examined the underside of the ship. "Maybe that's the secret."

The old cook stormed up to Innstein, driving him back with sheer will. "Talking about sailing isn't the same as sailing!" he bellowed. "What are you wasting time on here?"

"We were looking at some of the pictures in the book," said Innstein. "We think we know what they're about."

"They gave us an idea," said Utstein.

Kraki continued right up to the men, grabbed the backs of both their heads, and pulled them in close so that his face was inches from theirs. "Haldor says you should have the ship ready in three days. But it is my ship, and I say you have one. *Otherwise, you will take your idea boat and sail it straight up Njord's ass when I throw you into the sea!*" The man was turning from snow-white to beet-red as he shouted.

"Kraki." That didn't even make any sense.

"*Up his ass!*"

"Kraki!" I shouted. Though nowhere near as loud, it was loud enough to get his attention. "They understand. They will get it done. They just wanted to make improvements to the ship. Am I right?"

The 'Steins were not easily taken aback, but a crazy old *berserkr* two inches from your face shouting about asses will do that to anyone. Both men nodded, and Innstein handed me the codex when I asked for it.

"*We* can't read it," I said. "But *someone* wrote it, and that means *someone* knows how to read it. This is my responsibility. Until then, you know what the ship needs."

Kraki growled something unintelligible and stalked off. I waited until he left the area where the *Sea Squirrel* had been raised to say anything.

"I know he may seem crazy, but he is not," I said. "He's sailed this ship for more than twenty years. Shit!" I exclaimed in sudden realization. "He's been sailing this ship and raiding slavers since before I was even born. He is just protective of it. If you need three days, I will make him understand."

"It's not that," said Innstein. "We like this ship. We're so close to making it even better!"

"Close in theory," added Utstein. "We think there are valuable secrets about ship design in this book."

"Among other things," Innstein added. The brothers grinned.

Though we could not read the book, the 'Steins had imagined what the codex *might* say based on the few drawings and what any ship design would have to include. The two of them knew how to build and repair ships, and they had never seen a codex before. How would they know what it might include? Their instincts were on fire that it contained something valuable, even if they couldn't determine how.

"Look here," said Innstein. "Don't these runes look familiar? A few are just like our letters, but backwards."

"What languages do you *not* know, skald?" asked Utstein. "That might hint at who can read these letters."

I had never thought much about that. "I don't know the language of the Irish, for one. Or languages, if they have more than one."

"They are far from here," said Utstein. "And we never see trade from them."

"That's because their ships are terrible," added Innstein. "If this is Roman magic, why not Roman language?"

"I know the Roman letters," I said. "These look nothing like them. Could be related, though. And we are going to a monastery—perhaps one of the White Christ's followers will know."

"Why are we going to a monastery?" asked the brothers simultaneously.

"I need to see Varg Tiorvi about a matter."

"Does the matter involve killing him?" asked Innstein.

"More important, does Varg Tiorvi have much treasure?" asked Utstein.

"Yes?" I said. "But more explanation will only slow you down. We need to put to sea. The sooner, the better. Save improvements for another time."

That was one of my less graceful changes of subject, but I did not want to answer any more questions. They might get complicated. I left off with the codex and found Kraki by the shoreline. I told him how much the brothers cared about his ship and that they were only trying to improve it. He did not argue; his frustration had already poured out.

I even added "Three days," contradicting his earlier statement. He just nodded and waved me off.

"Now to the other errand," he said.

"What is that?"

"You will come with me, ask no questions, do exactly as I say. And then, maybe, you will have an explanation."

I had never known the old man to be so cryptic, but the look on his face was deadly earnest. My curiosity piqued, I agreed to his terms and followed him back along the path from Roskilde.

He turned from the path once we were deep into the forest. Huge trees of many types towered above us. Huge trees of many types also littered the forest floor, their decaying trunks covered in a deep green of moss and lichens. Pine needles and branches blanketed much of the rest. No path had been beaten here.

I had to physically bite my tongue to prevent the asking of questions like, "Why are we going this way?" Almost slipped, too, but with a great effort, I kept my mouth shut.

"Ask nothing, remember? But turn your intent toward the wizard's house. That is where we are headed."

Kraki knew how to find his way to Ketill's house? It seemed much had been afoot since last autumn that I had not been aware of. I set my will toward finding the way and found the forest obliged us as easily as ever. Where exactly the house lay in the forest was unclear. I wasn't convinced it had a fixed location. I wasn't convinced the forest had a fixed anything, in fact. But the *landvættir* inhabiting the place were friendly and always brought me through. Us, this time.

Wisps rose slowly out of the smoke hole in Ketill's house. Strange, since he had just been in the longhouse with us. The door opened, and out came Huld. Finnr stood in the doorway, holding the door open but not venturing out. The dwarf stood there, making it clear we had not been invited inside.

"Oh, hello," I said. I turned and noticed a foul look from Kraki. "That was not a question."

"Shut up a moment," barked the old man.

"Interesting company you bring," said Huld. "It seems to me there is little space left in this house at the moment."

"That's understood," said Kraki, his tone deferential. "We don't come seeking hospitality. The skald said some things I found interesting, and I decided this is where they needed to be heard."

What a bizarre way to phrase that, I thought.

"I'm all for listening," said Huld.

"Let's hear him speak then," said Finnr. "Loud and clear."

"I don't know what you three are up to," I said, "but this is getting stranger by the second. Fine, I'll speak. What is it you want me to speak of, exactly?"

"The *vǫlva* must know where we're headed next and why," said Kraki. "And Finnr as well. Tell them."

"We're going to Gotland. I have business with Varg Tiorvi, the kind he won't walk away from."

"Many have said the same," said Huld. "He's holed up in the middle of the island. He's been assaulted many times by armies much larger than the limited host he keeps. He's got a cow that moos, and mooing, it turns men mad—turns them against one another. Those armies have all torn themselves apart after hearing it. You've already made an enemy of one powerful sorcerer. Why go after another in the interim?"

That was not what I'd hope to hear about this cow, but the description changed nothing for me. "It was something I saw when I was in that ritual with Valborg. She wanted to help, to show things she could not normally see. I went too deep with her, and I saw a thing from her past she did not mean to show. What I saw can't be laid to rest as easily as her body."

"What is in this for you?"

An end to my nightmares? I stood there a long moment, balancing what needed saying with what I was willing to reveal. In the end, I decided shorter was better. "Some men just need killing."

Kraki grinned and patted his bone club. "A strange sentiment offered toward a witch who was his enemy. And with no possibility of reward, I noticed. Not many are willing to seek revenge on behalf of a former enemy. I wonder if that matters to anyone."

"Goat's breath and cat piss!" I said. "What is going on with you all? Why are you acting so damned strange?"

Huld cocked her head at me. "Can you keep a secret?"

"Yes!"

"This is a serious matter. Do not respond on reflex."

I took a deep breath, widened my stance, looked down, and closed my eyes. Could I keep a secret, not tell anyone? I took three more breaths before speaking again.

"I won't keep any secret that endangers the crew or would be dishonorable to them. Nor any secret that would offend my friends. Otherwise, yes. Does that satisfy you?"

Finnr looked back into the house. "I don't know. Does it?"

The dwarf stepped aside to make way for one more occupant to come out.

Her hair had been radiant blond the last time I saw her, and it was now streaked with different shades running through it. She held no wand to strike me with this time and wore simple, clean clothes. The last time I saw the witch, Aldis, she was in Alfhild's cave, reeling from a blow to the head. And, I thought, that is where she must have met her end.

"Skald," she said.

I gawked. Whatever I had been expecting, it had not been this. I think I was more surprised than when I'd encountered Valborg's severed head talking to me.

Expressions were unreadable. They were all trying to read mine, and I was a ball of confusion.

"Aldis has had a change of heart since last summer," said Huld. "She learns from me now, not Alfhild. Though she bears some lingering suspicion of you and yours, and that includes the king. I wonder if that suspicion still rages. After hearing the skald speak so freely—and seeing that he has clearly not been prepared for this—does that change the answer to Finnr's request?"

Aldis nodded. "Things are not as they seemed before," she said, her voice tight. It seemed women could deny their emotions showing just as well as men.

"Better get started right away, then," said Huld. Aldis and Finnr went back into the hut without another word, and only then did the *volva* step closer to us to explain anything more.

"Finnr has made a sword for the king. One he will no doubt need soon.

But the sword is not complete—it does not fit the king's way yet. Another part is required, and for that, Finnr needs Aldis' help. You can see why she might have been hesitant to give that help before and why she might agree to it now, I think."

"I think King Hrolf will be very suspicious himself," I said. "He was not happy to see Valborg in his hall, even just her head. I have a hard time seeing why he would accept a gift from another of Alfhild's old handmaidens, whether under your instruction now or not."

"That's good, very good!" crowed Huld. "You need not be a *vǫlva* to see some of the future! That's an understood thing you've just described, and it is perhaps the biggest reason you are sworn to silence. The king will need to accept this gift without knowing Aldis' involvement, that's true. And we will need you to play along with the giving of the gift to make that happen."

"Shit," I said, unable to see any way other than Huld's. I turned to Kraki. "So Aldis is forgiven and acts as an ally now. What happened to all signs pointing toward revenge?"

"Too much revenge is like too much . . ." he trailed off. "I don't know," he snapped. "You're the skald. Come up with something poetic about it."

GIFTS AND REPAYMENT

"YOU HAVE A KNACK FOR STIRRING UP TROUBLE," BEIGADH SAID as he let me into the hall.

"No idea what you mean," I said. *At this point, there are so many different possibilities.*

It had been two days since I'd seen Aldis and taken instructions from Huld. I had every indication that she was right about Hrolf needing a dwarf-forged sword and was not about to second-guess Aldis' involvement. Still, I had been a ball of tension. Deceiving the king for his own good is still deceiving the king, and Hrolf could dam his temper a long time, but I did not want to be nearby when that levee broke.

The king was a patient man and a stubborn one when it came to his own endurance. He would take fewer rations along with everyone else when necessary, dig holes when they were needed, and, on occasion, jump into a blinding ice storm to save one of his guests. He demanded little in return, as I think he considered these things part and parcel with his responsibility as king. That responsibility weighed heavily on him and had to be the cause for his getting overly lean during the winter.

Many of the new hangers-on coming to his hall sought nothing but their own fortunes. They were not like Haldor's Heroes and definitely not trusted. So while many in the hall boasted of their talents or past deeds and much ale sloshed about freely, I saw the king stewing on his high seat. A bear one should not poke at, if I ever saw one.

"Remember to breathe," Svipul told me, appearing out of nowhere, as was her practice.

It was easy to remember and less easy to do as I approached the king's high seat and joined the general throng of onlookers observing the latest decisions. Hrolf was receiving new guests again, those requesting hospitality and claiming to be of some worth. I found Huld and Finnr in the crowd looking on. Ketill was with them, as I should have guessed. It was his house they had based their conspiracy out of, after all.

"Maybe we could leave the sword and whetstone and have Aldis offer them together," I said. "After we set sail."

"Hmph," said Huld. Which was as much response as I would get.

Ulf had continued duty as the king's *þulr*, helping to organize those requesting hospitality and calling them up for their turns to speak. It was a good use of his time and skills. And probably the only thing that kept Hrolf from strangling certain people. Ulf stood a few paces away from the king, observing, speaking, and generally looking important. Hromund stood closer to the king, just to the side and behind, hand ever on the pommel of his sword.

The king looked like he wished he was bored, but was too annoyed for that. "Who are these?" he demanded.

Two stinky men with broad chests and thick arms stood before him. I noticed they had been disarmed by Beigadh at the door. Our lot carried weapons freely through the king's hall, but we were known and trusted. A few others, like Jarl Gorm Tin-Whisker, had similar status. But not these two.

"They say they are *berserkir* who would be your champions," said Ulf. His tone disguised his contempt, but I could hear it by what he had not said. And he had not bothered to say their names. "They say that with them at your table, you will never need to flee from either fire or iron."

"Hromund," said the king, gesturing the champion forward.

I'll say this for Hromund the Hard: He did not have his name for nothing, and he loved his job.

Two hundred pounds of armor-clad ill luck headed toward these supposed *berserkir*. Hromund was a fair sport, though, so he took off his helmet before headbutting the first one in the face. When the second took offense at this, he took a swing at the champion and cuffed him hard in the head. Hromund took the punch but swung back immediately, his blow knocking the man on his ass.

"That's enough," said a very tired King Hrolf.

Hromund nodded, grinning, as he retrieved his helmet and took his position behind the king again.

"There's many a man coming to my court claiming to be more than he is lately," said Hrolf. "You two may join us for the evening meal. That is, assuming your manners are very good. You will leave in the morning, however, and you will tell everyone you meet that King Hrolf flees neither fire nor iron, regardless of those at his table."

The two men carried one another away. So much for going completely, mindlessly berserk.

"Who is next?" asked the king in a decidedly incurious tone.

"This seems like a bad time to give the king such a surprise as is planned," I said.

"So you would assault a sorcerer next, one who has laid waste to entire armies," said Ketill, "but the thought of this king's disapproval fills you with dread?"

Maybe?

Nanthild elbowed me in the ribs, and in doing so announced her joining of our little group. I nodded. She nodded back. I got the impression she had been there for a minute or two and was enjoying my discomfort.

"Next is Toki, a blacksmith who asks for a place within the city to set up," said Ulf. "He has a gift to offer—an example of what he creates."

"If it pleases the king," said a man, stepping forward. "I have this helmet. A helm of awe to strike terror into your enemies."

"Hromund," said Hrolf, gesturing the champion forward again.

Hromund took the offered helmet with only the briefest flash of disbelief across his face. As I saw more of the thing, I could see why he was surprised.

Hrolf craned his neck forward and waited for Hromund to place the thing on his head. It was not easy. Though the helmet seemed to fit all right, it was weighted in the most absurd way possible by two aurochs horns sticking out from the sides.

Hromund made a good effort to balance the thing before letting go. The horns were small for an aurochs but still huge on the helmet, and one was bigger than the other. As soon as Hromund let go, the helmet fell to the side of the heavier horn, off the king's head, and clattered to the floor.

Finnr held his belly as it shook with silent laughter.

"A gift always looks to be repaid," said the king. "I do not want this thing, and you do not want me to repay you for the insult of wearing such absurd headgear. You may join us for the evening meal and stay the night. However, you will leave in the morning, and you will take this helmet with you. Sell it to some pretend *berserkr* if you can—that is my best advice to you."

Toki bowed as he picked up the helmet and scurried into a dark corner of the hall.

"My penchant for assaulting sorcerers is not at issue here," I said. "This is bad timing!"

"Hush," grinned Huld. "I want to see what happens to the next one."

"How many more, Ulf?" asked the king.

"Three more."

"Get on with it, then."

"Gullveig, a *vǫlva*. She offers to advise you on matters of great import." Ulf said all this with a straight face, which I had to credit him for. Gullveig was the most famous of all witches, a name so deep in myth that no two tellings of her were the same. If this woman had taken the name by choice, she was certainly setting herself on a high pedestal.

A woman who was definitely not a *vǫlva* stepped forward. I've encountered *vǫlur* before, even if you don't count Huld. Some are itinerant tellers of the future. Some are mysterious wanderers or healers for hire. All of them bear a worldliness that only far travel can impart.

So when this woman claimed to be a *vǫlva* and at the same time was asking for a stationary position in Hrolf's hall, that was immediately suspect.

But her appearance gave her away long before the claim. A flowing dress of yellow. A crown of antler-like twigs atop tightly woven hair. Dark lines circled her eyes, and a singular dark line shot down her lower lip and chin.

Painted fakery.

"She must know what matters are of greatest import that I would take advice on, then," said the king. He was holding back his tone, but even holding back, I could hear the grinding in its background. Hrolf tried to keep a civil court, but anyone who knew him knew he was not pleased.

Gullveig smiled and shifted her hips. "There is much to be learned from the right ritual. Knowledge that cannot be known otherwise."

"And what fires such rituals?" demanded the king. "I've seen spells fueled by sacrifice before, and I won't allow that."

"Certainly not!" said Gullveig, taken aback. "It is in the king's bed I might cast my spells. The spirits speak in an ecstatic state, and I can achieve such at will. I ask for a seat at the king's table—little enough for the many benefits I provide." She pushed her ample chest out at the word *benefits*.

Huld laughed so hard she snorted.

Hrolf, however, was less amused.

"Get out of my hall, you witless shit-for-brains!" he bellowed, rising from his seat.

I imagine there was some pent-up hostility for Alfhild leaking out there. Alfhild had also been a beauty and also claimed to be a *vǫlva*, all the while speaking poison into his uncle's ear. Hrolf might have offered the same meal as to the other pretenders, but this one had touched a raw nerve. Hrolf was a good king, but he was human, too, and not perfect by any means.

Gullveig started at the king's shout, frozen in disbelief. She quickly became a believer when Hromund stepped down and came after her. She made a quick exit after that, and Hromund returned to the king's side once she had left the hall.

"Ulf," barked Hrolf, "if there are any more offerers of prophecy-on-demand, you should advise them to leave my sight with utmost haste."

"That's easily done," said Ulf. "Next is nothing about prophecy, though. Vogg the Skald wishes to join you at court."

A nondescript man in a patched cloak and tunic stepped forward. There was not much to him as it looked like he had gone a long while without a proper meal. Tentative in his movement, he did not seem very skald-like to me. I may lack the martial valor of most skalds, but I at least know how to perform. Vogg gave the impression that most of the poetry he had composed had been in his head and never spoken aloud.

"Well?" growled the king.

It was not great timing for the timid.

"I eat very little," offered the skald to a chorus of laughter through the crowd.

"That's more than you could say for the last few, at least," someone called.

The king held out a hand to stop any further comments from the crowd. "And yet, eating little is not a primary characteristic I seek in a skald. What do you offer? Praise and poetry? Wit and wisdom? What is it you can tell me right now that would be of use?"

Vogg's eyes bloomed huge in the hall's firelight. I thought he might faint. But the slight skald had more to him than my eye could see, and he answered in verse:

> "The spear-king's
> space holds
> an unkindly menu
> for its master, I think.
> Who feeds
> this fine fellow,
> that heroes could call him
> Hrolf Kraki?"

I didn't know Vogg or where he'd come from, but his verse was brilliant.

Kraki's name was really a byname. It made sense if you knew he already had a name from Down-Below, and it especially made sense since Kraki meant "skinny pole" or something like it. He was tall and gaunt, and Hrolf had grown increasingly similar in body type as the stresses of being king were heaped upon his shoulders.

Hrolf wore those burdens without complaint, but he had grown increasingly skinny and irritable—increasingly like Kraki the man and like a skinny pole—as the winter had worn on.

Now, someone had said so. And Hrolf had a byname, whether he wanted it or not.

"So, I am Hrolf Kraki then?"

"Um, yes," said Vogg. "And I would advise a good meal as soon as possible."

The skald said this with such nervousness but such honesty that he had the entire hall laughing. The entire hall minus him. Vogg looked down and plainly thought he'd fumbled his one chance to gain the king's favor. To his mind, he'd failed and made himself a laughingstock all at once.

Only when I looked back to Hrolf, I saw he was smiling.

"Vogg, in one verse you've given me two things I've found difficult to come by: A byname and the truth. The name I'll have to share with Kraki Bentleg, there," he said, pointing to our captain. "And I'll take that as an honor. Tell me, truly, did you know his name already or that we fought back-to-back in the battle for this city last summer?"

Vogg's eyes were too wide and he looked too frantic to know what Hrolf was talking about. Eventually, he managed to shake his head.

"It's not an easy thing to choose the truth over flattery when your supper is at stake. Take this." Hrolf removed a golden ring from his arm and tossed it to Vogg. "You may stay for the evening meal. And then you may remain as a skald at my court."

Vogg's face went pale with excitement as he caught the bracelet and slipped it on. I couldn't hear his next words exactly over cheers from the crowd all around. It was the swearing of some oath or other and a great deal of thanks. I was cheering with them. After all, Hrolf needed a skald, and Vogg seemed uniquely qualified.

"Well done," said Ulf. "There is only one more offer this evening, and from a more familiar source. Finnr the dwarf offers you a gift."

Hrolf stood up and addressed Finnr in a voice meant for the rest of us in the hall. "You say you bring a gift. What for, I wonder? Is it one seeking repayment?"

Finnr and Nanthild stepped forward past the crowd with a wrapped parcel. I looked back, expecting Huld to step forward as well, but she had disappeared. I looked at Ketill with one eyebrow up. He just grinned.

"I don't know who you would repay," the dwarf began. "Not me, that much I can promise. There is no commerce to this gift, though there is art. Perhaps you would like to know what it is before deciding whether to accept it."

"Is this your forging alone, then?"

"Nanthild has been an assistant during the process. More of an apprentice, really, though that apprenticeship has now ended. She will sail off tomorrow, and I will return to the Down-Below for work I must pursue."

That was disappointing. And sudden. I considered the dwarf one of us and would miss his humor and wisdom.

To the surprise of very few, under the cloth wrappings Finnr carried was a sword in a polished wooden sheath. A heavy, almost triangular pommel and small, simple guard surrounded the off-white grip. Though the light was low and I only caught a glimpse, I could tell from the color that the grip was made of bone.

Dragon bone, I guessed. Huld really had harvested every part of that beast.

"Here is Skofnung," shouted Finnr, raising the sword high above his head and turning around so all could see. "I made this sword, and it will never break or blunt. It will cut through stone as easily as through skin." He drew the sword then, revealing two sharp edges on a broad blade. Then he addressed the king directly. "This weapon must draw blood if it is unsheathed."

I held my breath. What was the dwarf playing at?

Nanthild held out one bare arm, and Finnr drew the blade across it. Blood bloomed where she was cut. I shook my head as if to shake off the confusion, but it was no help.

Finnr then produced a slender whetstone about nearly a foot long and held it up for the king to see. "And here is the Skofnung Stone," he announced.

"What use is a whetstone to a sword that will not blunt?" asked the king, expression unchanged.

Finnr bade Nanthild hold up her bleeding arm. "Wounds from this sword will not mend as from a normal sword. But here," he said and drew the whetstone over the wound, "you may heal an injury done by the sword, as long as you have the whetstone."

Nanthild held her arm up once more. There was no cut, not even any blood. The whetstone had undone the sword's work entirely. Nanthild then produced a clean cloth and took the sword from Finnr, cleaning the blade well before resheathing it.

"All kings cut men down," said Finnr. "That is little challenge. A good king brings back together what has been severed. This is a sword for such a king."

Hrolf sat, staring at the dwarf, hand cupping his short beard. It seemed a long time before he said anything or even moved. I had been holding my breath and finally exhaled when I realized what Finnr had done. He was not asking for payment now or even later. Powerful as this sword was, it was just that power coupled with its rules that made some kind of demand on the king.

A good king brings back together what has been severed. The setup for Aldis returning. Indicating the king should forgive her.

"You said you made the sword," said the king. "Did you make the stone as well?"

"I was there for the stone's making," said Finnr. "But it was crafted by the *volva*."

Oh, that was sneaky. Hrolf was going to be furious.

"And what payment does she seek?"

"She seeks no payment from you other than your hospitality."

"She has that!" said the king, shaking his head. "These are very fine gifts. A gift always seeks to be repaid, and I will repay it now. Where is Huld? I would have her come forward and take a good place at the table."

"I am glad you accept these fine gifts," said Finnr. "I think you will need them very soon, given your enemies. But Huld is not the *volva* who crafted the whetstone. The *volva* was Aldis."

Hrolf's jaw ground his teeth such that they could have turned granite into dust. "Explain yourself, dwarf."

"It is an art to make such a weapon. I hardly know what its properties might be before I am halfway done forging it, and then even in the honing process, there are surprises sometimes. I knew this sword would be a powerful one and that it would need balance. You don't want a sword like Tyrfing—make it too fond of killing, and the blade begins to wield itself."

"This tells me nothing of a conspiracy to harbor a sworn enemy."

"As for conspiracy, that was before my time. I knew what I needed but did not know how to make it. So I locked the sword away until such time as I could find the necessary help. Aldis could provide that wisdom but was hesitant to do so."

"How was she alive at all?" demanded the king, not even trying to disguise his anger. The floorboard vibrated at his every word.

"I found her," said Huld, reappearing on the other side of the throng. The crowd around her moved, and she stepped toward the king. "Found her bleeding and stumbling in Alfhild's cave, still not recovered from a head injury. I healed her and brought her around."

"You should have killed her!"

"Should I?" Huld shouted back. "Here you are after Alfhild's blood— did you condemn your uncle for listening to her as much as you condemn her acolytes for doing the same thing? I'll remind you of them: Of those three handmaidens, one of them died on the battlefield seeing your side to victory. Another made every effort to help you despite your ungenerous response when she reappeared here some months ago. Now you find one whole, who has helped to deliver a gift you called a fine one, and you say kill her? Well! I said I would teach her, and so I have, and here is the result:

"A skilled *vǫlva* can do much healing. What can a dead woman do?"

Hrolf was fuming, but he'd already promised hospitality for Aldis, even if he hadn't realized it at the time. There was no backing out now. But he could identify the conspirators.

"Who else knew of this?"

Ketill stepped forward. "I knew after a time. I let the woman stay in my hut, though she was loath to do so. Apparently, Alfhild told her hand-maidens that I was not only a hermit but an outlaw and a rapist. This sat badly with them, as you might imagine. I won't claim Aldis did nothing against you, but she did so in being misinformed."

"I have known for some time," said Kraki, not bothering to step forward. "I think it's of little matter."

Nanthild stepped forward with a great smile and pointed at herself. I wished I could share her single-mindedness.

I took a great breath and stepped forward with far less confidence. "I also knew a few days ago. I was sworn to keep a secret before finding out what it was."

"The old man, I can understand," said Hrolf. "He and Finnr and these sorcerers are four of a kind, whatever kind that is. And the silent apprentice was not about to talk. But you? Why were you involved?"

"By my choice," said Kraki. "The witch had repented her allegiance to Alfhild, but she was not inclined to aid you. I brought the skald where she could hear him speak about her sister, Valborg, openly."

"It was the skald's words that convinced her to help create the whet-stone," said Finnr. "Words of healing for a healing item."

Hrolf Kraki walked with a weary gait until he stood nose to nose with me. Skinny as he might have been, I had no illusions. Hrolf was strong, fast, and tough. Even if his current state was emaciated, I suspected he might make up for that with sheer brutality if it came to a fight.

"So I have you to thank for this," he said.

"If you give me credit for all the good that sword and whetstone do for you," I said, "I think you will be giving away a lot of good reputation."

King Hrolf stood there a good while before he ripped that burning gaze from me. "Bring food," he shouted. "My guests are overdue for it, and I won't be called Hrolf Kraki because no one in my hall can eat."

Vogg started to say something. It was something in verse, something about a *vǫlva*. Hrolf waved him off.

"No more advice this evening, Vogg. Truth is like mead. One should not indulge in too much of either in a single night."

CHAPTER 21

THE DEAD MAN'S PANTS

THE CREW WAS IN HIGH SPIRITS WHEN WE BOARDED THE *SEA Squirrel* two days after presenting King Hrolf with his surprises. Those surprises went over with mixed results, as expected. Hrolf could not deny the sword's power or that the whetstone was essential. He was ill pleased about Aldis, a thing he communicated with every syllable, every look in our direction. We had done right by King Hrolf, but we'd tricked him in the process. It would be a while before he forgot the sting of that trickery.

King Hrolf did not hesitate to allow Aldis into his hall, but he grit his teeth as he did it. He had immediately ordered every person to seek treatment for their ailments from her, if they had any, and left Aldis without a free moment day or night.

When each one had come back better off for having seen her, Hrolf grit his teeth less. Even gave her a golden armring as a reward. He seemed less grudging of her presence by the time we set sail.

The 'Steins had not been fast hands at ship repairs but had been meticulous. Once they started working and not obsessing over my codex, of course. Even Kraki was pleased.

Still, the brothers took every opportunity to imply they could do even more. If I could translate the codex.

Finnr had said his goodbye the previous evening, taking his leave from the hall and, I assumed, disappearing into the Stone Road soon after. I would miss the dwarf, though I couldn't blame him for avoiding a long sea voyage.

Nanthild's company was not unexpected. She carried a sword by then, her own make rather than Finnr's. The dwarf would have done a better job, but Nanthild wanted to do it herself. Or so the 'Steins told me, who seemed to hear the young woman even though she did not speak. But her reaction to even slight swaying of the ship was not good. She kept her food down but remained pale and angry as soon as we set sail. It would be a long voyage for her.

Huld was coming with us, to the surprise of many but the disapproval of no one. Haldor offered the *vǫlva* an armring if she would only make it plain what she had done during the previous summer's battle. He knew she had been there, he said, because they found her tending to me. But where had she come from, and what had she been doing? Huld answered that her arms were old and saggy and an armring would only slip off. She thanked him but told him to put his jewelry on an arm that would bear it better.

Ketill could have seen us off and gone home to his hut. He probably didn't even need to burn charcoal to trade anymore. Coming to Hrolf's aid last summer had earned Ketill favor with the new king, and I'm certain he could have lived quietly and comfortably in his hut after that. But I think sobriety reawakened the wanderlust in Ketill, and he was set on coming with us. And where he went, Humor followed.

Some of the men who had flocked to Hrolf's hall elected to come aboard the *Sea Squirrel*. Out on the sea was where a man might win a reputation for himself, they said, especially if we were to kill Varg the Charmer. In all, we were two dozen total and twenty for rowing.

Huld smiled sweetly in disbelief that we would have an old woman strain her heart with rowing. Hemming was useless at it, even worse than I was. And Ketill just glared when anyone looked at him.

Kraki remained at the rudder, a new energy in him as the salt air coursed over his bare skin. He was in his element once more, riding the whale-road on a mission to kill a man. And he was the cook once more, doling out horrid rations he had smoked or dried or fermented. The old man was so happy he almost smiled.

I was more comfortable at sea than I had been the previous year. After taking a few serious head injuries, shitting myself nearly to death, being dragged underwater by a witch and then beaten, stabbed, and slashed, well, a ship swaying on the water no longer seemed all that uncomfortable in the grand scheme of things.

The sun was low in the morning but lit a bright sky as the *Sea Squirrel* pulled away from its mooring. The ship cut a smooth wake through calm water. Scents of tarred lumber and salt overpowered those of semi-washed humans. The air was far fresher out there on the sea than in the longhouse. We each sat on our sea chests, rowers all facing aft, though not where we each might prefer. My seating assignment was at port, staring at Svein's backside, the smelliest crewman among us.

I tried to keep my mind off the big man's odor and my penchant for throwing up while at sea as we rowed. At least we could ease into things in calm waters.

"Odds on when we see the first sea monster," shouted Innstein after we were underway. He and his brother sat opposite one another to port and starboard, just one row behind me. They were pulling their oars with so much glee they threatened to get out of time with the rowing. "Who wants to bet?"

"Only a fool will make any such bets," Ketill roared back from the aft, more to the rest of the crew than to Innstein. "I heard of your previous incident. The Midgard Serpent indeed! I carved runes to prevent another such visit, as these two well know. Bet against my spells if you wish."

"The last time you carved runes into something, it made people explode," said Utstein. "Does that mean we are protected or that the ship is doomed?"

"I will bet on the ship not exploding," I said. "But what did you carve?"

"Carving was only on the bow and the rudder," said Ketill. "You could carve the same runes onto a stick and let it trail behind, but the rudder is better. For the oars, I burned the runes on."

I watched my oar as it broke the water on my next stroke. The rune burned onto it had escaped my attention until Ketill told us what he'd done. It was just *laguz*, the rune for lake or water, which surprised me. "The oar is already in the water. Why use this one instead of, I don't know, conjuring ice or poison or a horse to make us go faster?"

"Because all those things draw attention," said Ketill. "And if you want to avoid sea monsters, you don't draw their attention."

"This is not helping us with the bets!" hissed Innstein. "How are we supposed to make any money this way?"

"Why are we going to Gotland first?" demanded Svein, who never did enjoy the 'Steins' humor as much as I did. "It's always a long stop before we go where we're supposed to be going."

"We're going exactly where we need to go," I said. "Besides, I hear Varg is a rich man."

"There's treasure?" asked Svein.

"Seems that way," I said. "Sorcerers always have the best treasure. They're awfully stingy, and they hoard everything they can find."

"Hmph!" grunted Ketill. He sat on his own sea chest in the aft of the ship, close to Kraki at the rudder and Huld nearby. He kept himself covered with his gray cloak. "Some shitman finds himself an animal to do all his fighting for him, and for that, he's called a sorcerer. If he is so strong with lore, perhaps we should have him translate your codex when we find him."

"Aren't we going to kill him?" asked Magnus, who sat across from me. "We should probably have him translate before we kill him."

"Yes, order of operations," added Innstein. "Because some people kill everyone before finding out where the gold is buried."

"That only happened once," Utstein shouted back, despite sitting right next to his brother. "And it was not my fault!"

The 'Steins were just getting started. I had heard this argument before and figured I would hear it again.

Kraki did not try to intervene, just ordered the rowing pace to increase as we made our way out of the fjord. It was a narrow inlet as I was familiar with from my homeland, but not surrounded by the same high cliff walls. The land of the Danes was too flat for that, so we rowed from a calm inlet to a mostly calm open sea with little difficulty.

From there, we cut northeast along the Sjaelland coast. There was wind enough to sail without rowing, but Kraki kept our oars in the water. I was about to ask before the answer occurred to me: Rowing a lot now would get us used to it before we were in hostile waters.

Late in the day, he ordered a break and let the wind carry us after a few hours. My shoulders burned, my arms ached, and my fingers felt like they would fall off. We hadn't even cleared Sjaelland yet, much less turned the southern tip of Scania. It was going to be a long voyage for me if I did not get my mind off my sore muscles.

"So, Ketill," I called out, "did I hear in your voice before that you think not so much of Varg's power?"

"I think I will judge that when I see it," said the wizard. "Or if there is anything to see. What reputation does he have other than his cow?"

I shrugged. Kraki had laid out the danger before anyone stepped on board, but most men laughed at the idea of being mooed to death.

"He has a few ships," added Kraki. "They trade with the Balts and the Finns—when they aren't grabbing Balts and Finns for thralls. Most of his men will be on those ships along with plenty of goods if we catch them fully loaded."

"Are we attacking three ships and then his stronghold?" asked Magnus. "An interesting plan."

"We attack the stronghold," said Kraki. "Unless we need to fight on the sea. I know where we will go ashore to keep the ship safe. We can scout the area and make a plan of attack from there."

"Get ready, my friends," said Magnus. "Our base will be a cave, no doubt about it."

"No cave," said Kraki. "A monastery."

Silence all around. Most were surprised, though none wanted to admit it.

"I stopped there once, some years ago," Kraki continued. "We needed provisions, and all we found on the coast there was the monastery. Once those cheese-blooded Christians realized we were willing to trade in silver rather than steel, we had all the provisions we needed. They did not haggle much."

"And it may be that someone at this monastery knows how to read this codex!" I said.

Svein snorted and shook his head.

"Ha!" spat Ketill. "That book is a dangerous thing. Wild and unpredictable. Throw it overboard, I say."

"It might contain secret knowledge," said Utstein.

"We love secret knowledge," said Innsein. "That's how we learned to build ships."

The wizard stood up, lit bright by the sun. "Of course, it has secret knowledge!" he shouted. "That's the dangerous part! It's like putting a sword into a toddler's hand."

"But what if they create codices at this monastery?" I asked. "You could have them write down the things you know so that knowledge is passed on."

"That is the worst idea I have ever heard," said Ketill. "If I did that, some fool would come around later and read it. If that person was you, he would probably skip to the end, ignore all the necessary preparations, and try a spell to make himself rich or some other idiocy. No," he continued, the crew's attention rapt. "No, I only pass on what I can see is ready to be passed on, and only to someone ready to wield that sword. The student must learn by experience, and the teacher must observe it. Giving such to random bumpkins without any guidance or control is folly."

A *galdramaðr* was a rare thing, even rarer than a *vǫlva*. Ripples on the water seemed to flow out from him as he spoke, and the strakes holding the ship together shook. Some of the new men on board concealed what I was sure was terror, while some, like the 'Steins, were in awe.

And then there was Svein.

"Are you saying," said the huge man, "are you saying you know spells that could make you rich?"

Ketill stared at the man in disbelief before his demeanor turned to something I had never seen. The wizard grinned a toothy grin as he stared at Svein and answered. It was half predator and half jester. "Yes," he said.

And soon, I realized why I did not recognize this expression: Ketill was going to play a joke on this fool.

"Well, why didn't you just do that then?" demanded Svein. "Why not do it now and make us all rich?'

"So eager for money! But the Dead Man's Pants is no easy conjuration," said Ketill. "It is an ill thing to even consider, let alone do."

I looked behind me to see Utstein make a rude hand gesture at Svein's expense. Both brothers were holding back laughter to keep from exposing the joke.

"But how do you do it?" I asked. "This must be a unique spell since you never taught it to me."

Svein grinned. "Yes, tell us."

The wizard looked over his audience in feigned hesitation, stroking his long beard and seeming to consider the request. Should he really share this esoteric lore with them? Well, perhaps they were trustworthy.

"You must swear never to try this," he said. "I will tell you only so that you might understand such things better."

I could feel the 'Steins shaking in their seats with laughter, holding their mouths closed.

"I do so swear," said Svein, transfixed.

"In that case, I will tell you how to cast this spell. But take heed: Though it will make you rich, there are better ways to get money. In this case, you would dig up a dead man buried in a churchyard. This man must be bigger than you are, or you will have trouble later on. You must cut away the skin from his lower half."

"All of it?" asked Svein.

"*All of it!*" Ketill shouted as he grabbed his crotch. "And keep it well intact. On the inside of his ballsack, you must carve the rune *fehu*. Now if the skald recalls what *fehu* represents—"

"Wealth," I said immediately.

"Wealth! Well done. Carve that rune into the inside, not clear to the outside. And before sewing the scrotum back up, place a gold coin into it. You will lose the coin but gain something more."

Innstein slapped me on the back, he was laughing so hard.

"And then I would be rich?" asked Svein.

"Not yet. Remember I said you must find a man bigger than yourself. And remember the name of the spell, the Dead Man's Pants! Once you sew the scrotum back together, you then slip into the skin and wear it as pants. As you go about town, you will have the greatest possible luck. As long as you walk slowly and don't try to force any situation, things will begin to happen such that you become rich."

Seconds passed in silence, and Svein considered the spell. Some of the men grimaced, others grinned. Finally, Svein spoke again, saying, "It is just as well. I have never met a man bigger than me."

"Strange that would be the put-off," crooned Huld. "With all the handling of another man's balls involved."

Svein's face went red at the laughter that followed, but he said nothing. He had a plan now, and I was confident that he would ask our soon-to-be hosts if they had recently buried any large men in their churchyard.

Some people will believe anything if the prospect of getting rich is involved. Or do anything if the dragon sickness is on them. At that time, I believed a man's oath was stronger than any such sickness. Later, I would see what depths the power of gold could plumb, and I would never be the same.

CHAPTER 22

MOSTLY HARMLESS

THOUGH HROLF HAD PROVISIONED US WELL, KRAKI WAS AGAIN the ship's cook. And the ship's cook had somehow found time last year to hunt one of those slow-moving sharks, butcher it, bury it in the sand, and let the flesh rot until it was fit for human consumption. Again, he served the hated *hákarl*. I would have counted the days until we reached Gotland if only I knew how many days that would be.

Nanthild fared little better than I. At her first bite of the stuff, she shot Kraki a disbelieving look as if he had played a joke on her. But on he went, and to each person he gave a ration. It was not a joke, just a terrible reality over the next week as we hugged the coast.

We could not stay near the coast forever, though. Soon, we were headed north and drifting away from the land and into bluer water. Gotland is a huge island. Kraki found it easily enough and navigated us to the southwest corner.

The sail was taken in and the oars went out, despite the wind. The shores were rocky rather than sandy, and the water leading to them was lousy with rocks big enough to damage the *Sea Squirrel's* hull. It seemed to me we would be better off, as in less tired, if we kept the sail up and let the wind take us to an easier place to beach the ship. Kraki was intent on finding a place along this one stretch of Gotland to put down, though.

On the fourth or fifth approach to the beach, grumbling started. Facing the aft of the ship, we could all see a small island about two miles distant. I pointed in between strokes and said, "Are you sure we're not better off camping out there instead?"

Kraki turned to look but shook his head soon after that. "That island is cursed. So bad it's supposed to make this part of Gotland full of spirits with ill intent."

"The spirits of dead Goths?" asked Innstein.

"Or Geats?" asked Utstein. "We've heard it both ways."

Kraki shrugged.

"And it's to the cursed part of Gotland you're taking us?" demanded Ulf.

"Varg does not come to this part of the island. The only ones who live there are the White Christ followers. They pay Varg; Varg leaves them alone."

Ulf snorted. He sat behind me so I did not see, but I suspect he was shaking his head.

"We could land in another spot," said Kraki, leaning lazily on the rudder. "Varg would know right away in that case."

"This sounds a like good spot to me," said Haldor. "However long it takes us to navigate through the rocks."

Fighting the current was difficult work, and we had to back out and go forward a few more times before Kraki was satisfied. He was right, though— we came right up to the rocky shore without any lone boulders scraping the hull. Tired as we were, carrying the ship up the beach and into the trees beyond land seemed more of a relief than anything else.

Haldor took council as soon as the ship was secured and somewhat hidden from view. He wanted to know more about this "cursed island" and its influence across the water. A strange thing for the influence of spirits to cross water, and not at all expected. Apparently they were powerful enough to keep the local *landvættir* at bay, but not powerful enough to scare off followers of the White Christ.

I was not part of the council and left the conversation to Haldor, Kraki, and Ulf. Meanwhile, I convinced Humor to fly inland a little bit, promising a greater likelihood of "a feast for ravens" if we weren't the victims of a surprise attack.

He returned shortly and confirmed the presence of "men with targets on their heads."

"Can you believe it?" the bird said, eyes wide. "They shave the middle part! It's like they're asking—begging—for me to hit that area right there!"

"Never met a monk before, bird?" said Utstein.

"They are peculiar," said Innstein. "Mostly harmless."

"Mostly," said Huld.

Ketill made a wordless growl.

Haldor said to bring only what was needed, but I couldn't tell what that was. I ended up carrying my whole sea chest since I figured I might need my lyre, the codex, and well, everything. My sling and bag of bullets were always on my belt. So were my carving knife and bag of wooden discs for carving the spells Ketill had taught me. I waved off a spear, saying I had Need, but Magnus slung a shield onto my back, saying I had need of protection.

Me carrying a shield. Can you imagine the absurdity?

We trekked inland past the small forest we'd secured the ship in. The monastery was in a clearing not far beyond it. The greeting we got at the monastery was not warm. Nor did our presence probably seem much welcome, especially as Magnus picked his way through every part of the main stone structure.

There were a few inhabitants when we arrived. Some tended to a cordoned-off herb garden, some worked the main structure. A larger farmed area stood a stone's throw away, though none were there at the time we arrived. Lots of barley there likely meant plenty of ale in the storehouses. Beyond the larger garden was a long, flat area that might have been expanded. With only about a dozen mouths to feed, though, there was not yet any need.

Ulf took responsibility for communicating our intentions. We soon realized they spoke Norse, or at least the abbot did.

He was the oldest man there. He was burly and with a face that spoke of a history of fighting and a lack of skill at shaving. A Swede, based on his accent. He poured us ale, despite the massive dent that must have left in their supply.

The main structure was made of stone, and I wished Finnr could have seen it. All that time surrounded by mostly wood, he would have been pleased to have stone walls around him for once. Not nearly as big as one of our mead halls, but still bigger than I had thought a stone hall might be. It went down one long way and then shot out at an angle. The room we entered was clearly for meals, and we found places to sit or stand there while I wondered what was around that corner.

"Where is Candidus?" asked Kraki.

"Died a few years ago," said the old Swede. "I am Tafi, and I continue his work here."

Niceties continued for some time, and I decided I was not needed. I slipped away from the group past the main hearth fire to have a look around.

Stone can be awfully cold when there is no fire, though. Past the bend, I could feel the lack of warmth. The next room was nearly empty but for a few tables and chairs. All the tables lay covered with light cloth, and I thought it strange to see a feather poking out from one of the tables. What I saw when I lifted the cloth would forever change my life.

It was the codex I saw first. It was more ornate than the one I had, both inside and out. It lay open to a half-written page, and next to it were a goose feather and a small knife. This was how they did it. There was nothing here most vikings would want to steal. But the unfinished book on the table belied other books besides, and when I looked around and saw the pile—a pile!—of codices these few men had written.

I charged back into the main room, heedless of who was speaking and what manners were expected. "Can you read this?" I said, stammering like a madman as I thrust the codex at Tafi.

"Please forgive our skald," said Ulf. "It has been a long trip. And you are good at forgiveness, I think."

"Ansgar, were you listening?" demanded Haldor. "You will go scout the area with Hemming."

"Right," I said. "And why am I going?"

Ulf sneered at my flighty attention. I couldn't help it. Someone might be able to read this codex, and no one was properly excited at that prospect.

"Because you know a bit of *galdr*," said Ketill. "And more importantly, you can run fast. I am not so quick on my feet anymore. There may be a need for both on such a trip."

"Varg will make you come to him," said Tafi. "I will offer what advice I can: Leave. Many have attacked this man and with bigger forces than yours. None have survived."

"I'll take that advice in the spirit it was offered, but I won't follow it," said Haldor. "If you have advice on how to deal with his cow, that I might follow."

Tafi shook his head. "I've already given the best advice I know of."

Haldor nodded and motioned for me to follow him outside. He pointed vaguely northeast to the center of the island. "Out there is where you're headed. Hemming will keep you both unseen and unheard on your way. And he will help you scout the layout and defenses near Varg's longhouse. Try to be back in three days or so."

"Three days!" Three days of cold and likely wet. Three days without a fire. Three days with nothing but some *hákarl*. I almost prayed to Odin for something other than fermented shark.

"Or more. Hemming can decide that."

I turned around and saw Hemming was already prepared. And by prepared, I mean he had covered himself in mud and sticks.

"And then we kill Varg?" I asked.

"We are considering the best way to approach that," said Haldor. "The *vǫlva* and the wizard have an idea that may get us close. We will need more than that. And we will need you to do this thing first."

"This way, skald," said Hemming. "Only one good way to travel unseen in the forest, and that is to look like part of the forest."

I kept my complaining to myself. In my mind, though, I raged about scouting with Hemming instead of talking about translating the codex. Now I reflect that Hemming's idea, applied to Valborg's prophecy, might have helped us figure things out sooner.

I doubt it, though. We had important mistakes to make, first.

Chapter 23

Pawn Protection

I did not believe we could travel all that way unseen and unheard, but Hemming's woodcraft was that good—little surprise from the man who spent his nights sleeping under trees when he could have a warm spot in a hall.

It was a sick place. Hemming said so at one point, but I had already felt it. Beyond the treeline of mostly ash that traced a soft boundary for the monastery were huge specimens of sweet chestnut. When they had lived, they must have been ten times the height of a man. Now they lay decomposing on the forest floor. The roots had soured and the trees had fallen over, unable to bear the weight of their great trunks. Plenty of other trees were fine, but those dozen or so sweet chestnut trees had gone down years ago. Maybe decades. And nobody had harvested from them despite the value of their wood.

"Watch our backs," said Hemming. "And follow me."

We stayed off trodden paths and kept to the thickest parts of the forest, often hunkering down in silence when any remotely suspicious sound came up. Hemming almost always had us moving shortly after.

I did a lot of that the next three days. It reminded me how tiring it can be to move slow rather than fast.

We found the longhouse on the second day and remained to observe the activity there. The compound was a small area walled off with the longhouse inside. We caught glimpses of the structure when the gates opened, but it was those gates and walls we would be assaulting, not the hall.

The area outside the gate was flat and open, leading to a land bridge over the deep trench that circled the compound's walls. There was plenty of activity we could see even from the tree line, including many animals taken out and shepherded along to do their business outside the walls.

"Do you see the cow?" I asked.

"I see *a* cow," said Hemming. "Doesn't look very intimidating to me."

There were plenty of cows, each one more mundane than the next. So we sat and watched.

There are logistical concerns with that kind of surveillance. Boredom is one, the bane of my existence. Some men do stupid things because of too much drink, whereas boredom is just as potent a poison to my mind. There were also practical matters involving olfactory pollution inherent to two men sitting around the forest for three days. Use your imagination.

A wooden tower stood high above the compound walls, giving its lone inhabitant a clear view in all directions. The guard changed every four hours during the day and every two hours at night. Their closest warning system. It was a long view from that tower over fields with deep irrigation trenches that would double as a means of slowing the quick advance of any oncoming groups.

Supplies had to come in, and no doubt they would need to cart things away. The road from the main gate snaked around and around, especially while still within bowshot of those just behind the palisade. Inconvenient if you wanted to bring in a wagonload of ale. Lethally inconvenient if the wagon you approached with was hostile.

It takes a while to move unseen and unheard. With a wide open area around the longhouse and eyes in the tower above it, it took us even longer to get around the sides and back. We did so, but it all proved fairly fruitless. The walls were even higher there, and deep pits filled with stakes waited for anyone falling off those walls.

Varg had designed a way to funnel attacking forces to the front. Slowly, though, so that there would be plenty of time to deploy his cow.

Even then, I wasn't sure I believed in this cow. It seemed too strange to be literally true. Stories change quickly as they move over time and distance, and if these stories were true, there were no survivors of those who had attacked Varg to give good accounts. I did not doubt Varg's sorcery or that he was extremely dangerous, but what exactly we needed to be wary of seemed like it was still a mystery.

It continued to be a mystery until the fourth day.

Hemming seemed to be happier than ever living in the woods. I was just about ready to murder him, wanting a fire and some ale and literally anything hot to eat. I had a small amount of relief when he decided to go forward on his own in the dark of the morning. I stayed behind, hidden in a copse of trees, still closer to the compound than I wanted. It was a break for me and exciting for him. He said he would be back before there was enough light for the watcher in the tower to make him out. Meanwhile, he would use the earthworks they'd put up all along the way there and back as cover.

I wasn't expecting any activity when I heard the gate open. It was not quite light yet, but it soon would be, the undersides of clouds heralding the rising sun. Not quite light, but too light, as I realized Hemming had not returned yet.

He had not returned yet because he had gotten very close. Now he was slipping under the land bridge and into the trench to avoid the tower guard's gaze. The gate opening was ill timing.

The animal waddled out with a minder alongside. The man was wrapped up warmly, especially around his head. As I stared, my vision seemed to hone in closer and closer despite the distance between us. And I knew that cow was The Cow.

Expression madder than Kraki's. Body fatter than Svein's. Yellow eyes staring out of sunken sockets seemed to long for a trip to the butcher. If that was just a cow, an erupting volcano was just a mountain. I didn't need Huld to tell me there was some kind of malevolent spirit trapped in there. If it had been Varg's doing, he would indeed be a hard man to kill even if we got his cow first.

The minder leading the cow was an unhappy man wearing the kind of beard that only men not intending to have beards wear. A too-tight leather helmet had straps drawn straight over his ears. As I looked closer, I could see the padding beneath the ear straps. Whatever he was using, it stopped up his ears, and the straps held it all in place.

Man and cow plainly could not see Hemming in his hiding place as they walked out, which was good. How long would that last, though?

The copse of trees I hid in gave me enough cover to act. If I could think of something.

Need? Not even a consideration at that range.

Spell? Maybe. What spell, though? I was not prepared to take this thing on directly.

Sling? I was an excellent shot, but even if I hit the thing in the head, it would be a high, lobbing throw. I could kill a man at range, but that's a man. Even at close range, I would not target anything with a skull that thick.

But I could create a distraction. Hopefully a very small distraction, because a distraction bringing a few dozen armed men out of that longhouse could be detrimental to our survival. I loaded a stone into the sling and broke cover to let it fly. The target was a good 400 to 500 feet from the tree line, outside my range for accuracy but inside my range for simply lobbing a stone.

I had broken cover before checking that the tower guard was conveniently looking away. Svipul tsked at me. "You're a lucky skald indeed," she said. "You might want to check things like that before risking your life in the future."

"Who are you, my mother?" I whispered under my breath as I launched the stone. I ran back to what cover I had before it came down. As intended, it came down to earth somewhere to the side of the cow.

The cow's herder made no reaction. Shit! Of course he wouldn't hear that; he had his ears stopped up. But the cow heard it and knew the sound for something unexpected. The thing turned back and set its demon eyes on the earth nearby. Then, it let out a groaning moo that pierced my ears.

Whatever the opposite of music is, whatever the counter to melody, that was the sound coming from the beast. It was a low rumble, not nearly the volume an animal that size could muster, and did not last long. I still recoiled at the pain it caused in my head and kicked at the nearest tree, wanting to lash out at whatever was nearest. The worst of the feeling dissipated with the kick, but I held onto that unfortunate birch and let it support me for a few more moments as I recovered and considered.

That was a powerful animal. And it would be far more powerful with a sacrifice to fuel whatever malevolent spirit was trapped in that body. Wishing I'd thought of this already, I stopped my ears up with cold mud, hoping that would blunt the thing's power.

Even if it did, I still needed to think of something for Hemming. I could see him behind one of the earthworks, cringing in pain beneath sharpened stakes. He was closer, getting more of the effect of that moo. But he couldn't move without being seen now, and he couldn't stay there forever.

As I considered what was next, a terrifying thought occurred: Stopping up my ears would not be enough. Surely someone had thought of this already and brought an army around full of men with plugged-up ears. Yet here was Varg, still sitting in his hall, so either no one had ever tried that, or someone had and failed. Maybe I had gotten just a small taste of its power. Either way, getting closer was not an option. I needed to do something from where I was.

"You could run," said Svipul. "Tell them Hemming got reckless, which he did."

"No," I whispered, my right hand reaching for Haldor's axehead armring.

"Well, you were chosen for your abilities to run and to cast spells. If running is not what you'll do, better think of something to carve."

"Ideas," I hissed, my back against a tree trunk as I tried to think. I looked around, but my *fylgja* was gone. Or if not gone, not about to help me further. I could come up with a spell, but what? And then, how would I cast it? I needed time more than anything else, and that was running out.

The loud croak of a raven called out in a wordless bid for attention back at the compound's palisade. Blue-black wings beat the air as the raven came to rest on the top of the gate. "I heard there was a battle cow here," said Humor in his loudest voice. "Is this the cow?"

"WHAT?" came the call back from the cow's minder.

"You should unstop your ears if you want to hear," continued Humor. "I was trying to ask you about the cow! Are you taking the cow for a walk? You're going as slow as a CRAWL. I saw a lot of FOG coming up when I flew here. You should be careful you don't get lost in it."

That was some great bird.

The ground was wet, but there wasn't a bit of mist up yet, much less a fog. If I could conjure one, though, that might be enough. Hemming could low crawl through it and stay out of sight, and then we could be away from there.

I fumbled out a disc and my carving knife. I had to try something. The disc was birch. Was that the right wood? *Stop overthinking, just carve.* Fog is water on the air. I had a rune for water but not for air. Hail is water on the air, would that work? No, I knew no way to change it that dramatically.

I shook my head, thinking my odds were so long at succeeding that Innstein would probably bet on me. One thought led to another along those lines, and it was the 'Steins on my mind. The 'Steins and their games of *hnefatafl*, where one side is trying to get its king to safety.

I was trying to get Hemming to safety as if he were a game piece on a board. The echo of Ketill's disapproving voice rang in my ears as I carved *gebo : perðo* for roughly *gift to the game piece*, hoping my will would carry through for the meaning intended. I cut my hand, bled on the carving, and felt a power flow into the piece as I'd never felt before. It was the correct side to bleed onto this time.

A dizzy moment had me leaning against the tree again. I recovered in a few breaths, noted the minder and tower guard both had their attention on Humor, and threw the disc.

It did not go nearly as far as the stone. I didn't need it to. I thought I saw the disc melt as it struck the ground. A gentle wind picked up, just a bit warmer than it had been before.

"I'm trying to ask about the story of the cow!" shouted Humor down to the minder.

"WHAT?"

"Oy, we don't need stories about the cow," shouted the tower guard. "Why don't you move along?"

"But I would trade!" said Humor as he spread his wings. "I have so much to trade! Do you know how popular horned helmets are getting in Denmark?"

"WHAT?"

"How popular are they?" asked the tower guard.

"Not very," said Humor. "But they might be soon. The king there is a real trendsetter!"

The tower guard put his hand over the top and sides of his helmet, seeming to feel for where such horns might be fastened. I marveled at the bird's bullshitting ability.

The conversation continued this way as air moved over the cold earth. Low clouds mushroomed up to my ankles as if the Down-Below was breathing out in slow but regular intervals. Soon, they were up to my calves.

A whining moo blasted the bird from his perch on the gate. My heart skipped a beat when I saw him fall, but Humor flapped and saved himself in the last few feet, then flew off, cursing the cow and its handler.

My head throbbed. Even that low moo and even with my ears stopped up, that had been painful. The desire to strike out moved my right hand to Need, the image of hacking Hemming down with it seizing my mind. I fell to one knee before I recovered.

Hemming was no longer visible. Panting, I crouched down again and narrowed my eyes to scan his most likely path back. Still nothing.

Minutes later, Hemming pulled himself up behind the tree next to mine. He was wet and out of breath and dirtier than usual, which was saying something. I locked eyes with the tracker, and for a moment I was not sure if he had taken some worse effect from the cow's moo.

"Had enough?" I asked.

"That is no cow," whispered Hemming.

"It is a cow on the outside, but I saw its eyes. Something else is inside."

The short tracker brushed himself off as his chest heaved. With one more glance toward Varg's compound, he shook his head. "Maybe it should stay there."

CHAPTER 24

THAT ROMAN MAGIC

A COMICAL ARCHITECTURE OF STICKS AND HAY STOOD ON ALL fours in an empty field. Its face was a grotesque mask of scrap leather bits sewn together in what was not even a rough approximation of a cow's head —a rough approximation of some mouthless, eyeless, noseless troll from a nightmare, maybe. But there it sat, laughing at us and the 'Steins' machine despite its lack of a mouth.

"Two cranks more this time," said Innstein, wet thumb stuck up to gauge the nonexistent wind.

The 'Steins had launched four stones already, and still, this model of our target stood stock-straight. I stood with them, eyeing the wooden beast they'd built. A stone thrower, they said. Capable of throwing stones big enough to cave in a cow's skull and more.

A small, mousey monk stood with us, and we four braved being near the machine. The rest of our crew stood at what we all assumed to be a safe distance behind us. After feeling the war machine's wild kick when it launched its stones, I didn't blame anyone for hanging back.

The wind was quiet as if holding its breath to avoid giving the 'Steins an accidental win. They would need to earn it.

Once again, the 'Steins turned the crank of the windlass to pull the great arm of the weapon back. Taller than any of us, the sling arm drew down against its neutral state, butting up against the padded crossbeam.

195

"The last rock went too far," said Utstein. "That will send the next shot even farther."

"The last one was the size of Svein's brain," said Innstein. "This one is more like . . . "

" . . . bigger than that?" I added.

"Much," said Innstein, his brother nodding.

Utstein huffed and shook his head as he continued to wind the crank, pulling the arm ever closer to the machine's rear. "Could have gotten more uniform rocks," he muttered.

"Patience, brother," said Innstein. "We are not yet so rich we can afford whatever rocks we want. We must use the rocks we have. After we kill the sorcerer, maybe then we will be so rich as to have the rocks we want."

"I told you, he is not a sorcerer," shouted Ketill. "He just has a magic cow! A real sorcerer would call up power when needed, not have it lumbering around at random all the time."

The wizard stood in front of the rest of the crew. Some of the monastery's inhabitants had come to watch as well. I was quite interested in anything that might kill Varg's cow without getting too near it, but at the same time did not want to be too close to anything capable of killing it. They insisted I stand with them as they made the thing work. I stood close to the weapon, awed and anxious at the same time. A step behind me was that little monk, who they'd also insisted be there for the testing.

"You go kill the cow, then," Utstein shouted back.

"Is there really a sorcerer?" asked the monk in Latin. This he addressed to me, as his Norse was good enough but clearly not what he preferred to communicate with. The approximation was close, but I knew *magi* had a very different meaning for him. Spirits were just a part of our world. We had no single word for "magic," as he understood it. And he understood it to always be malevolent. That complicated things. It even left me describing Varg as a troll.

That part was fine with me.

Tensions had been high since Hemming and I reported what we had seen. The brothers did not want their project to fail, and the others did not want to die horrible deaths. I still had confidence the brothers had found the magic we needed in that book, but every rock coming down on a place that scarecrow was not shook that confidence a bit.

"Perhaps there are more details in the codex," I offered, still a bit jealous I had been absent for the monk's reading of it.

"There is nothing about the operation in the codex," snapped Innstein. "We went over it up and down and sideways with Efraim here."

"Literally," said Utstein. "It is not enciphered. Just insane."

"Yes, well," said the monk in Norse, seeming to agree with only one part of Utstein's comment. "*Boustrophedon.* Very old." He traced a line in the ground with a single finger, then doubled his tracing back to create a line under the first but in the opposite direction. "Like plowing," he added.

I had heard of this but never seen it. What little Norse writing I had seen had been carved onto sticks and rocks and (sometimes) bones. Usually just a few words in one line. If there was more to it, like on a runestone, it was written left to right, starting left to right again on following lines. Alternating that with right to left did seem deliberately confusing.

"To make it difficult to understand?" I asked. "Maybe to allow only certain people to read it?"

The monk shrugged. That and half a dozen other reasons were possible.

"Don't tell the wizard that," said Innstein.

"If you do, we'll never hear the end of it about his wisdom in writing nothing down," hissed Utstein.

"I already heard you," shouted Ketill from the main group. "Because a real sorcerer can hear such comments. *Another thing I would not write down.*"

"By the burning balls of Surt," muttered both brothers.

"But what language was it?" I asked.

"A language of old Rome," said the monk. When I made a face indicating disbelief, he added, "Before the empire. Etruscan."

"A language *before* Latin?"

The monk nodded. It was not an original, he explained, but likely a copy from long ago. It contained many useful things, but all jumbled together and without coherence to it. Nor did it include appropriate praises of Yahweh, he added as he crossed himself, as the original was probably from the pagan Republic.

"Efraim here was hesitant to translate at first," said Utstein.

Innstein clapped the monk on the back and added, "But we offered him some ale and our friendship, and then he could tell us many things."

"Many numbers, more like," said Utstein. "Lengths and widths and weights."

"And the power of twisted rope," said Innstein as he brought an angled hook up to secure the throwing arm. "Though few drawings, and none to show you the finished thing as it should look." He shrugged. "Perhaps they were trying to hide their magic from anyone who did not know their old lore."

With the arm secured to the base, Utstein then detached the rope that had pulled back to the arm. "Thank Njord they failed so completely," he finished. "It is your turn, brother."

"Wait a moment," I said. "What do you mean *you* offered *him* ale? He would have offered *you* ale, I thought."

"Well, it's a rather complicated thing!" said Utstein in the voice he used when he was caught in a lie.

"I think you'll agree that our decision was a wise one given the circumstances," added Innstein, in the voice he used to rationalize his worst decisions.

I stared at them in turn as it became obvious what had happened. "You bastards drank my memory ale!"

"Somebody had to!" said Utstein.

"Just think about it like this," said Innstein, "if we were to march off to fight Varg and we lost, you would have never drunk it at all. And then some monk would drink it, and all he would remember is how bored he is here, tortured for the rest of his life with a perfect memory of everlasting dullness!"

"Now we can recall how to build this thing, and a few other things, too," added Utstein, nodding in time with his brother. "It was that or chance memory ale torture inflicted on an unwitting ally, which would have been most dishonorable. I think we've done you a great favor."

I am certain my face indicated that I did not feel like a great favor had been done for me.

Innstein approached the rear of the weapon. "Perhaps we should let the skald do it. He is lucky, after all. And he has been ass-deep in sticks and mud while we've been building this great weapon."

"What do you say, skald," said Utstein. "Have a try?"

I was angry at losing my memory ale, but I also wanted to launch that thing. It was one of the most fantastic contraptions I'd ever seen. And the thought of raining a skull-sized stone down on the head of that cow had me in its grip.

"See here where it is fastened now?" said Utstein, pointing to the angular hook holding the arm to the base. "You just take the butt of your axe and knock that backwards. It is already aimed—as far as we can, at least."

I drew Need. It came up as a hammer rather than an axe, which seemed to me a touch contrarian rather than needful. It did the job, though, and one smack from that hammer released the arm. The concussive thud of the arm against the crossbeam I felt in my chest as much as I heard with my ears. The rock they had laid in the arm's sling flew high and far.

"Ah, I've lost it already," said Innstein.

"Me too. The sky is even more gray than before," agreed Utstein.

I had not lost sight of the rock, however. I watched it tumble end over end in a slowness contrasting with its great velocity. I could lift a rock of ten pounds without difficulty. Maybe Svein or Haldor could throw one at an enemy effectively. What I saw this machine do with such a rock defied belief. Or would have if I hadn't seen the previous four attempts.

In a few breaths, there was a great crashing of sticks and hay, low cheering from the group, and primal shouts of victory from the 'Steins.

Efraim crossed himself again. He said a short phrase that was nothing like "By the burning balls of Surt" in content. I think that, nevertheless, he meant something quite similar.

CHAPTER 25

SAXA EX MACHINA

"Varg Tiorvi, I am Haldor Skullsplitter!"

There was little else that needed saying. No overt threat or demand was required, just a simple identification. Our numbers and the way we held our weapons said the rest.

It was an overcast spring afternoon when we approached Varg's gate and made our challenge. Still a ways off from the gate, we did not care to be easy targets for arrows. Varg's tower guard must have seen us coming for some time as we wound our way around the path in front of the compound. Technically, we were in the range of their bows, but it would be long, blind shooting from behind their walls.

The march from the monastery had been a long and laborious one. Every one of the crew was there. Svein stood at the front with Haldor. Magnus held a shield, though it wasn't his preference to fight that way. Even Hemming was in formation with us. Huld had marched with us from the monastery early that morning, but there was no telling where she was.

The 'Steins, normally a great relief to have in the shield wall, were well outside it. Those two manned the new weapon from well behind our line. They had named it "Cow Killer," our main counter to Varg's sorcery.

I was not involved in this naming, so don't blame me.

The stone thrower was mobile, with large wooden wheels built into its base. But we'd had no pack animals to pull it and so had taken it in turns to be our own pack animals. This was easier to do on the dry ground we left behind and more difficult once the overcast weather turned into a light rain, especially given the weight of the ammunition.

We were tired. But we were more tired of waiting.

"Varg Tiorvi," repeated Haldor. "Stay behind your walls, then! Though we stand in the rain, it is you who is wet. Wet for the *jǫtunn* that uses you like a woman every nine nights. Some men ride their horses, but Varg Tiorvi, we hear your horse rides you!"

So that was between two and three insults Haldor had made for which Varg Tiorvi could legally kill him. Being called "wet" by itself was borderline, a good ramp-up to the other insults.

"Perhaps it is best we go tell the Swedes in Uppsala of your cowardice," Haldor continued. "Surely, you would prefer that to facing me in the open."

That was a serious threat.

We wanted open combat to have a clear shot at the cow. If we didn't get it, we were too small a group to scale the walls successfully. If he wanted to, Varg could sit in behind his walls and do nothing. Then we would leave, telling about how we'd challenged Varg the Charmer and lived to tell about it, that Varg had been too afraid to fight.

That would forever damage his reputation. His trade would suffer, and suffering trade meant unpaid and, therefore, unhappy warriors. Unhappy warriors were the kind who took matters into their own hands and killed lords before suffering too long under their ill luck.

That was the internal threat. The external threat was from Uppsala. The king there liked expanding his treasure hoard and his lands. If he sensed weakness in Varg's hold on Gotland, he might take the opportunity to break that hold completely.

Varg's power was based on the fear that anyone who challenged him, even with greater numbers, was doomed to a terrible defeat. And to maintain that brutal reputation, we knew he would have to come out.

That was the reasoning behind the plan as we'd talked it through the day before. Ketill's contribution had been a lot of head-shaking. When Haldor finally demanded he speak his mind, the wizard replied, "No battle plan survives the first arrow's flight."

I thought about that when somewhere behind that wall, a woman screamed. It was a language I did not recognize. I could hear a scuffle of some sort, and then the woman's cries turned into a long, slow wail.

I heard nothing for a while after that. Then the gates opened, and it was time to apply my ear protection as the others had. Somebody had to keep their ears open—up to a point. Haldor had chosen me for that job. Meanwhile, everyone else had their ears stopped up with Huld's mix of tallow and wheat. Tallow to blunt the noise, wheat because it was strong against sorcery.

The mixture applied, I stepped over to Ketill. The wizard stood behind the shield wall, his bow strung. I bent down a bit so that he could etch an inverted *uruz* rune into the mixture I'd just applied to my ear. The tallow, wheat, and rune together should, we were told, stop the worst effects of the cow's mooing.

Once applied, even my keen hearing was almost completely gone.

It was hard to speak without being able to hear. There was little for me to do, anyway. Haldor had already gotten out most of the good insults.

The rest of us stood in a loose wedge angled back from Haldor and Svein. I was holding a shield, so I felt stupid. Never could get the hang of shields. The wedge was part of the plan, though. If the enemy closed ranks and protected the cow, we would charge, part their shield wall, and send Kraki through the middle to kill the cow. Assuming Cow Killer had not got it first.

If they charged us, the plan was much the same, only it involved more of a melee to approach the cow. Which is exactly what Magnus wanted to happen.

That was the plan anyway, and no plan survives the first arrow. I suspected our "plan" would turn into a general melee, for which I was ill-prepared. Need was a long but well-balanced spear in my hand, the simplest and best weapon I could have in an open fight.

Six champions walked through that gate. Or so I took them to be because they had good, steel helmets and shiny chain shirts. Expensive arms and armor were not so common for wandering mercenaries, of which there were also more than a few. These all spilled out little by little, all men staying behind that little land bridge. To cross that would be to give up an excellent natural defense.

An older man, not as ancient as Ketill but more bent, held the cow's reins and brought it right up past the champions to be front and center. He had been the minder I saw days earlier, but he had no ear protection this time. A cruel smile curled on his lips as he scratched behind the cow's ears, and I saw that his hand was bloody. He looked rather bovine himself, his mouth moving in a slow grinding motion as if he had cud to chew.

He motioned for some of the less armored men to form up with shields around the cow.

I looked behind me at Ketill, who had already nocked an arrow on his bow. He shook his head as if I even needed to ask. It's not easy to shoot straight in a wet fight, especially targeting a tiny opening among all those shields. Depending on how the fight went, he might need to start shooting anyway.

"Where is Huld?" I asked. She was supposed to be somewhere nearby, ready to heal the wounded. I suppose I was worried about my prospects in the coming fight to even think about her.

Ketill shook his head, and then I remembered nobody would be able to hear me through the tallow mixture. It was certainly effective, though I could still hear a bit. It mostly felt a bit itchy, and not just to me. Svein, too, was scratching at his ear.

A man appeared just behind the palisade, standing on some fortification, no doubt. A pink smile curved into a high forehead, which rose into white hair. Not gray or silver, but really white. He had gained some weight since the memory I had seen him in, but that was Varg Torfi for certain. His cheeks bulged sideways while a short beard betrayed a second chin.

"It has been a long time since a group of fools like yourselves tried such a thing," he shouted. Though muffled, I could still hear him a bit and read his lips for the rest. "Do you not know me and mine?" He exchanged a look with two of the best-outfitted warriors below, who raised their swords—his sons, no doubt. "Surely those stories are common enough that you would know what happens to those who attack me, even in numbers much greater than yours. You are on a fool's errand. It is a pity you will be unable to tell Arrow-Odd of your failure."

I nodded at Haldor to indicate I had understood him and shouted the man's words inches from Haldor's ear.

Svein looked over and tried to listen, then scratched at his ear again.

"What a random thing to say, referring to Arrow-Odd," Haldor replied to Varg. "Dropping unrelated names won't distract us or help you. Come out and fight me one on one, and your men can keep their lives. I will face you bare-handed against whatever weapon you choose. Few men find better offers than that."

Varg laughed outright at that and looked at the cow's handler. The smaller man gave him a nod and kept moving his mouth. Something about the handler unnerved me. Though I knew Varg to be a villain, he still looked like many other jarls. The handler, however, had an ill look to every part of him, from his shabby leathers to his grimy teeth to the cruel look in his eye.

I caught the scent of blood and rust on the air. I knew the smell of that sort of *seiðr* on a battlefield. Lejre was coated in its mist when we fought Alfhild, her sacrifice of Leif augmenting her already considerable power. It had flowed around and beneath us, dragging at our very feet.

Judging from the look on Ketill's face, he smelled it, too. Perhaps it was the cow, or perhaps the screams I heard had been a sacrifice to the cow, and the air of it only now wafted down. It did not seem quite right in that way I often find myself sensing something is very much not right but unable to find anything out of place.

Svein scratched at his ear, harder this time. We would need to fight soon instead of just stand around.

"'Random,' says the sea-king!" bellowed Varg, pausing for his men to laugh. "Either you are a most unnecessary liar or a most ignorant fellow! There are but two sides to choose, and a man who chooses neither walks toward his own death."

I again related Varg's words to Haldor as he inclined his head toward me. At the end of it, I thought I heard something else, something in the background. A low hum, not the cow. What was it?

"Every man walks the path toward his own death," said Haldor. "Some carry their courage with them and leave the same in their wake, though they have lost nothing. But you left your balls behind long ago, and it is no wonder you walk with a pain in your ass."

Varg's smile fell. Something about this insult had cut deeper than the others, and I tensed for a potential charge. Ours or theirs, who knew? We drew into a tight wedge, shields up, weapons ready. The hum increased and my face twitched from the itching at my ear. To my right, Haldor was holding steady, but Svein had put his axe into his shield hand and was aggressively scratching at his ear.

In the instant before the clouds burst, I saw the handler one more time. He was not chewing. He was chanting.

In the next moment, the demon cow raised its glowing yellow eyes to moo.

As we had drilled, Haldor raised his axe and our crew began to make as much noise as they could. The cow's moo rolled into that wall of shouts. The angry challenges from our side lessened at that thing's power. In the midst of all this din, I was desperate to get a message to the wizard.

"*Ketill!*" I screeched after turning around, "*The handler is a sorc—*" but I was cut short. Svein's shield boss had collided with the side of my face.

I went down seeing stars and twisting the shoulder of my shield arm in the wrong direction. When I rose, it was to see the reason for Svein's behavior. He had clawed away too much of the ear filling on one side, and he was taking the full force of that cow's power, swinging wildly at our own people.

Our wedge was in disarray. Haldor bade the others stay away and engaged Svein himself, banging his shield against the fat man but avoiding lethal strikes. He shouted for Svein to regain his senses, but for once, Haldor's command went unheeded.

For the others, it was confusion, especially those new to the crew: Where to stand, who to fight. Haldor pushed Svein back until he was far from the rest of the group while Ulf shouted at him to regain his senses. But I could see Svein's face when I rose, and whatever madness that cow could conjure was on him as long as it still mooed.

Plans and first arrows and whatnot.

Undistracted, Ketill loosed an arrow at the cow's head. One of the guards around the animal raised a shield to stop it. The arrow struck hard and pierced the layers of linden and hide but stuck fast at its fletching. Other guards moved into position to block further arrows.

Varg was through the gate then, just behind his champions. The less well-equipped men crossed the land bridge at the head of their group, all apparently unfazed by the cow. I reckoned we were outnumbered at worse than two to one.

The first rock came down wide of any warriors. The one with an arrow in his shield pointed and shouted to the rest. If the rock's thud put them on edge, it did not slow their advance.

I ran to Ketill as he nocked another arrow. "*Shoot the handler!*" I shouted into his ear.

"What?" he asked over all the other noise.

"*The handler! Varg is not the sorcerer, the handler is!*" It was not working. Though I could hear a small amount, Ketill could not.

I backed off a pace and made an expression like a man chewing cud, and then ran one finger across my throat.

The wizard looked to the handler, undistracted by Varg the Charmer, Varg the Distraction. Sudden realization crossed Ketill's face. He read the battlefield, and I followed his gaze to Svein. The fat man had left off fighting Haldor. He was running in the direction of the 'Steins. Toward Cow Killer.

Something changed in Ketill's face. Not the drunken glee from last summer or the capricious frustration of former times. An old fury, the kind that can only emerge from long years of nurture, formed in his eyes.

He wiped his bowstring as dry as he could before nocking the arrow again. "Stop the fat one," he commanded, his voice ringing through my ear protection.

I dropped that stupid shield and took off after Svein. Behind me, I could feel the vibration of Ketill's counter-chant. Maybe that would stop the sorcerer from burrowing into our ears to make them itch. Even if it did, there was still the cow to deal with.

Ahead of me, the 'Steins launched their second rock. What I would not give for that to take out the cow sooner rather than later. As it was happening, I had no real plan to stop Svein. All I knew was that I could run much faster than he could, and I would overtake him before he reached the 'Steins. What would happen when I caught up to the behemoth? I hoped for inspiration as I ran.

The cow mooed again, louder and angrier this time. I felt that demon voice in my bones. The sound pierced my ears but did not drive out my sanity, so that was something. However, it meant the rock had not found its target.

"Svein!" I shouted, coming within twenty feet of the man. "Cover your ear!"

The red-faced warrior looked back at me just long enough for me to see his lip curl in disgust. On he rumbled toward the 'Steins. Shouting the obvious was not working. A verse, perhaps! A verse sounded much better than trying to tackle a man twice my weight.

I had only seconds to compose, so don't be too judgmental.

> "Haldor's man
>   huffs and puffs
> running the wrong way.

He'll gain no
    glory this way
with that cow left unKILLED!"

I needed another line at least to make it *galdralag*, but I hadn't finished yet when Svein made it clear how badly the verse had failed. He stopped and pivoted, face full of rage, and threw his shield disc-like at me. Hence the unpoetic, high-pitched end to that particular verse.

Nimble as I was, I could not dodge the shield. Shields are made from linden because it is light and strong. "Light" is a relative thing, however, and light enough to deal with axe and spear blows is not light when it is sailing at your face at high speed. The shield clipped my right shoulder while I tried to dodge. I let the blow spin me as much as I could but stumbled and fell in the process.

The 'Steins had launched the third rock and were loading another. That was the first thing I noticed as I tried to get up. The second thing I noticed was that Svein had turned away from them and was heading for me, axe in hand.

"Keep shooting!" I shouted at the 'Steins. Whether the brothers heard well enough or not, they understood. Of course, even light rain might have an effect on all that twisted rope, and our enemy might just move our target at any time.

On my feet, I could have danced around Svein and forced a chase he had no hope of winning. But I slipped on the wet ground, and my rolling was not as fast as my running. Svein's huge movements telegraphed where he would swing in enough time for me to roll away. After the third attempt, he let out a howl of frustration.

Svein brought his axe down directly at my face. I turned my head away and brought my hands up, at once flinching and wishing I could face my death with more courage.

Need was still in my hands, though, and it was a shield at that point.

Svein's axe clanged violently off the shield boss. I rolled and blocked a few more times, but the force of each blow kept me from rising.

I caught a glimpse of the 'Steins. They had launched the fourth rock and were cranking the arm back. The cow continued to moo. It had taken them five attempts to hit their target in practice. If I could give them time enough for this shot and one more, that might be enough.

Between the rain and the clang of steel on steel, Svein lost his grip on the axe. In a rage, he took my shield in both hands, wrenched it out of my grip, and came at me with his bare hands.

I knew I could not win in a grapple. Despite all my negative comments about how dumb the man was, how slow and fat, he was incredibly strong. I kicked him hard on the knee, hoping to create an opportunity to inch away.

Svein saw it coming and shifted his weight. Had that knee remained solid to the ground, I might have made enough room to scramble away. I kicked against his knee all right but moved his whole leg as he had shifted his weight off of it to the other. All my kick did was move his leg back a little. Svein grinned and grabbed my kicking leg, pulling me closer, inch by inch.

That close-in fighting on the ground is difficult to describe. I tried to draw Need and realized I'd already lost it. One giant paw of a hand grabbed my right wrist and held it fast against my body as Svein edged into a better position. It was a slow struggle, slow and sure as a good grappler works. Svein did not need to end it quickly, only to avoid making a mistake I could use as a reversal. All my efforts, then, were little more than delaying tactics.

He punched me in the head a few times, pressed his advantage, and edged us both closer to his axe.

Seconds passed, and the cow screamed. Not mooed. Shock and anger rolled into one final shout, and then it went silent.

"Svein?" I said.

Svein reached for his axe.

Fear wrapped me in a blanket so tight I forgot how to breathe. I was pinned down with my hand clamped to my own body, seeing what was coming and unable to do anything but wait. The panic of Valborg's vision came back to me as if I was on that straw bed again. To die on your feet was one thing, but to be held down waiting for the end was worse.

"Svein!"

Svein seemed to raise his axe very slowly, one hand holding me down. For all his efficient maneuvering on the ground, he would revert to his big overhead swing now that he had his axe again.

A flash of white fur blurred my vision, and the world stopped moving so slowly. Ears back, claws outstretched, a huge forest cat hooked into Svein's beard and hair with her paws and bit down hard on his ear.

Svein dropped his axe and howled in shock. Grabbing the cat with his other hand freed mine and I wasted no time. I reached for Need, the shield, and did not stop to think before stabbing up into his shoulder, the shield becoming a long, thin spike as I struck.

The point found his shoulder just inside the socket, and the combination of spike and cat teeth was too much. Svein reared back and pulled Need out of his shoulder, then grabbed the cat and flung her away.

Maybe those pains returned his sanity. I would never find out because some things are better not left to chance. One 'Stein bashed him in the forehead, shattering the shield. The other connected with the back of his head right after, hammering Svein's skull with the shield boss so hard, Finnr must have heard that steel ring all the way in the Down-Below.

The madness drained from the giant man's eyes, as did all perception and consciousness. He fell forward, and the force of his body knocked the wind out of me.

Two grinning faces stared down for a moment and then disappeared from view. It was the last image I remember before falling unconscious myself.

CHAPTER 26

BLOOD EAGLES ARE OVERRATED

I WOKE LYING ON COW KILLER, ONE OF ITS HUGE WHEELS turning over and over as the war machine rumbled forward. Sitting up wasn't easy, but I did it anyway. We were moving toward the compound at a leisurely pace. Svein was pulling the whole thing himself, head down, not interested in conversation with the 'Steins on either side of him.

"Welcome back," said Magnus. He walked by within arm's reach of me and gave me a shove. "How many times did Svein hit you in the head?"

"I don't remember," I said truthfully. Then I realized the unintended joke and grinned. Blinking away the haze, I sat up, slipped off, and landed on my feet. I was not steady at first but still standing. I could walk, at least. "Wait!" I said, needing to know something at once. "Did a cat come on board with us?"

"A cat?" Magnus looked at me as if I had two heads. "On the ship? Maybe. Who cares?"

"It's just," I paused, not even sure my flashes of memory were to be trusted. "It was a cat that saved me from Svein. Before the 'Steins got there. Same cat that attacked Alfhild when Gudbrand and I charged her last summer."

"Are you sure it's the same cat?"

"Yes. No. As sure as I might be?"

Magnus leaned in close. "Your *fylgja* intervening, perhaps," he whispered.

It would explain the cat attacking Alfhild last summer, assuming Svipul could wear a cat's skin—or any skin. But no, that couldn't be if Svipul was that spirit that had turned me into a bear. I shook my head, and Magnus shrugged.

The light rain had stopped, and a few rays of sunlight poked through the clouds as we wound our way down that twisting path behind Cow Killer. Magnus' face and hands were stained with blood, but he looked cheery all the same. It seemed I had missed the battle, so I asked to know what had happened.

On that walk, I learned several interesting things. One was that we had indeed won. Two was that we had sort of won because Varg's sons were holed up in the longhouse and had yet to be dealt with. And three, Varg was still alive as our captive. Injured, but alive.

Magnus was eager to tell me the story. The second rock did not miss. It missed the cow, that was true. But it hit the sorcerer, the cow's real keeper, and that was not a bad result. Well, bad for the sorcerer. That itching spell to open our ears had been a brilliantly subtle move. Subtlety, however, is often undone by well-aimed projectiles moving at high speeds.

The resulting chaos was as bad for Varg as his cow had been for us. Worse, even, after Ketill began to chant and our crew locked shields again.

The third rock missed everything, but by then, all eyes were on Varg, who couldn't afford to disappear back into the compound and couldn't afford to wait for another rock. His people waited desperately for the cow's mooing to work, only it wouldn't. Then Varg drew his sword and ordered the men to form up.

That meant Varg's men were looking at a very different battle than the others they had fought. The cow must have usually done in most of the attacking force by making them fight amongst themselves. They would have normally had to walk over and finish a few men off as the hardest part of their fight.

Some of Varg's men held back, holding their shields over the cow. It was too risky to charge, they seemed to say. The cow will work.

The fourth rock landed on one of the men at arms who could not afford expensive armor. That was good luck for us because if he had been wearing good armor, it would have been ruined, and we wouldn't be able to loot it after the battle. He was a bloody mess, the cow was frothing at the mouth and rearing up, and Varg's contingent was showing signs of breaking back behind the land bridge.

Haldor did not order a charge at that point. The 'Steins' weapon was working too well. So he offered Varg single combat one more time. "That was fun," said Magnus, "because nobody could hear what Varg was saying with all the shouting and chanting, least of all Haldor. So Varg kept coming forward, shouting and urging his men to follow. Which they did, at a pace of two steps forward and then one and a half steps back."

The fifth rock came straight through the linden shields above the cow, breaking its back.

Varg turned to see that and froze in disbelief. Haldor waved the Brotherhood forward to charge.

The crew rolled over Varg's people. A few champions held and fought at the other end of the land bridge, and there they fell, giving Varg's two sons a chance to retreat. Varg tripped himself up, but Kraki dragged him back before he could get away, injured but alive.

"The gates are open and the compound is ours, just not the longhouse yet," Magnus said in his conclusion of the events. "That's where the survivors ran. The archer in the lookout tower is also not yet dealt with, so most of us are still outside under the cover of the palisade. Now you are all caught up with the day's events!" said Magnus, his cheery expression not at all undercut by the bloodstains on his face.

"What do we do about the archer?" I asked.

"Ulf is talking to him right now," said Magnus. "He's standing behind the gate so he doesn't get shot."

"Why is Ulf talking to him?"

"Oh, as a distraction! Hemming is climbing the ladder to the tower as we speak. Just very, very slowly so he isn't noticed."

Not so far away, I heard a prolonged scream. It cut off at the sound of an earthly thud.

Magnus shrugged. "Hemming climbed faster than I thought."

That left only a few warriors in the longhouse. Dangerous work, assaulting a longhouse. "So we have Varg. Do we let his sons live if they leave empty-handed?" I worked out a crick in my back and then rotated my shoulder. It felt fine compared to my swollen head and face.

"Kraki told Haldor you might have an opinion on that," Magnus continued. "Want to tell me what that is about?"

"No," I said, more abrupt than intended. "I mean, I don't know anything of the brothers." Meaning Valborg's brothers.

"You mean the sons?"

Whoops. "Yes. What did I say? Oh. Still groggy from being punched in the head."

"Hmm," said Magnus, his dissatisfaction with my answer plain.

"Why not just tell him?" asked Svipul. "You could tell him the general idea. You don't need to tell him every single detail."

Where were you when I was fighting Svein? I wanted to yell. But she had picked her timing well enough. For some reason, her sudden appearances never seemed to startle me, abrupt as they were.

"There are details of Valborg's vision I do not wish to relate," I said. "I don't even wish to think about them myself. They involved Varg only; I saw no one else. And Varg needs to die."

Magnus nodded, satisfied I had at least addressed the question. "Hung meat?" he asked. "Blood eagle? Something else?"

The image of Varg hanging from a rope running through his ankle had some appeal, but it would not kill him. Or not for a while.

"Maybe the blood eagle," I said to Magnus. "He needs to suffer."

"Oh, you don't want to do that then! Let's think of something worse."

"What is worse than that?"

"Cutting his toes off for one," said Magnus, eyes skyward as if that was where to look for ideas about torture. He began counting said ideas on his fingers. "Cutting his thumbs off is another. Thumbs and big toes! Hard to get along without them. Tar and feathering. Gelding. Lots of ideas! But not the blood eagle, that's stupid."

"The blood eagle sounds like the worst kind of dying imaginable!"

Magnus shook his head. "Have you ever seen a man get an eagle carved into his back?"

I shook my head.

"I have. Blood eagles work for dramatic presentation, but only for the audience. Sure, there is pain as the skin on the back is peeled away—skinning, there's another possibility, especially if you start with the feet—but this big idea that you will carve out the man's ribs from his spine and pull his lungs out like wings is for storytelling. I can tell you what happens: By the time you pull the lungs out, he's been dead for ten minutes! The blood eagle is just corpse mutilation." After a moment's thought, he added, "Which is fine if that's what you want. You'll get no judgment from me."

"It is good to have such open-minded friends," said Svipul, the bloodlust heavy on her breath. Maybe she really was a valkyrie. "Come now, did your humor fly away with that raven?"

Ah, Humor. He could be infuriating, but I liked him anyway, wherever he had got to. That thought led to another, which led to another, and then I knew what I would do.

Most of the crew was in the open area well outside the gate, cleaning weapons, adjusting armor, or seeing to injuries. Kraki was walking around the longhouse, tap-tap-tapping on the walls with his bone club. Ketill sat, examining which of his arrows were recoverable. Hemming climbed down from the tower, his task finished. He stepped around Varg, who had been tied to a post, and then over the body of the fallen archer.

"Do you have to do that now?" he asked Humor, who was pecking at one bulging eye.

"If not now, when?" he said and returned to the meal.

Behind me, Svein stopped pulling the cart and argued with the brothers.

"This is close enough to throw a rock onto the longhouse," he huffed. "Carry it yourself if you want it pulled further." Blood ran down the man's nose. He sniffed as he wiped it away with a sleeve.

"Haldor said pull it up past the gate," said Utstein.

"But by all means, be your own man," added Innstein.

Svein considered the barb in that last statement. Who knew how addled his brain was after hearing that cow's moo and then taking such a hit with the shield boss? He trudged off again, huffing all the way.

I got off the thing and turned to Magnus. "If Haldor takes my counsel, we will not need it again."

"What is your counsel?" asked Magnus, eager to hear what I had decided.

"I will tell it in good time and after a story," I responded. Then turning to the 'Steins, I added, "If Haldor likes my idea, I will need a goat and a length of rope. Can you two find such things?"

What a stupid question.

Nanthild had gone to sweep the rest of the compound with Ulf and some of the new men. They were just returning as I told Haldor my idea.

"I know it is more of a production, but I have not told a story in a while," I said. "And there are other things I cannot explain. The vision in the forge showed me something, and that something demands a ritual before it is well and truly done."

"Sounds like a lot of time for something that could be done more quickly," said Haldor. "Or by caving in the longhouse roof with rocks from the war machine before we go in." I noticed Haldor did not use the name *Cow Killer*. He didn't like it either.

Nanthild crossed her arms and shook her head. Not at me, but at our leader. Her face said all: She was furious and grabbed me by the arm to drag me back behind the longhouse, waving at Haldor to follow. With no idea why Nanthild was upset, I trusted she nevertheless had good reason.

I saw the body before we got close. Nanthild did not stop pulling me along until we stood within a pace of the sacrifice. The woman had been tied to a post, her wrists and ankles bound. She still wore her clothes, once colorful and now faded other than the new red stains. The style was not Swedish or Geatish. Perhaps she was a Balt or a Finn. Sami styles varied widely, so she might even have been related to my grandmother for all I knew.

Wherever she had come from, she had ended up here with her throat cut. This was the sacrifice that made the cow as powerful as it had been, and I regretted that Varg's sorcerer was not still alive to join his fate.

Staring daggers at Haldor, Nanthild pointed at me.

"It seems Nanthild has a strong preference for your idea," said Haldor. "I will gather the rest. Do what you will, but if no one surrenders after, we are going in."

Ten minutes later, I had an audience gathered outside the longhouse. Varg was stripped naked and tied to one leg of the tower, the tower guard having been left where he fell.

"Little help?" Humor asked me while I prepared. The guard had fallen face-down into the mud with only one eye up. I knew what he meant right away.

"It would be better if you listened instead of eating more eyeballs," I said.

"I can do both!" he persisted, but I told him to be more patient.

"There has not been a good story in some time," I announced louder than necessary. This performance would be as much for those inside the longhouse as our own crew. "Let me tell you one about the power of laughter.

"You all know Skadi, that fair daughter of the *jǫtunn* Thjazi. Many a hunter has called on her favor, and many more travelers have done so to keep their skis fast and sure. Skadi came to dwell among the *Æsir* after they slew her father, but it was armed and armored she came to them, looking to do battle. That was some brave woman.

"Gifts from the gods were not enough to placate her for her father's death. A husband she could choose, and that was no small thing, even if the rules of it were in Odin's favor. Choosing by feet alone, she picked the prettiest pair, thinking them Baldr's. She got Njord instead of Baldr, but call that no ill deal. Njord treated her with the respect she deserved, even if he was not as handsome as Odin's son.

"To honor her father, Odin cast Thjazi's eyes into the sky where they would remain as stars. Enriched and married and her father memorialized, it was telling how far the *Æsir* were willing to go to court this woman.

"But Skadi required another thing. Something the *Æsir* could not give out like gold, something so difficult she thought it an impossible task. Skadi's grief could not be addressed by a gift or a husband. Only laughter would bring her around fully.

"And so it fell to Loki to make her laugh. He was responsible in the first place for the ill that had befallen Skadi's family and the *Æsir* themselves. So he had rope and a nanny goat brought, and he tried his best in a tug of war. The nanny goat pulled with its horns, and Loki pulled with his balls. And eventually, Skadi laughed!"

Here, the 'Steins approached. Innstein had the rope I requested, but Utstein had done a slightly different thing. He was carrying a ram under one arm, holding one of its horns with this free hand. It was a young one, his horns just beginning to turn downward, and he willfully tried to buck side to side.

"Couldn't find a goat," said Utstein. "Will this do?"

"You should not do this," said Varg, who did a fair job of keeping his voice even. "I have silver buried in secret places. Chests of it! You will all be rich men if you let me go."

"Ah, silver," said Utstein.

"Worth its weight in gold," added Innstein in a long, dry tone.

The brothers grinned at Varg's expense. Despite their great fondness for winning money, there was no talk of securing Varg's treasure from those two.

I took my time looping the rope around the ram's neck and chest and tying it off.

"So, Varg," I said, raising my voice again, "You are the cause of much trouble, but we are reasonable people. If you can make us laugh, we will be in a mood to spare the lives of those now locked in your longhouse. Look at how much good you can do!"

Both brothers set the ram down and held him steady, scratching behind his ears and speaking softly to him. No matter if it calmed him down a bit. He was a young male, and soon he would be running all over the place.

"Magnus," I said, calling over my most reliable friend. "Hold his ankles to his ass for just a moment, if you would."

Magnus obliged. It was not too thick a rope. Which was good because Varg's ballsack was trying to draw up into him like a shy turtle.

Not shy enough, though. This was not pleasant work, but it was work that needed doing, and I found enough purchase to pull that knot taut.

"Silver," whimpered Varg. "Chests of it. And jewels."

"Didn't you hear the story?" asked Utstein, incredulous.

"A good laugh is worth more than treasure," said Innstein.

Magnus let down his feet and cut Varg loose. Hands still tied behind him, he was at least free to move. I signaled the brothers to let the ram go, and Innstein gave the young sheep an encouraging slap on the rump.

Oh, the sounds Varg made. None were words, but all were intelligible.

He chased the ram to allow as much slack as he could, but not fast enough. Again and again, the ram tugged on him, jerking him forward until Varg fell.

The entire crew laughed at the show.

Varg vomited and fell unconscious. The ram, lamenting the game had ended, butted him to little effect. Varg stirred, and I walked up to him as he wept.

"Why?" he asked through his tears.

I bent down and leaned in so that my lips were not an inch from his ear. "I knew your daughter," I said and slapped the ram on the rump to send him running off again.

The ram was happy to oblige me. This time, he ran free, dragging the rope behind him. It had not come undone, but part of Varg had, leaving a red streak in its wake.

Varg gasped, tried to stifle a scream, and failed to do so.

Loud exclamations from the crew joined Varg's voice. A few banged their weapons on their shields in applause. Among the clamor, I thought I heard the briefest laugh from a woman, but Nanthild was silent and Svipul nowhere to be seen.

As the applause quieted, I noticed the sounds from inside the longhouse. A lot of movement and thuds and some shouting. More than I had expected for a group of men preparing to surrender. Even more than expected if they were readying to fight.

"Weapons!" commanded Haldor. Then, when all were ready, "You in the longhouse! You may leave, but you will leave with nothing but your lives. Not your weapons. Not your armor. Not your clothes. Or you can choose to die fighting, but it seems to me you could have chosen that already if you were so inclined. Run from here and do not return to this island. And wherever you go, tell them Varg Sorrysack is no more."

Nice line, that, and some of the men chuckled.

Silence from the longhouse, then low murmurs. The door opened, but only a crack. I could see a figure moving but no details. Then that figure, now clearly a short and squat man, took half a step out. He tossed a severed head toward us.

The helmet came off the head after bouncing on the ground. It came to rest facing us.

Another helmeted head followed. This one must have had better straps because the helmet stayed on.

"Those are Varg's sons," said Ulf.

"Caw!" cried Humor. "Were his sons. Now they are dinner!"

The man in the doorway extended his arm out for us to see the two-foot-long seax he held. The blade was not just bloody but dripping in gore. He made a show of tossing it to the side, then put both hands out in front of him as he crossed the threshold.

His square face looked familiar, though worry lines were cut deep into it around his mouth and eyebrows. He was short, about Magnus's height, but built thicker all around. An iron collar was fastened around his neck. Once fully in the light, he said something slow and clear.

I had no idea what he was saying. The language was vaguely familiar but nothing more than that. His clothes were of the same style worn by the woman who had been sacrificed.

"He's a thrall," said Ulf.
"Not anymore," said Kraki.

CHAPTER 27

HARPING ON

THE MAN WHO HAD CASUALLY TOSSED OUT THE SEVERED HEADS of Varg's sons did not speak Norse. I determined the man's name was Joni. Soon after that, I determined I couldn't understand anything else he was saying.

This was not like hearing a few familiar things when Harbard spoke and then working them out. This was far, far more difficult. A few vowels were like the Sami my foster mother taught me, but the language was too far removed for me to converse.

Magnus made entry into the longhouse first as the fastest and most impetuous fighter, Haldor right behind him. They found more bodies and other (former) thralls but no one to fight. The stench of blood and entrails was heavy in there. A lot of men had died quite suddenly, and I saw how: The bodies were mostly against the wall we had faced from the outside. Sunlight shot through cracks in the beams and tiny holes they must have been peering out of.

They watched while Varg screamed himself hoarse. They watched but did not watch the thralls behind them.

Ulf questioned the survivors outside and in front of everyone, so there would be no confusion. Most were Norse and could converse with us, unlike Joni. Ulf confirmed what I had suspected.

Varg's sons and those few warriors left to them had shut themselves away but had no plan for what came next. Descriptions were fairly neutral at first. Once we shared some food and water and made it clear we would not enslave them, the descriptions Ulf received became more candid.

Joni had led a wordless but well-coordinated attack on those warriors while they peeked out to see what had Varg in such a state. Our little show had held their attention, and Joni took advantage right away. The thralls left none of Varg's warriors alive. Hoping we would take it as a peace offering, they severed the heads of Varg's sons and offered them to us.

Which made us very good friends, indeed.

Kraki insisted on talking to Joni despite the latter's total inability to comprehend anything he said. And despite the fact that Joni was wary of the old man in the extreme. You don't always need to speak the language to recognize crazy.

Or to recognize grief. We left Joni to grieve in his own way after showing him the sacrificed woman's body. I didn't know if her rites would be burial or fire, but Joni nodded when I brought a shovel.

Nanthild took the shovel off my hands and shooed me over to Huld. It took me a moment to realize why when I remembered my throbbing head.

The *vǫlva* had reappeared and was already preparing a tea. She donned her white gloves to grab the pot's hot handle and pour water into a few cups. At first I wondered at what must be in those cups, but her open hood caught my attention. I'd seen it before, but only now considered what it might mean that her hood was lined with white catskin.

"Drink this, and no ale or mead tonight," she told me. "Unless you enjoy having a big head."

Drinking was difficult enough without voicing my suspicion, but I was starting to suspect the cat was not really a cat at all. I resolved to let that lie for the time being.

The tea took the worst of the edge off my sore head, and then I got back to work. There was a good deal of cleaning up to do. We would want the use of the hall for the night, at the very least, and preferably not while it smelled liked spilled blood and intestines. All of us busied ourselves with one thing or another, moving things into the hall or out of it. Amid the activity, the 'Steins stopped me.

"What are we doing with Varg?" asked Innstein.

"I think his value as entertainment has diminished," said Utstein.

I did not want Varg to see the next morning, but every time I imagined putting a blade into his heart, the smell of straw filled my nostrils and stopped me. Even if Varg spent another week living in pain, it would be only a small measure compared to what he'd done. The gods devised an everlasting torture for the traitor, Loki, tying him up and having a serpent drip venom into his eyes for all time. I couldn't think of an equivalent for Varg.

Most of the men were busy stripping the bodies and dragging them into the trenches outside the gate. We took steel helmets, a few chain shirts, some decent weapons. I hated steel helms, but claimed a thick leather skullcap. The wolves could have the rest.

As for Varg, I tied him to the base of the tower and kept his hands and feet bound. I decided that Varg seeing the next morning and suffering all the way to it was just fine. The only issue was screaming, which he didn't seem to have the energy for. I gagged him just in case.

"You want this one's eyes?" I asked Humor.

The raven burped. "I've had enough for now."

I would deal with Varg in the morning.

The smell of death still lingered in the hall once we'd cleaned up a bit, but it was less than it had been. It was a late night for us, as nobody wanted to sleep much. Varg had stores of smoked mutton and barrels of mead to crack open. Hero and former thrall drained many a horn together. We feasted and celebrated late into the night.

To the dismay of the crew, there was no silver to be found. Ulf made this point many times over the course of the evening. There were plenty of provisions, though, from smoked hams to fresh ale. Much of which we enjoyed that night.

"I'm glad we don't have that cunt's silver," slurred Innstein, well into his horns. "I'd rather be rich another way."

"Rich in other things, perhaps," added Utstein from one corner where the barrels were kept.

"Yes, rich," retorted Ulf. "Rich in honor, but can honor buy food and weapons?"

"Apparently, it buys a fine drink, indeed!" exclaimed Innstein. "Look here! This isn't ale or mead, this is wine!"

Tucked well away in the corner was indeed a barrel of red wine. This was no small thing to us and was prized more highly than the best mead. We had nowhere to grow grapes well, and a trader who acquired them from afar would only return with raisins. Wine was too expensive but for the richest men and ladies and had to come from far away.

"Whoever Varg stole this from would want us to have it," said Utstein to the energetic agreement of his brother.

"That will be the spoils we take, then," said Haldor. "And there were enough good weapons and mail shirts that we can call this raid a profitable one. But," he said, affixing the brothers with his stare, "we must give up a good weapon here rather than take it with us."

"Not Cow Killer!" they exclaimed.

But it had to be so. Even if we could take it with us, we could not very well have it on the ship. And there was little sense in leaving the thing in working order for whoever might find it here. It had to burn.

The brothers each poured out a little mead for their construction. It had been a good weapon, and they would miss it.

"There may be other hidden treasure here," said Ulf. "Skald, what have you gotten out of that man?" Meaning Joni, though Ulf did not use his name.

"He doesn't speak Sami," I said.

"That is helpful," said Ulf. "You might go down the entire list of languages you speak that he does not."

"Some men have longer lists than others," I growled back.

Before the argument could escalate, Kraki took me and Joni aside. He wanted to know where the man was from and when he was taken. "We can't send this man off with the others we've freed. No one will understand him, and they will make him a thrall again. But if he comes with us, we should know who he is, and he must know where we are going."

"I have not been able to make more progress than a few words between us so far," I said.

"Well, what are the words?"

"Ale. Knife. To piss. People. Discerning plural from singular might be subtle. And the past tense—"

"You are thinking too much," said the old man as he shoved me away. "Let me try with gestures."

Kraki gestured wildly and shouted at the same time, increasing in volume and repetition when he was not understood. Joni had that stoic stone face that told you of apprehension by its lack of movement. Eventually, I had to intervene.

"Kraki, you understand not a word that man is saying. Why do you still bother him?"

"I can tell much from the way he speaks!" cried Kraki. "And he may take my measure as well, eventually."

"He thinks you're a madman," I said.

"He has taken my measure. Good, then."

I tried simple words the rest of the evening, and Joni was more receptive to that approach. I put my hands together and lay my face against them and understood his word for sleeping. I conscripted the brothers to sit on a bench opposite me and got his word for rowing. Iron, wood, stone, food; I got closer to his language and he to Sami, as Norse was just too far a stretch. But each time I tried a sentence or even a short phrase, it broke down. The logic of connections between words and how words changed in different contexts frustrated me.

I tried one last thing before intending to bed down for the night. In trying to convey that Joni should come with us the next day, I pointed to him, pointed in a circle at those men around us, and then made a walking gesture with two fingers on the table.

Joni replied in full sentences, knowing I could not understand them. In the end, he nodded and held out his hand for me to clasp.

The night wound down, and I ignored the further jibes from Ulf. Not that I did not want to respond, but I was exhausted and had enough troubling thoughts already. I would deal with Ulf in the morning if he still needed dealing with.

A few minutes went by before the sounds of snoring filled the hall. Wolves howled outside, having found the fodder we left for them. I turned in fitful rest but could not get comfortable. Perhaps I would be better off sleeping under a table as the brothers did or under the stars as Hemming preferred.

I opened my eyes and thought I saw the outline of a woman looking at me. "Svipul?" I whispered, but she turned and walked to the open door in silence. Moonlight, soft as silk, spilled onto her features, revealing dark hair that contrasted against a pale face. She carried a solid, short piece of hardwood with a small iron fitting at the top.

Valborg's eyes met mine for the briefest moment as she stepped through the doorway. I knew I had to follow.

She slipped through the compound's gate, open just enough for me to follow by turning my shoulders sideways. That was the last I saw of her.

We had shut that gate to secure the compound, I was certain of it. But I also knew what lay beyond that gate, and that was not what I stepped into. Instead of a long, grassy area with a twisting path into the forest beyond, I was indoors again.

I was inside a great hall. Little of it was lit, but I recognized I had been here before twice already. It gave the impression of midnight in Asgard. Where this had been a boisterous hall in the light of day, the hearth fires now burned low, the hall's servants absent and probably sleeping. Two figures sat at a table conversing in low voices as if not to disturb the shadows too much.

I tried not to disturb them myself. I wanted to hear what these two were talking about, so I kept still for a few moments.

Heimdall was speaking, the watchman of the gods. His blond hair shone with red tones in the low firelight while his bright blue eyes fixed on me despite my efforts at stealth. A ring sword showing the marks of long use lay sheathed on the table, his left hand never leaving it. A wool cloak sat on his shoulders but lay open enough for me to see that he still wore the strange leather cuirass embossed with the ram's head.

He had a smaller audience than he'd had when I met him in council with Frey and Thor. This time, he spoke to one guest only, a woman. She was bright and beautiful but not dressed to please men in a delicate outfit and jewelry. A bow and quiver sat beside her on the bench, wet skis propped just beyond to dry off.

Her skin was pale and smooth. Pale is the wrong word—my skin is pale. Her skin was like an unspoiled snowdrift in the dead of winter, her tunic blue as a frozen sea. Her expression showed neither happiness nor distaste, a neutrality that felt balanced rather than apathetic.

Not a goddess of Asgard. A *jǫtunn*. Skadi.

Heimdall said something to awaken a dim memory. A phrase I'd heard him mention but forgotten. These dreams in Asgard are never easy to recall. But now I seized on it, and I would not forget, and I would even demand an answer while I was here.

"What is the Spear of the Gods?" I asked.

I walked closer. Heimdall regarded me without surprise. Skadi was less certain of me.

"You mentioned nothing of another guest for this conversation," she said.

"This guest comes and goes," said Heimdall. "He has important friends."

"What is the Spear of the Gods?" I reiterated. "You said it last year, mentioned it in conversation with Frey and Thor. I could barely remember it, but I do. And there it was, in Valborg's prophecy. And here you are mentioning it again. What is it, this Spear of the Gods?"

"It seems our conversation is at an end," said Skadi, picking up her skis.

"You want to know so much so quickly, skald," said Heimdall. "But you learned why a wise man's heart is seldom glad. Are you so sure of wanting to know more again?"

Skadi stopped and looked me up and down but said nothing.

"There's much I would yet know. I think there is much arrayed against me, or at least planned without my consent. I would at least see the whale itself rather than have it keep brushing against me, more a mystery each time."

"Some men might panic at seeing a whale," said Skadi.

"Not this one," said Heimdall.

"I could use a skald such as that. Perhaps he would come with me to Thrymheim. There is a thing my husband might use a skald to help with."

"You are quite beautiful," I told Skadi. "The myths hardly do you justice. I would come with you for a time if it won't take me away from my friends. But first, I would have my answer."

Heimdall took a deep breath, his thin smile never wavering. Then, he locked eyes with me, and that bright blue gaze held me while his smile dropped. He spoke a verse I knew well.

> "I see a winter,
>   but not of snow,
> when hospitality
>   turns hostile
> and ancient lore is
>   likened as useless.
> Inspired fables
>   are fully forgotten."

"I have heard this before from Valborg."

"What happens if the old stories are lost, skald? Where comes inspiration? Does wisdom matter anymore, or is it just as good to go on knowing nothing of what came before?"

"You speak like the end times are coming. As if it's the doom of the gods. But that is not how *Ragnarǫk* plays out. People know the stories, but there is a great battle, and the gods fall."

"That is one story of the end, and I don't know that the source is a reasonable one. The stories ceasing to matter, though, that's a slow doom. The gods are not apt to intervene in much directly, but we would bring our own spear to bear if it prevented the forgetting."

I shook my head. "So you want people to tell more stories?"

The watchman nodded. "Among other things."

"It seems to me you're leaving something out."

Skadi took up her bow and quiver and turned away from us. There was no door to the hall in the direction she walked. Wait, yes—yes, there was. It came into focus only as I was looking for a door.

"Seeing the entire whale at once won't help you much," said Heimdall. "And staying means you'll miss your visit to Thrymheim. A wise man takes an opportunity when he has it."

I snarled in annoyance at Heimdall's indirect manner, but he was right about the opportunity. I followed Skadi into the darkness and stepped through the door into another hall.

This hall was brightly lit. Cheerier, less brooding. Wolves howled in the distance and winds whistled as they can only on a mountainside. Thunder rolled over the rooftop in a constant rumble. At the far end of the hall, a man sat by a roaring hearth fire.

"I cannot understand how he did it," said the wind-worn figure, shaking his head. His face had the tanned skin of a man aged many years at sea, and his furrowed brow revealed more wrinkles than his voice or manner indicated. He put a harp down on the bench beside him as he shook his head and then snatched up a horn of frothy liquid.

Njord, the sea god.

"I've brought a skald," said Skadi as she laid her things down. "I would try first, however."

"Think you can do better?" he asked. "Maybe you are closer to the thing than I am after all. Here." He handed the harp to her looking glad to be done with it and gladder to return to drinking.

I had been preoccupied with Skadi and Njord but now noticed the harp itself. I say harp: This is the closest thing I might call it. It would be played by plucking strings short to long, unlike the equally long strings of my lyre. But it was not made of wood as a normal harp would be. The frame looked to be made of a giant fish's lower jaw, its strings each fastened to a sharp tooth.

Skadi took it with more grace than Njord offered it, and she stroked the entirety of musical notes a single time and held it to her ear. "We had a visitor at our meeting," she said. "Did you call him to it?"

"Ha!" laughed Njord between gulps. "He is not one of mine. Not even close."

"But did you call him?" she asked with continued patience, plucking a single tine. The thing played the same note every time, but each pluck offered some variation of too flat or too sharp—never quite in tune and never consistent.

Njord shook his head from behind his horn.

She sighed and beckoned to me. "Well, do come forward and sit down. We cannot very well keep you standing and staring."

"There is ale," said Njord, looking elsewhere in the room and sticking his thumb out at the back of the room where a large barrel sat.

A wise man does not turn down free ale, especially from those hosts.

Skadi glanced at me with a smile and then went back to her musical experimentation. "It still sounds off," she said.

"I know, and you are doing better than I managed," offered Njord, sounding impressed. "Keep trying. At the very least, it will tamp down the sound of the wolves."

Skadi ignored the jibe. Her playing continued as I drew myself a horn full of ale, rich and fresh and sweet. It hinted of spruce, probably from the filtering, with a bit of brine in the back. The first swallow gave me that realization and brought back some of my senses. Obviously, there was something that needed doing.

So many curiosities might be satisfied in a place like this, but I was fixed on one in particular.

"Why are you staring at my boots?" demanded Njord, no longer patient or placated.

"Come on!" I said. "Everyone knows the story. I've told it a hundred times! Skadi had to choose a husband among the *Æsir*, but only based on their feet, and yours were the prettiest. I have to see if it is true."

"You shit!" he bellowed, to my utter apathy. "I should drown you right now!"

"You are not allowed to offer hospitality one moment and threaten drowning the next," said Skadi with a grin. "At least stop offering that ale. It sets the mortals quite apart from themselves."

"It is good ale," I added, feeling quite apart from myself in the best possible way.

"And his feet are beautiful," Skadi purred, turning back to me. The intensity of those ice-blue eyes could have melted my heart. If ever I thought a *jǫtunn* had to be brutish or ugly, I would never think so again.

Njord rose and made for the barrel as he drained his horn.

"Does Baldr really have ugly feet?" I asked.

"All you male types have ugly feet," she said with a mild tone. "Except his, scrubbed soft by salt and sand. Much unlike his personality."

"You see why I prefer to stay by the sea?" called Njord from the other side of the room.

I gulped my ale. The beverage was so delicious I thought I would not care about Baldr's feet so much if I could keep drinking it. But now an angry sea god was guarding the barrel, and I predicted I would have little more than what was left in my horn.

Music from the fish harp came in fits and starts. Skadi had the measure of it for several seconds, but then the instrument would betray her and play an off-note or no note at all. She sighed and placed it on the table.

"This harp is not a thing for us," she said. "I can feel it. It is close, but not quite. A skald who has crossed many thresholds might have more luck. Perhaps he would try it."

"It is from the sea, and the sea is my domain."

"It is of a lake pike from lands you cannot even pronounce, not from the salt sea. Or are you the king of every pond and puddle?"

Njord grumbled at that but gestured that I should take a turn. I suspected he drank and grumbled frequently when this far from the sea.

The instrument was so light as to give the feeling that the slightest touch might break it. But on testing it, no amount of force bent or broke the frame. I tried the strings with my fingertips and then my nails with mixed results. They played off-tune for me as much as for Skadi, but consistently off-tune.

I breathed deeply and closed my eyes, feeling and listening while I tested the instrument again. It did not work at first, the sounds making no sense based on my efforts. But I heard something in one of the notes, something like breathlessness. Focusing on that, I loosened my hold on the instrument and breathed in as I played the same note.

The note played true and hung in the air as long as I savored it. I played another note, and then another, and finally, I was playing note after note without thinking, without intention, and music flowed from the thing like a distant wind blowing through a valley.

I saw with my mind's eye as if I were the wind riding the treetops. I saw a great lake, the likes of which I had never seen before, and campfires around it. I saw fish and people and reindeer all around. And I saw a darkness I did not recognize in the distance. Shadows, indistinct but irregular. Shifting, growing, receding. But ever approaching, bit by bit.

The last note held as if questioning whether the song should continue, and I lost my focus. The music ended, and I breathed out as if drifting weightless in the silence. How long that silence lasted, I could not say. It was like falling asleep within a dream.

When I opened my eyes, it was Midgard I looked on once again.

CHAPTER 28

THE QUEEN IN THE ROCK

THE SHAGGY REDHEAD WAS STANDING OVER ME AGAIN, STARING with concerned eyes. Drops from his beard pattered onto my face. Doubtless he had just used the morning washbowl, swirling with all the sweat and snot and blood from the previous day's battle. Some of the water got into my eye, and I reached up to wipe it away, for whatever that was worth.

"What was that tune you were humming?" asked Magnus. "Whatever it was, Haldor says enough. We need to get back to the ship."

I was up late, a rare thing. Magnus and the others had just finished washing and were already packing. The 'Steins were organizing a wagon load of spoils and eyeing that barrel of wine as if the gods themselves had sent it. I couldn't blame them. It was the most valuable thing we had found.

Shaking off the morning drowsiness, I found a pot with steaming oats and scooped a portion into the nearest bowl I could find. "Joni," I said, getting the man's attention. *"Have some oats first. It will be a long walk."*

Confused, the man strode over to the cauldron and took the offered food. He chewed without taking his eyes off me, a look of suspicion on his face.

"What?" I asked as it was becoming awkward.

"You did not want to let on that you spoke Karelian last night?" he asked.

I nearly dropped my bowl when I realized we had just conversed in his language. Without thinking, I had just done it.

231

"It seemed to me you did not understand," he continued. *"But now it is clear you do understand."*

The fish-jaw harp had played an odd tune at first, the same as Joni's speech. Now, the song I played echoed in my mind—a different tone, but one I understood. Not everything, not by any means. But simple speech I could understand and speak, its music attuned by the instrument Njord and Skadi could not quite master.

"I slept on it," I said.

As we worked to load up weapons, armor, and provisions, Joni increased the complexity of his speech until I had to give him a sideways look at why he was holding back. It was not long after that he ventured into his own questions. And there began the real conversation.

"He is insane. I am grateful for his efforts, but you must know he is insane."

"Kraki is . . ." I tried to find a word that was more subtle than *insane,* but it was out of my reach. *"He is not so different from the others, I think."*

"No, he is different. I have known others like him. A brain-damaged person bent on revenge. Wherever he goes and whatever he does, there is strife. He is most dangerous."

"The cook has saved my life twice already," I said truthfully. *"He is not so unhinged as you think,"* I added, not quite as confident in that statement's truth.

The Karelian turned a bit sullen at that, and we worked for a while with no more conversation.

There was one other matter to tend to before leaving. Nobody had touched Varg's body. Haldor had ordered that Varg was my responsibility, living or dead.

Well, he was dead. Keeled over forward, ass-in-the-air dead. I kicked his body sideways and saw his eyes had been eaten.

"Humor! You told me you didn't want these."

The raven was splayed out on the ground as if he'd overdone the mead last night. Which was doubly strange because we didn't give him anything to drink. He rolled to his feet, belly bulging, head woozy. Then he projectile vomited in my direction.

"I, uh . . . what?"

"The eyes," I said, checking for what might have splashed onto me. "I offered you Varg's eyes last night, but you said you'd had enough."

"I had such a strange dream," said Humor. "There was a lady, a pretty one. She said nice things. But she said I looked so hungry . . . and I hadn't noticed it before, but I was *starving*. And I told her that, and she said, 'Oh, the best thing if you're starving is fresh eyeballs before the person is even dead.' And that seemed like the wisest thing I had ever heard. And then . . ."

Humor trailed off as he took in the dug-out eye sockets of Varg Tiorvi.

"Oh, well then," said the raven. "I ate too much. Better now. You're welcome."

I dragged Varg Tiorvi's eyeless body to a ditch and laid him among the half-eaten others. Let someone else try to figure out which one he'd been. He would get neither funeral pyre nor burial.

We set off back to the monastery under a clear sky, Haldor's Heroes and a bunch of former thralls. A few had already left our company. Perhaps they knew another place on Gotland to seek their fortunes. But most would follow us to the monastery and either join the monks there or sail with us.

A thin plume of smoke rose from the spot the 'Steins had set Cow Killer alight. Some kindling and whale oil ensure it would not be not found intact. Haldor was right to prevent anyone else from having that weapon. I, too, was sad to see it go, but Haldor was right: We could not take it on the ship.

About a mile away, I turned back to notice the smoke had gotten much thicker. It was as if the longhouse had been set on fire. Perhaps Cow Killer's pyre had expanded, a stray ember blown onto the roof. It was Valborg's hall now, one way or another.

On the way back, Ulf spoke loudly that a Finn should not be allowed on the ship because they had evil magic. This was to Haldor but for all to hear, I assume in the hope of influencing the general sentiment.

I countered that he had said the same of Huld just before she saved all our lives. Also, Joni was a Karelian, not a Finn.

"What's the difference?" demanded Ulf.

I shrugged. "One takes longer to say."

"You must carry a sharp knife, skald," Ulf said as he smiled, "in order to split a hair that fine."

"There's no man who is flawless," I countered. "Nor any man who is good for nothing."

"The Karelian can decide where he goes," said Kraki. "He does not need to speak in order to row. As long as he knows where we are going." He turned to look at me then and said nothing more.

Ulf got Kraki's attention. "He should decide knowing full well where we are going. It's a long way around the peninsula and then back up north. It's still a long way east from there to the White Sea if that's really where we're headed."

Kraki shook his head. "We're far off that way, but we could go the shorter way. Through the Gulf of Suomi."

"I know something of that gulf," continued Ulf. "We would need a guide to go that way and find a route through the rivers and lakes."

Kraki shrugged.

"Getting lost there would be a poor result," Ulf continued. "Besides, we have a few things to sell. Better to head back the way we came and work our way around so we know where we're headed."

I did not like the idea of a voyage that long or that much delay in finding Alfhild, but Ulf had Kraki's ear for the moment, and what he was saying was reasonable. We were only even on Gotland because of me in the first place, so I could not very well dictate yet another course for us.

I told Joni he would soon have to make a choice about where to go. The other former thralls seemed to think they had an idea. They knew where Varg had kept his ships and would shortly head for that to get off the island. One of them asked who had taken the hall. I told him Haldor's Heroes had taken it on behalf of Varg's daughter, Valborg. Let them all spread that story.

"You can go with them," I told Joni. *"You can probably also stay at the monastery. Or you can come with us, but I don't yet know where we're going. Or at least not how we're getting there. We will stop at the monastery first, no matter what. You can decide then."*

This was a surprise to Joni. He had expected his newfound freedom to include a lot of forced rowing and fighting, probably even farther away from his home.

I had heard of Karelia, but only as a vague area somewhere east and north of here bordering Bjarmaland. Joni had lived on the shore of a giant lake. Far from Gardariki, or so he'd thought, but it had been Rus venturing northward who captured him. He thought he had lost his life until they collared him and set him to marching. They took others from his village as well. He would not say what happened to his family, and so I did not press him.

"Anything is better than that place," said Joni, nodding back toward Varg's former compound. *"No, that's not true. They took me to an even worse place first. Not for very long, at least."*

"Where was this?"

"On the White Sea. They put us on a ship after the march. We sailed out, but soon there was nothing to see, only fog. How could they sail the right way if they couldn't see? I don't know. But then they docked on a big rock in the middle of the sea. Not a rock . . . I could not see it all for the fog. A tall building carved into the rock. They took us in there."

The hairs on the back of my neck pricked up at recalling my prophetic vision of the fog-shrouded island. *"What was in there?"*

Joni shook his head. *"Screams. A bad place. I was there for a few days? A week? And some of the others were taken away, but they looked at me once and put me in a cell. They brought me to the queen in that rock. But she did not want me, and they took me back to the cell. Then, Varg's son was there. I think he brought people. But then he took people like me from our cells, and he put us on his ship. And then we sailed south!"* Joni laughed, but it was tinged with bitterness. *"South through the rivers and the great lakes through the heart of my home to get to this place here."*

"This queen," I said, *"how did you know she was a queen living in the rock?"*

Joni shrugged. *"Maybe she just visited from her other rock."*

"How did you know she was a queen, though?"

"Oh! She wore very fancy clothes and so much gold. Bright gold, like her hair. People bowed to her. Deep bows as if they feared her. She had creamy, flawless skin except for the scars on her face."

I whipped around on that man faster than the North Wind could have even thought of moving. *"What did you—here, look at me. Look at my face. Show me where on her face was this scar."*

Joni hesitated for just a moment.

"SHOW ME."

Two fingers traced lines from my left nostril to the back of my jaw.

"Ha," said Svein. "They are face-touching." He was not the only one to grimace or express some distaste, but I had more important things to worry about.

"It was her," I said in Norse, addressing anyone who would listen. "It was Alfhild."

"What was Alfhild?" asked Magnus.

"Joni has seen Alfhild. He's been to her tower."

"Can he find his way back?" asked Magnus. It had been a question innocent of any ill intent, but I could see Ulf's eyes narrow. Magnus had only been thinking of the practical.

"Skald," said Haldor, interjecting for the first time. "You will learn all you can of this man and what he knows. Kraki and I will hear from everyone tonight and decide what's next. I won't speak for the sailing part, but I would put more faith in a guide we've just done a good turn for than in a prophecy as far as finding our way."

I was to be part of Haldor's close council? That was a step up for me. I hadn't even been privy to the plans set by Kraki and Finnr for finding out where Alfhild had gone. Now, I would sit among the most important advisors, including Ulf. I suddenly missed Kari all the more.

"This queen," Joni continued. *"She is important?"*

"Her name is Alfhild. She attacked us last year," I said. *"A powerful sorcerer. She used one of our crewmates as a sacrifice. She would have burned an entire city if she had her way. We will have her head. Now, we're headed north to the White Sea to find her. It appears that Arrow-Odd also pursues her, but we don't know why."*

The mention of Arrow-Odd's name stopped Joni cold. I could read it in the clenching of his jaw and his sudden reticence but could not understand why. Then, I realized what a fool I'd been. Joni was Karelian. His people would not tell stories of Arrow-Odd as a legendary hero. They would tell stories of him as a villain who raided their shores. I put my head down and tried to think of a better way forward.

"We are Haldor's people," I said. *"We are Kraki's people. Not Odd's. We don't even know why he would attack Alfhild."*

"How do you know that he does, then?"

"A prophecy," I said, hoping to go into no more details about that.

Joni nodded. He seemed to react a bit better. And it was my turn to be uncomfortable.

"Did you know she was pregnant?"

I shook my head as the blood drained from my face.

Magnus slapped me on the shoulder. "You light-headed, skald?"

"Joni says," I stammered. I tried to swallow, but my mouth was too dry. "Joni says Alfhild was pregnant."

Reactions among the crew varied. I could hear laughter, cheering, groaning. One pair of eyes was locked on mine in a deeper and darker knowledge than the rest.

Ketill stared at me because he knew that child might be mine. Could it be? I was not entirely sure. The whole episode of Alfhild glamouring herself as Fanya to take advantage of me was unclear. He was the only one who knew about it, though.

Oh no. Humor knows it, too. Would the bird trade that story?

And did the 'Steins just give me a knowing look, or was that just my imagination running wild?

I said nothing more the rest of the way back to the monastery.

It was late in the day when we arrived, the orange light bathing the forest in a warm glow. Tafi met us outside the monastery's low walls with a pensive look. He'd welcomed two dozen strangers without even a hint of worry, but here we were with every indication we'd won, and something bothered him.

"I was not certain you would return," he said. "But it pleases me that you did. What news of Varg then?"

"His luck fled with his courage," said Haldor. "He did not die well."

And with Haldor's words, that chapter seemed to close for me. I felt better rested than I had in months. Somehow, I felt Valborg was satisfied, and so was I.

But Alfhild being pregnant? That was an entirely new thing I would start worrying about.

CHAPTER 29

THE COURAGE TO LOOK

TAFI TOOK THE NEWS OF VARG'S DEATH WITH MILD SURPRISE, giving little more reaction than to say he was glad to see us alive again. He spoke with Haldor for some time while the rest of us saw to the many things that needed doing: Loading the ship, mending clothes, tending to weapons and armor. I wondered what the two of them spoke about, though, and why Tafi seemed to grow more comfortable through the conversation.

There was plenty to feast on from the spoils we'd taken from Varg's hall, so we did that for a second night and shared food and drink with our hosts. There was ale enough to drink and to leave some extra for the monks, who'd been generous with their own stores in the first place. I asked Haldor if we owed them something more and he told me no, we owed them nothing.

"But I've never met a man so generous or hospitable that he wouldn't welcome repayment."

Sometimes, obligations are invisible as well as unspoken. Had I been obligated to seek revenge on Varg? It was something I knew I had to do, but I couldn't tell anyone exactly why. Only that it needed to happen.

Haldor must have sensed something amiss with me because he shoved a cup of ale into my hand. "Not too much tonight, though. I want your wits there for the council."

That was an obligation but also an honor. I supposed I could have resisted it, but no. It was something I had to do, or else I wouldn't be me.

The monks had not enough room to feed us all inside, so we feasted outside their little stone buildings. A few of them even came out to join us.

Haldor and Kraki sat side by side during the council to confer. The rest of us summoned sat opposite them. Ulf spoke first and reiterated what he thought. I did the speaking for Joni, asking him questions when clarification was needed.

We covered mostly what I had already spoken to Joni about—recognizing Alfhild inside this island fortress with the tower. He even knew where this was, more or less, as it was on the White Sea, far to the north and east. As far as we'd already come, the White Sea was still half a world away. And when we approached the topic of Arrow-Odd, things became even more complicated.

"Varg said a strange thing just before the battle," I said. "He spoke like we were in Odd's employ, doing a job for him."

"How would he know we are going after an enemy of Odd's?" asked Haldor. "Even we don't know why he and she are enemies."

I translated this for Joni, and he patted my shoulder. Soon, I was translating his words to the rest.

"Joni says there is a big war going on right now, just like twenty years ago. Arrow-Odd and Ogmund Tussock are both fighting again and recruiting lots of others to join them. He thinks if Odd is attacking Alfhild, then Alfhild must be on Ogmund's side. Otherwise, he wouldn't be concerned with her."

"That's not what the prophecy said," Ketill coughed. "It said, 'the Arrow points ever at your enemy.'"

"She could be someone Odd is trying to recruit," said Ulf. "Or has recruited. That would make things complicated for us."

"I saw Odd's war council in the prophecy," I said. "There was no woman there. I think he and she are enemies."

"Still complicated for us then," said Ulf. "We're picking sides either way. Better not to get caught up with one or the other."

"We have a side already," growled Kraki. "Hrolf Kraki's side. The ship will remain independent of Odd and Ogmund."

"Then we have our answer as to why Varg would make an assumption about us working for Odd," said Haldor. "It must be because he had been recruited by Ogmund. That would be consistent with Alfhild's allegiance to

Ogmund, as she controlled the place Joni was brought to. The arrow points at Alfhild because she is Odd's enemy."

Ulf shook his head. "I won't say no to that, and it seems our destination is set. Only, consider the situation will not be so easy even when we get there. Ogmund has more allies than we would have guessed, and we don't yet know how many of them are arrayed between us and Alfhild. It's a long way to retrace our path so far and go north around Finnmark. And Odd—I say just ask the Karelian about this—he is known for many things. One thing he's known for is getting his allies killed. We'll need to step cautiously when we reach the White Sea."

Joni got the translation and nodded with vigor. He had one thing to add.

"Joni says he can guide us through the lakes and rivers. Says he will take us back the way Varg's men took him. He says he'll fight for us on the way and do whatever else is asked. He only asks we let him go when we get near the White Sea, as he doesn't want anything to do with Arrow-Odd."

Haldor turned to Kraki. "I like that idea better than the long voyage around Finnmark."

"If we take the shorter route, we could stop at Uppsala first and sell the wine," said Ulf. "The crew would like that."

Kraki sneered. "King Athils is not one I wish to linger around."

There was some argument about Uppsala and Athils, but the major thrust of the conversation was over. We would sail in the morning and head north. Joni was excited about returning home and went to work off his restless energy. Just as well, I had a conversation that could not wait if we were sailing so soon, so I left our feasting area as soon as I was able.

I got the attention of the 'Steins and asked them if they could teach me the language of the codex. As I had suspected, they could not. They could remember what Efraim told them about it but nothing else. Worse, they indicated they only knew a part of it.

"He read it all but skipped a lot in telling us about it," said Utstein.

"Skipped over the beginning, for one thing," added Innstein. "I wonder if there is something interesting in that part."

Twilight was on us, and I knew we had little time before we left, so I went to find Efraim while I still had access to the monk. Soon, I would again have a codex I could not read, and even I could not learn an entirely new language with a new alphabet in a day. While other monks remained at prayers, Efraim continued the copying in the little room. I found him there and startled him, yet to my surprise, it was he who spoke first.

"What will you do with the codex?" he asked in Norse.

"That depends," I said, having no idea what to do with it. "I have had little opportunity to find out what it contains."

"I know what it is," said Efraim, eyes wide. He put down the feather in his hand. "It is a weapon. It should not be in the wrong hands."

"My hands seem good enough to me."

He shook his head. "What you did to Varg—that was evil. And even if you forswear such evil things in the future, it could be taken from you by someone much worse."

"You sound like the wizard."

Efraim's face puffed up at that, at once announcing he took umbrage at the comment and that he had been trained to keep such thoughts to himself. He switched to Latin, however, his more confident language. *"I am a good Christian!"* he finally got out. *"I should not have helped before. I can only repent now."*

"Repent, eh?"

"Yes!"

I nodded. *"I am no Christian, so I think you will not listen to wisdom I know. But I am a poet and teller of stories. A skald. Do you understand that?"*

"I think your stories are heresy."

"I can tell you one story about a thing I just saw. Perhaps it is heresy to tell about such things? No? I tell such stories so people will remember them, so they won't be forgotten. Here is one story: There was a man who lived on an island, a powerful man who could have lived among others but kept to himself. He was rich because he took people from other lands and sold them as thralls. Why not live in the city where the trading would be easier? Because he wished to conduct himself in ways he did not want others to know about."

Efraim muttered something and crossed himself. He winced at the thought and clearly wanted me to stop.

"Don't look away, little monk! If you care anything for truth, you cannot look away. Because that was not all he did there. He kept his house defended with powerful magic. He had a sorcerer call an ill-tempered spirit and bound it inside of a cow. That cow's voice was painful to hear but could drive men mad enough to attack each other if only the spirit was given a sacrifice. So when

stout-hearted men showed up at his doorstep, he had the sorcerer slit the throat of one of his thralls, and that made the cow really dangerous."

The corners of Efraim's mouth hung down as if anchored to the floor. This was not what he expected. I held his gaze, and the little monk looked as though he might cry, so miserable was this story.

I approached and put my hand on his shoulder, squeezing too hard. *"But a monk read a book and shared its knowledge. And with that knowledge, the man was slain. And his sorcerer. And his cow. So when I go to tell this story later to those who have never heard it before, I want to know one thing: Do you still repent sharing that knowledge, or would you rather things had been as they were?"*

Efraim swallowed hard. *"Judgment is in the hands of God,"* he said.

I fought the urge to slap the teeth out of his mouth, and the look on my face must have laid those thoughts bare. Efraim shrank away. I held back, though. It seemed too much like kicking an injured dog. Here was a recorder of events, like me in many ways, and therefore, I had expectations of his courage. Expectations he ought to adopt an attitude more like mine.

"Defer your own judgment then," I said. My voice began to rise, and with that, the monk shrank away even farther. *"Sacrifice your every decision and give it up for another to make. Make virtues of fear and weakness so that only the most pathetic man is honored. Crawl on your hands and knees to find the scraps of approval your master might drop because you have not the heart to stand on two feet!"*

Efraim fell off his chair. He squeaked a cry for help and curled into a ball, covering his head.

"Hold," said a voice in Norse.

Tafi strode past me to comfort the whimpering monk. He cradled the little man and held him close, whispering a prayer in Latin as he did so.

"Is your wrath so needful against a man posing no threat?" he said, turning to me.

"He is weak," I said, disgusted at the sight.

"So were you, once." The big Swede had not raised his voice, but the words hit me hard for their truth. "This is not a place to test your valor. It is a place of peace and forgiveness."

"Is that what Varg needed, then? Forgiveness?"

Tafi hushed his friend and reassured him. He whispered something to the effect of leaving the two of us to talk. "Go say your prayers in the garden, my friend. Too much work indoors makes you ill."

Efraim shuffled past me, his eyes on the floor, then ran as he reached the doorway.

Tafi rose and dusted himself off. I took his measure and found myself even more taken aback. There was no anger in the man. Only some pain. But he bore it without rancor, without even the hint he would lash out at me.

"You wished to know more of the codex, and he would not tell you."

"That is true, but not the heart of it. He would take back what he already taught us. I told him what a monster Varg was, but he looked away." I held up a hand at Tafi to stop him from responding. "A storyteller cannot look away."

The man nodded and fell heavily into Efraim's chair. "For everything we do, there is a burden," he said. His voice became distant for a moment as he continued. "And for everything we do not do. I understand your anger, but directed at Efraim is directed the wrong way."

"I am not likely to take direction from a follower of the White Christ anytime soon," I said. "I believe in my own will and intellect, not commands to govern my every decision."

"I would not ask you to take direction. But will you hear a story from a follower of the White Christ? Maybe two. They are short if that makes any difference."

I threw my hands up in annoyance. "As you like," I said. "You've given us hospitality. I will not ignore your stories."

"Here is the first one, then. There was a man who lived on an island, a powerful man who could have lived in a city and been rich. But he was wealthy enough because he took people from other lands and sold them as thralls. He did not sell them all. Some of the women, he used to his liking, as you can imagine."

"I think I know this story," I said.

"You think you do," said Tafi, "but listen closer. Where a story begins and where it ends are just decisions we make in the telling. And at the beginning of this story, the man acquired a young boy. Where the boy came from, I could not say, other than to guess his family had been killed by vikings as they traveled. The man thought this boy was quite valuable for two reasons. For one, he could speak Latin. And for another, his skin was very smooth. Unblemished, even."

I crossed my arms. I thought I knew where the story was going, and it would not be pleasant.

"He used the boy to talk to the monks here. They were harmless to him and paid good fees to build and maintain this monastery when no one else would come to this part of the island. And the man did like collecting money. He also used the boy to his liking, as you can imagine such a man might do."

"Were his men not disgusted at this behavior?"

"His men were paid and they had their responsibilities: Go here, fight there, bring back thralls. Did they know of the behavior? Probably most of them. But their first priority was to earn money, and sticking one's nose into another's business is asking for trouble rather than money. Especially when the other person is a powerful man."

"Is that the whole story?" I asked as Tafi had gone quiet for some time.

He took another breath before continuing. "In weaves another story. There was once a fool who took money from the man to be one of his champions. This was years before the boy arrived. And the champion had amassed a great deal of treasure through the years because he was a good fighter and knew very well to not stick his nose into business not his own. He even liked the man, as he seemed a wise and cunning sort. So he was also very protective of the man's daughter."

Blood rushed to my face. I no longer knew what was coming, but I feared it nevertheless.

"The man's daughter was beautiful in body and mind. The champion liked her very much and looked forward to winters in the hall when he would not be sent out to capture thralls. She was like family to him, since he knew little of his own family. One winter, the champion returned and found she had left. He inquired about her whereabouts, but no one would speak of her. The champion was puzzled about this."

I swallowed hard. "The champion knew nothing."

And here, Tafi's voice rose for the only time I heard it, a shout that shook the stone walls around us. "The champion knew nothing because he chose not to look!"

This was not going as expected. Tafi did not continue to shout, but his tone thrummed with an intensity that volume alone could not achieve.

"But the champion's ignorance was so deep and desperate that he could not stop asking. One day, the lord yelled at his champion for asking. And one day, a tearful boy called the champion aside and told him stories. Stories that could not possibly be true.

"The champion's spirit broke, and he looked away. Away and too deep into his mead horn. Only when he had become too useless to employ any longer did he find his way out of it and into this place. And the man your friend knew, Candidus, picked up what was left of him."

I tried to swallow and failed a few times before succeeding. So Tafi had been one of Varg's champions and had come to regret it. I nodded in understanding, but that left at least one other question. "How did the boy get here?"

Tafi continued as if the great wave of fury had passed, much to his relief. "I bought his freedom. Candidus' idea. I had some money left, and Varg was less entertained by him than he had been in the past, so it worked. There are no thralls here, just as there are none on your ship. So now you know more of the story of Varg's home, and what it is to call this place home. Some are here for forgiveness for what they failed to do as much as what they did."

"So Efraim forgave you?"

"I do not ask that from him. Varg's daughter, I cannot ask for forgiveness because she is gone. Candidus forgave me. That is the way of the White Christ. The story cannot end there because I will never forgive myself for things undone. My inaction cannot be taken back, and I will carry the burden of it until I die. But until that time, I create another story, and that story is how Efraim and a few others may heal here, in a place of peace.

"I know what he said is offensive to you. It is not your way. It is not even my way, if I am honest, but I choose to walk this path in spite of my nature. This is why Candidus asked me to take over for him despite my junior station."

"Because he knew you were loyal?"

"Because he knew I would not turn away from these men, even at the cost of my life."

"You could have taken up arms with us."

Tafi shook his head. "I swore an oath not to. A man cannot seek both forgiveness and revenge."

"There is little need for Efraim to forgive Varg. As I see it, he should be happy he contributed to Varg's demise."

"That is as you see it," said Tafi. "But not as he does. And it is his decision how to deal with his pain, not yours. You know nothing of it."

He thought this ended our conversation, and I considered this might be the best way to leave it. "Wait," I said. "There is a story I might tell, but you would need to guard it with your life."

"A story about what?"

"Valborg." That got the big man's attention. "I know. You never mentioned her name, yet I know it. And I knew her."

And though I had not told anyone what I had seen of her, I told Tafi the story from the burning hall to her final dawn. I told him what I had felt, though I disliked even thinking about it. I told him how I'd made a show of Varg's torture and how I'd heard a laugh I could not place.

"Did it give you peace?" he asked when I had finished.

"I slept better last night than I have in months."

"Maybe that is true now," said Tafi, "but do not think too quickly that others should be as you are. I know the nightmares you speak of. They are a difficult thing and take a long time to deal with. Perhaps Efraim will feel differently if you leave here and come back without demands. For now, go out and make more of your story. I think you will fight for something more important than revenge before your story is finished."

CHAPTER 30

No Fish Is an Island

I had my mind on Tafi's story as we boarded the *Sea Squirrel* the next day. I was still not sure what to think of it. My mind had difficulty getting off the path it was on. And the path it was on marched right from "you will need every weapon against Alfhild" to "the codex is a weapon, but you can't use it." There would be other weapons, of course, but I hated that I did not have the knowledge to use this one.

Maybe I hated knowing Tafi had been right even more.

Kraki did not outright say he refused to sail to Uppsala to treat with King Athils. Not that I heard, anyway. But he and Haldor announced at our departure from Gotland that we would skip Uppsala in favor of bringing the wine to Arrow-Odd. We might need a favor or information from him and were far more likely to get it after delivering an expensive gift. Ulf grumbled at failing to get good value for it, but it was on his own advice we would tread carefully with Odd, so he soon stopped complaining.

It was a week of sailing just to reach the Gulf of Suomi. It was not a foreboding body of water to sail through. You didn't get a chill that you were being watched or that trolls were about to set upon you. But the further we went, the closer we were to the Rus, and they were strong in those waters.

The 'land of lakes' Joni spoke of might be accurate, but we were not there yet. First, it was the land of islands along the coast as we sailed. The more isolated the island, the better for our purposes. Fireless nights were cold, but cold was better than attracting potential raiders. Spending nights at sea was a possibility, but also dangerous in case we might run aground. So island hopping it was.

That made for early mornings and late evenings as the sun lingered in the sky. Navigating those islands meant a lot more rowing than sailing. I tired of the rowing quicker than most but did my best not to mention it.

One day well into our journey, I felt a great deal of relief when Hemming spied a small island that looked good to him one afternoon. It was well away from the sharp rocks that would wreck our ship. It was high enough out of the water to be safe but not so steep we would have trouble pulling the boat up its banks.

Even better, we saw the island had heather growing all over it. The bright purple flowers were a friendly sign. So friendly that we opted to stop there early, even though some daylight was left for rowing. Good spots did not appear everywhere, after all.

Heather or not, it was our practice to scout a place out before fully disembarking. The stem of the ship glided onto a gentle upward slope and stuck there. Haldor leaped down first and sloshed through the remaining shallow water before he met dry land. Hemming was right behind him.

"Now what?" I asked Magnus, restless as I was.

"Seems very fortunate," he said through a yawn. "Fortunate things are often traps. Also, the landing site could be rough, and we might need to row to another side. Just be patient!" He finished with a stretch and another yawn.

Rowing made me antsy. It left me tired but feeling as though I had not done anything all day. Then, we would set up, eat, sleep, and repeat the process the next day. The only break from this was when we landed with a little time to spare, and I could explore a small area near our encampment. Or bother Ketill about runic wisdom, which rarely worked. Or try to pry more secrets out of Huld, which never worked.

"I could go help them," I said.

"Relax! Why don't you think of a song to play?"

But I could not relax that day. Here was dry land. It was time to get off my sea chest and walk around and do *something*. Anything that did not involve sitting.

At the stern of the ship, Kraki stretched his back and shoulders. That many days as a steersman was no trifling thing, even for him. On either side of him sat Ketill and Huld, neither of whom rowed. Ketill stirred, stood, and popped various joints with alarming volume. The stiffness of life on a ship made me wonder how these men found the strength to fight battles at sea. Huld remained slumped against the gunwale, hood pulled over her head.

"Are you asleep, Huld?" I asked.

She snorted and coughed a little.

"I said, are you asleep?"

"Ugh," she said. "Any man who asks such a question loud enough makes his own death prophecy come to be."

"Or woman," Ketill added, grinning.

"It's always a *man*," replied the *volva*. She spoke her last word with a long groan, pulling her hood further over her face. I had never taken her as the seasick type, but perhaps the waves wear us all down eventually.

"Can you make anything with heather?" I asked, unable to keep the nervous energy out of my voice.

"I can use it to make a tonic for diarrhea," she said. "But not for diarrhea of the mouth, unfortunately."

Ketill went from grin to laughter, as did some of the others listening. I did not care.

"If you are feeling unwell, I will gather it for you," I said.

Huld's still-hooded face came down to fix me with an eyeless stare. "Gather it where?" she asked as if I were an innocent but still annoying child.

"It's all over the island," I said. "Take a look."

"I may be old, skald, but my nose is a keen one. If it were all over the island," she said as she pulled back her hood and then stopped. She could plainly see over the edge of the gunwale but stood up for a better view. "I would have smelled it already."

Ketill's smile disappeared, his look replaced by wide-eyed recognition. "Shit," he said. Then it was "Shit shit shit!" as he ran up the deck to the fore. "Back to the ship!" he shouted over the prow. "Back to the ship now!"

I stood and followed him, wondering what could be wrong. Was this heather some secret plant that was actually poisonous? Did he suddenly recognize the markings of an ill-omened burial mound?

"What is wrong here?" I asked.

"The runes!" he said, gesturing as if he had too many words to say and not enough time to say them. "Sea monsters can't find *us!*"

"Well done, then!" I said, even more confused. "No sea monsters, then."

"Except this one!" he said and turned back to Haldor and Hemming, shouting at them to get back to the ship.

Something was indeed amiss, and we all felt the first jolt through the ship.

"Surt's flaming ballsack!" said Magnus. "It was a trap?"

Haldor and Hemming felt it too. A great shudder, as if the earth beneath the ship had moved. It had moved, and it was not earth. Both men stumbled, and then they heeded Ketill's call. Haldor was behind the tracker but gaining on him with long, powerful strides.

"Ready to push off!" said Ketill.

"Where is it?" I demanded, looking over the starboard side. "How did it find us with your runes carved onto the ship? Did you miss an oar?"

"It is beneath us," Ketill shouted back. "And it never found us. We found it and rowed right onto its back!"

The ship's fore lowered as the island shivered. Haldor and Hemming were close but already running through inches of water.

The deck was chaos. Kraki was in charge but remained at the stern, where he would be most needed in just a few moments. Some of the crew stood up, some came to the fore, some stared over the side in disbelief. Nanthild and Joni sat with oars in white-knuckled hands, ready to row, but few took after them.

Desperation in Ketill's voice was not something any of us were accustomed to.

Over the din of questions, Kraki called out that the 'Steins had the deck. Up the brothers sprang and pulled down any man still standing while they gave orders.

I went back to my seat at their command and explained to Joni what was happening.

The 'Steins called Ingolf up to the fore. He was not the strongest, not the fastest, but he had long limbs and, unlike most men, the ability to follow simple directions. Innstein tied a rope to the handle of a shield. If Ingolf could not reach far enough to help Hemming and Haldor, Innstein could throw the shield like a disc and get them a rope to hold on to. Utstein readied an oar to push off.

"Faster!" yelled Ingolf.

The movement of the island, or whatever the island really was, had turned the ship a bit. I could see then that 'faster' would not be enough for both men. Maybe Haldor could make it, but Hemming would be swimming. Innstein saw it as well and threw the shield across their path. If one did not make it, at least he might grab the rope and be pulled back up.

Haldor turned, slowed, and ran just behind Hemming for the last dozen steps. At the last moment, he grabbed the tracker's belt with both hands, bent his knees, and launched the man forward and up.

Hemming flew with such force that he crashed into Ingolf's chest, and the two toppled backwards onto the deck.

With a groaning exhalation, the island disappeared underwater, pulling Haldor down with it. The *Sea Squirrel* shuddered at being pulled down by the sudden current. The ship came down almost to the water's edge, and I felt my balls shrivel into raisins as I saw just a slosh of water over the gunwale.

The current abated, however, and the ship rose again. The shield floated on the water, but I saw no rope or sign of Haldor. Then I realized I could not see the rope because it was pulled taut by the 'Steins. Something was pulling both men nearly off their feet.

That was a frightening sight. Not as frightening as when the rope suddenly went slack.

"Oars in! Spears ready!" shouted Utstein.

"If there is a wizard with some explanation, now is the time," said Innstein.

The crew traded oars for spears. Except for Ketill, who strung his bow and nocked an arrow. "Lyngbakr waits for men to land on it and then swallows them," he said. "We've run right up onto his back, so now there is nothing for it but to fight."

Lyngbakr: Heather-Back. No wonder Huld smelled nothing; it was only a visual trick. What we might accomplish with spears and arrows against an island-sized sea monster, I did not know. "Can we run to shallow water?" I asked.

Ketill growled back in grim determination. "Not much room to run. It is here." He turned to the 'Steins and shouted, "Eyes! Go for its eyes if you see it!"

"Hard to go for the eyes if it swallows us whole," said Kraki. "Going to have to cut our way out then."

The wizard stopped at that, sudden realization on his face. "Skald, how are you with a bow?"

"Fair?"

"Be better, then," he shouted, tossing me his longbow and quiver. "I have other work." Ketill drew his carving knife and looked around the ship, settling on one of the strakes near the rudder.

"It is coming up from below!" Magnus shouted just as we felt the sea lurch beneath us.

Lyngbakr's nose lifted the ship's prow out of the water briefly before it slipped off. I dropped the quiver and almost lost my balance, which was better than most others fared only because I ran into the gunwale for support. Ketill had been leaning over the edge and nearly fell off the ship, but Kraki pulled him back on by his robes.

"Better to swim in different directions," Ulf shouted over the confusion. "This thing will swallow us all at once otherwise! If we swim, half or more might reach another island."

Svein's head turned in sudden panic, which I took to mean the strong man was not so strong a swimmer.

"Shut up and let me work!" Ketill spat back. "If I can finish this carving, it will not have the ship so easily."

"I see its eyes," I said, nocking an arrow.

There was still no indication of Lyngbakr's full size. The bulbous body gave way to a short neck pitching below the waves before its massive head rose above the water. A spearhead-like nose and upper jaw gaped so wide I thought we would sail straight into the expanded lower jaw and sit there until it closed on us. Giant, grinding teeth that lined its jaws looked as though they would bite our ship in two if it chose to make us two swallows instead of one.

"Don't shoot!" warned Huld. "This is no time for stray arrows. Look, there, over its side!"

One tiny eye stared out from the side I could see, and close to it was the reason for Huld's warning. I would never hit the eye at that range. And I might hit Haldor, who was holding onto the side of its head.

Lyngbakr swayed once, twice, and then groaned as it tried to buck Haldor off. The beast was so huge that every movement was slow. Haldor held fast, one fist holding onto the fake heather while the other sought a new handful.

The monster closed its mouth and plunged its head down, tipping the *Sea Squirrel* again. As it rose back up above the water, Lyngbakr opened its jaws again and made slowly for the front of our ship.

"The tongue!" said Huld. "Shoot the tongue!"

I raised the bow and readied to loose an arrow. "Whatever your plan, wizard, I hope you have time to explain it one day," I said. The arrow flew into the back of Lyngbakr's mouth, but if the monster noticed, it did not react.

Ketill shook his head with the rocking of the ship but did not break his chant to curse under his breath. His attention was fully on his task, a combination of chanting and carving. This was something more advanced than what he had taught me, and soon the rhythmic chants of the familiar rune sounds gave way to something more verbose. The wizard was not speaking a verse in *galdralag*; it was something similar but felt older, more arcane.

It was not in a language I knew. Not Norse, but familiar enough for me to hear the commands the alliteration made. This was something old, something closer to Ketill's origin.

Ketill shouted at the height of his verse and sliced deep into his palm. He opened the wound freely and held it to face the sky as the last words left him. Then he slammed his palm down onto his carving.

"The tip of the tongue, not the back!" shouted Huld.

"Goat's breath and cat piss, woman! Cast a spell to guide my arrows, then!"

"Or just move to the fore and shoot from closer," said the *vǫlva*.

It was too late to move to the front of the ship. Lyngbakr was on course to collide with the *Sea Squirrel* head-on, so I put my back against the gunwale and one arm over to hold on. My hand searched for even the slightest grip and found none along the sea-wet wood. In desperation, I tried to dig my nails in, but that was impossible. They scraped the ship's hull as if it were cold stone, and then I realized: It was.

"The ship is hardened," Ketill shouted.

Lyngbakr's jaws closed over the prow. Most of the crew there retreated toward the aft. The 'Steins alone kept to the fore, stabbing the beast's mouth with their spears even as the front of the ship was about to be bitten away. Those huge teeth crashed down with a horrible grinding noise, but the prow held.

The monster bit down a second time, and our ship tipped forward again. Again, the hull remained intact, and the curling design of the *Sea Squirrel's* prow still stood.

Behind Lyngbakr's head, Haldor crawled slowly onward, slipping on seawater but still hanging on.

"To the aft! All hands to the aft!" shouted Innstein.

"Get all the weight to the rear!" explained Utstein.

Lyngbakr roared, the sound of a whale screaming in anger. It opened its jaws again and moved back. The prow was bloodied, having pierced the roof of its mouth.

The tongue. I could still shoot the tongue, but not over the heads of all our crew. I pushed my way forward on the swaying ship until I was even with the brothers.

"What are you doing?" demanded Utstein.

"The tongue!" I said, fumbling for an arrow.

Lyngbakr pitched its body down in order to come at the ship from a lower angle. Seawater flooded into its gaping mouth and slowed its advance even further. Haldor slipped backwards but caught himself.

"That arrow will not be much of a taste," said Innstein.

"If you have a better dish to serve," I said, "now is the time."

"I have—" said Utstein and then stopped mid-sentence and slapped his brother's shoulder.

I nocked the arrow and missed the rest of what Utstein said, but I knew that look. The look of an idea had by two at once.

"If it fails, it's not as if we can drink it anyway," said Innstein with a shrug.

"Shoot that tongue!" added Utstein. "We need a moment or two."

I hopped up as far forward as I could stand for a better shot. It was a strange thing to find myself holding a weapon I had little skill with at the fore of a ship full of warriors facing down the second biggest sea monster I had ever seen. A year prior would have seen me vomiting over the side of the ship or frozen in terror. And there was fear, have no doubt about that. But this was the first time I felt a taste, just a little bit, of maybe what drove people such as my crewmates.

I was excited.

That feeling lasted about a quarter of a second before I drew and loosed the arrow. As it flew, Lyngbakr closed its huge mouth so that the arrow struck it directly between the eyes. The arrow bounced off of Lyngbakr's scaly armor.

"That's perfect!" said Innstein. He and his brother were lifting a barrel out of the shallow hold in the ship.

I thought he was joking until his brother added, "Keep its mouth shut until we say!"

Excellent, outstanding, good. I had a simple job then. No one could screw it up. Unless one fumbled his arrows and dropped them one after another, which is exactly what I did twice before nocking another one. I drew and pointed threateningly at Lyngbakr's snout, but it would not open. Instead, the monster rammed us head-on, sending such a shock through my feet that I accidentally loosed the arrow, dropped the bow, and almost fell overboard.

If I hadn't grabbed the prow and held on tight, I would have been swimming. I looked down for just a moment and saw the huge mass of water gathering into Lyngbakr's partially open mouth. There was more than enough room for a man to be sucked into that thing's jaws.

I swung myself back onto the deck and ran for my life. The monster was no longer trying to swallow the stone-armored ship whole. It reared up with its mouth closed and brought its chin, insofar as such a monster might have a chin, down onto the ship.

The *Sea Squirrel* pitched forward, almost too far for any of us to keep our footing. Had it come down with more precision, we would have all been dumped straight into the monster's mouth. As it was, sea chests tumbled forward and loose oars and spears fell away. Everyone was still hanging onto something: The gunwale, the mast, or just each other. I found a grip at the edge of the hold to pull myself away, my feet so close to the monster's jaws I could feel its fishy breath.

Most precarious were the 'Steins, who hung from the mast by their legs while they clung desperately to a barrel of wine.

"You can't take it with you!" I shouted.

"That's the whole idea!" Utstein said. "Open it!"

"What for?"

"We'll explain it in Hel if you wait any longer!" shouted Innstein. "We can't hold it forever!"

I pulled myself up and braced against the deck, reaching for the bunghole as far as I could stretch.

"The sword," Ketill was shouting from the back. "Use the sword!"

I drew Need and waved the blade at the bunghole. If I could dislodge it, the wine would spill out as the 'Steins had suggested. I could reach, but the ship's rocking was too much for me to put the blade on the stopper and dislodge it. At last, I let out a curse of frustration just as Lyngbakr moved forward, trying to shake loose every crewman.

Moving Need just outside my peripheral vision, I closed my eyes for a moment and whispered my need, hoping the weapon would hear me. I pushed up and sat at the edge of the hold, gripped Need in both hands, and swung upward as hard as I could.

The splitting maul Need had become broke through the barrel's head, wine gushing out in torrents as it spilled into Lyngbakr's mouth. The beast's eyes went wide as the liquid hit its tongue, and it went still while the wine poured in.

As I looked up, a dripping figure crested the creature's head. Haldor's bright teeth gleamed through his dark, sodden beard in a murderous grin as he crept ever up the creature's head. As the barrel bled its lifeblood away, Haldor crested Lyngbakr's skull, crawling to the point between its side-swept eyes.

Innstein lost his grip. Utstein held the remaining weight himself for the briefest moment before the barrel slipped his fingers as well. It seemed to me enough had already poured out. Knowing their intent, I spoke a verse to help seal it.

> "A hard thing to swallow,
>   this sea castle.
> The island-fish
>   finds a rare drink.
> Better to eat
>   elsewhere—
> A gift always seeks
>   a good return."

Haldor did not seem a very poetic man to me, or else his poetry was in deeds and not in words. Perhaps he understood the 'Steins' plan as well as I did at that moment, and that is why he did not raise his great axe to bring it down into the monster's skull. Gripping Silence in two hands, Haldor spoke as if to convince himself to not strike.

"Wine instead of steel, then. That is some good gift."

Lyngbakr's eyes pointed up toward the man sitting on its skull as if to recognize its indebtedness. Slowly, the creature paddled its massive fins backwards until it was no longer atop the *Sea Squirrel*.

It was slow but still no gentle thing when the ship's prow shot up. I toppled backwards into the hold, straight on my head. The 'Steins, still holding onto the mast, pitched bodily into the mass of our crew.

Few stayed on their feet. Haldor was perhaps the only one, leaping off Lyngbakr's head as the thing dove down along the side of the ship. I can't exactly verify this, given my ass-upward position at the time, but that's how I understood things as I crawled out of the hold.

Oars and spears lay strewn about the deck. Sea chests had tumbled forward, and though not lost, some of them had been crushed by the underside of Lyngbakr's jaws. I scrambled to find mine.

It lay open among some of the others. Most of my things were there. My heavy wool cloak was wet, but my lyre was dry and intact. Everything was there, I thought for a moment. Until I realized it was everything but the codex.

I searched. I asked if anyone had seen it. Haldor put a hand on my shoulder.

"I saw it tumble into the monster's mouth. I don't think we'll see it again."

The crew was jubilant, except for me, and I did my best to fake it. The celebration was all directed at the 'Steins. Even Nanthild smiled.

Trying not to feel such a loss, I asked the brothers how they knew their plan would work.

"We are good listeners," said Utstein, eyeing Ketill and Huld.

"We hear talk from sorcerers about balance," said Innstein.

"Even the king said a gift always looks to be repaid, so it must be a powerful thing," said Utstein.

"About the sword, you mean," I said. "He was suspicious because he did not want to accept it only to be in debt for a price to be determined later."

"The king is wise," said Innstein. "In this case, we could not converse, so we just gave the wine as a gift."

"And only for a trade of not eating our ship!" said Utstein. "I think that sea monster owes us yet."

Celebration was short-lived. Some of the crew were banged up. There were no broken bones or other injuries, but the crush of us against one another had a few favoring one arm or holding ribs. Hemming was not himself and sat against a gunwale, looking pale and drawn. The light would not last, and we still had to beach the ship, set up camp, and take stock of whatever provisions we had lost.

Other than wine, as Ulf soon reminded us.

"An expensive friend to buy," said Ulf as we collected ourselves and sat down.

"More expensive not to buy such a friend," Magnus countered.

"You'll row better with your mouths shut," growled Kraki.

It was not a suggestion.

CHAPTER 31

A SHORT HISTORY OF THE END OF THE WORLD

THERE WERE NO MORE SEA MONSTERS AS WE MADE OUR WAY along the coast. Or at least none that we ran our ship into.

Talk of sea monsters, however, would not abate as we sailed on. We needed something for entertainment during those long, dreary days at sea, and I could not compose poetry at all hours, so most conversation went on about the sea monster we had bested just days before.

Sea monster talk led to talk about Thor, the killer of the biggest-ever sea monster. That story led to talk of the doom of the gods, because Thor and Jormungand killing one another only happens when the end of the world is nigh.

Ragnarøk would be upon us one day, and nearly all the gods would die in the fighting. The world would burn under Surt's flaming sword. And all this would only happen after Midgard had suffered a years-long winter. Nothing would grow and kin would kill one another, or so I had heard it told. Many versions of the story existed with a few different details, but the themes were the same. It would be the end, period.

Ketill stirred at the talk of *Ragnarøk*. It was a story fit for a skald to tell in full, so I did that. The old man became more and more fidgety as I went on.

The story of *Ragnarøk* is not just the story of how the gods die and, in some cases, kill their enemies. It is a story about prophecy, and that prophecy is obtained by Odin when he raises a *vǫlva*, sometimes unnamed, sometimes said to be the old witch, Gullveig. Whoever she is, she is powerful in life and becomes even more so after crossing Hel's threshold. Odin questions her, and she tells him of the events he can expect.

Wise old Odin hears of the years-long winter and the chaos it brings. By the end of the telling, he knows how he'll meet his end, swallowed whole by Fenrir the wolf when that monster and many others all array themselves against the gods and the mortals of Midgard.

For all his wiles, Odin cannot prevent his death. Or the end of the world. Yet he schemes and fights anyway, as hard as he can.

I thought it was a good telling. I even folded in a joke about how men always ask about their futures but never profit from knowing. Huld rolled her eyes right into the back of her hood, not interested at all. But Ketill? Ketill had words.

"That already happened," said the wizard.

That got some attention.

"What do you mean it already happened?" I asked.

"Just what I said. The years-long winter, at least. And the miserable infighting that ensued, though to my mind, people needed little prompting for that. After, many were starving and fighting over what food was left. That already happened. And there was not a god to be seen helping in Midgard."

"When was this?" I asked.

"Long before your time. And before the time of any family you know. I am old, very old."

"As old as Finnr?"

"Not that old, however old that is. Old enough to have seen a different age, little as my like could do about it."

"You speak as if there were many wizards, once."

"More than there are now. That matters little, however. Long ago, I advised great men and rode with their armies. I sought deep wisdom like Odin, and I could charm or deceive, bind or heal. And I could do much more than that, but it was not enough."

The wizard hung his head, and I could tell it was painful for him to recall. But recall he did and told about the end of the world not as a story, but as his lived experience.

"You have never been hungry, I think. Not hungry in the way that drives a man to desperation. And so, when the sun hardly shone and we saw frost on the grass one summer, we joked. But the frost did not leave, and the sun was as if blanketed. Few things grew, and in few things growing, fewer sheep and cattle lived. That was the first summer.

"Those of us who survived the winter that followed spoke of the coming relief of summer, but no relief came. The next summer was cold and dark, and the warring over food began in earnest. Friends and kin betrayed one another and called it wisdom for preserving their own interests.

"But the third cold summer was the worst because by then, most had abandoned all hope. Or at least hope beyond their own survival. Kin slew kin for handfuls of grain. Men buried their treasure in droves as if that would help them. Good lords turned to sacrifice in the hopes that it might gain them some favor with the gods.

"We had already heard the stories of the coming mighty winter. Not like you just told, only that a long winter would fall on Midgard. Then it happened, and all my lore became useless. I appealed to the gods and sought protection and a return of the sun. I called out to Thor and Frey, though I called them by different names."

"And then a great battle was fought?" I asked.

"No great battle. Small, desperate fighting and murder. The gods did not take the field against their enemies and bring life back to the world through force of arms. They were nowhere to be seen or heard! Perhaps they were holed up behind their walls in the sky, as desperate as the rest of us. But make no mistake, they gave not one sour apple for Midgard.

"And so—that great battle? I made it up. Made it up and let those callous gods die in the narrative since I could not tear them down myself. They deserved no better, having left us all to our own misery after posing as heroes. Others changed the story I told a bit, maybe gave those gods some better endings. They still die. They have been dead to me a long time."

Perhaps for the rest of the crew, it was just another story. But here was Ketill, saying he was the *source* of the story. Not of the long winter, only the doom of the gods. But that was always part of the telling—as connected to the myths as Thor's hammer or Odin's sacrificed eye.

Myths did not have a single source to trace back to. They arose out of many tellings. Doubtless every god we knew the name of had their source in more than one king or hero. But to find the root of something, even just a part of a myth like this one, I realized I had never lived such a thing and might never see its like again.

Ketill finished and wrapped his robes tighter around him to fight the chill in the air. His bitterness was unfathomable. I knew what it was like to live among heroes. I had seen some die as heroes, and I would remember their names forever. But if Haldor, for example, turned tail and ran, leaving us all to our fate, I would turn bitter as well.

And Haldor was just a man. He asked for nothing but our honor. To give yourself in belief to the gods and hear their silence in a time of need—well, that was unthinkable. Breathing became difficult. My hands went numb.

"But summer returned eventually," I said, hoping it would mitigate the fear. "What did you do then?"

"Returned no thanks to those gods," replied Ketill. "It was hardly the end of trouble. Plague and politics killed just as many, and few heeded my advice. Eventually, I walked. No destination in mind, no reason to be. Fury drove me, and I found plenty of deserving recipients of that fury. There are fewer trolls in the world for that walk when I made my way through strange forests and mountains. And many a traveler and skald did I tell the story of the doom of the gods. But both gave me little comfort. I found my way north and crawled into a barrel of ale eventually, and there I stayed for a long, long time."

"You crawled out, eventually," I said. "Do you still hate the gods?"

Ketill laughed. "More than ever!" he shouted. "I finally understand their burden. Power and knowledge make demands on those who hold them. Otherwise, they are comical figures, flailing about in their own self-impor-tance until they come face to face with their own failures. And that is what they are: Failures."

"You must think little of the stories I tell then," I said. "Most of them are about the gods or have them involved."

"Stories are not worship. Good stories tell about people, even if they are in the form of gods. The stories of the White Christ reverse this, taking what people do and claiming those deeds for their god. That is worship, and not at all to my liking. One day, you will tell this story, I think. Will you tell how heroes succeeded only but for the grace of some sky-resident? Or how they earned victory with their own sweat and blood?"

"No one here was granted victory. We took it with might and main, will and intellect, courage and honor."

"There, then," said Ketill. "That is a story worth telling."

CHAPTER 32

THE ETERNAL SKALD

"TELL YOUR PEOPLE TO BE READY TO FIGHT," SAID JONI.

We had just left the gulf's waters and were finally sailing upriver. The sky was bright, the days were long. Daylight lasted longer, twilight lasted longer, and the night was no longer got quite as dark. We headed north from the gulf, no more sea chop or island hopping to deal with. Joni assured us he knew the waterways that would take us on our circuitous but not months-long route to the White Sea.

He had not said anything about fighting before we left, however.

"We are in Karelia, are we not?" I asked. *"This is your land. Why should we fear attack?"*

"My land," Joni said as he shook his head. *"My land is where I was captured. If raiders from Gardariki don't control every waterway, so what? They still roam the land mostly unchecked. The king has few riders to spare."*

"There's a king?" I asked, incredulous. *"And he keeps horse-mounted warriors?"* Not every people had a king. There were petty kings in the North Way, just not in the area I was from. There, we had a few jarls who met and decided things. I'd never heard of a king of Karelia, so I had assumed they were somewhat similar.

"Ha, I hope I am with you if you see them," said Joni. *"Not horses. Moose."*

Moose-mounted Karelian cavalry? If I lived through this adventure, that was a thing I would need to see with my own eyes.

263

"But not here. Too many Rus. That's why your people should be on guard."

Not every Rus would be hostile. Joni didn't like it, but we traded with some along the river for food and supplies, having lost more than my codex during the fight with Lyngbakr.

Further upriver, we found people Joni could converse well enough with to trade for information. Joni and I asked about news further north, but they shook their heads. There were bad things happening further north. Better to stay in the south or maybe go west. The Bjarmians had gotten bad, keeping land for themselves instead of sharing it. King Harek of Bjarmaland had grown more ambitious as he'd gotten older. Something unsaid told me "ambitious" also took on the meaning "cruel."

Worse than the Bjarmians were the Rus, who struck out all over to take people as thralls. I said this might be good, that perhaps Bjarmaland and Gardariki would be at odds, but I got strange looks in response, even from Joni. Clearly, I didn't know how it worked in this part of the world.

They told us there was a rumor that Gardariki's King Valdar had sent his wizard north, a powerful sorcerer who could change his shape into a winged dragon. Sent him north to King Harek of Bjarmaland.

Again, I thought this might be good news. A powerful sorcerer against a powerful king. Joni's comment cleared up my understanding.

"Who is this wizard from Gardariki who seeks an alliance?" he asked.

Who knows how it was that they all knew this visit had to be for an alliance? But that was the moment I knew I had crossed over an invisible threshold, the most dangerous kind. I was in the North, still, but no part of the North that was familiar to me.

"Grim Aegir," one of them said.

Joni nodded, glad I had my answer. But that was because Joni didn't speak Norse and didn't realize "Grim Aegir" just meant something like "Hooded Sea."

The few of us who treated with them returned to the ship with supplies and information. I relayed what I had learned to Haldor, but for all to hear, including about this Grim Aegir.

"That's a phony name if I ever heard one," said Utstein.

"Not even a good one," added Innstein.

I had to agree. I'd rather be called Tin Whisker, even if the description didn't apply. But no one knew anything of this man. Did he even exist? These were rumors far from their sources, full of suspicion and conjecture.

We stopped only to camp after that. Rivers and lakes wound us in every possible direction for days, but Joni was always certain we would come out going the right way. When we reached the first great lake, which Joni called Luadogu, it was so vast I wondered at first if he had navigated us into an ocean. It was not saltwater, though, and was much calmer than the seas we had sailed.

Joni said there were two options: Sail straight across the lake despite the other side of it not being in sight, or go north and hug the coast to come around more slowly. Kraki allowed popular opinion to win out, and we hugged the coast. The fish were plentiful and good eating. We feasted on carp, salmon, and sturgeon as much as we could, and all without burying the things for a year until they tasted slightly less like poison. We had enough of that already, and I savored the roasted fish every night for over a week.

That was a good place, and I knew I would miss it when Joni pointed us to the mouth of the next river to take. It was another week of rowing, though less maze-like than before. Lake Aainen was not nearly as vast, but the swampy marshes of its banks allowed us to take down plenty of waterfowl. We ate well on that trip.

"From here, is it complicated," said Joni as the *Sea Squirrel* cut north along the eastern bank of the lake.

"Why do you have us sail north when you look west?" I asked.

"North is the White Sea. West was my home."

"How much farther will you guide us then?" I asked. *"The longer we go, the further you will be from your home."*

"Maybe," said Joni with a shrug. *"I know where I will leave you already. Not all the way to the White Sea, but close enough. From there, I will go west and see what I find. Maybe some of my family still live."*

"You talk a lot with that man," interrupted Ulf. "And no others can understand. Why not share that knowledge of his language?" He looked back as if to beckon the interest of others. The 'Steins perked up at that and both nodded.

"It has been a long trip," said Innstein.

"Have you at least heard some stories from him you can tell? New stories are best," added Utstein.

The request from Ulf was a surprise. He had not wanted to take Joni with us at all, but now he was interested in learning to speak with the man. That would not be easy.

"It was difficult enough for me," I said. "We could start with a few words, but soon enough, Joni will leave us."

"So soon!" said Ulf. "As you've described, it will be hard to learn much in that time. But maybe you can tell us what he has to say. After all, you have been the only one to speak to him."

It was a welcome thing that Ulf would show some interest, both in Joni and in me using my skills. I thought he would be sullen and insecure about the situation, but instead, he was curious and even warm. Perhaps he'd had time to reflect on taking the long route to the White Sea during mealtimes and had to admit eating roasted fish for a few weeks in Karelia was better than eating fermented shark for a few months along the North Way.

I started with a few words: Ship, river, lake, fish. This was only to show how the Norse words were entirely different. I added the Sami words to show some similarities. We had no time for enough instruction that would allow them to speak freely with Joni. I might be able to do that, but I was no expert. I had only just crested the hill that allowed some free conversation, making errors in word order frequently.

I've spared you those errors as the reader because I didn't want to torture you.

I told the crew Joni would leave soon and why. Ulf seemed satisfied, but the 'Steins called for a story since they would have little chance to hear a tale from the Karelian. Joni agreed to this and took a moment to consider what story would be best.

The story he told went like this:

There was a wise old man named Vainamoinen. 'Wise' and 'old' do not really do him justice. He was the first man, born of the sky's daughter. He walked among mortal people even though he was very old when they were very young. So when they met him, they only ever knew him as an old man with a long, white beard. Yet, despite his age, he was a powerful singer of magic and a strong fighter. The Eternal Skald is what they called him.

Well-loved as Vainamoinen was, other men were jealous of his talents. One such man, named Joukahainen, attended a feast where he heard there was a skald much better than he. Joukahainen became angry and went south to find Vainamoinen, running into him on the road.

The younger man should have yielded the way, but Joukahainen claimed his qualities meant Vainamoinen should move. Joukahainen claimed superior wisdom and lore and a sweeter singing voice, as well. He suggested they test each other's lore.

As impetuous and angry as Joukahainen was, Vainamoinen was equally calm and unshakable. He claimed to have little knowledge and a mediocre singing voice. But he accepted the boastful challenge and invited Joukahainen to display his wisdom.

After two attempts, Vainamoinen was still unimpressed. He asked Joukahainen to tell him something of new wisdom, something he did not know. At this, Joukahainen claimed to know of primeval times, when the world was created and the moon set in the sky. He had been there when these things began, he said.

Vainamoinen had enough, and rightly called Joukahainen a liar.

Joukahainen then challenged Vainamoinen to a contest of arms. Vainamoinen refused, citing Joukahainen as too pathetic a man for him to fight.

("Not with one so vain and paltry will I ever measure broadswords," said Vainamoinen, and I thought he might mean more than broadswords. I liked the style of this Vainamoinen very much.)

The sneering youth tried to sing a spell on Vainamoinen. He chided the old man for his unwillingness to fight and declared he would turn him into a pig with his magic song.

Vainamoinen sang back, and the world heard his wrath.

Mountains trembled at his voice. Cliffs were torn to pieces. The ocean churned. Distant hills in unnamed lands shivered. Joukahainen, transfixed by the power of the spell, found himself sung into a bog where his feet stuck fast. Looking down, he found both feet turned to stone and not at all movable other than the fact that they were slowly sinking deeper.

Joukahainen pleaded with Vainamoinen and offered him many valuable things: His choice of magical items, including bows, ships, and horses. Failing these, he offered gold and silver in abundance. But the eternal skald already had these things, had them in such quantity that he found these offers worse than useless, and he sank Joukahainen deeper into the mire.

There was one thing Vainamoinen did not have, and that was a wife. When Joukahainen offered his sister, Aino, in marriage, Vainamoinen accepted. He eased off his spell and allowed Joukahainen to escape the mire. Both men went on their ways, Joukahainen carrying a heavy heart and Vainamoinen light in his steps with happiness.

Joukahainen broke the news to his family, and his sister was distressed. No tottering old man had she envisioned for herself as a husband! She was young and beautiful, and so it was understandable that she would think the marriage an ill fit. Her mother argued that it was a good thing, but Aino despaired and left their house.

"Better to be among the fishes," she said. And she drowned herself.

And so Vainamoinen wept bitter tears at that and offered advice to any who would listen: That in marriage, there should not be too great a difference in age that may lead to unhappiness.

Joni nodded, signaling the end of the story.

"Is that all?" asked Kraki.

"Did Vainamoinen find a wife later?" asked Magnus.

"Did he seek revenge?" demanded Ulf, sneering at the foolish story.

I checked with Joni and answered in order: "Vainamoinen's story is a very long one, but no, he never found a wife. And no, he didn't seek revenge. Who would he seek revenge against?"

"The younger man," said Ulf. "The pretender. The one who promised him a wife and failed to deliver."

I explained this to Joni, who asked me in a roundabout way if Ulf was mentally unhinged.

I told him I didn't know and I wasn't going to ask, but Norsemen generally sought revenge for anything that could embarrass us. Or we thought could embarrass us. Or we thought could potentially embarrass us if seen in just the right context. Losing face was just about as bad as losing your life.

Joni said this was the way of broken men and that Vainamoinen was sad, not broken.

I told Ulf that Vainamoinen was very sad and did not want to bring more sadness into the world by rekindling an old conflict. Ulf huffed at that. The 'Steins were satisfied, even if they thought it not a very exciting story.

No one asked the Karelian to tell another story, and I think he was glad of it. Of course, I wanted to know more stories, all the stories. And I should have asked for them earlier, but so it goes with many such decisions. One realizes the best road to take only by looking backwards. With perhaps only a few days left for all I knew, I asked to know more about this "eternal skald" Vainamoinen.

What Joni told me could fill many more pages, but there was one detail that made my heart skip a beat. Vainamoinen's instrument of choice was the kantele. They usually had five strings and were plucked rather than mostly strummed like my lyre. And he played not just any kantele. His was fashioned from the lower jawbone of a giant pike he slew. It was famously difficult, and no others could get it to play the right notes consistently.

Someone yelled at me for being out of rhythm and clinking oars, and that was when I realized my hands were frozen. The blood had drained from every part of my body and gone who knows where.

Joni didn't know why I looked so strange at the telling of these details. I could have explained my dream with Njord and Skadi and the strange stringed instrument made from the jawbone of a fish that neither of them could play. Yes, I could have told him and none of the rest of the crew would have known.

But if he then asked me what that dream meant, I would have had no idea what to say.

CHAPTER 33

WATER HAZARD

THOUGH MANY A CREWMAN SPOKE HIS THANKS AND OFFERED small gifts and extra supplies to Joni, I had no doubt that he was eager to leave us when it came time. You can tell much by the stories a man tells, and his stories told me he valued family over fame, unlike the rest of us on the ship. Not that I did not value my family, but I was not with them, was I? I was out trying my fame the same as Haldor was, only in a completely different way.

We would never have found our way without the Karelian's knowledge of the many rivers and inlets of that strange land. We traveled north on the river he called Vyg. I would have called that "a maze that opens up into a bay with no indication of where to follow it and then hides the way forward so that even Hemming would need to trip over it to find it." But to Joni, it was no trouble to navigate.

There was not much I could do to thank him. I decided to carve a rune, hoping it would aid him in finding his people. Still uncertain of my carving skill, I consulted with the wizard first, knowing the next day was likely to be Joni's last one with us. The ship was pulled onto shore early, and nobody really knew how late it was, so most everyone had found something to occupy their time. I found Ketill testing his bow, as he often did with his spare time.

"You want it to just be one rune?" he asked, confused.

"Yes, *algiz*," I said.

"What's the spell?"

I described Karelia's moose riders. "It is in the hope that he finds them, or they find him. *Algiz* represents moose."

"Docile animals," said Ketill as he stroked his beard. "But still wild and dangerous if you threaten them. They travel with the seasons. But you don't intend a metaphor here, you mean for your friend to find a literal moose in this case?"

"Yes, exactly," I said. "But the younger rune *maðr* takes the same shape as *algiz*, and *maðr* means 'person.' So: Moose in the old runes and person in the new runes. I mean to give it to him as a token of good luck, hoping he, the man, finds a friendly moose."

"Poetic. But you don't intend to cast it as a spell, then? Why ask me?"

"I, uh," I coughed, trying to camouflage my lack of confidence. "I have carved some things badly in the past. I want to make sure what I hand him will not do him any ill."

"You remember an early failure more than your most recent success," said Ketill. "Just carve the thing and explain it, and he can carry that memory with him. That is a gift not looking to be returned, and any sane man understands the value of such things."

I had grown close to the Karelian in the many weeks since our first meeting. When he pointed out our path down the next river, the last, almost a straight shot into the White Sea, I made a plea to Kraki to take us off course further west. That would allow Joni an easier starting point for his travel.

Kraki changed course immediately. A mile or so out of our way, we beached the ship, and the crew took a break while I walked out to the top of a nearby hill.

You never know what cresting a hill might mean. It might separate the way people speak or conduct themselves or change the stories they tell. This was open land, nearly as flat as Denmark, and I just wanted to see my friend off and make sure there was nothing on the other side of the hill waiting to eat him or put another iron collar around his neck.

The other side of that hill showed a vast country full of life. Marshlands dominated the field just below, with a creek running close by. Beyond the marshes was what seemed like a never-ending sea of pine trees, bright and green. Flowers dotted the marshes with color. Birds swooped in to find resting places or food. A flash of blue appeared at the edge of the creek but quickly turned back, showing its copper breast. Always good luck to spot a kingfisher.

It was already a hard thing to say goodbye to Joni. My shitty little piece of carved wood seemed so inadequate I almost didn't dig it out to give it to him. I did, though, remembering Ketill's words, and explained the intent behind it.

"This is some good thing!" he said, smiling. *"I will show this to the king if I see him and tell him the story behind it."*

It didn't seem very kingly to me, but maybe the story was worth telling. I wished him good luck and turned to go, but he stopped me.

"You never asked what happened to Vainamoinen at the end," he said.

That was true. As I heard more stories, "the eternal skald" was described more and more as a wandering wizard. He was no stand-in for bloody-minded Odin, but there were enough parallels that their ends might be similar. I was afraid Joni would tell me about Vainamoinen being eaten by a giant wolf. Or worse.

"Times changed," said Joni, continuing without me asking. *"His powers waned with the changes, and that made him feel truly old. So he sang himself a boat of copper and sailed away into the sunset. Perhaps people will recall his wisdom-sayings one day, he said, and wish him to again bring peace and plenty to the Northland. Then, one day, if we watch for him at dawn, he may return."*

The man turned and left, walking in the direction I had seen the kingfisher. A warm breeze brushed the pines and carried their scent. The landscape was so peaceful, I thought I could hear the grass growing.

I pondered Joni's parting words and whether this had really been a simple fisherman or something more. The *landvættir* of Karelia felt different from those I could feel in the North Way or even in Denmark—more quiet and wary, yet I sensed they favored Joni even if I was still suspicious to them.

I had met strange people in strange forests during my travels, sometimes suspecting them to be more than they let on. They would never give more than hints. If Joni really was something more than he seemed, I could not say what it was, as my lore of this place had been only what he told me.

"He is not Vainamoinen," Svipul said over my shoulder.

"I don't recall saying he was," I said, not bothering to look at her, the annoyance in my voice plain.

"A man thinks many things he will never say with words, but they're often laid plain by his face. And I know you better than you think."

I turned to face her, and my annoyance melted. Her snow-pale face seemed healthy and alive, even though I knew this must be the spirit of a dead woman. Her raven-black hair was bound back behind her helmet. Steel-gray eyes stared through the helm's sockets and fixed me with a stare that could have meant anything but for the smile on her lips. Her leathers and heavy mail were much for a warm day, but I suppose spirits don't sweat. She was more dressed for battle than usual, shield on her back, spear in hand, axe, knife, and sword at her belt.

"Hmmph. This is no great wisdom, and you come uncalled when at other times I had need of you. Why, so girded for war, do you speak now?"

"I speak as needed, as I think you know," she said, gentle but not sweetened as I would take false words to be. "You are right to think your friend's path a peaceful one. He will walk among the pines and breathe easy. He is a good man, and his family will be better for having him back."

"But?"

"But your path is down another river. You do not sail toward a peaceful place or a joyous reunion. You will need to be fully armed and armored to survive your journey."

I shrugged. "I hate wearing mail. It slows me down too much, and I can't move right. I am no Gudbrand Shirtless to wear multiple layers of the stuff. And helmets chafe and make it difficult to think."

"Your 'might and main' really are 'will and intellect.' You are more taken with the wizard's wisdom than maybe you admit."

"Why would I not admit it? Wit got me through that blizzard, not force of arms."

"Then keep your wits sharp as your sword. You will need both before long."

I stalked off in a huff. *That was hardly insight,* I thought as I marched down the hill. As I did so, I considered that I had not oiled my carving knife in some time. Did Need require oiling to keep the rust away? I hadn't even thought about it. Was my leather sling still strong, or fraying anywhere and liable to snap? I had not even considered the wooden discs in my carving pouch for weeks.

I reached the ship and looked back up the hill. There she stood, staring down at me, that unflappable smile seemingly visible at any distance. She winked at me.

I turned back and ran to the ship. The crew had disembarked, taking the time to stretch their limbs or take care of business that was easier to take care of behind a tree than squatting over a gunwale.

"You ready, skald?" Magnus asked as I approached.

"I might have a few things to do first."

"Ha!" Magnus covered his mouth with one hand. "I will tell no one you said that. It is past time to go, and Kraki is waiting."

So be it, then. I would need to find time to see to my equipment later.

We rowed back to the spot Joni had pointed towards and found the water going in the same direction we were. Though the current was in our favor, we rowed anyway, the anticipation of the journey's goal looming large in our minds. It was a bright, sunny day with a bright, cheery outlook.

It was about a mile down the river that we were ambushed.

We were pulling back on the oars, and when I say pulling, I really mean 'leaning into.' So I was leaning back, just like everyone else, and the ship came to an abrupt stop despite its speed. I toppled backwards into Innstein's lap. Some fared better than others but the result was mostly men falling all over each other and nobody knowing why.

The why of it was this: Some troll-cursed *niðingr* had set thick ropes across the river where it was narrowest and had tied the ends of these ropes to particularly large trees. We who were rowing didn't see these at all, being we were facing backwards, and Hemming saw nothing as our lookout until a few stout figures on the west bank pulled the ropes taut. The *Sea Squirrel* bucked starboard with the angle of the ropes despite Kraki's efforts at the rudder.

We were headed for the east bank no matter our next efforts, and Haldor knew it. "Forget the oars, arm yourselves!"

Even as he did so, grappling hooks tumbled onto the deck and snagged prow and gunwale as their owners drew back. We could see the warband now, and we were outnumbered. Two lines of men with spears and shields, all armored in mail and glinting helms, stood locked in a shield wall at the shore. Another five to ten protected each flank, not including those who had thrown the grappling hooks. Worse, one of those on their left flank was a giant of a man, and I don't mean big like Haldor. I mean, he had to be half-giant because men don't grow to be nine feet tall. Even worse than that, there was no telling if that was the entire group or not.

The crew of the *Sea Squirrel* drew on their mail shirts and helmets, grabbed shields and spears. Whatever the numbers we faced, they would have no easy time boarding the ship. I thought about armor myself, but as I had said to Svipul, it slowed me down. I ran forward and cut one of the ropes attached to a grappling hook, crawled beneath the gunwale in case an archer had caught sight of me, and cut the second rope. Then I scrambled back to get behind our own shield wall and readied my sling.

I felt the soft scraping of sand under the front of the ship. That meant about knee-deep water, but we were not fully parallel to the shore. That was not much attack surface for the enemy to use. They could keep their shield wall up as long as they wanted. It was on them to get to us, not us to get to them.

"Greetings," boomed the giant. When no response came, he took a step forward and spoke again. "Is silence your response to a courteous greeting? It might make a man suspicious, I think, being so uncommunicative in these uncertain times."

"Silence is my response," said Haldor, "though not the kind you might expect. To what do we owe the courtesy of having our way barred and our ship vandalized?"

"I think that's to be determined," said the giant. "We're very interested in who might be coming down this river and why. Maybe we aren't barring your way at all. Maybe we are just making new friends. Or maybe we are here to kill you and take your ship. The fact of your presence is not nearly as important as the why of it, and the why will determine what we're doing."

Huld peered up over the gunwale without the slightest hint of fear, fixing our ambushers with an evil eye. She spat down at them and raised her staff, whispering something to herself.

"That business is none of yours," Kraki said to the giant.

"We aren't in the habit of taking orders," said Ulf. "Every man on this ship is a free one."

"Even the women are free men?" asked the giant, as he pointed at Huld.

Old linguistic habits die hard.

"More man than any lot sneaking about with not a ship to their names," said Huld, undeterred by Ulf's gaffe. "What a sorry crew you all are. You know, vikings are supposed to have ships!" The old crone held the gunwale and stuck her head out as far as she could, as if the giant were a doddering old man hard of hearing, and shouted. "Dirt pirates, I name you. Now flee before I curse you thrice over and the skald puts your pathetic attempt to verse!"

Whatever points the giant had landed earlier, Huld was well ahead now for sheer boldness.

"That is no set of manners for guests," rumbled the giant. "And you are guests in this land. It is only right that you declare yourselves and your intentions for us to hold council on."

That last comment triggered a memory. "Haldor," I hissed, trying to get his attention before the next verbal salvo. "I know that man!"

"Who is he?"

"Well, I don't know," I said stupidly. "I mean to say my vision with Valborg showed me such a man. He was seated in council with Arrow-Odd. I do not think he is our enemy."

"Hold," Haldor shouted to the crew. Then he lowered his shield and spoke directly to the giant, his booming voice radiating energy. "Who are you to declare yourself a host here? We've helped one Karelian already, though he did not speak our language. I think you are not from here, either, but if you are, know that we've done one of your countrymen a good turn."

"It's true I was not born on this spot," said the giant, "but my father's army holds the area for now. You are a wordy bunch and I tire, so I'll declare myself. After that, though, I expect an answer. I am Vignir Oddsson, and this is no band of pirates, dirt or otherwise. I have been expecting unwelcome guests coming up this river and found more than a few who harbored ill intent toward my kin. So speak now, if you would. Or if you would not, then step down from your ship and we can mark off an area to see who is the better man."

"Oddsson?" said Haldor. "You don't mean to claim this kin of yours is Arrow-Odd, do you?"

"I do claim him as kin," said the giant. He pulled up the mail sleeve on one arm to reveal an arrow-shaped armring. "He is my father, and that's why I'm so short."

A half-*jǫtunn*. They weren't all giant in size, but some were, especially the mountain-dwellers. The coupling of Vignir's mother and Odd, at maybe half her height, must have been a strange one.

Shields were lowered, the threat of the whole situation evaporating like mist. We had no need to fight Odd's men, and they might even help us. Haldor stepped out to speak more clearly. "Then we have been well-led in our route. I am Haldor, some call me Skullsplitter. We do not come as enemies to your kin."

"That answers one reason you *don't* have for being here," said Vignir. "These are strange shores to visit for men seeking profit."

"There's profit enough to be had, but honor is more important," said Haldor. "We are friends of King Hrolf and enemies of Alfhild Smooth-Cheek. She made a sacrifice of one of our men and burned the king's city. We won, but she slipped away before we could finish her. We hear she is up in the White Sea, in an island tower somewhere. And that, for some reason, your father Odd is after her."

"You have part of that wrong. He isn't after her," said Vignir. "He's after Ogmund Tussock, as he always is. Alfhild just happens to be Ogmund's student and consort."

Which was, in many ways, not a surprise. And yet, in many more important ways, made our mission even more complicated than it had been before.

CHAPTER 34

A WISE MAN'S HEART SELDOM GLAD, AGAIN

WE HAD SUCH A CORDIAL EXCHANGE OF WORDS WITH VIGNIR that people put their weapons away. Eventually.

It's an easy thing to judge a man by actions rather than words, but when you have no actions to go on, it's all your own judgment about whether the words are true or false. That cut both ways, as Vignir was suspicious of us and we of him. It was the armrings that did it for us. Odd's armring wouldn't be worn as a trophy, so he had to be Odd's man, son or not. And he didn't know us, but he had heard tales of King Hrolf facing down a horde, as well as the king's hawk sigil. The hawk armring some of us wore was good enough for him.

I was one of the few who came down off the ship to speak to Vignir face to face. Or face to torso, as Vignir towered over us. He held a fine steel helmet under one arm, almost lazy about it. Perhaps a man that big needs to take extra steps to seem casual since every step seems intimidating. Light brown hair was pulled back into a tight braid. His beard looked like it grew freely, not groomed much in the last few weeks. And I don't know who made his chain shirt with links that thick, but he wore it like the thing was a light tunic.

No judgment, but I'm certain he stole a few glances at Haldor's axe, which was a good deal nicer than his own. Envy aside, Vignir wanted to know more about who we were and what we had seen, especially about our sea monster encounter. He was also generous with his own information.

It would be another two days' sail to Odd's camp, where we would be welcome. Just further up the river, as Joni had guided us, and then south along the coast of the White Sea, and there would be no missing it. Dozens of warships and thousands of warriors looking to win fame had surrounded Ogmund's cliffside fortress. He had few defenders with him and would not have provisions forever. He had to come out eventually.

"Is Alfhild holed up there with him or on this island we've heard of with a tower?" asked Haldor.

"The island, if it's one or the other," said Vignir. "As far as I know, it is only Ogmund and his eight followers chased into that cliffside. I think you should talk to my father and see if your interests align."

"Ours is an independent ship," said Kraki. "There will be no swearing of oaths to another man. I say where the *Sea Squirrel* goes. Haldor says where the crew goes on land."

"That's up to you, then," said Vignir. A good, standard Norse response. I had heard it many times in response to my continued argumentation, and it had taken me years to suss out the meaning. It could be anything from *I'm not interested in arguing* to *I think you're an idiot, but I'm not interested in arguing* to *I don't give a shit what you do, so be on your way.* "But if you speak out of turn, it will make me look bad, and I don't want that."

A wave of heat rolled through my face as he said that last part. Times in my youth when I tried to impress my father flashed back. It was a strong impulse to look good in our culture, even stronger for a boy to be thought well of by his father. Or at least not to look bad in front of him.

"We wouldn't do that," I said, maybe a little too loudly. I coughed and modulated my voice a little. "I mean to say, we've no interest in making enemies with Odd or his allies. Including the short ones like you."

Vignir laughed out loud at the continuation of his own joke. "I have no doubt of that. And I think you want to be off so that you can make use of the best light remaining in the day, but I will tell you a useful thing before you go: Odd's war council is tricky with politics. I could be there right now, but I offered to take men south and cut off enemy ships coming up this way if I found them."

"Can we trust any of these men?" asked Ulf.

Vignir nodded. "You can trust them all to be themselves, that's for sure. Gardar and Sirnir are powerful jarls and were sworn brothers before they ever met Odd."

Though Haldor was silent as Vignir spoke, his shoulders tensed at those names.

"Gardar is one you might know, since he is a Dane," continued Vignir. "A man with high spirits who buoys the mood of others around him. A little impetuous, though. Sirnir is a Western Geat, and you'll have to guess at why he and Gardar ever became friends since he is quiet and moody. They met my father, Odd, through a man called Redbeard, the fourth councilman."

"Where is Redbeard from?" asked Haldor.

"I couldn't say. My father met him in a dark forest years ago. He had lost all his men, and Redbeard offered him sworn brotherhood. He introduced my father to Gardar and Sirnir. The four of them all agreed they would go raiding together, all four sworn together so that nothing could beat them.

"And nothing has. Puny as my father looks, he is quite a good fighter, whether against trolls or men. Redbeard is not one I choose to spend much time with. He has a fair amount of lore to draw on and advice to give. But I haven't noticed much of his exploits when it was time to draw steel."

"I hear what you're saying," I said to indicate I heard what he was not saying. He was not going to say *Redbeard is a sorcerer and shies away from fighting*. Not outright, at least.

"There is one more you should know about, and that is Styrgrim, who some call the Bear. He fought for my father before but returned only a few years ago. He has fewer ships and men than Gardar or Sirnir and is older than they are, but he's much fiercer in combat. Whatever you do, you should not make him angry unless you want a fight. Even my father treads lightly around that one."

One of the worst aspects of having pale skin is that when you blush, you go bright pink. That was what my face was doing at the mention of my father, both out of surprise and fear. I felt as if all eyes had suddenly snapped to me, the weight of those gazes so heavy that my boots sank into the sand.

For three years, I had wondered about his whereabouts and even his fate. Gudbrand could not imagine him dead, and yet no ravens told a story that would lead me to him. Yet there he was, only a few days away. Would he greet me with more warmth than I remembered now that I had two armrings? Would that be enough?

Was anything enough?

The flood of emotions and the complexities of their interaction made me dread what would come soon. I would rather be standing on the prow of the ship, facing a sea monster with a bow and arrow. At least then, I would know where I stood.

"That's quite the war council Odd has assembled," said Haldor.

"It's a lot of talking," said Vignir, crossing his arms. "Odd is foremost, but remember, they can all have their say. Even if you think you're talking to just my father, you're really hearing the thoughts of other men along with his."

"We will take care," said Haldor and motioned for everyone to get back on the ship. It was a welcome gesture, and I nodded my thanks as he shepherded everyone away. Everyone except me, allowing me a final question with Vignir once the others were far enough out of earshot.

I had little time and thought Vignir would respect a more direct approach, so I just let out with it. "It's interesting you mention Styrgrim the Bear," I said. "Because I am Ansgar Styrgrimsson. I haven't heard anything about my father in over three years. I wonder if he ever mentioned his family at home since you've known him."

Vignir nodded, acknowledging this might be an awkward thing to discuss. "He did this sometimes. His parents, especially his father, who made his weapons and armor. We all know Halstein's work. And his wife he once mentioned, a brave and strong woman he missed very much. But she died in childbirth twenty years ago, and since then, he never met her equal or close to it."

"Died in childbirth?" I asked, my hands and feet going numb. "Maybe you are mistaken. My mother died of illness when I was very young."

Vignir shrugged but stepped forward and leaned in. One massive hand rested on my shoulder, and the half-giant's voice pitched low and warm, as only a man who knew the need for a father's approval could do. "I can only repeat the words he spoke, and they were that she died in childbirth. I wish you good luck, whatever you decide to do."

A wise man's heart is seldom glad. Pursuit of the deep lore led to some dark places, and again, I was reminded that Odin was both the wisest of the gods and the most drunk. Ketill, too, had seen more truth than he had intended, and it had driven him to drink as well. I still had questions—many more than Vignir could answer—about the hints of my heritage.

What roads would they lead me down? None I wanted to travel on was my fear.

I did not even ask if Styrgrim had mentioned his son. I had a feeling I already knew the answer and that confirming it would make me feel worse than I already did.

Chapter 35

The White Sea

We had to camp another night before reaching the end of the river Vyg, Hemming shouted his excitement upon spying the mouth of the river, and most of the crew shouted back their enthusiasm. Not I. My mind was a maelstrom of confusion. I sat sullen and quiet while others cheered. I only looked to the fore after several from Magnus to get my attention.

There are few experiences like riding a river as it opens into a massive, unexplored sea. Unexplored by me, at least. I was as deep in an unknown land as I was deep in the unknown of my own life. Calm, clear water showed us the bottom even though we were well away from shore and atop depths I could only guess at. Beaches, some sandy, some rocky, dotted the shorelines. There was some comfort in the uncertainty and adventure about the place. At least I was not the only one in unfamiliar territory.

We followed the coastline south as Vignir had directed. Soon, a wind picked up and we let the sail take us, a rare break from the constant rowing. That was a relief for most. But with no rowing, there was more talking, and the talking inevitably led to questions about my family.

"So, Kraki," said Ulf, "how independent can we remain with the son of one of Odd's war council on the crew? It seems to me we've chosen a side or had it chosen for us. Let's hope we don't end up fighting our friend Joni if he's opposed to Odd's presence here."

Some of the men murmured about that, mostly the new ones. Svein made a wordless harumphing sound.

My face flushed at the implication I had created a problem for the crew, and I fought the urge to jump up and attack Ulf right then and there. Heedless as that would have been of Ulf's vastly superior fighting ability, the breaking of both Kraki's and Haldor's rules, and the distinct possibility of being thrown overboard, I still thought about it. My nerves had been frayed since my conversation with Vignir, and that's the kind of foolish decision one makes when feelings are so raw.

"No," said Svipul. She lay sidelong on the gunwale, floating next to me, one elbow propping her chin. No helmet this time. She let her raven-black hair blow with the breeze as I looked her in the eye and saw how serious she was. She did not elaborate, but her look and firm tone brought my blood back down. A little.

"That's a good question," said Haldor. "Let's address it right now. After all, Magnus has sailed with Styrgrim the Bear and called him his captain. Skald, what do you think of this side choosing? Are we Arrow-Odd's crew after all?"

Arrow-Odd can sit on a sharp stick for all I care! was what I thought. The look on my *fylgja*'s face told me a more considered response would be better. I breathed in deep and found one. "I would welcome Arrow-Odd as a crewmate," I said. "As long as he swears to uphold the same rules as the rest of us."

Murmurs of dissent turned into low growls of approval. Odd was not captain of a single ship; he was a legend whose campaigns moved thousands of men. It was a bold statement to make that he might be just another crewmate rowing with the rest of us.

"Well, Magnus, how does that sound to you?" continued Haldor.

Magnus responded so quickly he almost interrupted. "He's as good a fighter as they say, but he's shit at rowing!" he said to laughter among the crew. "But I wouldn't mind if he joined us. Assuming he also swore to uphold our rules."

"Well, he can't have the rudder," barked Kraki.

There was more laughter, and Ulf did not raise the question again. It would be difficult for me to see Styrgrim again, but that was my difficulty. I would not share that burden with the crew.

"What about the others?" asked Magnus. "If Gardar is a Dane, where was he last year when he was needed?"

"Gardar is as powerful a jarl as Gorm Tin-Whisker," said Ulf. "He holds the north of Jutland, not so far from the Western Geats where Sirnir is from. Gardar's reputation is just as Vignir described."

"And Sirnir?" I asked. "He is a Geat, so—"

"Sirnir is my brother," said Haldor.

Hard to underestimate the collective intake of breath at that. Few could conceal their looks of confusion. Haldor was the brother of a jarl? And one he had never spoken of?

And here I was, a skald, and I had failed to get even his most basic story. Never even tried to square his contradictory titles, *the Great Geat* and *the Hero of Halogaland.* It is not so easy to be from two different places so far away from each other. I had assumed they were just alliterative flourishes.

"We will speak no more of him," he continued after a long moment.

That was a challenge I would accept. For now, we would speak no more of Sirnir, but I would discover Haldor's story one way or another.

"We should be wary of this Redbeard," said Ketill.

"A strange man Arrow-Odd found in the forest? I agree, be wary," I said. It broke the tension as if it were a joke, but I was speaking from experience. A delivery job I took a bit before ever meeting Haldor and Kraki took me through a strange forest to meet an even stranger old sorcerer. I'd come out of it well; maybe he'd even saved my life. But the impression I got from him was not warm or friendly, and I did not desire to meet him again.

"Fair jest, but I suspect he will seem fairer than I did and conceal more."

Ketill thought I was referring to him. Which was fair, though not my intent. I'd met the sorcerer I referred to on a delivery run. I still remember the power of his charm, and how he had saved me from a witch who might have dyed her clothes in my blood. That had been one scary witch. And the sorcerer had made her flee in terror.

"I only know Arrow-Odd from stories," I said, retrurning to the more immediate subject. "But the stories are less about him and more about what happened around him. Gudbrand told me a bit about the fighting, but Odd and Ogmund were off in the distance."

"He is something of a legend," said Ketill, whose tone indicated it was no compliment. Conversation died out after that.

We camped one more night, and this time, I felt the incredible wildness of the place. Hills and mountains even more distant in the north seemed to promise unending exploration and adventure. Wolves howled in the distance and sea birds sang in the twilight as we put up tents and gathered wood for fires. Wisps in the night sky danced, and I took them to be the spirits of the place, perhaps not so land-bound after all.

As the day grew late, the sun failed to fall. Twilight held until the morning. The evenings still demanded meals, however, and that was when we saw other fires. A few miles away, hundreds of them. An army, no doubt, as that was too many to be anything else. It would be a short trip the next day to find them, and then we would be surrounded by new people to meet. Not much time or space for discrete conversations, then. And there was one conversation I wanted in private before I lost the chance.

I pulled Huld away to the beach and walked well down the sand until I had no doubt of speaking in secrecy. She did not protest.

"You've never spoken a prophecy," I said.

Huld shrugged. "None to your ears. And why would I? Men never profit from knowing their futures."

"That is the thing we've all looked away from," I said. "You never talked about Valborg's prophecy, either. Not a word, even though you're a *vǫlva*. But she told us this would be a terrible trip. For us and for Odd. 'Looking for revenge, he'll find more regret, a yield he'll share with his yeomen.'"

"Not for the first time," said Huld. "How many friends has Odd led to their deaths? He always believes it will be different, and so he believes it now. You don't need a prophecy to tell you it will likely turn out like the last time."

"For Odd, yes. I don't know what we can expect if we aren't allied with him explicitly, though. It seems to me we make our own fate. But Vignir told me what he heard my father say, and I knew that was part of the prophecy, too. 'The raven banner buried a truth as well.' My father flies a raven banner, and I think he has lied to me about my mother."

"Why call me down to say such things?" asked Huld.

"Because I think you've known much more than you ever let on. Why have you said nothing?"

"You fools would not have listened."

"But we will listen to a cat, is that it?"

That got her attention.

"You were not there at the battle last summer, yet there you were, healing me as soon as I needed you. I always thought that cat had a human's eyes. I assumed it was a trick of the light at first. Then there was the cat again when

I needed help against Svein. That's you. You are the cat, in case I must say so directly. You keep that secret for a reason. I've said nothing of my suspicion, but I could easily do so."

"I do not advise that." It was a dead tone, the most serious I'd ever heard from her.

"Why? Tell me one solid thing about why."

"The hidden wolf."

I shook my head, uncomprehending. Part of Valborg's prophecy came back to me then. "'The hidden wolf waits and watches.' You think there is a danger we aren't seeing and want to keep your skin-changing a secret?"

"I think you and your friends will need every advantage when the time comes, and I don't intend to be upfront about what I might do in the meantime."

"Why help us, though? Why then and why now?"

"That is a long story. Too long for tonight. And I don't know that I wish to tell it to you. You are quite keen on knowing the history of others, and you assume it to be a service to them. Well, here is what service I want: Say nothing. My story is my own."

"This goes in circles. If you won't tell your story, tell me why you are with us."

"You aren't likely to succeed without me. It is likely to go badly for you."

"Why come with us, then?"

"There is important work yet to be done. As important as your pursuit of the witch. Would Haldor turn away from that even if he knew it would kill him? No, don't bother answering out loud since you know he would not. We all march toward our fates. It is the direction we take and what we carry on that march, as he said in the grove."

"Well, what is the work?" I shouted, immediately regretting raising my voice as I had intended the conversation to be private. I went on quieter. "What is so important that *you* go on a doomed journey?"

The *vǫlva* smiled at me. "So difficult to face your father you would call it doom! Will it kill you then?"

I refused to answer that stupid question.

"Exactly," she continued. "Something will come after it. As something will come after Odd's war. Haldor's time will come, and something will come after. Something always comes after. It is that something I am here for."

CHAPTER 36

ARROW-ODD'S WAR

OUR SMALL SHIP MUST HAVE BEEN HARDLY NOTICEABLE WHEN WE made landing among Odd's massive fleet. We were among at least five dozen dragon ships and half again as many smaller craft. We disembarked fully armed and armored, however, and that many men walking up the beach got noticed.

A rider, himself well-armed and armored, approached—and not to offer us ale. His helmet was worn with score marks but was as clean as his mail shirt. His face seemed vaguely familiar as if I'd met a close relative of his, but I couldn't immediately place it. Medium in height is what I guessed, though that was hard to tell as he sat on his horse. Not medium in width, though— he was stocky and strong, with a jutting jawline.

My father favored men of that physicality. I knew that from many comments he'd made about me being "too tall," which had led to "muscles stretched too thin" and the like.

The more obvious identifier was the raven emblazoned on his shield. I doubt any of our crew took him as a potential enemy, so we did not take fighting positions.

He pulled up a dozen paces short of us and reined in his mount.

"Ho there," he said. "It's a sleepy task to watch the ships these weeks past, but watch them I do. No more did I expect to land here, yet you don't seem to be a big enough force that you mean to attack us. Who are you, where are you from, and what do you want? That's what I'd like to know, and sooner rather than later."

I wanted to speak, but Haldor waved me off. There would be no need to translate, and Ulf was more diplomatic than I, no doubt about it.

"Ho there, yourself, brave guard of the coast!" said Ulf, matching the man's formal address. "One man approaches an entire ship and demands answers. I think that's very brave. You are right to think we're not expected and right to think we don't intend to attack if this is Arrow-Odd's camp. At least this is about where Vignir told us the camp would be, and it seems unlikely another army would be so nearby without him knowing."

"You have it right that this is Odd's camp," said the coast guard. "And Odd is one without peer among his allies, even if Vignir is much bigger. I am still Styrgrim's man, however. Hjalti is my name."

"I can see you're Styrgrim's man by the raven on your shield," said Ulf. "This ship is the *Sea Squirrel*, its crew Haldor's Heroes, and we want to know if Odd, Styrgrim, or anyone else here knows the whereabouts of a certain witch."

"I can't say if there's help for that," said the man. "But I will announce your arrival and see you are received well." He turned his mount but halted when Ulf spoke again.

"You may wish to tell one specific thing to Styrgrim," he said, glancing my way, and at that, I had to intervene.

"Tell him Magnus the Red is with us," I shouted. "He has sailed with my —with Styrgrim before."

The guard could see something was awkward, but not quite what. He nodded, accepting what information he had, and left us, galloping off the beach and up the green hill he had come down.

"Let's see if he remembers a man he fought alongside," I said. "That will tell us something of what else we can expect from him."

Haldor nodded. "Give that man a few minutes to make his way back. We don't yet know if any on that war council will speak to us, other than Styrgrim. It is fine to use Magnus' name for now. That way, it won't seem like we are trying to demand favors. But you should not hide yourself when the time comes."

I wanted to say, *Nor should you hide from Sirnir*, but now was not the time.

Soon, I was carrying a spear and shield again, even wearing my ugly skullcap. The getup gave me an out-of-place feeling I hadn't had since my early days on the *Sea Squirrel*. The feeling did not lessen in the time it took Hjalti to return and tell us to continue on now that we were expected.

Occupants of the camp's outlying tents gave a few curious looks. Looks and nothing more, though, because they were otherwise occupied. People busied themselves with practical things: Cooking, mending clothes, making shoes, sharpening blades. Some were still washing despite it being late morning. Few were dressed for battle.

"This camp is not very warlike," I said to Magnus. "Nothing is happening."

"It is completely warlike!" said Magnus. "You have never been on a campaign. Most time is spent on chores. To engage the enemy, you need to be in a spot where you want to fight. But it also needs to be a spot they want to fight, or they move to a different spot! Then they like their spot, but you don't like yours, so you move." He waved a hand at the camp around us. "And when anyone moves, they have to move all their things. Every. Single. Time."

"What if you catch the enemy where they can't move?"

"Good idea," said Magnus. "And good luck doing it. I think that is what you see here, though. Odd likes his position, or Hjalti would not have said he'd been watching for weeks. But no fight has come, so maybe Ogmund likes his position too, and neither is willing to move."

An encouraging hand slapped me on the shoulder. "Aha!" said Ulf. "That's a big problem Alfhild will have. However large her army is, we will be able to find her. A single ship moves much faster than an army can muster." He strode ahead, grinning.

Too much time on the sea could try any man's patience, and I tried to think this was more the Ulf of our crew, not so much the one who needled me continually. We were not Odd's men and not looking to be Odd's men, and so surrounded by not-enemies but not-friends, it was good to have a skilled negotiator with us to do the talking. And Ulf did love to talk.

"You should be up there with him," I told Magnus. "Let Styrgrim see you straightaway."

Magnus shook his head. "That would be too expected, given you mentioned me by name. Let him pick me out of a crowd if he remembers. I think it is you who ought to be up there with Ulf. Show Styrgrim your armrings and see what he says about those."

"Maybe you're right," I said. "But I will stay back for now. Ulf will do the talking. Svein will do the huffing. Haldor will do the deciding while they listen to Ulf and look at Svein."

"You just want to see your father's look of surprise when you turn up out of nowhere."

"Not just," I said, considering how good that idea sounded. I'd fought in battles since he last saw me and had the scars to prove it. Maybe I could finally get a hint of recognition out of the man.

Hanging back from the front of our group did well to conceal me, but I ran straight into Ketill's backside as I did.

"Shit," said the wizard. He had stopped all of a sudden with no explanation other than his one-word declaration.

"Better do that away from camp if you want to make friends," said Magnus.

I knew better than to joke. If Ketill thought he saw danger, it was time to lock shields. "What is the matter?" I asked, my eyes wide and searching. "I see men, some sleepy and some cheery. Are we being followed?"

"Worse," said Ketill. He nodded in the direction of a man with a broad smile and bright red hair. "I know that grin."

"Welcome!" said the man. Of middling height, he was well-dressed and not just for a war camp. High boots and a blue-striped cloak stood out the most to me. Even with all the mud of thousands of people tramping all over the place, those boots were somehow still clean. A long reed in his hand puzzled me since it was neither a weapon nor a symbol of rank or treasure. He had a courteous way about him as he introduced himself and seemed to address us all individually.

The man known as Redbeard seemed familiar, but I could not place him. A delivery I had made, perhaps, or a man I'd met in a mead hall?

Ulf matched the man's courtesies compliment for compliment. The two of them sounded something like this:

"Who is this man who speaks honeyed words with a silver tongue? He is no commoner, a man with that kind of voice."

"Words do justice to the man before me! Surely he is a leader here, who comes dressed as a jarl sitting in a mead hall."

And so on.

I've omitted more ego-stroking than I've described in this story so far. It's not what I would call necessary to the story, but this was both excessive and characteristic of Redbeard's ability to charm others. It is not quite something I can convey in text. More like something you had to feel. Redbeard knew how to pitch his voice, his manners, and his words to each person for the best effect. Even those suspicious of him.

"And here is a man of runes," he said, looking at Ketill. "I can tell he has wandered to many places and heard the thoughts of many others. Such a man is wise."

Something happened to Ketill's face. Each part twitched in turn such that it seemed to me he was resisting a smile.

I think Redbeard would have said something similarly ingratiating to every one of us had he been able to continue. Sweet as his words were, the voice that interrupted him was anything but.

"Why does Magnus the Red not step forward?" boomed Styrgrim the Bear. "Has he grown so short that he walks upside-down below the earth?"

I had not heard that voice in over three years. It was much the same as I remembered it, slow and grinding, like a wagon the size of a house being pulled an inch at a time. Long shirt sleeves reached down his arms beneath a thick mail shirt. His shield was strapped to his back. He took off his helmet and held it under one arm. His black hair had gained in silver since I had last seen him. That face was drawn into a tight line, his lips curving neither up nor down.

It had taken me years to realize this thin line was a smile.

Magnus stepped away from me before answering to avoid drawing attention in my direction. "Is that Styrgrim's voice, or is an aurochs choking down too many acorns at once?" He gave his spear to his shield hand and then reached out to clasp arms with Styrgrim. "No shorter, but I have walked below the earth," said Magnus.

"You've been to many places, it seems. What brings you here, though?"

"These fine people bring me here!"

That blood-draining feeling began again. I could see where this conversation was headed. Magnus began with Haldor and Kraki and then mentioned Ulf and Svein as they were right next to him. On he went with the others.

"Then there is Ketill the *galdramaðr*," said Magnus. "And Huld the *vǫlva*. Wait, where is Huld? Well, she disappears from time to time. Nanthild won't introduce herself, so I will do that." On he continued, even with the names of all those new crewmembers we had taken on. "There are the 'Steins, who keep the ship in good repair. Then there's Hemming, who stays with the ship to keep away the rabble. But perhaps of more interest is our skald, who has got us out of many tight places."

I stepped out from behind the wizard and gave my spear to my shield hand as Magnus had done. Without a word, I took off my skullcap and held it under my left arm, letting him get a good look at how I had a few scars now. Small scars, but well earned. How my shoulders were broader. How I looked more a man than when he last saw me.

"Still trying to grow a beard, eh?"

The biggest barrel on the insult wagon had rolled straight onto my face. Dear reader, I don't ask for your pity. I've known so many others with far worse fates. By comparison, I had it easy. I tell you this only to show there is no telling the power a father might exert over his son with even a light touch. I would rather have been stabbed in the guts than hear those words.

"Ha," I said in a cracking voice and could feel the respect of the others draining like the blood in my face. The man had left me no good options. I had to respond to the insult, but only enough that it seemed trading jests. Failure to respond would peg me as half-man, unable or unwilling to defend myself.

"Beards come and go," I said. "But a man's mouth is here to stay. The last time I stared into a mouth so big as yours, it was trying to swallow our ship." A bit weak and ham-fisted, but better than nothing. My belly lurched with the effort. Better had I composed a verse as a response, but I felt lucky to say anything coherent.

"Ha!" said Styrgrim. He punched me in the shoulder, not hard enough to challenge and not light enough to be levity. "It is good to see you."

Which it plainly was not.

"Come and follow me!" said Redbeard, addressing us all. "I am just a simple advisor. Let me take you straight to Odd so you may meet the man himself."

On we walked, a slow shuffle more than a military march. Redbeard pointed out important men among Gardar's Danes and Sirnir's Geats as we went. Others were Odd's own men, and these were from all over: Balts, Swedes, some Norse from Hrafnista where Odd's family was from.

Here was Haakon the Black, and there was Harald the White, friends despite their opposing bynames, both Swedes. Helgi Pike-Tooth was a Dane. He was not present at the moment, but we'd know him when we saw him. Birki the Obstinate was a reliable man but wouldn't tell anyone where he was from. Josur the Daring was from Trondelag and had the most ships of anyone not on the war council itself. And there was Asmund Barrel-Beard, from many places; sometimes you just needed a man who kept spirits up during the slow and boring times.

"Barrel-Beard?" asked Ulf.

"Barrels are mysteries, aren't they?" said Redbeard. "There's almost always something in a barrel, but you never know what it is. Usually, it's some sort of food."

That restored some of the levity to the situation, and the crew laughed along with Ulf.

All these descriptions gave the impression their presence in this place was Redbeard's doing. More than that, it seemed to me Redbeard and Ulf were becoming fast friends.

While Redbeard engaged with Ulf, Styrgrim tried to make small talk with Magnus and thereby engage me. I did not wish to be engaged after that insult, however, so I let them talk of old raids and close battles. I slipped quietly away from any further attention and to the other side of our group, where I found Nanthild.

At least she would ask me no questions, I thought. But soon after settling in beside her, I realized she was staring at me.

"What?" I said, too loud and gruff to maintain a veneer of cool.

Nanthild pursed her lips and shrugged.

"I don't want to talk to him right now. It is enough to have found him alive," I lied. "It is complicated. For many reasons."

Nanthild sighed, but I would not be baited. It felt better to remain silent in the loud world all around me, at least for a while. At some point, I would talk to my father. Hopefully without pleading questions subject to answers that might leave me no better off than I was before. Where were you all this time? Why did you send no word back? What happened to my mother?

That would not do. I did not come all this way and face all these dangers just to be dismissed like a thrall. I had countered powerful *seiðr* with verse. I had gone into the Down-Below and gotten us out again. I had stolen a book of Old Roman magic. I had gone into the places of deep wisdom and terror and returned. I had avenged a woman who had tried to kill me just on principle. And I had stared down a sea monster and not swooned.

I had earned my armrings.

The thoughts brought the blood back to my face and made me bold. Perhaps I would demand some answers right now!

Nanthild yanked me back toward her before I had gotten two steps away.

"Now what?" I demanded.

"You really don't know how to listen at all, Skald!" said Innstein.

"She's giving you good advice," added Utstein.

"How is it you two know what she means?"

The 'Steins shrugged. "Seems obvious," said Utstein to his brother's agreement.

"Family often makes a man insane," I countered. "As I've seen it go with you two at times. So give me a hint, at least, if you've got such secret knowledge that I don't."

"You might do for another what's being done for you," said Utstein.

"Think of you and Styrgrim, then think of Haldor and Sirnir, and you should get it," concluded Innstein.

Nanthild's look turned more hopeful. I considered this and considered what had been done for me. My father had lied to me and wasn't any more approachable than I remembered him. What did that have to do with Haldor and Sirnir when Haldor never spoke of his brother?

And then I had it: Haldor did not wish to speak to his brother any more than I wished to speak to my father, at least for now. And for now, Magnus was doing all the talking. Magnus, my good friend, put himself between me and my father. Therefore, I should put myself between Haldor and Sirnir when the time came.

And the time was coming very soon. There was a large canopy ahead of us standing over a grand table. Three serious men sitting in ornate chairs indicated the time was upon us.

I shoved my way ahead and set myself at the forefront near Ulf. He could have the distinction of speaking to Odd on our behalf, but I would need to insert myself at some point.

"You look a familiar face," Redbeard said to me.

"I was thinking the same," I said. "Perhaps we met at Hjalmar's mead hall on the Fordefjorden sometime?"

"I know that place well!" he said. "Many a good night's entertainment to be had and plenty to drink. Hjalmar is truly a generous host."

I nodded in agreement because he was right on in his description of Hjalmar. Only after he had turned back to Ulf did I realize he hadn't answered my question at all.

Redbeard turned to announce us before I could follow up on that thought. "Ho there, lords! I have found a ship full of heroes to introduce. I think you have heard of Haldor Skullsplitter and Kraki Bentleg, yet there are so many more! Here is Ulf Silvertongue, though. I will let him make his crew's introductions."

I had never heard anyone call Ulf "Silvertongue," but I suppose there is a beginning for every byname.

"We're pleased to meet such fine men," said Ulf.

The man I knew by reputation to be Arrow-Odd kept his seat as if it were a throne in a great hall. Though clad in a bright scarlet tunic and gold-embroidered headband, it was his arrow bag that had my attention. It was no normal quiver. It was made out of a goat's skin, and I mean the entire thing —horns and hooves still dangled from it. There were a lot of arrows in that bag. And they were bigger than most. Three of these were fletched with gold. Those had to be Gusir's Gifts, the dwarf-made arrows he had from his grand-father. Arrows not even a sorcerer could block, so the legend said.

"There's many a hero here already," said Odd without rising. "Though I won't deny any who wish to join us. Find yourselves a suitable campground to put down on." Addressing the other men at the table, he added, "We have ale enough to share."

"It would please me greatly if my brother, Haldor, might make his camp next to the rest of my men," said the one who was obviously Sirnir. And by obviously, I don't mean the content of what he said. I mean the stumbling pronunciation that marked him as a Geat. Whether it was closer to a Dane trying to talk while eating a potato or a Swede with a piece of hay up each nostril, I had not yet decided.

Why did Haldor have no Geatish accent? I was so distracted by the ques-tion, I almost forgot to take the advice the 'Steins had given me.

"We've not yet made ourselves plain, I think," I said. "We haven't come as joiners or hangers-on. This is an independent crew. We are contracted with King Hrolf Kraki and will need to speak with the Danes on his behalf. It is best we would set up camp among them."

Whether by tone or content, my comment cooled the conversation. I was brazen and bold, speaking beyond my station. I did not care, and my tone announced that I did not care. It was time to get between Haldor and his brother. Eyes were fixed on me, no longer in welcome admiration of the arrival of a new crew. That was fine. I would be the rude one and let Ulf mend relationships after.

"Yes, we heard ravens speak of the fall of Ragnvald," said Gardar. "So Hrolf is king now. He must have a lot of faith in you."

"Or he paid them very well," added Sirnir.

"We're here to do the same thing we were going to do absent Hrolf's wishes," I said. "Kill the witch, Alfhild."

"That's a bold boast," said Odd with that grinding tone I recognized from Hrolf. "She's yet been unable to come to Ogmund's aid. Or she's tried, and we've made it difficult for her. We, this entire army."

"An army may take a long time to move," I said. "A single ship can move much faster."

The pale, freckled arm of Arrow-Odd slammed down onto the table. "You think to defeat Ogmund's most powerful ally with a single ship? I already fought two wars when Ogmund had not so many allies, and few walked away when either was done. But here you are, with a single ship. You don't even have enough men to row a dragon ship!"

"Oh, it isn't a dragon ship," I said with far too much cheer in my voice. "It's a *karve*. A good one."

"A transport ship?" said Odd. "What are you going to do, defeat your enemies by bringing them presents?"

"Kraki has a delivery of bone to make," I said. "And Haldor a gift of steel."

"You arrogant shit!" said Odd. "Go off on your own and die then. I have fought Ogmund before and lost better men than you have ever known. I will fight him again if he comes out of those cliffs, and not with some paltry, over-confident force!"

To Odd's raised voice, I raised my own. "We already fought the witch once and won! And that was with her taking us by surprise and unprepared. Overconfident, you say? Share what you know of the witch's location then, and we will put that statement to the test."

"I think we have gotten ahead of ourselves," said Redbeard. "Ulf has not had time to introduce some others of note. Here is Ansgar Styrgrimsson, skald of the *Sea Squirrel*."

Odd stood over the table, splayed fingers digging into it like claws. "So.

The son of the Bear, who became a bear. A troublesome poet, if I ever met one."

"Tempers run hot for such a mild day," said Gardar. "I fear we'll have little left for Ogmund if we waste so much fury on minor things, Odd. I've known Hrolf since he was a boy, and I think he'll be a good king. He would not put his trust in just any crew. If he has sent these men—"

"And women," I added.

Gardar missed only half a beat before nodding and continuing. "If he has sent these men *and women*, he must think very highly of them, paid or not."

"Then there's little more to be said on the subject," said Sirnir. "And we did offer them ale, yet have not delivered. Let us make good on that promise first and come back when tempers and thirsts are quenched."

"Later, then?" proposed Redbeard.

"Later, then," confirmed Odd.

That conversation had not gone as planned. Then again, I never had much of a plan. Asserting our independence was good. Ale was good. Speaking over Ulf might make him angry at me again, and it was possible Haldor and Kraki were both displeased with my combativeness. They would not be so displeased at asserting ourselves, though. Asserting oneself, even inappropriately, was very Norse.

We left to find a suitable place to set up camp. As we walked, I looked up and there was Kraki, staring me down. I braced for a tongue-lashing. The old man rarely did what I expected, however.

"Not bad," he said. "I have not been able to displease such an important man in a long time."

"I'm glad it pleases you," I replied, "because I am not nearly finished."

CHAPTER 37

THE TROUBLE WITH PEACE AND QUIET

HAVING MADE NO NEW FRIEND IN ARROW-ODD AND HAVING NO clear way forward yet, we set up camp near Gardar's people. Redbeard had ale brought to us, and some of the Danes joined to commiserate eventually.

We shared tents, two to four in each. If I had my choice, I would have pitched mine well away from the rest of the army and slept by myself, but neither the positioning nor the privacy were options. Speak of an army to a young man and see if what's in his mind's eye isn't gleaming mail or the smell of the salty sea on the air. The reality is more like a lot of men walking through mud and the smell of sweat and fecal matter, and that's if things are going well. At least I was able to share a tent with Magnus.

Setting up our dozen or so tents in a circle took little time, and then we got a fire going in the middle of our area and found a few logs to sit on. Some men took their run of the place to see what was what, but most of the crew sat tight to discuss things.

As Redbeard had inserted himself so firmly into our situation, I redoubled my attempt to think of where I had seen him before. I stared at the man for a long time but got nowhere. I would have remembered the ostentatious dress and the way he did not compete for attention like a skald so much as he simply held it whenever he spoke. Ketill must have seen me watching because he had added his own thoughts to mine.

"Trust nothing that man says," said the wizard.

"What makes you say so?" I asked.

"Because what he says seems so easy to accept at every turn. Did you never hear the sticky-sweet beguiling in Alfhild's voice?"

I nodded, remembering a certain incident I did not wish to remember. It reminded me of the further complication that Alfhild was pregnant, possibly with my child. Who knew what to do about that, if anything?

"The most dangerous things sound all the sweeter," said Ketill. "Eventually, you may find you recognize it for the trap that it is. Eventually."

"Redbeard's voice is not so sweet," I said. "I do not see the connection."

Ketill looked around, agitated. He wanted to share a drink with us but knew he could not. Not without going farther down a dark place he wished not to revisit. "He is far better at his craft than she," he said, standing up. "It all makes sense and is so obvious that to contradict it seems a vulgar thing. *That* is charm."

"You said you knew that grin. You have met him before?"

Ketill looked back at Redbeard and was more agitated still. "It seems familiar," he said, standing and shaking his head. "I will have a walk around. Do not seek me out."

It was in keeping with the wizard's character that he would say something important but only just on the edge of understanding. I was not about to follow him after being told not to. Some statements were just suggestions, but that almost never applied with wizards.

Redbeard was calling everyone to attention. Apparently, his conversation with Ulf had either stalled or he wanted more of an audience. I looked down into my own cup of ale, still mostly full as others were getting new pours. I decided to stay for at least as long as it took me to drink it.

"Listen here, you," said Redbeard, pointing at Magnus. "There's good reason Odd only attacked Ogmund once he had assembled such a large force. You all, of the *Sea Squirrel*, you think attacking his closest ally by yourselves is a good idea. But you've only fought a small portion of Ogmund's forces."

"We're only looking to kill a small portion of Ogmund's forces," said Magnus. "What is the problem? Why are you and Odd so concerned about what we do? It seems to me you might be helping us, and we'd do you a favor. Then you can just deal with this Ogmund, whatever he is. Sounds like a troll to me."

"Ah," said Redbeard. "You've heard these names, but you don't know the stories, do you? Skald!" he suddenly called over to me. "Did you tell these men nothing of Ogmund Eythjof's Killer?"

"They know the name as well as I do," I said, wondering if this old man was positioning me to be upstaged. "The rest is rumor as far as I know. If you're so keen on telling the story, just tell it!"

Redbeard grinned from ear to ear. "Listen then, and I'll tell you how Ogmund got his beginnings. Long ago, King Harek of Bjarmaland looked for revenge against Arrow-Odd for his raiding there. Odd had very much gotten the best of the Bjarmians and made off with much of their silver. Harek was something of a sorcerer himself—still is, in fact, though he is very old. He found a troll woman living under a waterfall, herself full of ill magic, and he made a child with her. This child he named Ogmund.

"When Ogmund was three years old, they sent him to Finnmark among Sami shamans of the nastiest kind. He mastered their arts after a few years and returned when he was seven, already big and unruly and difficult to control. His looks weren't any better either: His skin was dappled with black and blue spots, and in the place of his forelock, there was a great tussock of moppy hair. So much the better it hid his face, because he was never handsome.

"Then, Harek brought his best acolytes to do their own rituals on him and strengthened him with sorcery. Ogmund is hard against steel for that reason, and no blade will bite him. But that wasn't the last of the enchantments they put on him, knowing it would be hard for him to kill Odd. Trollish as he already was, they made him even more so with sacrifices.

"Ogmund developed his own following in the next few years. Eight men of his own, all sorcerers in their own right and untouchable by iron, and they did as they pleased.

"While this was happening, Eythjof the Berserk caused a great deal of trouble and conquered a lot of land. He forced many lands, including Bjarmaland, to pay him tribute every year. Ogmund joined with Eythjof for reasons I can't explain other than perhaps they were two of a kind. They wreaked havoc wherever they went. Ogmund was ten years old at the time, and he raided with Eythjof for five years. Eythjof took such a liking to him that he exempted Bjarmaland from tribute. He was even about to formally adopt Ogmund as his son.

"Ogmund's response to that was to kill Eythjof while he slept and conceal the murder. Then he took two ships of his own, separating from the rest of Eythjof's men, and went to seek out Arrow-Odd."

I had heard of some of the things Ogmund had done and I wasn't about to sympathize with him. But I wasn't sure Redbeard's story was quite as convincing as he had made it out to be. If Ogmund hadn't been made out to be as strong as he had been with his own set of dangerous followers, I might have wondered if there was something very practical behind his murder of Eythjof.

Besides which, it isn't like King Harek was the forgiving type when it came to vikings taking money from him. I shook my head and drained my horn.

"A little suspicious of that story?" I heard a man say behind me.

He was as tall as I was, but I could tell he was more muscled even though his loose-fitting tunic did much to hide it. It was a friendly face that greeted me, welcome enough except I'd just had my mind on how anything friendly was likely concealing something sinister. Nothing marked him as a man I would recognize, though the bright green of his clothes and the red sash speckled with gold at his waist told me he was not wanting for money. His sleeves were too long for me to see his armrings, assuming he had any. It seemed to me almost anyone in the camp would have them to mark their allegiance to one of the war council members.

"He has a certain way about him," I said.

"Ah," he replied, still smiling. "A good, vague answer for an uncertain interaction! But soon, you'll know me, one way or another. I am Hallfred the Skald. Horsefly, some call me. I heard there was a new skald come into the camp. I haven't marked the wrong man, have I?"

I shook my head. "Well met, Hallfred. I am Ansgar the Skald." Here I paused, intending to give my byname as he had. But what was it? I had so damned many of them at this point I wasn't sure what people were calling me. Usually, they just shouted "Skald!" and that was all. I settled on the one I hoped most to be true. "Ansgar the Lucky some call me. You marked the right man, though I am not sure how," I finished, clasping arms with him.

Hallfred threw back his head and laughed. He looked half-wild then, his expression unmarred by the usual need for stoicism. His loose blond hair shook with each movement. "My lucky friend, you are the most markable skald in this camp! I knew it from a hundred paces away. I could practically hear your thoughts aloud. Some of the men were disinterested and some enthralled, but you were the only one who looked suspicious. Like you could hear truth or lies woven into the music of the story.”

“Can I take it there were both in what I just heard?”

“I cannot say for certain,” said Hallfred, lowering his voice. “But I can tell you the rest of us heard what you heard.”

“The rest of us?” I asked. “Whose man are you, then?”

“Ah, I am with Odd, but that’s not what I mean. By ‘the rest of us,’ I mean our little enclave in camp. An enclave of skalds.”

“I, uh,” I stammered, my heart pounding. I had only ever met a few skalds in my life, always brief encounters. “How many are there?”

“An even dozen of us before you arrived. If you’ll follow me, I will bring you around and introduce you. Then we may be a lucky thirteen!”

I tromped through the mud so fast that I was speeding ahead of the man despite not knowing my way. The wood chopping and water carrying were well underway by that time, and the camp was busy with men and women moving in every direction. It reminded me a little of a busy marketplace, only nothing was being bought and sold.

“Watch out!” said Hallfred as he shoved me at one point. Only I saw nothing to watch out for, and there was definitely a big something he pushed me into. “Damned ravens,” Hallfred muttered, and only then did I see the bird droppings I had nearly walked into.

As I looked up, I took notice of the man I had bumped into when Hallfred shoved me. He turned around and gave me the most frightening sneer I had ever seen. Sharpened white teeth gleamed as his lips peeled away from one another.

“He’s with me,” said Hallfred as he grabbed me by the shoulder and kept me moving forward. He shouted back, “Move out of the thoroughfare if you want to stand still!”

And we were off, Hallfred moving me forward without another word.

“Was that Helgi Pike-Tooth?” I asked.

“Oh, you know him!” said Hallfred.

“Redbeard said we would know him when we saw him, so I suppose I do.”

“True that! He’ll come by later for satisfaction. It would be embarrassing if he did not. But don’t worry, he is a friend to us skalds. He’ll take satisfaction in the form of a verse if you praise him, and then the matter will be done.”

We continued past the busiest parts of the camp, then took a turn away from the war council tent. Piles of rowan branches marked a circular area maybe thirty paces in diameter, and this was our destination. No one lingered nearby or even within ten feet of the circle. Did the skalds here really have such status and respect?

"Over there," said Hallfred as he led me to a break in the branches. "Enter and exit only through here, but come and go as you please. This is our meeting place."

Ten other skalds sat on makeshift benches that triangulated a small central firepit. As I sized them up, I realized Hallfred was right that we skalds had a look about us. It took me a moment to understand why or even what it was.

Not the dress—Hallfred had bright colors whereas two others were in undyed leathers. It was the way they smiled, I realized. They were happy and were pleased to meet another like them.

Two of the skalds were women, one of many new things I had yet to take in. Could a woman be a skald? I didn't see why not, yet I'd never encountered one.

The two women sat next to each other. One wore a light chain shirt. She raised a suggestive eyebrow at me. Many a weapon sat in her belt, and the scars on her hands and face told me she'd seen some fighting. Her partner had a more delicate look to her, but I was not fooled. She was seeing to her horn-bow, a style I'd never yet seen. She took less notice of me.

The other skalds came in all shapes and sizes. Two were quite fat. Some wore chain shirts or thick leather inlaid with iron rings. A few had swords. I realized I had given much more of my interest to the two women than any of the others.

"Welcome to the Grove of Poets. It's not very nice as groves go," said Hallfred as he looked down and kicked mud off one of his boots, "but it does well for our purposes."

"What are your purposes? I mean, I have never even thought this many skalds might be in one place at one time."

"It's a strange thing, that's true. That's why we marked off this space for ourselves. A little place of our own when we might need it individually, a general meeting place to share stories and thoughts. And a remarkable opportunity to keep one another informed. The lords of this place are of two minds for bringing us here. One mind is bent toward having their stories told. But there is a more practical mind as well, and that is to prevent stories from growing too much on their own. Few false stories live more than a few minutes in this camp when we come together."

"So you each tell what you know," I said, considering the implications of this, "and then you all know the same things."

"Then we all know something," said the woman in mail. "And it's a rare thing one of the others doesn't know a thing to confirm or deny it. So we hold our own councils here on hard matters, and after discussing it, Horsefly here has the difficulty of telling Odd something he might not want to hear."

"Not always what he doesn't want to hear," said the woman with the hornbow. "Just most of the time."

"Thank you both. I think. Here is our new friend, Ansgar. Ansgar the Lucky!" Hallfred gestured toward the first woman, "Ansgar, this lovely maiden is Steinvor, and here next to her is the battle-hardened Jorun."

The two women exchanged a knowing look. It was clear just from looking at them that Hallfred had reversed their descriptions. It was Steinvor who was the more battle-hardened. Her large seax, with maybe a two-foot blade, was her most prominent weapon. Two other twin knives about half that length also rested in her belt, and the handle of a fourth blade peeked out from the small of her back.

For all that, it was her burgundy hair that got my attention most of all. It was darker than Fanya's had been, and she wore it shorter, but I gaped in much the same way as when I'd first seen Fanya. I took a deep breath and tried not to get too distracted.

Jorun had a softer look about her and no scars, or at least none visible. She put down the bow and absently tuned a lyre while Hallfred introduced me. She wore a fine blue cloak clasped with a silver brooch. Those clothes were altogether less worn and stained than Steinvor's and were considerably nicer than mine, making me wonder if I had neglected my appearance somewhat in our travels.

"Nice to meet you," I think I stammered, or something else that seemed appropriate. I was trying to sound polite and ended up sounding intimidated.

"A virgin skald," said Steinvor, crossing her arms.

Jorun pursed her lips as I went from pale to pink. Before I could defend my honor (is that really honor? I'm not sure what else to call it), a beating of black wings took my attention away. The raven's noisy descent landed him on the table Steinvor and Jorun sat at.

"He's not a virgin," said Humor. "And apparently, his luck has grown. I almost had him in the main thoroughfare, but that one plucked him away. He has powerful friends, it seems to me."

"'The Powerful!'" said Hallfred. "So much better than 'Horsefly.'"

Humor cocked his head. "Not you! I mean unseen friends. SPIRITS. My gods, the *landvættir* were practically lining up to lick his balls last summer." Humor turned toward Jorun and Steinvor. "Even more than you two are now."

Steinvor leaned in to give the bird a backhanded swat, but he was too quick on his feet. He croaked a little laugh after her hand missed and walked down the table, further out of arm's reach.

"Do you have stories?" asked Humor, addressing Hallfred. "You must! I have good stories to trade, too. His crew killed a sorcerer already. And they were almost eaten by a sea monster. Good trades, good trades!"

"In good time, raven," said Hallfred. "But not for barter. The ravens bring us information freely, and we tell them what we know in the same way, to the benefit of both. But there is no negotiation nor calculation of trade."

Humor flapped his wings and fell over.

"This is Humor," I said. "He's been with our wizard a long time. He likes being dramatic and shitting on people's heads."

"Mostly just yours," said the raven, still keeled over.

"This may not be much," said Hallfred, "but for the skalds, it is a sacred space. We expect no ill manners here. In fact, we don't allow anyone else in the circle, including ravens. Be off now, and go find the others."

"But I did all that work to get those stories!"

"It seems to me you now have many stories the ravens here do not, and so you're likely to be very popular," I said. "And you've missed all the stories they can tell about this war so far; you're likely to get quite a lot out of meeting them."

Humor popped up and flew off.

"That's an odd one, for sure." Hallfred paused and counted heads. "Where is Bjorn? I see he's the only one missing."

"Right here," said a voice behind us. "Pike-Tooth had to bend my ear and then Styrgrim wanted to know all about what he was saying, and then they both had a little to say to each other. You know how it goes. This him?"

The man was no more than my height but bigger in every other way. He had less of the lightness of Hallfred's strides, instead adopting a heavier, more purposeful gait. It would be heavier, as the man was both wider and wearing a chain shirt that stretched down to his knees. A sword hung at his belt in addition to an axe and seax.

"This is he," said Hallfred. "All right, we're all here. Gather round and listen."

"Am I supposed to perform?" I asked.

"I daresay so," said Steinvor, winking at me.

"Stop, stop that right now," said Hallfred. "We don't have time for jokes. Or even introductions of everyone, so excuse me, my lucky friend, this will be a bit one-sided. We will tell you about ourselves later. What we have time for is for you to introduce yourself and tell us about your crew, where you come from, and what you're doing here. There's a rumor of a saucy bunch of heroes coming in with high connections. Some of the lords are grumbling about their lots in this whole business, and if you don't know what it is to live in a camp full of killers speaking ill of each other, well, let me tell you . . ."

"It's dangerous," completed Steinvor.

"Dangerous! That's what I was about to say. Here's a few thousand warriors with no active war to fight. Rumors will be the death of us if Ogmund isn't. So—"

"I understand!" I said. "I know how rumors work. One tells another tells another, and it changes each time. But you all come here to find out what's true and then tell your lords so there is no more rumor. I get it. Listen then: The *Sea Squirrel* is an independent crew. Technically, we are working for King Hrolf, but only insofar as we want the same thing he does. Kraki Bentleg owns the ship and decides where it goes. Haldor Skullsplitter leads on land. Neither man will swear allegiance, not even to our friend, King Hrolf. We did agree to pursue Alfhild the witch, who we heard was an ally of your enemy, Ogmund."

"That's something," said Steinvor. "But who are you, specifically?"

"Ansgar the Skald. Ansgar Styrgrimsson."

"Exactly," said Bjorn. "Questions about that. Questions about favorites."

The skalds all seemed to speak at once, so I couldn't hear anything clearly. I also had no idea who was speaking. That was fine, I would let it die down.

Except in the dying down, I heard someone mention, "A small beard for a big favorite is what they're saying." Whatever goodwill I had walked in with turned icy inside me as I ground my teeth. My insides hardened and pushed out my uncertainty and, with it, any warmth in my tone.

I would answer questions for the time being, but soon, I had my own to ask.

"You have more answers than I," I said. "I haven't seen or heard from my father in over three years. I did not come here to see him. As for favor, we didn't ask for any other than where to find Alfhild. Which I would presume is in Odd's own interest to help us with."

"You're hunting a bear with a wet stick doing that alone," said Hallfred.

"I was a bear last year," I said. "However briefly. Alfhild brought up her army and all the magic she could muster. Surprised us all, too! She fled, panicked and bleeding."

"We heard of the bear thing," said Jorun. "Can you explain it?"

"No," I said, oversimplifying for conciseness, maybe playing a little fast and loose with my interpretation of a valid way to answer.

That was an unsatisfactory answer but spoken in the sort of way that makes it final as well. Hallfred left the subject alone. "There was mention of a sea monster. Surely that you can explain."

I nodded. "We happened upon an island that looked to be an inviting place for us to camp. It was full of heather and would give us high ground to fight from in case of attack. But it wasn't heather, and it wasn't ground at all. It was Lyngbakr, and he tried to eat our ship."

"Where was this?" asked Hallfred.

"Somewhere off the north coast of the Gulf of Suomi."

Some of the skalds shook their heads. "That's far from here," said Hallfred, "and Lyngbakr is Ogmund's pet. We would expect him somewhere in these waters. Are you quite certain it was him?"

"And have you seen him in these waters?" I asked. "Unless you know of another sea monster with heather on its back, then I'm as certain as I can be."

"How did you defeat it?"

"It tried to eat our ship, but our wizard Ketill hardened the ship as if it were stone so it could not bite down. It tried tipping us out into its mouth, and that nearly did us in. But a gift always looks to be repaid, and we sent our most valuable gift, a full barrel of wine, right down its throat."

"That's it?" said Steinvor. "You fed it wine, and it left you alone?"

I shrugged. "It had the choice of accepting that gift in the spirit it was received or ignoring it and getting Haldor's axe through its skull. It chose the former."

Hallfred spoke next. "There's the question of favors from Sirnir," he said. "I'll speak plain as one of Odd's men: Some of his vassal lords are wondering if there isn't overmuch favor being paid to your man Haldor. Sirnir's vassals are wondering if they are about to take a demotion. That's the kind of uncertainty that plays in men's minds when they've not enough to do."

"They're brothers, and that's all I know."

"So surely he might be elevated—"

"Surely nothing. I never heard Haldor mention he even had a brother before hearing Sirnir was in this camp. And when Sirnir invited us to camp near his men, that was declined. I don't know what's between the brothers. If Sirnir's vassal lords want to know, it seems to me the one who they should speak to about it is Sirnir rather than each other."

"So you're just here to find out where to go next?" said Steinvor. "Not to enlist aid to find Alfhild?"

"She is likely in a tower somewhere on the White Sea," I said. "We heard that from a thrall we freed. He'd been taken there, then sold to Varg the Charmer of Gotland. That's where we found him. He helped navigate us up this way before we let him off in his own land. We plan to find the tower, kill the witch, and go back to Lejre," I said. "To a very thankful, very generous king. Why are you all here, is what I might ask."

Quizzical looks all around. "What do you mean, why are we here?" said Bjorn. "We're here to fight and to tell of great deeds and adventures of our times. What could be a better place for new tales than this old conflict between Odd and Ogmund that draws in so many kings and lords?"

"You make my point for me," I said. "It is not the first time it's happened. Twenty years ago, Odd had hundreds of ships at his command, yet only one sailed out with a handful of badly injured men. Styrgrim was one of the few who survived. And even that war was not their first conflict. Just tell me this: How many of Odd's friends and allies has he gotten killed in his pursuit of Ogmund?"

"We all will die," said Bjorn. "All that matters is how."

"Follow who you like, then," I said. "I wear Haldor's armring for loyalty and Hrolf's for friendship, and I've had more from both than they've ever asked of me. If you prefer to serve Odd, that's your business."

Hallfred nodded and looked back to the group when no one else spoke. "Now we've all heard the same thing. Take it back to your people and tell them what you heard." He pivoted from his serious tone in an instant, making his voice higher and twiddling his fingers as he raised his hands in the air. "Now fly, little skalds, fly!" he sang to Steinvor's rolling eyes.

"There is one more matter," I said, myself pivoting in tone, only with that change, I became more serious. "I told you I knew little of Styrgrim, and that's true. But we ran into a man named Vignir on the way here, and he said something about Styrgrim's wife dying in childbirth."

"That's right," said Bjorn, not knowing the quagmire I was shoving him into.

"That's not the story I was told before," I said. "I was told she died of illness when I was very young. So I told you why we came here, for Alfhild only, and that's true. But I am not leaving this camp without finding out why Styrgrim the Bear lied to me."

CHAPTER 38

A TROUBLESOME POET

COULD I HAVE LEFT THAT PART ABOUT STYRGRIM LYING TO ME alone and pursued the question of my mother's death privately? Of course. But I was angry about that small beard comment, and that explains all.

The other skalds passed by me on their way out. I left the grove myself, wandering a bit instead of heading straight back to our campsite. Maybe I would find Ketill and bother him just to aggravate as many powerful men as I could in a short amount of time.

No way could Styrgrim ignore an insult like being called a liar. Maybe he could claim misunderstanding, but that would just look like evasion and, therefore, cowardice. Calling him out in a way that the entire camp would know about guaranteed me an answer. It's just that the answer might involve a fight to the death to defend his honor.

I wandered the camp in that sort of search that sometimes happens when I don't know what I'm looking for. I found myself at the edge of the camp, where boulders lay haphazardly across the soft sand before hitting the steep line of sea cliffs. Here, among the boulders, was where the ravens clustered. They flapped and cawed at my presence. Once Humor saw me, he flew right over.

"Are you making a feast for ravens?" asked Humor. "You have that look sometimes. Like right now!"

"If I am, it will be a small one," I said. "More likely, there will just be a lot of shouting. Maybe some pummeling. But not so bad you will be able to eat my eyes."

"I wish *somebody* would make a feast for ravens," droned Humor. "We're staaaaaaarving!"

"Ogmund had not enough men to give battle? I thought he had been hiring men since at least last year. Halfdan the Toothless mentioned it. Perhaps he stayed in his new hall instead of coming out all this way."

"Don't know about Halfdan, but Ogmund is up there with his eight followers, whoever and whatever they are. Odd's fleet came upon Ogmund's and chased it across the sea. Strange happenings, then. Ogmund lost most of his fleet in a storm and holed up in those cliffs. Odd's army has been sitting here ever since."

"So why not attack them in the cliffs?"

"Can't find a way in," said the raven. Flapping his wings to show off, he added, "Or a way up."

"There must be a way in if Ogmund found one."

Humor shrugged. "That seems obvious, yet they've found nothing. They would like to attribute that to Ogmund's skill as a sorcerer. I think it is mainly due to a bunch of dumb brutes looking for their asses with both hands and coming up empty."

"You're only saying that because it's funnier that way."

"And your point is?"

I left the raven to his machinations, whatever they were. The skalds had left to tell their captains and lords what they had heard. I should do the same for mine instead of wandering aimlessly. I had no trouble finding my way back to our crew's campsite. I still watched the sky for raining bird shit, but none was forthcoming.

Redbeard must have finished his tales because he was gone from our little campsite. My crewmates were all engaged in the various tasks to prepare an evening meal. I found Haldor carrying two giant pails of water.

"I have spoken with the skalds," I said. "All the other skalds in the camp. They wanted to know more of our journey here, among other things. I told them, and they are taking those stories to everyone else to prevent rumor and misunderstanding."

"Good," said Haldor without breaking stride. "That's good."

"I also called Styrgrim the Bear a liar in front of all of them."

Haldor was not the sort to drop what he was carrying in surprise. He was not the sort to make any kind of reaction that would indicate surprise. Surprise, as I've described, would be unmanly. So he made as big a reaction as he was likely to do.

"Hmm," he said. "What wisdom was behind that?"

I folded my arms in front of me. "It seems to me family can be a complicated thing. Relationships exist whether they are acknowledged or not, wanted or not. And we can turn away from them, I suppose. But I have decided to confront my situation and not leave unsaid things to simmer as if in a cooking pot."

There was no rage in Haldor's eye, but it was a hard, long stare nevertheless. He was no fool, and he knew what I was saying. It did not make him like it, but he would not deny the truth of my words. He would need to make his own decision with Sirnir as I had with my father.

"I would have a plainer description from you," said Haldor, "but I think one may be forthcoming from another source."

"An explanation, boy?" shouted Styrgrim as he strode up behind me. His voice broke like thunder over my ears, pushing out much of my recent word courage. With no less volume, even as he got closer to me, he continued, "You'll have your explanation here and now then: I told you your mother died of illness because it was technically true and to spare you the guilt. But it is also true she died giving birth to you. You were the illness! You killed her! Does that explanation satisfy your troublesome tongue?"

"None of this is your fault," said Svipul, who had just walked into my field of vision. She stood off to my right, but I did not mark her appearance because my gaze was locked on Styrgrim. Her voice, though, was not the sweet or playful tone I knew. The change to its gravity told me of worry, maybe even fear.

"I thank you for your prompt if over-pitched explanation," I said back, loud enough for many others to hear but not as desperate for volume as he.

Styrgrim's eyes were nearly level with mine and only inches away. I could smell his breath, at once the familiar warmth I had craved for most of my life and also the hot stench of present-day threat. Though I was taller than him, my height advantage did not make me nearly as large. He was broader, thicker, harder. If he wasn't twice as big, however you wanted to measure it, that was the impression he gave. The black and silver shaggy beard and hair matched his black tunic, the only brightness from him coming from his shining mail shirt and those burning eyes.

"There is no need to egg him on," said Svipul, the tension in her voice increasing.

Where did we go from here? He could not kill me without a great deal of dishonor. He could not beat me without the entirety of our crew falling on him, including Haldor, who was little more than arm's reach away. I had my explanation, though it seemed to me too simple a thing to be the whole truth.

"Of all the foul luck and misfortunes I have suffered," he said, his tone more even now, "I mark you as the greatest taker from me and the least of my rewards. No greater disappointment for all I've given to Odin than a trade of you for my wife. Now you play at adventure and come 'round demanding answers from me?"

"Mark yourself if you want. It wasn't I who put a child in your wife, nor I who ran off scared while others fostered the last bit of her in Midgard. That was you."

"Scared, am I? Boy, you know nothing of fear, but I am a willing teacher." Sweat beaded on his brow and ran down his face. There was no mistaking that for tears.

"Stop this!" shouted Svipul. But the only way I could think of to stop the confrontation was to win, and to win meant either to fight or to force Styrgrim to walk away. The former would be impossible, but the latter I might do in verse. To force Styrgrim to the point of striking me would do it. Either he would stop himself at the last moment or carry through, however foolish that seemed. So I took Styrgrim's hard words and the story I knew from Gudbrand and sent them back at the man like a javelin at his heart.

> "How boldly roars
>   the bear about
> the sorrowful life
>   he's led and why!
> If only that arrow
>   were an inch higher,
> he'd have been a
>   happier man."

Then I smirked at him like the little shit that I was.

Svipul winced at the verse. In a moment, she stepped forward, cupped her hand, and whispered something into Styrgrim's ear. She stepped away after a moment and disappeared outside my field of vision.

"The arrow," said Styrgrim, almost in a whisper. "How do you know about it?"

"Gudbrand Shirtless," I said, and I think I could not have spoken another word at that moment.

Realization dawned on his face. "Of course. How else? You know part of the story, then. So you came looking for more of it."

After several deep breaths, I mastered myself again and spoke. "I came seeking Alfhild the witch. Finding more than that has been by chance."

Slowly, miserably, he nodded back at me and took his time boring into my skull with his eyes. "May you find only what you seek then," he spat. "A wise man's heart is seldom glad." He turned and walked back the way he had come, every eye for two hundred feet following him.

My feet were like lead in my boots as I watched my father walk away. It was not what I had wanted, strange as that may seem from my actions. Never underestimate the need for a father's approval, even when you know it isn't coming. Especially then, perhaps.

Unknown to me, many of the crew had risen and come up close behind me. Close enough to fight, I realized. I had nearly drawn us all into a conflict with the last person in the world we wanted conflict with—a man even Arrow-Odd trod lightly around.

And my Brothers had been ready to back me.

"If it pleases our leader," said Ulf, "I would do the talking for us from now on."

I was still too raw to respond to Ulf's sideways insult. Ulf wasn't exactly wrong in implying I had been a terrible diplomat, inserting myself out of ego and personal interest.

"Go talk to the council for us then," said Haldor. "I will know the skald's mind on something in the meantime."

CHAPTER 39

HALDOR'S STORY

I MOVED ONLY WITH GREAT EFFORT AND FOLLOWED HALDOR to a log. There were not many places to sit and certainly no tables or benches to spare. But someone had found us a few logs to put round our fires, and that was something.

"It is no secret there is tension between my brother and I," he said. "There are issues greater than—" he paused and pointed at where Styrgrim and I had our brief standoff.

Greater than mine, I thought. Which was a bad sign if I ever saw one.

"If I ignore the past, then only I have its burden," he continued. "But if I speak to him about it, as I think he'd have me do and as many of the crew are interested to hear, I think the confrontation will go quite badly. I don't want that. What are your thoughts on this?"

"If it is likely to go as well as things did with my father," I said, "then I don't blame you. Though I doubt there are similar issues between the two of you."

"Similar, no. There is more anger buried there. More than you might imagine. I chose to walk away from it long ago."

"Anger that strong might be buried, but it will walk the surface of its burial mound like a *draugr*. That will be a hard thing to control, and you will confront it eventually," I said, realizing I was speaking of myself.

"Hard to control indeed," said Haldor as he nodded.

"If you won't speak to Sirnir yourself, you could send Ulf. He is plenty willing to speak with lords."

"That's true as far as it goes for diplomacy, but I cannot have Ulf confront my past."

I paused a moment to think. "Confront it now, then," I said.

Haldor shook his head. "I'd be a hair's breadth away from challenging him to a *holmganga*, and that won't help us at all."

"I don't mean that. I mean confront it now, here, with me. Tell me your story. You know me; you know I won't repeat it unless you wish me to. It wouldn't be the first story I swore secrecy of. Some secrets gnaw at your roots like the harts that eat at the world tree's roots. But to me it will be a story, something more I know, and not a burden. And I am only one man."

"Trust in one, never in two," said Haldor.

"Trust in three, and the whole world knows," we said in unison.

Haldor grinned. He had heard the same line from *Hávamál* as I, and those words of wisdom were a comfort in our conversation. "All right, then," he said. "I'll tell you something from when I was very young, and then you'll understand why I don't wish to speak to my brother. I know you like understanding the why of things, and it may do me good to tell one person. I don't wish it to be repeated, however."

"Never? No wisdom in it you wish to be shared?"

Haldor considered this. "Never for trade with a raven. Never for humor or levity. And not amongst the crew unless I have died. But if you come across another in Midgard also interested in the why of things who would gain wisdom from the story, then you may tell it."

"There's nothing more important than the why of things." I nodded, and Haldor began his story.

"Our father was jarl among the Western Geats. He had us fostered by one of his landowners. That was a man named Skygni. Skygni was neither big nor strong nor rich nor with any great quality I could see. Being far bigger and stronger than the other boys, I thought little of Skygni at the time. But Skygni had a way of seeing things before they would happen, and I think that's why our father chose him.

"We had the run of our village, forests, rivers, and plenty of small islands to explore just off the coast. Sometimes, we would row out and explore. Sometimes, we would see who could swim to an island and back faster, and I always won. Especially to Dog Island. Dog Island was our name for the one with old Vifill on it, who kept two dogs we played with. Sometimes, we would camp out with old Vifill and he would tell us frightening stories over the fire. We saw our family often, including our parents and our uncle, Olaf, who kept land just east of our village.

"When I was ten years old and Sirnir twelve, Olaf came into disagreement with our father and killed him. I do not know the details, only that as soon as Skygni heard this, he had us pack clothing and supplies for ourselves, but only as if we were planning to camp for a few nights. I complained, but Skygni said there was no time for an explanation.

"He rowed us out toward Dog Island as fast as he could, and we could tell something was wrong even though Skygni let nothing on. While still in water over our heads, he told us the bad news about our father. Again, I wanted more explanation, but he said there wasn't time. He said our next steps were very important, even if they made no sense. We were to jump off the boat and make our next decisions as we thought best.

"We did that, and Skygni rowed away.

"The obvious choice was to swim the rest of the way to Dog Island and find Vifill so we could dry off. His dogs leaped all around us, thinking it was time to play, but we were in no mood. The old man took us in warmly and asked why we'd come into his house, dripping wet. We told him what Skygni had said. Vifill said it was ill news about our father but that Skygni had done the right things.

"Olaf was power-hungry, he told us, and that meant he wanted to have what our father had. Sirnir understood this right away, but I took longer to come around. Vifill explained that our uncle meant to have our lives so we could not claim any inheritance.

"But that was also why Skygni had to make such a strange decision in dropping us in the water. He was our father's retainer, so he would now owe loyalty to Olaf. By taking us away and getting back quickly, he could hide us and give no indication where we had gone. By dumping us in the water, he could honestly say he didn't know where we were.

"Sirnir thought it was only a matter of time before our uncle searched us out, but Vifill said we would not need to worry. He may not look like much, he said, but he had a good deal of lore he could call up when the need arose. One thing he would need to do himself was rename us Hopp and Ho, the same names as his dogs. That way he could introduce his dogs to any visitor.

If asked if he'd seen anyone else, he could always say he had seen only Hopp and Ho.

"So we stayed with Vifill for the better part of a year and made the best of it we could. Sometimes, he would tell us to hide. I couldn't see anything to hide from, but he said he could feel it when there were eyes on his island. I didn't know it at the time, but Olaf had hired wizards to search for us, and they could see things from afar.

"Vifill always made his lore seem trifling to us as if he were just a silly old man who knew a few tricks. But I saw him in a trance once. His clothes were soaked through, and his eyes had gone pale white while he chanted. I heard him, and the strength in his voice set my hair on edge, it was so overwhelming. I think it was no small thing to keep those far-seeing gazes turned away. As gentle as Vifill was with us, I could see he had a lot of power behind that gentleness. That is what I remember most about him.

"Olaf had his suspicions despite all our efforts. Three times, he came out to the island and questioned old Vifill. The old man would seem to shout commands to his dogs when they were really commands for where we should hide. Three times out and three times frustrated, Olaf left, and we wondered if he had given up.

"Sirnir asked to learn some of Vifill's lore, which he did. To me, it was nothing I wanted to deal with. Spirits and unseen things and forces operating in secret reminded me of my father being killed because that had also been this thing that happened in secret. I stuck to hard work and got even bigger and stronger, but Sirnir learned some of Vifill's art. I learned something as well, but not like Sirnir. I heard the voices on the island, the way they spoke with the wind and the trees.

"One day, an old thrall came rowing to shore and we hid near the house. He came right in to talk to Vifill and said, 'Skygni thinks it's time for Hopp and Ho to join the pack because there are plenty of other dogs who would prefer their company.' Then the man left. Vifill explained he thought this meant it was about time for us to return and attack our uncle, for which Skygni had secured some aid.

"I was excited to go back and avenge our father. We had lost him, but we still had each other. And we had those loyal to my father's memory. It buoyed me to know that even in bad times, there were people you could rely on for help. I swore to be loyal like they were and gentle in my strength like Vifill.

"My brother was the greater thinker between the two of us, and he suggested we take both boats from the island instead of one. I wanted to return together, but Sirnir cautioned me against this. Better to take two boats and different courses. In case the plan was found out and something went wrong for one, the other might still carry on. I could not argue with that, though I liked it less.

"Sirnir shoved me off first and bade me take a more northerly route. There was a heavy fog and it folded in around me thick as wool. I thought this might be good as far as hiding my approach. Then I heard it, the chanting. It was Sirnir's voice, and he was casting a spell. Soon there was shouting, and that was Vifill, and then he was chanting.

"Out across the water, I heard Vifill call out to me. 'Row!' he shouted. 'Row until you can row no more!'

"I could already row a long way, easily to the mainland and back many times over. But though I rowed for hours and hours without cease, I reached no land. There was nothing I could see in the fog, but I knew this could not be natural. I rowed until my hands bled, and then rowed some more. Sirnir had learned much—too much, maybe—and had sent me into a between-place. I did not know that then, only that nothing was right.

"I think Vifill must have added a counterspell on that shore. Too late to bring me back, but enough to see me through to safety. As long as I kept rowing.

"Sleep took me at some point. I woke to my little boat scraping the bottom of a rocky beach, a light coat of snow upon the sand further in. My hands ached and were crusty with dried blood and splinters. The paddles of my oars were worn down to nibs. I was in no brave state as I got out, but at least I had some things with me: My clothes and a small handaxe and knife, some food and water. There was a house nearby. Smoke came out of a smoke hole at the top. The next thing to do might be obvious to you, but I was full of fear and suspicion.

"What if I had been wrong that even in bad times, one might find good people to rely on? I had thought that of my brother, but he sent me away. Could Vifill have helped him? Could his command to row have been what sent me so far from anything I knew? I had been wrong about such a basic thing. Maybe I had no idea how the world was.

"I was dressed warmly enough, but I shivered and knew I needed shelter. Knocking on that door was the hardest thing I ever did.

"The family gave me hospitality. They talked funny and thought the same of me because I had rowed through all that fog and been dumped all the way in Halogaland. I'm not sure if they believed my story, but it was also hard for them to square how else I would be so far from home. They were a good family, though, and not apt to turn away a stranger willing to put in some work.

"They gave me food and shelter. It was a long time before I grew to trust them. The injury from my brother had cut me deeper than a sword wound, though he had not touched me at all.

"But there, I learned to hunt seal and whale and scale mountains like a *jǫtunn*, and eventually, I called them family.

"You're wondering why I did not return to kill Sirnir, I think. Well, that was on my mind every day for years. It would have been a dishonorable thing to kill one's own brother, but such was his betrayal that I thought it only fitting for him. I was caught between vengeance and moving on from it for a long time. It was a visit from a *vǫlva* that made my decision. She said the weave of my fate could take on one of two patterns.

"In one, she said I would be a king. I would see my brother again and become more powerful than he, though I would have little responsibility. I would live a long life as long as I stayed indoors most of the time and only faced a challenge when I was favored to win. It would be a comfortable life.

"In the other weave, I would see my brother again and have his power lorded over me. I would have the merest of titles with the greatest responsibility to shoulder. I would not live a long life, and it would be hard and uncomfortable. But as long as I never challenged a lesser opponent, never broke my word, and let Sirnir keep his life, I would never again be brotherless in any sense of the word.

"It was then that many of Skygni's lessons came back to me. Things he said that had not been in the form of lessons, but now I understood them. I told the *vǫlva* that she was wrong—my life could not have two different weaves. I remembered Skygni and Vifill, and what they had taught me about being a *drengr*. And that was the only way I knew how to be.

"I met Kraki Bentleg soon after.

"My brother wishes to make amends. I want for no amends. His voice threatens to free my axe arm of its senses and hew him down. I don't want that either."

The huge man shifted in his seat. He had come to an end point but wasn't sure how to finish the story. Which made sense since his story was not finished.

"Sirnir used you as a sort of sacrifice," I said. "Not to the gods, but all the same. He betrayed your trust in order to see his own gains realized. That is why you have the rule against sacrifice."

Haldor nodded. "There is nothing worse than betrayal," he said, gravel in his voice.

Here was Haldor Skullsplitter, the word-fame seeker. Always intent on making a name for himself. Or so I had always thought and had always been wrong about.

"You must let your brother keep his life for your own sake. But you owe him nothing and can't get anything of value for yourself. I was wrong: You should not confront him."

Haldor grinned. "Says the man doing all the confrontation!"

I put my hands up. "And where has that got me? Well, at least confronting my father."

"Yes, my question to you is that exactly." He was serious.

"Nowhere, as far as I can tell," I said. "I joined the crew in part to prove myself to him. But that's a fool's errand, I can see now. I will never prove myself."

"Never to Styrgrim, maybe, but you are our Brother. You've already proven yourself to us, otherwise you wouldn't wear the armring."

I nodded heavily. "We need to kill that witch and get out of this place as quickly as possible."

So, of course, it wouldn't go like that whatsoever, would it?

CHAPTER 40

THE SOLUTION TO IDLE HANDS

ARROW-ODD INVITED OUR CREW TO JOIN HIS COUNCIL FOR THE evening meal. It turned out the evening meal was to begin very early that day. It was much more polite than demanding our presence to answer questions. Maybe Odd was smarter than I gave him credit for.

Hallfred came to deliver that invitation. He used the gentlest and most complimentary words to describe our presence, and that was how I knew I had pissed Odd off. Our days in that camp were numbered, and surely that number could be counted on one hand.

Ulf responded about how honored we would be to share a table with Odd. Hallfred grinned, and when Ulf wasn't looking, he winked at me. The Horsefly was a canny skald. I hoped I would have a chance to learn what I could from him later. Or failing that, at least I would eat a lot of Odd's best food.

We arrived at Odd's council area to generous pours of ale for all of us, with plenty more behind. Three large cauldrons hung over cooking embers. Two of Odd's men slid rich chunks of whale meat into the bubbling stews. Drink was plentiful, but I was looking forward to the food.

After sitting down and exchanging some pleasantries, we found that Vignir had returned to camp. "What puny little people you all are!" he shouted in jest. "It's no wonder the camp has been here so long. Feeding an army must be easy when all its warriors can eat two or three grains a day and be satisfied. I have a greater hunger."

"Is one of those all for you, then?" I asked, pointing to the three cauldrons.

"You mean is one of them for all the rest of you?" asked Vignir. "Maybe I will leave you half of one so you can fatten up your skinny bones."

Though the lords of that council all sat at one long table, Vignir had made his way there slowly. He had traded jibes with many a man who walked with him but who were not important enough to join him at Arrow-Odd's table. He knew their names and joked about where they were from. Men with sullen faces earlier in the day drank and laughed at Vignir's jokes. He was a popular man, and they were sad to see him leave their company.

"I think you know my son," said Odd when he finally got a word of introduction in. "It seems he had good information from you."

And with that, the feast we were expecting was turning into a political game. Odd was implying we had been less forthright with him than with his son. I wasn't going to have any of that.

"He asked good questions," I blurted out before being nearly tackled by the 'Steins.

"Shut up, you!" hissed Utstein.

"You want fresh stew for dinner or rotten shark?" demanded Innstein.

The brothers shook their heads, and I was duly chastised. Pride was worth defending, but sometimes good food and drink were worth enduring a few verbal barbs. Better to let Ulf speak for us.

"We nearly came to blows with Vignir," said Ulf, eyeing both me and my father. "But cooler heads prevailed."

Oh, spare me.

"My skalds possess cool heads," growled Odd. "I think they made the best effort, in fact. They even included one detail that Vignir wasn't aware of when you spoke to him. I don't like to make a man eat and talk at the same time, and that's why I thought it best for you to come early. I am very interested in this sea monster you encountered."

Odd sat at the head of the table with Vignir to his right and Redbeard to his left. Gardar and Sirnir sat across from each other, and then came Styrgrim and Hallfred on either side. There was no chance that setup happened at random—those men knew their seats well. Styrgrim nodded to Bjorn, who sat next to him. So Odd's skald had a regular place there, but my father's skald was not always included. *That's good to know,* I thought, though I wasn't certain why.

Our crew came after Odd's men and only at his bidding: Haldor and Kraki, Ulf and Ketill, other familiar names to you, and then the rest of our crew whose names I have forgotten or not noted in the first place. It was that last group Ulf directed me to sit with. I was about to protest, especially since it was Ulf. But the 'Steins dragged me with them over into the middle of nowhere, flanking me on the bench in case I got any ideas.

This conversation was for cool heads, and the less I was involved, the hotter my head became. I drained my first cup of ale in a few gulps and had it refilled. Heels dug into both my feet at once, and I got the message.

"How do you think we feel about it?" said Innstein.

"We're two of the heroes of that sea monster story, but here we are at the ass end of the table," said Utstein.

"But for whale stew, I have no issues."

"Nor I."

"At least let me listen, then," I said. "I want to hear what they're saying."

Wordless, the brothers acquiesced, and I heard our future unfolding in the conversation that followed.

"Redbeard tells me this sea monster you ran into was likely sent by Ogmund," said Odd. "I find that a strange thing, given he has been stuck in those cliffs for weeks now."

"It seems obvious to me," said Redbeard. "Ogmund may have sent it, but Alfhild knows many of his tricks. She could have sent Lyngbakr against enemies she failed to kill last year. What I don't understand is how Lyngbakr found them."

"It did not find us," said Ketill. "We found it. Ran the ship right onto its back."

"And from where did Alfhild send it?" asked Ulf. "We heard of a tower on an island where she kept prisoners and sold some as thralls. These cliffs are no tower, however."

"What of a tower?" asked Odd. "Where did you hear this?"

"A Karelian we freed on Gotland spoke of it," said Ulf. "Said he saw the witch herself. He was taken there and sold later. An island, he said, hidden in the mist of the White Sea."

"That could be a lot of places," said Styrgrim. "This sea is lousy for weather."

"No, it can't," said Vignir, and all eyes turned to him. "Well, if I had known what you were looking for, I would have said something. You didn't mention the mist."

"You mean you know where this island is?" asked Ulf.

"I've never seen it if that's what you mean. But we all know that part of the White Sea in Risaland. We don't go there any more than we run our ships onto the backs of obvious sea monsters. Really, who ever heard of a random island sitting around with nothing but heather growing on it?"

"Are you sure of this?" asked Gardar.

"He knew where to find Ogmund," said Sirnir.

"You strange little people!" said Vignir, shaking his head. "I guess you just don't frequent the same lands. Or maybe your ships are no good. My uncle taught me to fish, and he made sure I didn't go near there. There's sorcery afoot there, and all I know of it is that nobody on that island wants visitors."

"So this tower cannot be reached?" asked Odd.

Vignir shrugged. "It must be reachable if the witch is there. Maybe it's her magic that hides it."

"Where is this tower, then?" asked Odd.

"Right out in the middle of the sea," said Vignir. "Exactly where you wouldn't want to take any of your ships. Right about where Ogmund's fleet was headed when that storm came about and destroyed it. If the storm hadn't been there, I would have told you to go nowhere near there. But as it was, we were avoiding the place anyway."

"So Ogmund's most powerful ally is able to send a sea monster against her enemies from that place," said Odd. "And it must have some importance. Why take a thrall all the way out there only to sell him?"

"He was not the only one," said Ulf. "He told us others were taken, but not all were sold."

"And you trust this man's word?"

"Well, strictly speaking," said Ulf, "I did not understand a word he spoke. All we had to go on was what our skald translated for us."

Everyone looked at me just as I was downing a huge gulp of ale. Innstein poked me in the ribs, and Utstein chuckled at my startling.

Odd had to raise his voice to address me so far down the table. "Only you could speak to this man?"

"That's right," I said. "He was a Karelian. It took some time to figure out his language."

"Figure it out," said Odd, slapping the table. "And if you misunderstood something in your 'figuring it out,' what then?"

Then you can sit in your camp and have people call you Odd the Smug!

"I don't know," I said. "Maybe it is not Alfhild. Maybe when he described her as beautiful and richly dressed, he meant ugly and dressed in rags. Maybe when he said the woman had scars on her cheek, he meant scars on her ass. Maybe when he said queen, he meant trollwife. Maybe when he said he was taken prisoner, he meant he was taken as a concubine. Maybe there is a big, ugly troll woman in the tower waiting to seduce young, virile men who sail too close to her tower. What then?"

"In that case, we should investigate immediately!" shouted Vignir.

Laughing at Vignir's jest was cut short by a wave of Odd's hand. "This place is how far from here?"

"Day and a half by sea, unless there's a good deal of hot air," said Vignir. He locked his fingers behind his head, taking a relaxed pose. "Which there rarely is around these parts."

One of the veins on Odd's forehead throbbed beneath his gold-embroidered headband. It seemed to be in time with Vignir speaking.

"That's where we're going, then," said Kraki to no one in particular. "Tomorrow at dawn."

"A fine idea," said Odd. He must have been pleased to know the troublesome crew of the *Sea Squirrel* would be out of his camp so soon.

"I should come with you," said Vignir.

The vein on Odd's forehead bulged again. "Afraid to stay here in case Ogmund and his louts come at us?" he said.

Vignir was no longer relaxed at that. "It seems to me finding this tower and its witch are a better use of my time than waiting."

"That's a fine thing," said Odd, his turn to be droll. "There's one great sorcerer here and eight of his followers with him. No one could blame you for going after a smaller threat in this singular witch."

Vignir sat up and stared at his father, one huge fist on the table. "I think that's a jest you'll come to regret," he said. "But I will stay here since you are so in need."

The table became silent as father and son returned icy glares. After a long and tense moment, Styrgrim noisily drained his cup and slammed it onto the table, the only one willing to break the silence. "Odd and Vignir will fight Ogmund and his eight lackeys," he said. "But we don't want to be surprised by a witch and her minions. It makes sense to send a man who knows this sea with this crew. How about you, Redbeard? You've been around. What do you think of being their guide?"

"Even if some won't take my advice," said Redbeard, "the camp here is where my advice is given."

"Advice. So much advice," said Styrgrim. He rose up all of a sudden, shouting, "I piss on your advice! Better counsel than his own, a man can't keep."

"And what counsel have you for us then, Styrgrim the Bear?" said Odd. The vein in his forehead was no longer pulsing. It looked like it had created a permanent dent on the outside of his skin.

"For you? Nothing! Look to your own mind if you will, or not. I have had enough of waiting. If the witch sits in the tower, I will relieve her boredom. Make a sacrifice to Odin, I say, and then go off to war. A real war."

"I won't spare any ships for this," said Odd. "Not when victory is so close here. And if I haven't made it clear, I think it's a fool's errand. We have the enemy cornered. Risking ships and good warriors to weather and sorcery is pointless."

"I have few ships under my command. The great majority would remain here."

"Few or many, you swore your ships under my command when you joined this council," said Odd. "My decision is final unless you want to take off your armring and leave it on this table."

Odd was under stress from what Vignir had said and, frankly, from a mouthy skald on a ship with no loyalty to him. His aggravation built and built. Though my father had taken little part in the conversation, I could tell he chafed at every new sentence. Tension between our crew and Odd had become tension between Odd and Styrgrim, and neither man would back down. Would my father really break away from Odd, the hero of a legend he had so attached his own identity to?

I saw a way out that I did not like at all. But my dislike was not dangerous. Not yet, at least.

"He could join our crew," I said. "Just for this mission, I mean. And then return to the camp."

Silence again. Haldor took a drink of ale with practiced slowness and then wiped his beard. "He would need to swear to uphold our rules. That means no sacrifices."

"And he would need to row like the rest," added Kraki.

Styrgrim blanched. A warrior who had become famous as a sea king in his own right reduced to rowing on another man's ship. Or reduced to a man with no armring. Or a man sitting idle in a war camp with no war in sight. I knew his choice before he did.

"Tell me these rules then," he said. "A man who can't row his way to a fight might as well be dead already."

Chapter 41

Freely Offered

We did eventually consume something other than ale that evening with Odd's council. The stew was rich and meaty. I forced some down despite the anxiety filling my belly. If you've never been the son of a famous warrior, maybe it's difficult to understand my not very coherent actions in the camp. I was afraid of what he would think about me, yet eager to push him to the brink of homicidal rage. I was dismissive and pissed off at him but suggested he come with us. Then, getting what I suggested, I was so anxious about it that I could hardly eat.

Sounds about right.

Family is complicated, especially when you don't fully understand your own self. To change my story and make it seem like I did nothing contradictory or even downright stupid in that camp would be a lie.

I took my leave of that meal early, grabbing a bowl of stew and muttering something about Hemming deserving no less than we did. He was still with the *Sea Squirrel*, ostensibly to guard it but mostly to keep him away from the crush of people. Too many people in one place was something the man could not tolerate for long, and this gave him an excuse to be alone.

I arrived late, but late mattered little to the light that hardly dimmed so far north. Hemming was sharpening one of his many knives when I arrived at the ship. I'm not sure what else the man did to pass the time.

For all the gold I've seen jarls give in friendship, I think I've never seen a gift received as warmly as that bowl of stew. It meant little to me and was almost an afterthought. I still didn't like Hemming much, but he was a Brother and someone should have seen to him. I told him I thought he should share in the same food we were getting. He started to say something in response, choked up, and played it off as a cough as he took the bowl. I did not linger.

Hemming's reaction puzzled me at first. Why so thankful for a bowl of stew? He was not known for his great appetite.

There is wisdom about gifts everyone knows, and that is about gifts always seeking a return. Only in the cracks in reality do you find the world's magic. I didn't realize it at the time, but one of those cracks holds another secret about gifts: A gift seeking no return can sometimes have a power greater than any trade or contract.

I headed back to the center of the camp, hoping some of the skalds would be at their meeting place—not for any information in particular. I suppose I was hoping to figure out what I was looking for.

Steinvor and Jorun were there. The women sat across from each other at the same table, discussing something I could not hear. Jorun looked up and smiled. "Look who is here!" she said. "With a mouth like that, you must be lucky if you are still alive. Come join us."

Steinvor sharpened her long seax, almost as long as a sword. But it was not the way I had seen Hromund or Beigadh do it. They obsessed over their fighting kits with the practiced care of long-experienced professionals. Steinvor's long, slow strokes against the whetstone told of a woman whose mind was elsewhere. This was a distraction for her.

"I meant no interruption," I lied.

"None at all!" Jorun replied in kind. "It is good that you're here, so I need not leave a friend alone." She strummed her lyre once more, now very much in tune, and took it with her as she left.

Steinvor gave me a half grin and a nod that said she didn't mind the interruption.

"So, what is it you've gotten Bjorn into?" she asked. "You talked about towers and witches and whatnot, and now he's bound for some invisible place on this freezing sea."

"Should be a good story," I said, shrugging. "Why must Bjorn go? Only Styrgrim swore himself that I heard."

She shrugged. "You may have noticed the many conflicts in Styrgrim.

Bjorn is as patient a fighter as Styrgrim is wild. He is a good balancing influence in an unfamiliar situation, and he is quite loyal to your father."

"I thought he might need to stay as Styrgrim's stand-in here."

"Styrgrim's second is Helgi Pike-Tooth."

"That freak is his second in command?"

"Don't be so quick to judge!" she snapped back. "Helgi is a strong leader and crafty. His teeth are a great distraction from that. I would follow him too if I were not already sworn to Gardar."

"Hmph," I said. I sat down and crossed my arms. "I have given enough thought to my father for one day already."

"As you like," she said, laying her seax and whetstone on the table. She smiled and moved closer to me on the bench. "To what would you rather give thoughts instead?"

All rational thoughts fled me as one overwhelming new thought occurred. Had Steinvor been flirting with me before? Had I just been too dense to notice, or was there really no outward sign?

I stammered some wordless sounds, trying to sound deep in profound thought. Certainly, I was not taking notice of trivial things like the whiteness of Steinvor's neck or the way her green eyes flickered in the firelight. And if locks of that burgundy hair fell from her neck like the richest satin, that was something far outside my interest. Obviously.

"A balancing influence?" I said, more asking than saying.

She pursed her lips and suppressed a smile as I looked her in the eye. I have traded looks with some powerful sorcerers in my time. Looks from Huld and Alfhild that bored into me. Looks from Ketill that burned. And others I haven't told of in this saga. But I never felt as if my mind's voice was being heard so easily as when Steinvor read me like a runestone in that one look.

"That's why you're here, of course!" she said, her expression now more casual and less lustful. "Here in this circle. Because though you know your crew and you don't know us, we think closer to how you think. Certainly closer than your father thinks. Sometimes, it is good to seek out what you have in common."

"Is that what you were doing with Jorun just now?"

She tossed her head back in thought, hair flowing like waves behind her. There was a playfulness about her manner, one informed with scars and weapons, no doubt. I had a brief flash of the combination of lean muscle and female curves her armor must be hiding. Everything about the way that woman moved set my mind on fire.

"Something like that," she said. "Actually, no. Sometimes it is easier to talk to another woman."

"What did you discuss?" I asked. "I mean to say, I am curious."

"Ah!" she said, her teeth gleaming white. "We talked a little about music and breaking in new lyre strings. But that was not the deeper part of the conversation. I will tell you what we talked more about if you tell me why you think we talked about it."

"What do I need to bet?"

"Bet?" she said. "This is no money matter!"

"Oh," I said. "Betting is a habit on my ship. Please continue."

"We spoke about Arrow-Odd and Ogmund. You know the story of the beginning of their feud?"

I nodded. "Ogmund slew one of Odd's friends, and Odd vowed revenge."

"Aha," she said with obvious disappointment. "And if that is the whole of the story, do you at least know his friend's name?"

I did not. It was a long time ago, as Odd was very old. Hundreds of years old, some said, as the legendary heroes are sometimes unnaturally long-lived. "Was he even real?" I asked. "Stories change over such long periods."

"I think he was very much real," said Steinvor. "That was his sworn brother, Thord Prow-Gleam."

"I thought Hjalmar the Brave was Odd's sworn brother," I said. "I mean until he was killed in battle from Tyrfing's wounds."

"It's true they were sworn brothers," she said, "but Hjalmar's end from that malicious sword came later. Thord fought alongside Odd for a long time, including against Ogmund Tussock in their first meeting. You know Odd and Thord and Hjalmar were the only survivors on their side? It's likely Odd only survived that encounter because of his shirt—the one that prevents him from being bitten by iron. And Ogmund and his eight followers—or whatever you'd call them—they were the only ones left living on his side. So Odd and Ogmund agreed it had been a draw and went their separate ways."

"That doesn't seem very feud-inducing."

"It was a few days later that the feud began. Odd and Hjalmar were scouting an island, and when they came back, they found Thord was gone. They found his body stuck in a cleft in a hillside. A spear was stuck through one armpit and came out the other, and they knew it had to be Ogmund's work."

"It was murder, then," I said. "The stuck body and strange wounding don't sound at all like combat."

Killing happened all the time in my world. If you declared yourself, it was just killing, and that was fine. Maybe you had to pay weregild, but that was something to be worked out. Murder was different—something done in secret, a vile act.

"Exactly," said Steinvor. "And so: Why were we discussing it?"

I had gotten lost in the story and forgotten where it was leading. Now that we had arrived, I had no idea. "That is why Odd is so focused on Ogmund as an enemy?" I said. "Oh! So Odd has many reasons to kill Ogmund, and he would probably want to kill all of Ogmund's allies himself for satisfaction. That would mean our presence here is disruptive to his plan for revenge. Is that it?"

Steinvor swayed her head from side to side. "Well, it was a good try."

"Did I miss the mark?"

"You're a man. You shot at a different target."

"Oh." I cast my eyes downward without intending to. As soon as I did, I straightened up, not wanting to give away the depth of my disappointment at being wrong about that question.

"I did not mean it that way," said Steinvor, some of her confidence replaced by what sounded like disappointment in her own mannerisms. She put a gentle hand on my back. "We were not talking about what a legend might do, Arrow-Odd, Odd the Traveler. We were talking about Odd the man."

"What of him?" I shrugged, ill at ease and yet excited at the same time. "He may be a man, but he is long-lived. If the legends are true, he can call up the wind whenever he needs to sail, and that shirt does more than keep him from being bitten by iron."

"Now we're closer. Listen." She leaned in as if in conspiracy. "He had that shirt from a witch in Ireland. He nearly killed her after Asmund, his first sworn brother, died there. But the shirt she offered was too good not to accept, so he spared her. Ended up marrying her, in fact, not that he paid her much attention after the fact. That shirt has kept him alive longer than he would have been otherwise. It's what he wore to protect him in the first battle against Ogmund when he saw twenty ships worth of his men killed. Soon after that battle, Ogmund murdered Thord.

"Not long after, Odd had two ships finally manned again. And then Angantyr the Berserk and his brothers killed every man aboard, including Hjalmar.

"And Odd survived again, regretting that if only he had fought Angantyr himself, Hjalmar's life would not have been wasted. Have you never felt the weight of regret hanging from your neck?"

"I might know something about that." My gaze and voice trailed off as I considered how I might have saved Fanya.

"Odd says he pursues Ogmund for the murder of Thord. That is the legend speaking, and I wonder if he can separate the legend from the man anymore. We were talking about the source of Odd's bitterness and how it is his shirt."

"His shirt? It sounds like an excellent thing to have."

"Initially, yes. And then consider that in a battle you are routed in, you will survive, but you will see all your close friends die. Again and again, Odd has seen that happen. He's lived a long time and suffered that many more tragedies than the rest of us because his shirt has kept him alive. But in keeping him alive, it has deprived him of his friends and kept him lonely. Now, he channels all his misfortunes into his hatred for Ogmund. Ogmund had nothing to do with most of Odd's misfortunes; they were due to his own choices. Even Ogmund himself is a result of Odd's choices. But Odd is a man, and men are not apt to find a better way past their own guilt than focusing on revenge. It won't alleviate the guilt he has for his sworn brothers."

"I think you are wrong about revenge," I said, shaking my head.

"I have touched a nerve. I did not mean to."

"I should go," I said, rising from my seat. "I am expected."

"You need not, though!" she said. "You defy expectations. Unlike Odd. Unlike Styrgrim. If you did not, I would never have opened my thoughts to you."

A bitter laugh boiled up in me. "So much for defying expectations," I said. "The greatest defiance of expectations I ever made had me as a bear, and even so, I was a failure."

"Here is a place we can speak of those things freely. Can that be said about where you are expected?"

I searched her face. There was no play or flirt to it. I had fought and lost, and I stared into the eyes of someone who had done the same. Understanding is what I saw there, and it bade me to sit back down.

Steinvor edged closer to me. We sat shoulder to shoulder. For a long time, we just sat there in silence in the night-long twilight. I closed my eyes for a few breaths and tried to make my mind go blank. It would not. Even if Steinvor had not physically been next to me, knowing she understood something about me gave me a feeling I had little experience with.

There is nothing quite like acceptance.

"A friend told me to remember that Odd was not a good person," I said after a while. "Not as bad as Ogmund, but not a good person."

"As long as he lets the world define who he should be as a man, he will be such," she said. "His son seems a good influence. Maybe that will help. But he has failed to kill Ogmund before, and if he fails again, I fear he'll seek other means."

"Other means than an army? Like what?"

Steinvor took a deep breath. "Understand this is only speculation. But though Ogmund is hard against steel, just like Odd is with that shirt, I think there are some things they would not be able to withstand. If he fails here, I think Odd might pursue some desperate measures. Maybe even abandon his independence and sacrifice to the gods after all. Certainly, Styrgrim would support that."

"Strike a deal with the gods to get what, though?"

Steinvor shrugged. "To have Odin point his spear? There would be a great cost if he asked for that."

"Goat's breath and cat piss, he'd be insane!" I shook my head.

Yet, Odd wouldn't be the first fool to make a foolish deal with Odin. What victories he granted were always cut short. Odin answered one such call and gave his favorite warrior the sword, Gram. Then, he broke it in the midst of battle to make sure his 'favorite' warrior died. Odin is fickle and capricious, but there has rarely been a shortage of men of Midgard desperate enough to seek out that fickleness.

Desperate like a man who had already spent a lifetime seeking revenge.

"I see your point," I continued. "Odd might be driven to the edge of his sanity by something like that. What to do about it, then? I am still going after Alfhild. You are still here until Odd sees his fight with Ogmund through."

"So long as I am Gardar's skald, that's true. And it is as I knew it would be. I did not join to compose poetry about adventures only but to live them, and here I am. You are right not to stay in camp, though. Odd has a history of getting his armies killed."

"Please don't die," I said, turning to her suddenly. It was only three words, but I was out of breath.

"Nor you," she said with a smile.

"I think I will come out alive. I am a lucky skald, after all."

Steinvor hummed a pleasant sound and put her arm around me. She let her head rest on my shoulder, and I hugged her to me. "Ansgar the Lucky. That is a good name," she said. "Better than mine. 'The Slim One' they call me. Or Gardar does. He already had two skalds when he took me on. You saw Gizur and Kormak but didn't meet them. They are both fat! Gardar said he couldn't afford another skald who ate and drank so much, but he would take on 'the slim one,' pointing at me."

"'The Slim One' could be worse. It hardly describes you, though."

"Oh," she said. "Have I gotten fat myself?"

"No, no," I said. "I only meant it barely scratched the surface. There's nothing in it to convey your wisdom or beauty. It's like naming Hallfred 'Pretty Beard' or—"

I couldn't say anything else because she had pulled my face into hers.

We kissed long and deep, deeper than I thought possible. I ran my fingers through that thick, soft hair and pulled her close. The smell of her hair sent my heart racing even faster than it already was. After a minute or ten, we pulled only inches away, both breathless. I cupped her cheek in my hand as we stared into each other's eyes.

There were no more words necessary that night as she led me back to her tent. It was not my first time with a woman, yet very much the first time experiencing anything like that. You can fill in the details with your imagination. I'll only say that I hope you find such an experience yourself at least once before you die. I was happier in those moments before sleep than I may have ever been.

The moments after sleep took me, however, were a different story altogether.

CHAPTER 42

THE BRIDGE TO HEL

THE NIGHTMARE FLOATED THROUGH THE TENT LIKE LIVING smoke and grabbed my ankle in its toothless maw. Somehow, there was enough pressure to hold me steady without breaking the skin. Steinvor had been asleep beside me the moment before, but as I looked over, she was gone. The thing dragged me out of the tent and into the mist where the camp should have been, flying into gray nothingness.

I had felt this happen before. It had been more than a year since then. A year and a lifetime of experiences. And just like the last time, it felt as if it were real. Only this time, I did not just find myself alone on the road in the middle of a forest. I was dragged for what seemed like forever through the forest road and then off the road and then, somehow, down.

Very far down. As if it dragged me through the Myrkwood and into the Down-Below.

Cold air filled my lungs. Breathing out was practically making snowflakes. I was in a tunnel or a series of caves. Heading downward without falling, my body flopped around but somehow didn't bash against the walls. The musty smell gave way to an odor of decay, mild at first, then increasingly pungent. Darkness blotted out my sight for a while, but I blinked back some ability to see. By then, things looked different than I expected.

Finally, I dropped into a deep cavern. I was underground, but the ceiling was so high I couldn't see it. Foxfire glowed in patches on the ground and the walls behind me. My eyes adjusted enough to see what my ears could already hear as running water. A river flowed from one end of the cavern to the other, disappearing from sight in both directions.

I was a stone's throw from the nearest bank and closer even to the bridge that led across it. A bridge that stretched back as if to infinity. There was no mist to cloud my vision, only the never-ending length of the thing disappearing from sight.

This was the River Gjoll, or I had my lore wrong. The river that separated the living from the dead.

And as I had my lore right, I realized I was not alone.

The troll stood on the bridge another stone's throw from the path on the bank, dressed in rags and holding a gnarled iron staff. I had seen this figure from my previous nightmare, though I knew no more about it than I had then. I at least knew not to be surprised when the white pockmarks on its staff turned out to be teeth.

The bridge keeper made no effort to hide his face under a hood. Or was it hers? I couldn't tell anymore. The elongated nose and chin crinkled as if fungus grew haphazardly beneath the skin. Greasy forelocks fell over the rest of its face but hardly concealed the widened yellow eyes.

It took a step forward in a click-click-thud series of sounds from its feet and staff. Another step and it pointed at me.

"Keep to your own realm, troll," I said. "I am not dead yet, and you cannot have me."

I reached for Need, but the sword was locked in its sheath. Abandoning that weapon, I slipped on my sling but found no ammunition in my bag. My carving knife was gone, too.

In retrospect, maybe I should have given thanks that I was still wearing pants in this dream. It could have easily happened without them.

The troll answered me in verse, its voice a shouted whisper through a desiccated throat.

> "Troll they call me
>   cradle of the moon's minions,
> scion of monsters,
>   storm-sun's misfortune,
> witch's friendly companion,
>   watcher of the dead's boundary,

> trampler of the sun,
>> what is a troll, other than that?"

Fear washed through me. I tried to think but only the thought, *there's nothing you can do,* repeated over and over in my mind. The troll on the bridge was coming, and I had nothing to fight it with. In the previous nightmare, I had curled into a ball, all my ideas of courage washed away by a tidal wave that laughed at my resistance.

One weapon still remained. I could respond in verse if only I could think of something. The first line was obvious. If I could just begin and declare myself, maybe . . . "Sk– sk– sk—" I stuttered, unable to even call myself a skald. My tongue rolled in my mouth, my lips numb and ineffectual.

On came the troll, and its laughter pierced me like a spear. Nausea brought me to my knees. Fanya's voice echoed dimly from afar, asking why I let her die. Ulfberht's voice joined her, and then Kari's. The shame of failure to protect my friends ran cold through my veins. I doubled over, seeing stars through my closed eyes.

I wanted to fight, but I didn't know how. I knelt there, dry heaving, my body refusing to obey my commands until all my senses faded into nothing.

CHAPTER 43

RUIN

A HAND WAS OVER MY MOUTH WHEN I WOKE. THAT WAS A GOOD thing because I was inclined to scream, and screaming would have woken Steinvor. The hand was telling me not to scream, with just enough pressure to make that clear but not so much as to indicate my throat was about to be cut. The other hand held a single finger to a wizened old mouth.

I was still breathing like my air was running out, but the sight of Huld's face was oddly comforting.

The *vǫlva* removed her hand from my mouth. Without a sound, she backed out of the tent and gestured for me to follow her into the still-not-very-dark of early morning.

I tried to do this without waking Steinvor. I even thought I had succeeded once my pants and tunic were back on. A glance back showed me a single green eye open, watching my every move. I stepped back to her, wishing I could stay.

"I have to go," I whispered and kissed her on the cheek.

As I turned, she grabbed my hand. "Why now?" she whispered. "Just a little longer."

I shook my head. "Huld woke me. Our *vǫlva*."

"*Vǫlva?!*" she hissed. "You know Odd hates them!"

Sudden realization dawned on me. "Probably why she disappeared as soon as we got into camp," I said. "If she indicates I am needed, I believe her."

Steinvor squeezed my hand once again. I did not want to leave. I wanted to stay by her side and never get up again. At last, she flashed a sad smile, resigned that I would need to go at some point. "I hope to see you again," she said.

I nodded. "I hope to see you again as well." Oh, the lameness of that statement. I should have made the woman a promise. My present self knows that. But my past self was still not very mature when it came to romance.

Huld was right outside. At the sight of me, she began a quick stride away from Gardar's enclave. I had to run to catch up with her.

"They are looking for you," she said. "An early departure. And you were not to be found last night after it was decided. So strange, the skald going missing." She eyed me with an appraising look.

"Unlike a *vǫlva* disappearing," I said. "You have a great advantage here, knowing where I've been but keeping your own whereabouts unknown."

"That's right," she said, rounding on me. "And I will take every advantage I can find. There is no wisdom in entering a hostile place by the front door. Walk in carefully. Take a look around before you do anything rash."

"Perhaps you should say so to Haldor."

"I already have," she said and turned to go again. "But you know why I don't tell men their futures. They never listen."

"It's told that long ago, Odd hit a *vǫlva* in the nose with a stick after she told his future. He must have been listening, he just didn't like what he heard."

"What's the difference?" she snapped. We came to the edge of where the *Sea Squirrel's* crew had made camp. It was packed up already, the crew gone. "Here, I leave you," said Huld. "If you run, you will surely meet them before they set sail. And you should be with them."

"You are not coming with us?"

"Would that I could be two places at once, but I must choose, and I choose here."

"Would that you told me what secret purposes are behind such choices. Why be coy now?"

Huld sighed. "You don't have time for the whole of the story, and part of the story would only confuse you."

I crossed my arms, my feet rooted to the ground.

"Stupid boy! Let your friends die, then, and tell yourself you still feel lucky for being the one to survive."

Survival was high on my list of priorities. The highest priority ever since I could remember. Something about her statement struck me deeply, though. I imagined myself in camp, wondering why the *Sea Squirrel* never returned. In that moment, I did not feel lucky to have avoided the fate of the rest of the crew. I felt alone and by my own regretful choice.

Brotherless.

I ran to the *Sea Squirrel* as fast as my legs would carry me.

The ship was still beached when I arrived. Crewmen loaded sea chests on board, everyone moving slowly in the fog that had rolled in. Little waves lapping at the shore looked like curled fingers beckoning us into the sea.

Styrgrim wore a dour look, but that was as common to him as a weapon at his side. The better news was that Bjorn stood with him. I was glad for Bjorn's presence, but it didn't make me want to speak to my father any more than I had to. I got Magnus' attention instead, but he cut me off before I could say anything.

"Oh, hello. Are you a skald? You look like a skald. Turns out we already have one aboard, though. How are you at juggling and other things jester-like?"

"Why do we need a jester, Magnus?" asked Utstein.

"We could put a silly hat on you, and that would be just as good," added Innstein.

"You all talk too much," said Styrgrim.

"Talking is generally the way of stories and humor," said Bjorn. "It will be a shorter journey with both welcome on deck."

"And one with a less welcome outcome for failing to give to the gods," said Styrgrim. "This prohibition won't please Odin at all, and it seems to me that sort of favor would be more welcome than idle tongue-wagging."

"I've never considered Odin's shaft to be very welcome in my business," said Magnus, setting off a series of further jokes and laughter.

Styrgrim stalked off at that.

Hemming broke off from the revelers as if to approach me. He was slow and tentative, though, and Bjorn had his own intention of having a word. The skald came up close to me, clearly to say something not for many ears as he moved me away from the ship.

"I feared you would miss our departure," he said. "Though I might have suggested where to find you, I thought it better to remain silent."

"I appreciate your discretion," I said.

"Oh, it was not for you. You, I hardly know. But Steinvor is a friend. Her business is her business and not subject to the judgment of others."

I nodded. 'Not subject to the judgment of others' might have meant he needed to protect Steinvor's honor from petty rumors, but I did not get that impression. Steinvor did not need protecting. But Bjorn would also not sit idly by if someone made an off-comment about his friend he didn't appreciate, whatever the rules on our ship were. Better to avoid stupidity altogether than try to quash it after it comes up. And it would be a bad look to volunteer to go on this raid only to get into a feud with one of our crew.

That skald had seen much. Maybe it was indicated by his blond hair turning gray or the horn he carried marred with the marks of much use. He had his full kit with him where much of ours was left on the ship, and so I could see the chain shirt and helmet he carried were both heavy and worn. I gathered Hallfred had seen much as well, but Bjorn had a sharper edge to him. No wonder my father took him on.

He smiled at me then, a genuine look showing the crow's feet around his eyes. "It's a good thing!" he said and slapped me on the shoulder. A good thing for me or for Steinvor or for him that I wasn't a complete idiot? It was not quite clear what he meant. Maybe all at once.

Bjorn was some good skald.

We were underway before dawn, or what passed for dawn when the sun never set. The fog cleared soon after we set sail, giving us a clear view ahead. Despite the warm feeling of the light at the height of summer, the sea was cold. The wind whipped across my frozen fingers, laughing at the worn mittens covering them.

That same wind took the sail as if it knew our destination. We put up the oars for a long while and let it take us. Vignir had been right about no shortage of wind here, though I think he had meant his comment to have two meanings.

It was unfortunate for us that Vignir had not come. He would have been a cheerier passenger than my father, who took no part in conversation. Neither did I speak much, though. My mind was on Huld. Had her words about my friends dying been literal? Or had she spoken more generally to remind me it was my right place to be here?

I wanted to talk to my *fylgja* very much. Ask her pointed questions and yell at her if she gave evasive answers, in fact. But talking to invisible people is a bad idea with others around, and as far as I could tell, she was not present. I decided to ask about something else.

"Haldor," I said. "Have you seen Huld?"

The giant man nodded. "Just before we left," he said. "She had some advice, though I'm not likely to be told how to proceed. She did not care to come with us."

"What did she say?" asked Ulf. I was surprised he had not been one to hear it already.

"Something about not going in through the front door," said Haldor. "A thing from *Hávamál*, not a prophecy."

"Sounds like good advice," said Utstein.

"Of course. We're plenty good as back-door men," added Innstein.

Bjorn grinned while Styrgrim shook his head. Some men just have no sense of humor.

It was a long journey to where we were headed despite the wind being with us—less than Vignir's guess of a day and a half, but a full day of sea travel nevertheless.

We first spotted a gray mass that looked like bad weather rolling across the water. It didn't move, though, and so we made right for it. Bad weather turned out to be low clouds of thick fog. I didn't like the look of it even before we saw any of the island.

I knew the look of that fog. It felt the same as what I'd been pulled through into that terrible dream. Whatever this was, it was more than just a spot on the White Sea. It was one of those places where the boundaries between realms are less like boundaries and more like suggestions. The smell of *seiðr* floated over us, close enough to be identifiable but different enough to suggest it was not Alfhild's doing.

As we lost sight of the sky and the water more than a few hundred feet around us, smaller waves sloshed against the ship. The wind left our sail, and we put back the oars. With no direction to go but straight ahead, we were damn near on top of the island before we saw the tower.

A small mountain of solid rock reached up out of the water like a desperate hand. In the grasp of that hand sat a stone structure, impossibly tall and jagged. If I had seen living stone in the Down-Below, this was dead or dying. Maybe once, it was a magnificent sight to behold, a tower atop a mountainous island. Now, it was a ruin and yet still in use—a thing reanimated like one of Alfhild's raised corpses.

A makeshift dock stood with only a few ships moored to it. From there was a rough path that led to a long staircase carved into the mountain. The rocky shore would allow a landing, but it would not be easy. More to the point, it would not be easy to depart from if we were in a hurry, and that seemed a likely scenario.

"Since you two are so keen on exploration," Haldor said to the 'Steins, "perhaps I'll send you both to scout away from the main group."

"Scout for what?" asked Innstein. "Weird things?"

"We're guaranteed to find those in such a place," said Utstein.

Haldor shook his head. "Anything besides the front door."

Kraki circled the *Sea Squirrel* around the island. The rear, as we guessed it to be based on the one visible entrance, had a shorter tail of sandy rock on its bank. The mountain was as steep in the back as in the front and pockmarked with dark holes all the way up. Windows, perhaps? But there was no rear entrance as there was in the front.

"No good for a main landing," said Kraki. "And the other side leaves the ship exposed. Could leave some to guard the ship around the other side, I suppose."

"This place reeks," said Ketill. "Nothing in there can be good. You will need as many as you can take. If I stay with the ship, I can keep it unseen."

"We'll do that then," said Haldor. "But first, it is time for our back-door men to have their chance."

"We've already found something weird, though," said Innstein.

"It's right here!" added Utstein, gesturing at the entire island.

"Can you climb?" asked Haldor. "I thought you could climb. Perhaps I need to choose someone more able."

No way could the 'Steins allow that charge to go unanswered, and so they reiterated their willingness to go.

"I can go with them," I said. "I've climbed worse than this before. Some rope and a grappling hook and crampons will do it."

Haldor rounded on me in surprise but said nothing at first. "No more than three, then," he said after a pause. "Go as high as you can. Maybe come in behind our enemies and give them a surprise."

"What if we can't get in?" asked Utstein.

"Then get out," replied Haldor.

"Get to those stairs in front," said Ketill. "The ship will be near them on the bank, even if you can't see it right away."

Haldor nodded. "If you can't find anything interesting, find us. Who knows if we'll need you to cover our exit."

"We'll find some way to make trouble," said Innstein.

"One way or another," concluded Utstein.

Those two might have been made for the sea, but they were nearly as ready for the mountain. Both tied crampons to their shoes, and each took a length of rope and a grappling hook. Other choices about what to take could be a matter of life and death. Need had already made the practical decision to shrink to knife-size. I would also take my discs and carving knife, but as we'd be inside, I left my bag of sling bullets behind.

The 'Steins thought I was crazy to not wear a chain shirt for the coming fight, and I thought they were crazy to put theirs on for the coming climb. Each one kept a metal helmet tied to his hip for later. I donned my leather skullcap only. It wouldn't stop many weapon blows, and it looked silly, but after being punched in the head by Svein, I had resolved to have at least a little protection for my head.

Oars in reverse, the *Sea Squirrel* backed away to leave us to our devices on that strange shore. There was not much shoreline before the sheer climb. Up went our hooks, finding purchase among the cracks without difficulty, and then up we followed. I had the greater skill scaling such craggy faces, but the 'Steins had long experience in overcoming obstacles of all types. They did not fall too far behind.

Higher up, the spikes under the balls of my feet dug deeper into the rock than I expected. It was hard there, but the surface was soft for solid rock walls, and my crampons ground fine powder out of some of those footholds. Progress was faster at that point, but the light had dimmed, and we had to gauge our ascent more carefully.

We were even farther north than Arrow-Odd's camp, and though it was night, there was no dimming beyond early twilight. Had it been the dead of night in Denmark, we would not have been able to see well enough to continue. The light was less than at noon and yet plenty to navigate by. I stopped at a flat opening big enough to stand on to catch my breath. I needed little sleep, but the previous night, I had gotten less than normal (no regrets) and ended it with a nightmare. Now we were into the evening time when reasonable people would be asleep again, and I was feeling the tiredness ache through my bones.

"I think it levels out a little higher," I said. "Could be an open area with access inside. Are we aiming higher than that?"

"No idea what we're aiming for," said Innstein as he looked for the next hand-hold. "I think we will know it when we see it."

"You won't stop until you're in Alfhild's larder, eating all her meat," said Utstein. He had stopped for a break as well and was making his brother laugh as the man pulled himself up.

"I would need to be a hungry man for that," said Innstein. He was higher up than his brother but was working out a series of hand-holds for his next few steps. "That's a lot of bird," he said.

"Are you sure?" asked Utstein. "I think she prefers pork."

"No, dammit!" said Innstein.

Some men are all about good jokes. When the tone of such men turns deadly serious, you know something bad has happened. Innstein pointed up but not at the tower. He drew our gazes to his right, which was behind me.

"Eagle?!" said Utstein.

The bird was angling parallel to the rock face and descending. Eagle, maybe, only it was far larger than any eagle I had ever seen.

"If that's an eagle, Fenrir is a puppy," I said.

"I knew I should have taken a spear," said Innstein. "If it comes at us when we've leveled out above, though, we'll make that thing regret seeing us." He had found the holds he needed and was moving fast now.

"And if it hits us while we're on the rock face . . ." Utstein did not need to finish his thought. With fewer holds immediately above him, he tossed his hook up, where it found purchase. If it held, he could pull himself up the rest of the way with his rope.

So the 'Steins were fine as long as their luck held. I looked up and saw a bad situation about to unfold, unless my luck could be stretched very far indeed.

I had found an excellent spot to stand up and rest, but it was not a spot to ascend from. An outcropping above me prevented any direct route. Great climber though I am, I am not so great as to climb upside-down. This position also prevented me from seeing where my grappling hook would go, assuming I could get it anywhere. Every reasonable route would take me sideways before I could continue my way up, and that would take time.

Utstein gave me a sidelong glance as he moved steadily upward. "Get moving, skald!"

The outcropping. Perhaps I did not need to get as far as the 'Steins. If I could just get up to the outcropping, I might have more space. Enough to take a step or two would be a great improvement if I needed to fight. I tossed my hook upward. If it could grab onto something solid, I might pull myself up.

My hook bounced once and then scraped down the face of the outcropping.

"No good that way!" said Innstein. "You need to go sideways!"

Goat's breath and cat piss!

"Shit!" said Utstein as he pulled himself up over a ledge.

I didn't bother turning around before I drew Need. I would need to fight where I was and without the ability to move my feet more than a few inches. The eagle was not on me yet but would be in seconds. Need came out as a long seax. Light, fast, razor sharp. Better than swinging a sword in these circumstances and less likely to off-balance myself than with a sword or polearm.

"Come on, brother!" shouted Utstein. "I'll toss you my rope!"

"It's not me that thing is after!" replied Innstein. "Offense, not defense!"

There was a moment's pause. "Right!"

Whatever that meant, I was not looking. My eyes were fixed on the twenty-foot span of wings gliding toward me. The scream that thing let out was less a bird's call and more like a bird's call being torn in half.

I braced my back against the stone and bent my knees. Stay flexible and never lock your knees was one basic fighting principle I remembered. *And don't lean so far forward that you fall to your death,* my mind kept trying to add in the least helpful way possible.

With Need in my right hand and the hook in my left, I might give this bird cause to leave me alone yet.

That thing came at me perpendicular to the cliff and at a speed I knew I wouldn't be able to stop. One rake from those talons, and I would be tumbling down. I braced for one possible strike, hoping I would open its guts in payment for my life at least.

A grappling hook from above struck the eagle hard on the beak.

"Haha!" cheered Utstein. "Look, brother, I've hooked a great eagle-fish!"

It was a welcome cheer, though he had not gotten the hook in. Big as that bird was, it was not so big that a couple of pounds of iron hitting it in the face went unnoticed. The eagle veered away from me, only feet from where it might have attacked. It glided away from the rock face only a little, though, and would come back in a wide circle.

"We will see who hooks the bigger catch," said Innstein, now fully up to the ledge.

"Perhaps you two could pull up a friend rather than a giant, ugly bird!" I suggested, watching as the thing turned around to come straight at me.

"No time just yet," said Innstein.

"We'll make him pass once more and then haul you up together," said Utstein. Quieter, he added, "Oh, I see you found what you were looking for after all, brother."

I didn't know what those two were talking about until the eagle had to dodge two fist-sized rocks thrown from above. The brothers yelled obscenities about the eagle and its mother. Instead of an attack at full speed, the bird changed direction and then held back just a bit, flapping to stay airborne without flying away again. The gusts from those massive wings beating threatened to throw me off-balance, and the bird saw this. It came in slowly from above, open talons threatening to grab me by the arms.

Down came another grappling hook to strike the back of the bird's neck. It shrieked again, another tearing scream to assault my ears. Its breath smelled of rotting flesh and something worse I did not want to think about.

A second hook came down, but this one had not been thrown. This was dangling lower, then lower, until it was just beneath me. "Grab the hook!" yelled Innstein. "Hook the fish, and we will pull it in!"

I had nowhere to move forward, so "hooking" that "fish" would put me in range of its talons and beak. It seemed to me the 'Steins' idea was fine from afar but not so good up close. I looked at the eagle again, looked down, and considered that I might not have many other chances to win this fight.

I dropped my hook, grabbed Innstein's, and sheathed Need. With two hands, I might be able to give a little slack and snag the bird after all. I tossed the hook over that troll-cursed eagle's shoulder. With a triumphant shout, I pulled down on the rope to set it, digging the hook into its back and wing.

The eagle screeched and reared back as it flapped. The trouble was that as the eagle pulled away, I was still holding the rope.

Balance is a funny thing. I was already oriented forward, and just that small tug I felt before giving the rope more slack sent the top half of my body far, far over the ledge. I threw my arms back in reflex, but that was not nearly enough, and much too late. I was going to fall. And in the desperation of seeing the rocks below, I did the only thing left to me: I grabbed the rope with both hands.

The eagle flapped in random spasms as my weight pulled it down. It screamed in impotent rage. Those great wings had so much power behind them that the bird soon leveled out and flew away from the stone face of the tower into the open air.

"Shit!" I heard from two voices above.

The feeling of being pulled along in the air by that eagle is something I will never forget. My hands still cramp up a bit when I think about it.

I mosty remember fear and the single-mindedness of holding on and that it seemed to take hours. In reality, it probably took about one minute because even an eagle of that size doesn't intend to carry a man on a tour of its eyrie. Up it went at first, flapping to gain altitude, and then inexorably down from fatigue.

The great bird flew over the water and then banked all the way back around, heading for cliff face on the side of the mountain. I thought this was making my position a bit easier at first until I realized the intent. The eagle would fly just over the cliff face and then be able to land. Meanwhile, I would continue straight into the solid rock at high speed.

Not the face we had climbed up, the one with lots of hand and foot holds. I would slam right into the bottom of a rocky ledge. No way would I be able to hold on after a jolt like that. And there was little to break my fall from there.

I saw this play out in my mind's eye as the giant bird glided toward the rock face. I looked down and considered the freezing water of the White Sea. I might survive the fall if I dropped, but I would not survive being cold and wet with no way to warm back up. There was nothing to do but hang on.

Except for one idea I got at the last moment. Which would probably kill me anyway, but at least it would annoy the eagle.

I gathered up some of the rope's slack hanging beneath me and wrapped it around one fist. Seconds before the impact against the ledge, I let go of my higher grip and let myself drop, gripping the rope tight at the lower part.

And then the eagle was not just carrying all my weight, but suddenly feeling the great tug from my short fall. I dropped, and the eagle fell with me and just barely righted itself as it shrieked in what must have been a great deal of pain.

The rope above me hit the ledge, arresting most of my momentum and swinging me forward. I hit the solid rock face after swinging up. It was not as bad as it might have been, but it was about as bad as I had expected.

The rope strained against my hand as my right shoulder took most of the shock of the impact. My hands slipped down the rope. I tried in vain to grab something and lost all control for a moment. I reached out in desperation with one hand, finding a tenuous hold among the rocks for a good one or even two whole seconds. I slipped off but found a small tree growing out from the side of the mountain.

I held that tree and balanced my weight between it and the rope as my feet looked for purchase. Then the rope went slack, and all my weight was on the tree. Those were some stubborn roots to grow in such a hard place. Not stubborn enough to also bear the weight of a full-grown man, however. The roots tore away, and I fell onto what was not quite a sheer face but still quite steep.

I slid sideways and down, arresting my fall here and there. But the truth is I tumbled, barely able to keep my life, hitting every desperate plant and bump. Down and down and to the side until I was sliding more than bumping and funneled into a crack in the mountainside that plunged me down well away from the waves, beneath the ruin itself.

You can learn much in the deep places of the world like that crack I fell into. I certainly did. And I was never the same after.

CHAPTER 44

THE MAN WHO WOULD BE PREY

I TUMBLED THROUGH A SHAFT OF LIGHT SHINING INTO A HOLE I looked on as my likely grave. That last bit of light shone on one more thing to hold onto, however, so I grabbed a final ledge in desperation. Most of the wind had been knocked out of me, and that final hold lasted maybe half a second before I slipped down into darkness.

I landed awkwardly on my feet with no ankle twist and not with my knees locked, thank the norns, or that would have been the end of my story. The landing was quite hard on my ass, but that was a much better result than what might have been.

Solid rock beneath me clicked with each step until I unfastened my crampons to move in silence. Nothing jumped out and bit me, and no one shouted a warning, but I kept my hand on Need and took a few deep breaths as slowly as I could manage. That place had such an ill feeling that I had to take stock of what my senses were telling me.

The first thing that hit me was the smell. Salt and dried blood were the easiest parts to identify, but there was more. Entrails opened up long ago and never quite washed away. And something else, something musky in its decay I could not put a name to.

Constant churning rumbled all around. I was below the sea here, in the bowels of the mountain. The hole I had come down was wet—washed periodically by the highest waves of high tide, I supposed, even if the water didn't come close most of the time. Another sound, long and raspy, was so faint I wasn't sure if I was making it up at first. Like an ogre snoring softly. Inside that place, even the smallest sound echoed eerily in the darkness.

My eyes adjusted quickly, though details were still difficult to make out. Shapes of various sizes littered the ground, all seeming to be some shade of gray. I was in a cave rather than a room, it seemed, with stone pillars stretching from floor to ceiling in some places. In other places, only stalactites had formed, still drip-drip-dripping their way down.

My skin crawled and my lungs refused to slow down. I moved along the periphery of the place, feeling along the walls as I went. The wall was alternatingly smooth and sharp as if part of the area had been dug out rather than formed naturally.

Something squished beneath my boot, too soft to be alive. My stomach dropped as I looked down.

It was a leg, a human leg. Bloated skin moved loose across the bone in accordance with my boot.

I picked my foot up and stepped over it, careful not to look again. I was certain I would vomit if I did.

Eventually, I hit an open space in the wall, and my heart began racing at the prospect of a way out. That excitement was short-lived, however. The massive entryway cut out of the wall gave way to a solid wooden portcullis braced with iron fittings. I pulled at it, but it would not budge, and there was no obvious device on my side of it. On the other side was a room that looked very much like it must have a device for lifting the thing. A torch lit in the back of that room threw a hint of light my way. It mostly illuminated a set of stone steps in the back of the room.

Sadly, I realized the device being only on the other side was probably the whole idea. Wouldn't want whatever was snoring to wake up and have the run of the place up above this dungeon.

And something was just above, for certain, because I could hear people making a lot of noise. I walked toward the source and away from the portcullis to find a hole in the ceiling. Voices echoed and torchlight flickered above. Hurried whispers indicated a sense of urgency. I made out a few of the words:

"She's asleep" and "keep her that way" and "just get it done."

Slowly and with a few grunts, a man was lowered down head-first. He was covered from his ankles to his arms in coiled rope. A gag was pulled tight around his mouth. He had no blindfold, though, so as he spun around in mid-air, he saw me.

I wondered if he was more surprised to see me, or I him.

"Steady," someone said. It sounded like three of them were up there past the hole in the ceiling.

"Just drop him."

"You'll break his neck that way. She likes 'em to kick a bit."

Which was not comforting to hear.

The three unknowns lowered the man slower and slower as his head came closer to the stony floor. Eventually, his head touched, and then his neck, and then they let the man flop painfully down the rest of the way on his back and legs.

"We're done here."

"Other work to do. Let's go."

I cut the bindings off his hands first. Hand, actually. He only had the left one. With no right wrist, they had tied his left wrist to his right upper arm behind him. He wriggled away before I could cut anything else, even before pulling his gag off.

"I thought I was the only one to get sent here for a while," he whispered as he struggled to get free of the rope coiled around him. "How do you have a sword down here?"

I shrugged. "It didn't fall off when I tumbled down." I pointed to the dim shaft of light across the floor and the shallow pool it let into.

"You're from outside?"

"Where else?"

He shook his head in disbelief. "Why are you here?"

I was tempted to go on with some answer about a series of calculated errors that had somehow resolved in my favor, but I didn't want to wake whatever it was that *liked 'em to kick a bit*. "There's a witch. Pretty in an ugly sort of way, or the other way around. Big scar on her cheek. First, tell me who you are to her."

He looked at me like I was crazy. "A prisoner. I thought, same as you."

I shook my head and introduced myself, and then asked how we would get out of there.

"We don't get out of here," he said. "For what it's worth, I am Vilgrip. Son of Tyr."

It sounded funny the way he said it. "You mean Tyrsson?"

He gave me that *you must be crazy* look again.

"Do you not know what this place is?"

"It's where Alfhild is. Why, what is it I should know?"

He held up one finger and turned away, listening. I didn't hear a threat. That was the problem.

The snoring had stopped.

He leaned in and whispered in the quietest possible voice, "She's awake. We'll have to fight her."

My mind recalled the rotting limb I'd stepped on, and I concluded the limb's previous owner had probably fought whoever 'she' was as well. "There has to be a way out," I mouthed back.

Vilgrip shook his head and pointed at the hole in the ceiling. They hadn't even bothered to cover it. No way up. No way through the portcullis. And the way I came? That was the most one-way of all the ways.

Somewhere in the darkness, a voice made a series of happy grunts. Hungry. Excited. The sound of a blade on a whetstone followed, slow and certain.

Vilgrip glanced around but clearly couldn't see very well as he felt about for a rock big enough to swing as a weapon. I still had no idea what he might be swinging at, but I knew Need was more likely to be effective. I watched Vilgrip's back as he wrapped the rock over and over with rope so as to make a primitive, if potentially effective, weapon.

That gave me an idea.

"Is there a catch up there? Something a grappling hook could grab ahold of?" I asked, still in the quietest possible voice.

He nodded without looking at me, scanning the darkness for danger. "But so what?" he mouthed.

I spun Need around in my hand and came up with a grappling hook.

By then, Vilgrip was looking at me like I was more than crazy. Like maybe he had also gone crazy, and he wasn't at all certain of what he was seeing anymore. But he untied his rock, handed me the rope, and followed me to the hole he'd come down. All we had to do was toss it up there, have one of the claws catch, and climb out.

I made a bit of noise with the first toss. Maybe more than a bit. I tossed the hook, and steel rang on stone throughout that cavern when it hit the ceiling, missing the hole by a foot. It rang again when the hook clattered down to the rock below.

The happy grunts became quizzical. Something was about to come looking for the source of this noise.

"Hel's dragon!" hissed Vilgrip as he snatched the hook off the ground. Left-handed, he spun it a few times and launched it upward through the hole. It still clanged when it hit the floor above us, but not nearly as much.

He pulled gently at first. Then, finding the hook had caught on something solid, he lifted himself up one-handed.

"I can go first and pull you up," I offered.

Heavy footsteps thudded slowly our way. I was suddenly quite interested in my offer for my own sake rather than Vilgrip's.

Vilgrip grinned back at me.

I had assumed too much about what it meant to have only one hand. The story about Tyr makes it out to be one of the saddest things in the world. He was a great warrior but had only one hand after Fenrir the wolf chomped off the right one. Left him practically a cripple.

Vilgrip hooked the rope between his feet, one stepping on the other. He pulled himself up with his left hand, legs, and knees bent up towards his chest. Then he hooked the rope between his feet again, stood up, and repeated the process. This was better than my technique of shimmying, and he was up that rope faster than I could have been. He even pulled me up the last of the way with his left hand. Vilgrip had arms like iron.

"Thought I was a cripple for losing a hand?" he said.

"I had the wrong idea," I said in response. I was so surprised I nearly left Need behind. "Where are we?" I asked as I collected the rope behind the hook. I had a feeling I might need it again before too long.

Vilgrip took a look outside the tiny room we were in. It had been carved out as well, or else the floor would have been too smooth for the hook to find any purchase. "In the feeding room," he said without glancing back at me. "But they think the feeding is done, and they're probably asleep by now. I don't see anyone. It looks safe, but we can't stay here. You have a ship?"

"We do, but," and I realized I had a mission beyond what Haldor had mentioned. "Listen, we heard stories on the way here. One story was that Alfhild was pregnant. Is that true?"

"No idea about her being pregnant, but we did hear the wailing of a baby for a long time."

"Where?" I hissed too loud.

Vilgrip looked back at me and shook his head. "The upper levels when I heard it. But I haven't heard it for at least a week."

And just as the sun had risen in my chest, it fell with a thud. I didn't know what to think of the child. It might not even be mine. I had no real responsibility. Did I?

"Did she . . ." I stammered, "did she cast any big spells around that time?"

Vilgrip shrugged, looking confused. He was locked up, of course, and wouldn't know.

I didn't want to think about Alfhild draining the tiny body of blood. Would she do that to her own? If not, what had happened to silence it?

I gritted my teeth and shook off the questions. No point in fixating on what I couldn't do and couldn't know. "I was headed for the tower before. Exploring, seeing what I could find. Do you know what's up there?"

"The witch is what's up there, so I'd advise going in the opposite direction."

I shook my head. "We came to end her."

Vilgrip considered this for a moment. "That won't be easy. She is powerful, even without the necklace. She turned some of my siblings without even using it."

"Siblings?" I asked. "Necklace?"

Vilgrip put one finger to his lips. Then he leaned in and whispered. "You don't know what this place is, do you?"

I didn't. None of us did. And even when I heard it, I could hardly believe it.

Chapter 45

Upward Spiral

"And they tested these abilities you might have by cutting off your hand?" I said.

The idea was to find a way outside and, like I had started in the first place, to climb up and get to the tower. Vilgrip waved me off as we padded quietly through the corridors, looking for a way outside. I knew we needed to be stealthy, but every ten seconds or so, my mind would explode a little more, and I would forget, and I would start asking questions again.

Asking questions seemed like a reasonable response to the explanation *The gods have been busy making babies with mortals, and this is the place the god-children are all brought to after Alfhild captures them.*

So many implications and so many questions. But I couldn't wrap my head around why they'd cut off Vilgrip's hand if he was a son of Tyr. Assuming he was a literal son of Tyr, which I found difficult to believe.

"Tested my abilities by cutting off my *right* hand," Vilgrip whispered.

The corridor forked in two directions. One way looked to have a slight upward slant to it, and Vilgrip pointed us that way. A few turns later, I saw a small opening that looked out at the White Sea. We were not too high up, and looking for a faster way to ascend.

The inside of the place was bigger than I expected. And we were sneaking around at just the right time, when most would be asleep, so we didn't even have to dodge any guards making their rounds.

The thing about living inside a giant rock is you need air and light. Maybe not if you're a dwarf, but these were no dwarves. That first opening hadn't been big enough to crawl through, but it wasn't the only portal to the mountain's exterior.

We followed the sound of wind to a door that led to a small balcony outside. There was no overhang above it, so it was perfect for beginning a climb up. I scanned the sky for monstrous birds first. Seeing none, we used the grappling hook and rope to take turns climbing.

Up we went, and as we went, Vilgrip continued.

"My right hand because the stories tell that is the hand Fenrir demanded be placed in his mouth. The gods bound Fenrir, Fenrir failed to break them, and when the gods did not release the wolf, he bit down and took away one of the gods' best weapons in Tyr's sword hand."

"And so they thought that, as Tyr's son, you would become more god-like after completing a ritual to make you physically more like Tyr," I shook my head. "Did you have any abilities after that?"

Vilgrip held up the stump on his right arm and considered it. "I got more stubborn, maybe. I'm not sure what abilities they were expecting," he said. "Anyway, it was a stupid thing to try since I've always fought left-handed. Take after my mother that way. I suppose you never know what you'll inherit. Maybe I would have developed some latent powers if they cut the other hand off." He shrugged, grinning.

At least they had not amputated the man's sense of humor.

I shook my head. It made so much sense, but only if you knew how absurd the gods were and how stupid humans became in trying to emulate their power.

"Why?" I asked.

"Why what?"

"Why any of it! The sons and daughters of gods roaming Midgard, most of them knowing nothing of their parentage. The hunting and capture of them. This nonsense of 'testing' for supposed powers. And why bring your 'siblings' here—why this place?"

I swallowed hard. Siblings—or maybe cousins?

Olgram had called me cousin. Alfhild's son, the troll of Lejre, or according to Fanya, just a big ugly child with a penchant for drinking and a difficulty with following directions. Calling me 'cousin' was a riddle I'd never solved. A shiver shook my whole body as if I were again descending into places of deep lore to learn unhappy things. Deeper than I would care to go despite our direction being upward.

That's the scary part of wisdom. You can't measure and draw the amount you want as if from a well. When it comes, it comes like a flood.

Vilgrip laughed quietly as he whispered, "I think the simplest answers are most likely. Why do we exist? The gods were horny and took what they pleased without regard for others. The gods are not unlike vikings that way, even Thor sometimes. As to why they did nothing to tell us we were their spawn, I can only guess that they are lazy."

"Seems reasonable," I murmured. Maybe Ketill was right that the gods were never there when you needed them.

"Collecting us and bringing us here, though, that seems more obvious: They want power. We're the children of gods. Who knows what we can do? And so they will need to control us. They keep the means of it here and well-guarded."

"They. You mean Alfhild Smooth-Cheek?"

Vilgrip let out a barking laugh. "She's the newer warden."

"Who was the older warden?"

Vilgrip shook his head. "I've been here a while and Alfhild hardly rates. The one from before was Svart. Haven't seen that beardless bastard in some time. He's the one who took my hand."

"Svart, not Ogmund?" I asked.

"Ogmund, Arrow-Odd's old enemy?"

"That's him. You never saw Ogmund?"

"No idea. A few big vikings have come through, but mostly to buy the undesirables as thralls. God-children like me, they keep us and work on turning us."

"What do you mean, turning you?"

"Turning us to their will. Enthralling us. The necklace gets almost everyone, Alfhild's specialty. I almost gave in this last time. Perhaps it was being that close and failing that drove her to send me down here."

"What necklace is that?"

Vilgrip shook his head. "I can't imagine why you would be here if you didn't know this. Only reasons to come here are for thralls or treasure, and this is the biggest treasure of them all. I suppose they've guarded the secret well if even you don't know, though."

"Know what? Speak plainly."

"The Brisingamen. She knows how to use it. Had a way about her more gentle than Svart's. Less chopping off of hands and whatnot."

My chin hit the floor. After I picked it up enough to speak again, I was still in denial. "You don't mean– I mean– the actual—"

"The Brisingamen. The torc of yellow gold that Freya paid for with her body. Gave a single night to each of four horny dwarves in exchange for it, or so the stories tell. Don't ask me how, but the witch has it, and well does she know how to use its charm." He spoke in between deep breaths as he climbed after me. "I can't see your face very well, but you have the sound of disbelief about you. You can believe I am a son of Tyr, but not that there is a dwarf-made necklace upstairs?"

The myth went that Freya had seen this torc being made and knew she had to have it at once. So she negotiated with the dwarves making it. She offered them gold, but they refused. Gold was easy to come by, they told her, and they had plenty of it. What they wanted was a night with Freya each. She didn't like sleeping with them, the story goes, but the torc's beauty was such that she had been willing to pay any price for it. It became Freya's most prized possession. How would a thing that coveted by one of the most powerful goddesses come to Midgard?

Vilgrip reached the ledge I was on and I gave him a hand up even though I knew he didn't need it.

"Every answer you give spawns two more questions," I said. "We came here for Alfhild, to end her and honor our Brothers. I did not suspect we would overturn one secret after another. She couldn't have built the tower, though. She had been with the Danes for many years. Did this Svart build it?"

Vilgrip shook his head. "Some of us speculated it was the Romans, with all their ancient magic in building things. I never heard of them coming so far north, though, not even close. Probably *jǫtnar* from long ago, though whatever they intended, I think it wasn't this. There's a corruption here. Like it was made for one thing and then bent to another purpose, but one at odds with its original conception."

"Sounds like Alfhild herself." Whatever that witch's story was, it was hard to imagine she had always intended to be the way she was.

I wondered if Alfhild had used the necklace on Hrolf's uncle Ragnvald and that was the cause of the Danish king's awful judgment. No, Ragnvald just had awful judgment. And was probably lonely, though you weren't supposed to say that about men. Didn't make it any less true, though—Ragnvald found as much comfort in Alfhild's embrace as her handmaidens had. If Alfhild had used the Brisingamen before, she would not have needed it much.

We had reached the jagged top of the mountain, high above where the *Sea Squirrel* had let me and the 'Steins off. A hundred feet away on flatter ground, the tower sprang up as if it had grown out of the stone itself. The conical shape made that impossible, of course, but I could not see where it ended and the mountain below it began. The craggy boulders we walked on had to be the roof of what we had seen inside, a hollowed-out mountain teeming with life. And, apparently, with children of the gods.

Vilgrip stared at me as if taking my measure. "How many of you are there?"

"About thirty," I said. Judging by the look on Vilgrip's face to be less than impressed, I added, "I am not the best fighter among them."

It was shaping up to be a day of understatements.

The base of the tower still looked just as much a part of the mountain as the rest as we got closer. Only the ground around it had been chipped away to create a walkable area. The tower's existence made no sense. It was not built of stones or any craftsmanship I could see. To look at it, it was undeniably a tower as if it had grown up out of the rock beneath it.

"Thirty won't be enough if Alfhild wakes her warriors," said Vilgrip, shaking his head. "I think it's better to find your people and get out while she sleeps rather than try our luck against her. Don't want to wake her eagle, either." He pointed to a set of steps spiraling up the right side of the tower and put one finger to his lips.

A few makeshift steps led up to a heavy oak door. Just looking at that door made me want to turn around and take Vilgrip's advice to retreat. I shook my head though, knowing I had to go in.

"As you must, but wait," he said, his voice low. "You wouldn't know from looking at it, but there is a door back there." He pointed at a large, flat rock standing at an angle among the edge of those jagged boulders. I blinked and could barely make out the outline of what might be a door. "That's how they would bring me here. If you survive killing this witch and I don't, that's your way back inside."

I nodded heavily and held him back a moment. "If it goes the other way, though, listen. Take my sword if you can. I think it will let you. But also take my beaver skin bag and carving knife. And one more thing: You said the child might be in there. If we find it, and it's alive, swear to me you'll bring it to safety."

We clasped arms, and he swore, and there was no doubt in my mind that Vilgrip's oath was ironclad.

The oak door at the base of the tower beckoned. Perhaps we could take Alfhild by surprise. Maybe we could lock her in if we couldn't kill her.

I had the worst feeling about it as if we would all be far better off sailing away immediately and never thinking about it again. But we had come this far, and that was not an option.

There was no way but forward, so forward I went.

CHAPTER 46

BRISINGAMEN

"A GUARD MAY BE SITTING INSIDE. PROBABLY ASLEEP. GO quietly, slit his throat."

I remembered trying that on an old woman once. It had not gone well. This would need to go much better. And Need would only listen to me, so it would be me who did the killing.

The door opened to a small room with a straw bed at the opposite end. It was empty. Supplies were stacked neatly around a small table and bench. To the side, a great blowing horn hung over a mostly empty rack of weapons and shields. Mostly empty, but not quite, and Vilgrip made straight for what was left there.

"Where is the guard?" I whispered, eyeing a spiral staircase up along the wall.

Vilgrip shrugged. "No telling," he whispered back as he slipped an axe through his belt and hefted a short spear. "Stay quiet, though."

There was little light inside once I closed the door behind us. Night had fallen, but that meant just a little darkening during the time of the midnight sun. A few tiny holes in the wall opposite the stairs were the only illumination, and then it was the light of dusk only. We made our way up the stairs by feeling the wall as we went.

I had less trouble seeing in the dark than Vilgrip, so I went on ahead. My heart hammered in my chest at what was next. Up I went, fighting the urge to charge forward and get it over with.

Each level was its own circular room. We passed a few outfitted as sleeping quarters, but none I thought would belong to the witch. It was a long way up to Alfhild's level. I couldn't say how high we climbed—not to the very top where a hatch might open to the eagle's eyrie, but the last stop before it where the stairs ended.

A hearth in the center of the room burned low. Holes were carved through to the outside high up on some of the walls, probably less for light than to be rid of the smoke. A bed stretched out long and luxurious, its head-board of carven oak. Dresses and furs hung neatly along the walls. No benches at the table, this room had chairs with fur-lined seats. Bright jewelry hung from pegs along a board on one of the walls. Ornate chests, vials filled with colorful liquid, and a work table full of dried ingredients all hinted at mysterious contents.

"She is not here," I said. Indeed, no one was there. "The necklaces—is it among them?"

I already knew it was.

One torc hung apart from the rest as if pushing other items away from it. Dozens of strands twisted among one another down from two dragon heads at the ends. The pure gold shone like the surface of the sun like it had never even been seen before, much less touched. I looked into it and it looked into me, and it seemed all the soreness in my body was melting away.

Vilgrip slapped me across the back of the head. When I came to, I realized I had walked across the room and was standing there before the Brisinga-men, having no memory of walking up to it.

"Did you hear me?" Vilgrip demanded. "I was saying you would know it immediately if you saw it, but apparently you did. If she wears it, she is most difficult to resist. Even if she takes it off, it calls to you. The twisting of the metal bores into your brain and you can think of nothing else but how lovely it is, how lucky you are to be graced with its presence. But make no mistake: It is a slave collar, prettied-up and more subtle."

I took a deep breath and pried my eyes from the thing. "How did you resist it, then?"

Vilgrip shrugged. "I never was much like the others around me. And I was still angry about my right hand when she came 'round with it. I'm not the only one, though. There are some other god-children who just never liked that witch's smell. Others, I suspect, are not even god-children—just caught up and imprisoned with us. Those don't usually last long. They're fed to Grimhild below or sold as thralls. With me, Alfhild took her time. I guess I wore out her patience, though, since she had me thrown down as food."

"You should carry it then."

He shook his head. "I said I resisted her. I don't know about that thing on its own. I can feel the temptation to put it on and try my hand against her magic right now. You should carry it if you can."

I looked at the thing again and swallowed hard. This was a powerful thing, no doubt. No wonder Freya had wanted it so badly. How would I carry it without succumbing to its use? A bag full of sling bullets would be ironic company for that torc and I grinned at the thought, but I'd left my sling ammunition on the ship. All I had left was to tuck it into my belt . . .

. . . or stuff it into my beaver skin bag of rune discs. That bag had survived being in the middle of a burning hall without so much as a scorch mark. If it could keep fire out, maybe it could keep this thing's influence contained.

I could feel the jolt of the torc's call as I grabbed it, hear the voices assuring me of ease and comfort as well as power and influence. Perhaps I should just put it on and see what happens? I was good at trying things and seeing what happened.

Need's angry hum got so loud I thought I could feel it vibrating. The weapon brought me out of my spiraling thoughts. I stuffed the torc in with the discs and pulled the bag shut, and the voices quieted.

"That's some good bag you have," said Vilgrip, apparently feeling the torc's pull even as I'd held it.

"More than you know. But this is as much a problem as a victory: It is night, but Alfhild is not asleep here. Where else would she be?"

"She was done with me, and I thought done with prisoners for the night."

"What did she say exactly?" I said, a vague but sudden suspicion growing.

Vilgrip shook his head, uncertain. "Just that I'd had enough chances. She said there were enough of 'us' already, and they wouldn't need me."

"But you resisted many times," I said, almost to myself. "Why stop now?"

Though the nights were not dark, we had come upon the island when the sun had been lowest. Vilgrip's description further confirmed that most would be sleeping. Why not Alfhild? Why not the guard at the base of Alfhild's tower?

And then that part of the verse came back to me.

A hidden wolf
    waits and watches,
biding time
    to break cover.

"Goat's breath and cat piss!" I said, turning to a confused Vilgrip. "Those who threw you into the pit, were they dressed as normal or dressed for battle?"

Vilgrip stood still as he considered. "For battle."

"This is no lucky coincidence. They knew we were coming!"

I flew down those steps as fast as my feet would take me, heedless of Vilgrip behind.

"The eagle told her?" he suggested.

"It is much worse than that," I said. "We are betrayed."

I had gone deep into places I could not even name for a prophecy that I had soon forgotten about. Huld had been right. Men never heeded prophecy and went on to their doom despite being told every detail they needed to avoid it. There was no wolf outside lurking around us. There was a wolf among us who'd sent word of our arrival.

"How many are we facing?" I said, my voice hard as we descended the stairs. Fear and tentativeness were shoved away in place of anger and frustration. Who else was supposed to see the warning for what it was, if not the skald?

"At least a hundred just in god-children," Vilgrip said. "More if there are vikings here to do business and buy or sell thralls."

We had dealt with worse than that before. But this time, there were no Spear-Danes to rally alongside us. The wizard was out of position to help. There was no witch to counter Alfhild's magic. And the cat, though I knew her to be much more than a cat, had stayed behind with Arrow-Odd.

Back at the base of the tower, I eyed the guard's empty seat and the nearly empty weapons rack. No one expected us to be here—not in the tower itself. I ran to the front door and slammed it open, beckoning Vilgrip to hurry.

Soon, I got a reminder of the need for stealth when the giant eagle came screaming down from above. I dove away and rolled on the ground to avoid it.

But when I say screaming, I mean that in the most literal sense. The bird had not flown so much as fallen, flapping wildly, and crashed into the stone about twenty feet from me. Groggily, it rose and picked at its shoulder, and only then I saw a grappling hook set into it. The hook was tied to two huge rocks set as an anchor.

Vilgrip shouldered me aside and lowered his spear at the thing. I stepped back and drew Need.

"It's not dead," I heard from above.

Seconds later, a head-sized rock whispered through the air above and slammed into the bird's back. Having approached the eagle with his spear ready, Vilgrip leaped back at the impact. The eagle crumpled under the blow, and I knew if it moved again, it would only be death spasms.

"It is now," another voice from above continued.

Stepping back to get a better view of the tower's pinnacle, my eyes confirmed what my ears told me. The 'Steins had found a way up and had devised a way down for the eagle that suited their needs.

"Is that the skald?" said Utstein.

"We didn't avenge him after all, then, if he's not dead," said Innstein.

"Pre-avenged, brother. Now he owes us if we die."

"I would rather have something before I die than after. Maybe we can negotiate. A special poem, perhaps."

"You two, get down here as fast as you can!" I shouted. "We need to find Haldor!"

"I think he can take care of himself for the most part," said Utstein.

"He doesn't even need to worry about giant eagles anymore," added Innstein.

"It doesn't matter," I shouted, full of exasperation. "They knew we were coming. Alfhild isn't in her quarters—she is setting a trap."

"How could they know we were coming?" asked Utstein.

"Because there is a traitor! A hidden wolf, the one the prophecy told of. We need to get back to the ship!"

That gave the brothers pause. The details of how I knew and disbelief at such a claim would take a reasonable man minutes or hours for discussion. We did not have that, but we did have something more. The 'Steins were not just crewmates. They were my friends, and they trusted me.

"We are coming," said Innstein.

Both men disappeared from view.

"Are the rest of your friends that resourceful?" asked Vilgrip.

"All in their own ways."

"Thirty might be enough, then," he said, opening the door in the rock wall he had pointed out before. "Let's waste no time in finding the rest."

Down the steps and corridor we ran, Vilgrip leading the way. With the door open, the dull light of evening spilled in to show us our initial direction. There was only one passage at first, a single tunnel leading to a corridor that ran in both directions.

Each way branched off into more directions, with no indication of which way would take us where. The tunnels were humid and musty. Small blooms of foxfire glowed along the ceiling and walls, the only illumination once we no longer had the benefit of that open door at the top of the mountain.

"How do you know what direction to take?" I asked.

Vilgrip shrugged. "I can't see at all. And I know *a* direction to take. The one they brought me through when it was my time to go to the tower. We'll go right here and then take the first left. That will bring us to—"

I grabbed the man's shoulder at the sound of light footfalls around the next corner and drew Need. Would the man be armored? Probably. Better to attack part of him that was unprotected then. I readied the sword for a quick thrust to the face.

Hemming turned the corner. No mail, as it was never his practice to wear any. He held his seax at the ready until he saw who it was. He was more surprised than I was, which surprised me further in what was about to become a never-ending upward spiral of bewilderment.

"It's . . . good I found you!" he said.

I kept Need in a position ready for a quick thrust. "What are you doing here, Hemming?" Every ounce of my distaste for the tracker told me to be wary, that here might be the hidden wolf himself.

"It's not like that!" he squeaked, seeming to sense my distrust. "Haldor sent me to look for you! Have you seen the 'Steins?"

"I was expecting your people to be more resourceful and less nervous," said Vilgrip.

"He was just about to explain how he got this far up without being spotted," I said, watching every move Hemming made. I did not doubt that he'd been sent to look for us, but had it been by Haldor? How could I tell?

"I sneaked around! It wasn't difficult with all the side rooms to duck into. I was about to give up looking, but you can help now that I've found you!" His tone was full of fear, and his eyes darted back and forth. All of which made sense given where we were. It would also make sense if he was the traitor, looking for the last stragglers to find.

Vilgrip walked up to be inches from the tracker's face. "Help what?"

"Free the prisoners." Hemming shrank away and looked at me for assistance. "Haldor's orders! We found many cells but no guards. He sent me up to find you, said we were leaving with them."

Hemming's voice was as small as Vilgrip's figure was imposing: Tall and broad-shouldered and with the look of a man who was always losing patience. I had no doubt he could pick Hemming up and break his back if he felt the need.

"If they're in the prison cell area, they'll be trapped," said Vilgrip. "Long way between there and the exit, even if they have more people to fight alongside."

"Sword arms without swords," I said. "Vilgrip, is there an armory nearby?"

"No idea. It's not a thing they would have introduced me to."

"There is an armory; I passed it on my way here!" said Hemming. "We can bring weapons down to the prisoners."

"Let's be quick about it, then," I said. That *no way but forward* feeling intensified and sent a shiver down my back.

CHAPTER 47

THE WOLF INSIDE THE DOOR

VILGRIP AND I FOLLOWED HEMMING THROUGH THE DARK, twisting corridors until our path opened up into a huge cavern. A stone banister stood at the edge of the walkway, the only thing between us and the open area beyond. We were up on the highest floor of the place, looking down at several more floors, all carved into the side of the mountain.

Holes in the ceiling also let in a few faint rays of dull light, dripping with the water from above. It would be cold and wet down there. No wonder it's where they kept the prisoners.

Much of the mountain had been hollowed out. Walkways ran along the edges. Balconies were built out from tunnels like the one we had just emerged from. We stood looking out and down on a central open area. More foxfire grew wild and untouched along the ledges, though there was more light from torches five stories below.

We looked down and to the left to see four of the crew formed into a shield wall, Haldor and Svein most easily recognizable. There was no gate or door to the prison area, just an opening where two walls left a gap between them. It gave them the advantage of having to defend only a small area. My friends bided their time, occasionally lashing out against Alfhild's people.

A much larger group pressed in on them but did not seem to want to fully engage. Children of gods or not, they were too loose to have a real formation and did not charge in with much courage. More than a dozen

372

bodies lay prone already, a testament to what happened when they got too close.

"There they are," offered Hemming. "Just like I told you! Are you ready to help now?"

I wobbled back from the low (very low) would-be banister at the edge of the path overlooking the cavernous center of the place. It seemed to me it would be very easy to get down as long as you weren't picky about the means, but that was not helpful. Nevertheless, it was easy to see and hear what was going on but not so easy to see how we would get down to Haldor and company to aid them.

The sound of steel on steel rang out in the dim cavern. The clatter of breaking shields and rent armor served as background noise for the occasional stifled scream. Low laughter reverberated from Alfhild's people. They could see this ending in their favor, however long it might take.

I exchanged a look with Vilgrip, who must have been even more suspicious than I was. He patted the short spear he held, and I thought I took his meaning. He would hang back a little, and if Hemming led us into a trap, Vilgrip would try to get me out of there.

"This way," said Hemming as he led us toward a staircase closer to straight above where the battle was taking place. "The stairways nearest the entrance only go up one floor. But they keep the armory near the stairs up here in the middle. These stairs that lead all the way down."

He ducked into a room with lit torches inside. I braced for the unexpected as I followed him around the corner.

Armory? It was a supply room Arrow-Odd's army would have been impressed with. The walls stretched back a hundred feet from the entrance. To my left was nothing but spears and axes along the walls. To my right were simple helmets, no protective mail hanging from their backs. Barrels and crates of tools, clothing, shoes, and the like were all available. It was just about everything an army would need other than provisions.

In the back were shields. Lots of them, and all painted with the rune *opala*. Only it was a variation on the rune, showing little upturned feet. I may have been a poor student of Ketill's at times, but I remember Ketill's reaction when I carved something similar.

"Do not carve it that way. It is wrong, and something about that particular wrongness makes it foul."

Foully painted shields were better than no shields, however.

Hemming turned to me with a tentative smile. "You see?" he said.

"Hmmph," said Vilgrip as he entered.

"This is good," I said. "Spears into barrels. Hemming, as many shields as you can carry."

"Are we carrying them?" asked Vilgrip. "Or sending them down the fast way?"

I thought we would carry them, but "the fast way" sounded like we could just drop the wares straight down. Maybe? I would need another look to decide that.

With our arms full of spears and shields, we left the armory and went back to the banister. I poked my head just above it, hoping not to be seen.

The mass of foemen were being commanded to "reform and maintain discipline." Actually, I think you can't maintain what you don't already have, but I held my tongue. We could drop crates or barrels and maybe drop them on the heads of our enemies. But the space between them and the crew was too fluid, and depending on the timing, we might just drop the weapons within closer reach of our enemies. That would do us no good and would alert everyone to our presence.

Another group of god-children had massed at the opposite end of that cavernous main level, largely huddled on the staircase opposite us along that first floor. The large staircases around the sides of that cavernous area indeed only went up one story as Hemming had described.

An archway twice as tall as I was loomed in the darkness beyond. I guessed this was the main entrance and probably the only way out. Haldor would have to lead us in that direction at some point, and at that point, the crew would be surrounded. Greater numbers want a more open field of battle. All they had to do to get it was wait.

Vilgrip joined me as I pulled back from the banister. "Is there another way out of here than that main exit?" I asked.

"Not unless you dive out the waste chute into the freezing water below."

We would be fighting our way out then. Out through every warrior Alfhild put between our people and that archway. I hoped those prisoners had strong sword arms.

"Well? Dump the weapons here?" asked Vilgrip.

"Don't want the god-children to grab them in the chaos," I said, shaking my head. "We'll need to carry them down."

And fast. I knew we could not remain unnoticed forever, but it seemed not-forever was coming sooner than expected. A fast *clack-clack-clack* sound told me of two in fast pursuit. Where exactly they were was too difficult to tell with all the echoes of battle and the sounds of many other feet through the hollowed-out mountain.

Hemming motioned for us to join him. Vilgrip and I stepped away from the banister to follow before Hemming disappeared around a corner.

But Hemming did not turn the corner. He stopped short, not the action of a man who realized he was in the wrong corridor. He had the look of a man who had just run into something very, very bad.

"Wait!" shouted Hemming. "I have—"

Vilgrip and I dropped our barrels and drew our weapons.

An arm reached out and spun Hemming, then wrapped around his throat. Hemming's hands pulled at the arm but to no effect. The blade of a long seax came fully through him and punched out through the front of his tunic. Hemming's body went still with the stab from behind.

Hemming locked eyes with me and would not look away. His lips moved without sound, but his intent to convey was clear. Blood ran out of his mouth as he stood there wide-eyed, held up only by his attacker.

The owner of the blade let go, and Hemming fell to his knees. As he fell, he spent his last breath on a single word, only audible to one possessed of the keenest hearing:

"Svein."

Out from the shadows stepped a man with a long, bloody seax. His beard and hair were black, and his teeth showed in a wolfish grin I had come to know but never recognized until that moment.

Need became a spear, and I pointed it at Ulf's face.

"The skald has a very fine weapon," said Ulf. "Make sure you don't lose it after you kill him."

Half a dozen figures rushed out of the shadows past Ulf while the *clack-clack-clack* sound of others sprinting our way followed behind them. Vilgrip and I backed into the hollow of a stair entrance. They would not surround us, at least.

"Vilgrip!" choked out a man holding a long spear. He was outfitted with better equipment than we'd found in the armory, including a chain shirt and a helmet with only one eye socket. Same shield with the footed *opala*, though. "I thought we fed you to Grimhild."

"You never could see what was coming very well, Vikar," snarled Vilgrip.

Vikar beckoned the rest to move back as he strode ahead. "You can see what is coming," he said, almost as if to make peace. "You denied your heritage, and look where it got you."

Clack-clack-clack.

"Maybe you should take a look yourself," said Vilgrip. "Your brothers and sisters want to kill you no less than I do, but you'll have to live with them. Watching your back at every moment—ha! Some life, that."

"You are a rat caught in a trap," said one of the female warriors. Like Vilgrip, she had one hand, and it held a shield. It was her handless arm that was the weapon, her forearm fitted into a sleeve with a metal cup and two-foot spike. "Vikar, let me at them, and let's be done with this!"

Clack-clack-clack.

"Approach, then," said Vilgrip. "I always wanted to be an only child."

The woman bridled at the comment, but Vikar held her back. "You must be favored by the gods to have gotten out of there," said Vikar. "We can't deny that. Neither can you! You were hopeless and now you are raised up. Accept us now, and we will accept you back. This is where you belong."

Two shadows ran through the darkness behind our assailants. The floors clacked with each footfall. Though I could see no more than outlines, I knew them right away. We needed only seconds more.

"I see your point," I said. "What you see done around you is by any hands but your own, for any motivation but yours. You think your heritage makes you strong, and in giving away your own attributes, you leave yourself just a puppet."

"So says the mortal child of nobody," said Vikar. "That's the sound of inferior blood bubbling to the surface. In secret, though, you wish you were Odin's spawn."

"If you like Odin so much," roared Vilgrip, "join him!"

Vilgrip's spear flew like a bolt of lightning and took Vikar in the throat just above his chain shirt. He had little to say after that.

That was the beginning of chaos in those halls. I surged forward to meet Vilgrip's half-sister. She swatted away my spear but could not get close enough to attack me. The other god-children all moved forward until Ulf pulled two of them physically away from us and toward the onrushing threat.

It was fast enough to save himself, but not much else. Ulf had just realized what that *clack-clack-clack* sound was.

It was the sound of two men in far too great a hurry to unfasten their crampons.

Innstein's axe came down against the first god-child in a brutal arcing slash. Part of the axe's blade clanged off the helmet, but most of it found the jaw just below the face covering. Teeth flew out of the man's mouth and skittered down the hallway as he staggered backwards, flailing.

The other warrior held his shield steady and tried for an overhand slash against Innstein. He might have had a chance to do it if Utstein had stopped to engage him, but Utstein never stopped charging. He picked up the man bodily and drove him backwards before slamming him down onto the hard stone floor, scattering nearly all the combatants.

That was a fortunate thing for me. Utstein had driven the man so far back he knocked into the Tyrsdottir, who was dangerously close to slipping past my spear point. I saw the crush of bodies coming and managed to knock her in the head with the spear's butt end as she fell.

Too bad the spike of her weapon found my shin.

It's one thing to have a piece of steel driven through skin. If it hits muscle, that's worse. But there is a whole other world reserved for the pain of steel piercing bone. I was no great warrior, able to shrug off such wounds. My body twitched backwards, my foot fell behind to catch me, and only then my brain registered the bad news.

There is no step right there.

Down the stairs, I went. I shifted my weight and rolled with the fall as well as I could. Which, on stairs, was not very well at all. It hurt, though not nearly as much as the spike in my shin had. Then came the difficult part.

The Brisingamen was a wormy thing indeed. My beaver skin bag may have shut it up for a time, but somehow, it had gotten loose and found its way out. The blazing gold of the torc shined such that it lit the small area by itself, a beacon to more familiar eyes.

"The torc?!" shouted Ulf.

Through the melee over the fallen, Ulf pursued and was on me before I could get my balance or draw Need. As desperate as he was to have that jewelry, I was desperate to keep it from him, and I held onto it with both hands. I don't know how he lost his seax, but I know that if he'd still had it, I would have died right there.

An elbow slammed into the side of my head once, twice, three times. Ulf screamed into my ear to let the torc go. The stairway I had come down and the corridor beyond spun. Heavy, calloused hands tried to pry my fingers open. I slid away, pushed back with my head, anything to prevent his grip. I lost my bearings somewhere in the chaos of that struggle. The rest of the world seemed to fall away, and I feared it would remain so if I let go of that thing.

I'll admit to screaming when he tore away my skullcap and bit off part of my ear.

Even the dulling of pain that came with my blood being up could not stop that sensation. A sudden flash of fear pulsed through my body. I was being held down again, fighting but unable to get away, pushing with my knuckles even as they went white from gripping the torc.

Ulf took advantage of my stiff posture and turned me over so that I faced him. I twisted away, belly to the ground, and refused to let him even touch the thing. Repeated blows to the side of my face were the price.

No aid was coming. Time slowed down, at least to my perception. Only my mail-clad *fylgja* stood nearby, leaning on her spear. "You know better than to give your back to an enemy," said Svipul. "And better than to match him in strength."

An elbow struck the back of my head again, but I did not feel it. The pain and fear were washed away by the hunger. Some will tell you about "blood rage" or *berserksgangr*, but anger is the smallest part of it. I could see myself from the outside looking down, seeing my enemy even as I was turned from him. And it was hunger, a dispassionate craving for violence, that seethed through me.

With my left hand, I tossed the torc a few feet in front of me. Ulf could not help but reach for it, as I knew he would. And when he did, I drove Need's knifepoint down through his hand.

Ulf howled in fury at that. I turned and laughed in his face.

No phony thing, that laugh. In that state, there is no fear. In fact, there is a great humor in violence. What had just happened was better than any joke I had yet played.

The struggle that followed was just as frantic but without the desperation. On my part, at least. Ulf nearly had it once, his hand beyond mine and coming straight down on it. I could just barely grasp the thing, so I flicked it across the floor, out of the reach of us both. He cursed and struck me barehanded. I laughed and slashed at his midsection. Need rent his chain shirt as if it had just murdered every individual link. They fell away, but the man himself was unharmed.

Ulf was not willing to engage an armed man barehanded. Then the *clack-clack-clack* was coming again, and he knew what that meant. Ulf withdrew and ran, disappearing down another corridor. From the darkness, he called out, "You would have done better dying early, fool! Worse for you by far still waits."

The 'Steins heard this as they charged from the stairs and swept the immediate area. Vilgrip came through next. He was bleeding from a head wound, but his eyes were bright and focused. Seeing no one to fight, the brothers helped me up.

"How did you know we were betrayed?" asked Innstein.

"We raided Alfhild's rooms," I said. "She wasn't there. Should have been asleep. And no guard was posted. It wasn't right. And then the prophecy came back to me. It was foolish to ignore it."

"Impressive you made it up there," said Utstein. "The last thing we saw was that eagle carrying you out of sight. We assumed you were dead, so we avenged you."

"Pre-avenged," corrected Innstein.

"You two can argue or help your friends, but not both," said Vilgrip.

That shut them right up.

"Get the spears. Get the shields. If we free the other prisoners and arm them all, there is a fighting chance of escape."

"How about escape after we kill Ulf?" said Utstein.

A roar rumbled through the halls from somewhere in that place—like the snoring I'd heard in the pit with Vilgrip, only now whatever it was down there had gotten out of the dungeon. Someone had opened the portcullis from the lower level.

"Grimhild is out. And you're far outnumbered, even if my siblings aid you," said Vilgrip.

"Who is Grimhild?" asked Utstein.

"How big is this family of yours?" asked Innstein.

"There is no time to answer questions!" I said. "We need to warn Haldor about Svein. Get the spears and shields and follow Vilgrip." I realized the 'Steins had no context for anything as I stooped to pick up the torc. "And no matter what, whatever the cost, we cannot let them get this back. If I fall, take it off my body and get it out of here. Destroy it."

The 'Steins looked at me and then at each other. Both were already headed back up to collect weapons and shields as they called back to me.

"So many questions," said Innstein.

"You'd better live long enough to tell us the story later," added Utstein.

Chapter 48

Last Laugh

It turned out that the single stairwell by the armory did lead all the way down to the bottom floor. Lucky for us, the level I'd stumbled down into was a place Vilgrip was familiar with, or we might have trapped ourselves.

"You two," he said, gesturing at the 'Steins, "get down the stairs. There's a portcullis there; be ready to brace it open with spears. The wheel to lift it is here, so the two of us will do that. Work fast because once it is lifted, we will count to ten and then cut the rope that pulls it up."

"And we wait until you're through to pull the supports away?" asked Innstein.

"Where will that leave us, though?" Utstein added.

"At the rear of the prison area, where your people are holed up."

That was good enough for the rest of us. The 'Steins made off, and Vilgrip watched my back as I cranked the wheel that pulled the portcullis rope. The process seemed to go on forever, and my head pounded with the effort of every heavy turn. My leg burned where I had taken that steel spike in the shin. Both types of discomfort were muted by the fear that we might be attacked by another retinue at any time, so I pushed through the pain.

Finally, the thing hit a wall of resistance, and I knew the gate was fully raised.

"Footsteps," said Vilgrip.

I counted to ten perhaps a bit faster than I would have if he hadn't said that. I could hear them, too, but they were headed away from us, down a different corridor. We hadn't been seen after all.

Vilgrip gave me a nod on the count of nine. It seemed I was not the only one counting fast. I drew Need and slashed the rope, which fell down into the crevice I'd pulled it through. While just outside my sight, Need became a huge hammer. I took the hint and smashed the wheel, leaving nothing to pull that portcullis back up once we were through. Then we were off.

It turned out that stairwell stank like a *jǫtunn's* outhouse.

"One corridor smells worse than another," said Utstein as we passed through the open portcullis.

"And that is saying something," added Innstein, pulling his spear away to let the thing shut behind us.

"They have to dump waste somewhere," said Vilgrip, pointing to a large hole in the wall. "Might as well be near to the prisoners since we all stink anyway. That hole sends it all straight to the sea."

That would have to be one long tunnel of a waste hole to get all the way to the outside of the mountain. But there was plenty more mountain that had been bored into and hollowed out, like the prison area we now stood in. The prison cells were in a low-ceilinged area surrounded by solid rock. They would have given the impression of a dungeon had I not already known we were on the ground floor.

Cells lay open to my left and right as I strode forward. Most of my crewmates were massed further up where those cells ended. There, it was open where four abreast could fight side by side and hold off any attackers. That was a narrow enough space to defend well with two rows of fighters. Behind them, former prisoners stood on their toes and craned their necks to see what was happening beyond or armed themselves with the spears and shields the 'Steins had carried down.

Styrgrim looked back to see what the new commotion was and stepped back from the line to us. He wanted a word with the 'Steins, apparently, less so with me.

"Thought you were under attack," said Utstein.

"If the path is clear, let's arm every prisoner we can and get out of here," added Innstein.

Styrgrim shook his head. "There's no pressure on the front line right now. They backed off when that monster appeared. We're to hold here for now, Haldor's orders. That monster will wreck a shield wall in two swings, and then we're done for if we're out in the open. He says wait until he and Svein have dealt with it."

"He's in danger!" I shouted, trying to get Styrgrim's attention.

But my outcry was drowned out by the voice of something else. Something massive—bigger than the lindworm I had fought last year. Every other voice in that cavern echoed within its mass, but this one filled the entirety of the void. It was animal, but not one I had ever heard before. It was human without language or sanity. Something more than feral was in that voice. It was a madness that wild animals never had.

"That's Grimhild," said Vilgrip. "She's out of the pit!"

Styrgrim rejoined the line, locking his shield with the others. Through a brief gap, I saw that Alfhild's god-children had halted their attack. They were even backing away.

"I need to warn Haldor," I told Vilgrip.

"Who?"

I turned away from him. Everything was taking too long to explain.

"Haldor!" I shouted as I approached the line, my eyes searching for both our leader and for Svein in case I ran afoul of him. "Haldor!"

"Look who joins us!" said Magnus. "Haldor's fighting that great scaly beast with Svein."

"*Stop him!*" I screamed as men held me back from charging in. "We need to stop him! We need to get out!"

"Stop him or get out, which is it?" demanded Styrgrim.

"Has he gone mad?" asked Bjorn. "That is a lot of blood."

"Stop your screeching, boy!" said Kraki. "Haldor's orders: Stay put and let them deal with this thing."

Even Nanthild's eyes silently questioned my sanity.

"You don't understand," I said, flailing as half a dozen arms pulled me back in. Too much was happening all at once. There was no time to explain. I knew my manner seemed too strange to be taken seriously, and I could not convince anyone of my need. The roars of the monster drowned out all but what I could shout into someone's face.

My father's hand grabbed the inside of my shirt and pulled me back, and that was one thing too much. That was when I punched Styrgrim the Bear in the face, probably the only person to do so and live.

He stood in stunned surprise for a moment.

"Svein is a traitor!" I screamed into his face.

He shook his head. "He fought with us," he snarled. "When you were not here."

"And how many did he cut down?" I demanded. "Was his axe bloody when he set off with Haldor?" I waited a moment for the man to search his memory. "I fought Ulf up above, saw him kill Hemming. I think Hemming was part of the betrayal but had a change of heart, so Ulf killed him. He died with Svein's name on his lips as a warning. Come on! You fought with Haldor Skullsplitter! When will he be more vulnerable to a knife in the back?"

Realization came upon Styrgrim, the realization he had made a mistake. My father breathed in what seemed like all the air in that mountain. His shoulders broadened like great muscled wings. Bone-white knuckles gripped his sword. His features hardened and his voice dropped to a hoarse growl.

Styrgrim the Bear.

I would not want to fight him.

That is what your father could do when he was half dead. He did much more in the days before that.

"Does this crew know *svynfilking?*" he demanded.

Svynfilking. The Swine Array. The charging wedge formation designed to break an enemy's shield wall.

"We do. But I don't know about them," I said, gesturing at the prisoners. Some grabbed spear and shield right away. Some stumbled, barely able to catch their feet beneath them. Men and women, most of them about my age.

Two came out who seemed to know one another and were truly strange. The first one had the padded feet of a hound, but he was far closer to a man than the bigger one, who was a moose from navel to foot. Navel to hoof, I suppose, and only halfway there since he still walked on two legs.

"They are the children of gods," I continued. "Or some of them are. Some were just caught up at the same time. Either way, the ones still locked up are those who would not swear loyalty to Alfhild. How much they've fought before, I don't know."

"Straight up the middle," said Kraki. "They'll get the idea."

Styrgrim shook his head. "And do you lead if Haldor falls?"

It was not an outcome I wanted to contemplate. The feeling was made worse by Kraki's lack of answer. He was a great fighter but chaotic and no good at giving battlefield commands.

"If you want to get out of here, I suggest you give your trust to Styrgrim and follow his commands absent Haldor," said Bjorn.

And then, the surprise of surprises, Kraki looked at me.

I would decide at that moment who would command the crew. A shake of my head would mean Kraki would do his best. Or maybe he would point to one of the others. Magnus for experience, maybe, or Ingolf for steadiness. But if I nodded, that would put us under the command of Styrgrim the Bear, my father and mental antagonist. Not one of us.

But I knew what he could do, so I nodded.

"Look here, you lot!" shouted Kraki. "Styrgrim leads on land until Haldor's return, understand?"

Magnus chanced an uncertain look back at my father and then at me. He grinned. He'd left my father's ship before, but I had no doubt there was something of fighting side by side with Styrgrim he missed.

"Put the ones who know that formation in the front," Styrgrim commanded. "Those without experience but with a shield, further down the line. Anyone without a shield stays in the middle and protects the flanks or punches through as soon as the boar's snout creates an opening."

"Most experienced are you and me," said Bjorn.

Styrgrim considered his skald's words. "Stay closer to the back and help organize the prisoners. Magnus will remember well enough to join me at the front." He turned and left us, disappearing behind a crush of men and women and heading to the front of our line.

I stared out beyond our defensive line. Out in the lonely middle of the cold, wet stone, Haldor circled the beast from the pit. I was behind most of the line but stood up to get a better look. No sign of Svein, so that was at least something.

"What is that thing?" I asked, hoping someone, anyone, might name it. That was a troll so big and ugly it should probably have its own word. There's a power in uncertainty, and humans everywhere have reduced that power by naming things. Trolls are harder to name the more powerful they get.

It was twelve or so feet tall, but that was only because of its stooped posture. Maybe you'd call this an ogre or a misshapen *jǫtunn*, but neither would be adequate to convey the wrongness about its whole body. Humans don't have scales or tusks, and spiders don't have opposable thumbs or ears. A tattered loincloth covering the thing from waist to thigh was its only clothing, but not its only protection. Its midsection was armored with scales like a lindworm, while its arms and legs were covered in prickly hairs.

Two mostly humanoid arms held swords, the likes of which even Haldor would have found heavy. Two longer, thinner arms originated at the shoulder blades and had an extra elbow each. Both of these terminated in sharp claws rather than hands. I would rather meet my end at one of those, I thought, than its horrid, dripping mouth full of yellow teeth.

"They call her Grimhild," said Vilgrip. "They feed her prisoners from time to time. I've never heard of her coming out of that pit, though."

"Grimhild, eh? I heard stories," said Bjorn, shaking his head. "But now I see it and I can't deny it." He made a gesture over his forehead, grabbing some of his hair and pulling it down. "Look at that dark forelock! That's Ogmund's mother, after all."

Yellow eyes without pupils glowed with a madness beyond anger. The black hair grew back wild as an untouched forest but for one part. In the middle of its head, a distinct black forelock hung down like a tussock.

Ogmund Tussock. You never know what you might inherit from a parent.

"You've never seen Ogmund, I suppose," said Bjorn. "But maybe you see what I mean."

And I would never be able to un-see it. "What would being sired by that troll do to a person?" I asked.

Bjorn shook his head. "She was a troll long ago if you believe the stories. Who knows what she was like then?"

Redbeard's story came back to me. I did not believe any king would mate with this Grimhild. Or if one tried, how would he have survived? No, something was missing from the story, maybe many somethings. And I wonder how much a troll Grimhild really had been, or if Harek might have weaved some of his sorcery to her detriment before Ogmund had even been born.

The torc was unnaturally heavy inside my bag as if pulling at my attention. I had a powerful item. Could I use it to our advantage? No, that was the sweet idea trying to trick me, just as Ketill had described. I cinched the bag tighter, and soon, the idea of taking it out was lessened.

As far as we were from Grimhild, I still flinched every time she shrieked. The high pitch of her wail pierced my ears as Varg's battle cow had, only it was not the urge to strike out that came with it. It was fear, just fear.

In between the screams, Bjorn organized the prisoners behind our crew. I moved to somewhere in the middle of the right edge, where someone had shoved me. I couldn't take my eyes off the fight that was already going on, though.

Haldor hopped out of the way of a long swipe from one of Grimhild's secondary arms. But only just. The monster had reached too far and could not follow up with a swipe from the other arm, leaving it vulnerable to an immediate counterattack. Haldor took advantage with a swipe of Silence that would have severed the arm of any human. The horn of his axe caught her arm by an inch and drew blood.

Grimhild screamed again and lunged, heedless of keeping her balance. Haldor raised his shield just in time to take a blow from the other long arm and was knocked backwards when his own shield hit him in the helmet. The giant of a man grinned as he backed off a few steps and circled his enemy. This would be a challenge unlike any other he had faced.

Where had Svein got to?

Alfhild's voice rose over the din. I had not heard it since last summer, but there was no mistaking that sickly-sweet tone. "You have something of mine," she said, her voice echoing from high above.

The monster paused in that moment, as if responding to Alfhild's intent.

"We will have more than you think," roared Haldor, never taking his eyes off Grimhild. "How far north did you flee? How high did you build your tower? Yet here we are."

"You are brave *and* resourceful," she said, drawing out the words as if seducing the man.

God-children piled up the steps, withdrawing even farther from the fight. At first, I had thought this self-preservation on their part, but no— they moved to the sound of her voice.

"And your little skald surprises yet again! I'm told he's stolen a torc of mine."

"Perhaps he would replace it with a different piece of metal at your throat," growled Haldor.

"No doubt!" she laughed. "But for that piece of metal, I will offer a fine reward, and one you will enjoy since you will have your lives as well."

"We can run for it now!" said one of the prisoners behind me. "The way is clear!"

"Shut up, you!" barked Bjorn. "They will cover that entrance before we're halfway across and surround us, that thing included. Wait now. Wait and stay with us." He turned to me then, as had many others. "What is she talking about, this torc?"

"An artifact," I said. "She needs it for what she is doing here."

Bjorn eyed me another moment and understood. Not that he understood any of the details, but sometimes the wise understand when there is no time for details.

"Where is that shitman you recruited from our crew?" said Haldor, his voice now matching her in sweetness. "Oh, I think there was more than the one, as Svein has disappeared. But he was not likely to make such plans by himself. I am certain he had a minder, the other one who I haven't seen much of lately. What was his name? Ah: *Wet Ulf.*"

Ulf's voice roared back from high up. "Shut up, Haldor! You pissed on your so-called Brothers more times than you can count! Never one for sharing fame, even if you were the smallest part of it."

"What friends your wisdom has gained you!" replied Haldor. "Bare is the back of a brotherless man."

"Shut up, Haldor! It was I who advised you, I who provided wisdom. But you ignored my best advice, and look where that has gotten you. You were a fool in life, and you're a fool as you walk toward your death."

"I have done many foolish things indeed," said Haldor. "Not the least was taking you at your word. But I don't envy your lot, Ulf. I walk proudly with my Brothers no matter where I go. You are a steaming pile of shit sliding from one place to another. You may get where you want to go eventually, but the trail you leave will not be one to speak about in verse."

"We'll shut you up one way or another, Haldor! And then the only verse made will be about how your skin was peeled away bit by bit, your fingers and toes taken one at a time."

The nerves of that one panicking prisoner would not hold despite Bjorn's assurances. Again and again, he implored that we rush for the exit now while we had a chance. After Ulf's description of torture, he broke from our group and ran.

I can't fault him for cowardice. Few people can stand their ground in a shield wall without shitting themselves, and fewer still when standing shoulder to shoulder with an unfamiliar lot. Holding that line is more a matter of trust than of courage. It was the breaking of that trust that made Ulf's betrayal so disgusting, worse than one of us dying in battle.

Grimhild marked the fleeing prisoner as he covered the ground between him and the exit. She waited at first, letting him distance himself from the rest of us. When he was too far to turn back, she sprang at him, away from Haldor. Her loping strides were awkward and looked like she needed two more legs, her longer arms neither helping her run nor certain what they should be doing. But each step was so long that even I would not have been able to outrun her for long.

It seemed she would snatch the man up with ease until I saw the second figure charging. Through the shadows came Styrgrim, his reddened blade resting on one shoulder. Black hair and black leather blended in with the dark stone of the floor, and he flew forward faster than any man his age should have been able to.

His shield abandoned, Styrgrim reached out to grab the panicking prisoner and flung the man backwards. One clawed hand swiped at him at the same time. It pulled back in pain when Styrgrim's sword came down.

That blade was Halstein's make, no doubt about it. The waves of steel layered one upon the other showed a distinct pattern that my grandfather and few others knew the secret of. And as Halstein's blade, it bit deep enough to draw blood.

Again, Grimhild screamed and raised her swords against my father. It looked like his end for certain, and the thought struck me like a fist to my gut. So many unsaid things, so much unresolved. In that moment, I realized I had never really known the man, never would, and had been a petulant ass in the camp when I could have remedied much of what had been between us.

The swords came down side by side with horrific force, clanging on the stone below and striking up sparks that lit the cavern like lightning. My father was not in their path.

A discerning listener undistracted by the great noise might have heard his low, derisive laughter as he hopped aside. He disappeared under a second attack to slash at her midsection, but it came to nothing as it glanced off her scaly armor.

That was of little matter. The power of Grimhild's unknowableness was no more. Twice she had bled, and that was something. But now she had been laughed at, and she would never be as intimidating again.

"Is this the best you have?" roared Styrgrim as the two slashed at each other, neither to any effect. "Is this Ogmund's greatest champion?"

"How distracted we've become," said Alfhild. "I have not even made my offer."

Grimhild pulled back again, this time plainly unhappy about it.

Haldor spoke low to Styrgrim and waved him off. I could not hear what he said. Weeks ago, I would have guessed he was waving him off to face Grimhild alone for the future stories that would make. But now I knew Haldor, and that was not it. He wanted Styrgrim in a position to help his Brothers, should he fall.

"There is no reason we cannot come to a fair resolution," said Alfhild. "Swear off your allegiance to Arrow-Odd and swear to Ogmund in his place. You will be well-rewarded. Of course, the return of my jewelry will be necessary, but that hardly seems—"

"What a strange creature you are," interrupted Haldor. "I have often wondered what it is like to value nothing. You are more like a spirit waiting to be called rather than the *vǫlva* calling it."

The biggest of the god-children, sons and daughters of Thor, no doubt, massed on one side of the cavern. Out from the middle of them all, a man half a head taller and twice as wide as any of the others shoved his way through. The stupid smirk on Svein's face was one I will never forget. Svein, the dimwitted giant, had outsmarted the rest of us in joining up with our enemies.

Hemming. Ulf. Svein. Had Hemming tried to warn me before we set sail? Had he bitten his tongue only at the last moment last night when I brought him a bowl of stew? Too late, he had turned back to the rest of us, and it cost him his life. Svein, on the other hand, showed no regret. Jealousy blazed in his eyes. He must have been an easy recruit for Ulf, who likewise craved more word-fame for himself. What would happen when the two of them had to share in the word-fame spoils, I wondered.

Perhaps thinking along the same lines as I, Haldor drew back and addressed Svein directly. "Better to have tools than Brothers, I am sure they told you. Better to direct the pieces on the *hnefatfl* board than to be a piece someone moves. You'll soon find you have neither Brothers nor tools. There you are, a piece directed on a board. Come on then, *tafl* piece, it is time for you to move forward!"

Alfhild's voice dropped like a cold rain. "The others may think differently when they see your fate," she sighed.

"There will be no bargain here," said Styrgrim, turning suddenly. "What have you other than an ugly thing and an army of brats begging for their allowance? Children of gods!" he hocked, loudly clearing his throat, and spat on the ground. "Dead children, those I've traded blows with! Pretend that heritage grants great boons if you like. I am Styrgrim Halsteinsson. Some call me the Bear, and not from accident of birth. No spoiled brats do I crave as cousins."

Grimhild hissed at him, far as he was from her at that point, but her steps were all toward Haldor.

Meanwhile, Svein descended the remaining steps, holding back the godchildren as if they were moving too fast. They were not. It looked more like he was buying time for himself, maybe hoping Grimhild would do the hard work for him.

"What are we waiting for?" I said.

"Haldor's orders," said Styrgrim. "We're to stay put until he kills that thing."

Haldor eyed Svein's approach while fighting Grimhild. That was a dance I will never see the like of again. Haldor was constantly in danger and Grimhild constantly lashing out. Yet every time she did, he dodged just to the side or just out of reach. The slashes of her swords came so close they could have taken whiskers off his beard. But never did they bite his flesh.

Likewise, Haldor's reflexes found openings to slash at Grimhild, but he could not do more than draw a little blood from one of her limbs. Her armor protected her from all but the strongest slash, and that Haldor could not find an opening for. She was slow and clumsy compared to the man, but two swords and two arms beside her left little space for him to work with.

Behind me, two unfamiliar voices bickered. "It's cowardly to stand back here and let others fight on our behalf," said one in a hoarse tone.

"They let us out and not to purchase us," barked the other. "I'm going to trust their judgment, and so should you, brother."

I turned to see the two part-animal prisoners. The one that was half moose let out an animalistic growl.

The one with hound's feet saw me turn and addressed my attention. "He'll hold," he said. "But best you let him through the middle before anyone else. He fights better on his own and with a shorter weapon than a spear."

"It's Kraki who goes up the middle," I said.

"Which one is Kraki?" demanded the moose-man. A bone club tapped him on the shoulder.

"You can wait your turn, Elk-Legs," said the old cook. "Grab a spear if you're so excited."

"I am Moose-Frothi," he said, scowling. "I have waited for my turn far too long now, and I work better with a short blade. Give the spear to my brother, Thorir, and you'll be better off for both."

Kraki gave the man a hard stare. After a moment's appraisal, he drew his own seax and handed it over. Moose-Frothi grinned as he took it.

"Stand ready!" shouted Styrgrim. He stood in the front rank next to Nanthild, Magnus having moved back. She was a warrior smaller in stature than we would normally see at the fore. Nanthild's frame looked so slight with her slender fingers gripping that sword. But I knew from experience she was stronger—much stronger—than she looked.

Styrgrim said something to her in a low tone. Nanthild shoved her shield at him and pushed him back. Farther than anyone should have been able to do. Styrgrim nodded—he had seen enough and addressed the rest of us.

"Do you want to get out of here?" he demanded. When he was met with confused looks and wordless mouthings, he shouted, "Well, *do* you?!"

Yes! came the answers.

"One man isn't an army," he continued. "One man isn't a shield wall. They have bigger numbers, and they can keep them. Big numbers don't matter much against a wedge that holds firm. So you all stay an army—*my* army. You stay a tight wedge, whether you're standing or running or re-forming. Listen to my voice, and don't hesitate a moment at my commands. I will tell you where to be, and you will remain an army. Hard for any entitled brats to fight an army. Follow my commands, and we will win free of this place."

By the gods, even I believed him.

He was readying us to charge for the exit. But that assumed Haldor would kill Grimhild. Haldor was a hero among men, larger than others in size and courage, strength and fortitude. There was never any question of him not killing Grimhild because that is what he did. But there he was fighting this four-armed thing while opportunistic killers waited to close in.

Grasping at revenge, more regret he'll earn, a yield to share with his yeomen.

We had insisted to one another that we were not Odd's yeomen. Yet here we were, fighting his enemies with two of his best men.

Dread took me. Not just of fighting in a shield wall, which was bad enough. It was Haldor's command to wait until he had killed Grimhild.

What if he did not? We might charge that monster, but would our spears turn and break on its scales? Would it hew us down three at a time with each sword stroke unless we helped Haldor to kill her?

The Wolf of Bees' weave wavers.

The prophecy was playing out.

"We have to charge her!" I shouted.

"Orders!" Styrgrim shouted back. "He knows what he's doing."

Grimhild's attacks started coming in planned series rather than haphazardly. She slashed at Haldor's right, forcing him to move his shield. Then the long claw on her other side shot out at the opening his movement made. He was too fast to let it skewer him, but those claws raked along his mail shirt and sent dozens of its tiny ringlets skittering to the ground.

Svein took that as a sign to attack. The fat man rushed in shield-first and tried to knock Haldor down. Again, Haldor was quicker, and Svein scored only a glancing blow. Haldor circled out from between his two enemies and set up to face them both at once.

He grinned and addressed Svein directly with a verse:

> "That witch matches her
>   wisdom only with
> how much hate
>   she harbors for herself.
> How long before
>   her foul spirits
> find the next hapless
>   hero to feed on?"

Enraged, probably at the truth of Haldor's implication, Svein rushed him a second time. Svein's oversized axe struck Haldor's shield again and again as our leader laughed. After four or five strokes, all turned so the power behind them was nil, Haldor struck back a single time. He lifted Svein's shield up with Silence's long spike, stepped to the side, and slammed the rim of his shield into Svein's mouth.

Haldor was fighting both Svein and Grimhild and winning. I wanted to cheer, to charge out and fight with him, but I held my place in the shield wall. If it came down to it, could I cast a spell that would help us? My mind raced for an idea.

Haldor kept Svein between him and Grimhild. If the monster had any inclination to kill indiscriminately, she was not willing to offend Alfhild's will to do it. Svein staggered backwards and fell. I wondered why Haldor had not followed up with a killing stroke. What was he doing?

And then I knew: He didn't care about Svein. He could kill Svein at will, or leave the task to Magnus. But Haldor *had* to kill Grimhild and would not take any bait that endangered that goal. Haldor had just baited his own hook.

Tired of waiting, Grimhild stepped over Svein to make her own attack, and then I saw Haldor's plan. It was awkward to step over that giant hunk of meat, Svein, and in doing so, Grimhild held her arms out wide for balance. And why not? Haldor was outside her striking range, leaving her far outside his.

Unless he threw his axe.

Silence flew end over end to take Grimhild high in the chest, where her scales thinned out and became leathery skin. No more glancing blows—the horn of the axe pierced her and stuck fast, the full weight of the weapon throwing her backwards. Grimhild stumbled back and tripped over Svein, who fell down a second time.

Haldor was on her as her back hit the ground, pulling Silence from her chest and holding it over his head with both hands, his shield discarded.

One sword licked out and took off his left arm at the elbow. It was not enough to stop him.

Haldor brought Silence down through the middle of her tussocked skull and into the rock beneath it, the hand of his severed arm still gripping the axe.

Silence had truly descended in that cavern where we had all forgotten to breathe. And then echoing throughout was Haldor in great, heaving guffaws.

Svein called over those six other warriors. They rushed all at once and hacked at him. One-armed and already dying, it still took them all to bring the man down.

And that is why Haldor Skullsplitter died laughing.

CHAPTER 49

HEROES

THE SHOCK OF SEEING HALDOR DIE HAD MY SENSES TIED IN knots. He had been our leader, sure. But I'd looked to him for more than leadership without ever realizing it, and suddenly the world seemed a very strange place.

Styrgrim pointed his sword, and we moved forward as one. He shouted something, probably about keeping a tight formation. There was not much point in formation if it wasn't a tight one. I saw but didn't hear him. The world was silent but for a high-pitched tone, making it difficult to focus on more than one thing for very long. My head throbbed. Every heartbeat felt like a drum beating on my leg and what was left of my bleeding ear.

Then, I was moving forward as the man ahead and to my left moved. I had a spear and a shield, but I was uncertain how to hold them—how to hold anything anymore because it seemed to me the whole of Midgard had been turned upside-down. I felt a tingling in my hands as if all the blood had drained out of them. They were cold, so cold. I slipped a little on the wet stone but caught myself.

We moved away from the prison area and into the great cavern in the middle of the mountain. So many people, so much shouting. The shouting rose in volume. We increased our pace. Soon, we were running. Not at my full speed, but maybe at someone else's. I was a faster runner than most. That was good, running felt good.

Then I looked at where we were running. We were running at a shield wall. As I thought this, my senses began to return. We were running at a shield wall full of spears pointed at us.

Shit, we were running at a shield wall full of spears pointed at us!

I felt the shock of the first collision all the way down the line. Styrgrim and Nanthild had the unenviable position of the closest-quarters fighting. Despite their fine swords, this was less like slashing and more like shoving and headbutting and occasionally biting.

The foemen pressed back against them, no better able to swing their weapons than Styrgrim and Nanthild. Other enemies not quite so close jabbed spears in our general direction but were on their heels. Meanwhile, our second and third ranks countered with their own spears, finding more gaps to drive them through with the surge of our momentum.

Vilgrip was one of those. Losing one hand had left him unable to carry a shield in the front rank, but the man knew where to stick his spear.

Someone shoved me from behind, and I shoved the man ahead and to my left, and so on. Those of us within range of the shield wall stabbed out and tried to avoid being stabbed in the frenetic back and forth. Those too close to stab set to shoving, trying to make room. In that space of about five feet was where the fight would be won or lost. Would the defenders hold fast long enough for their kin to overwhelm us from behind? Or would we punch a hole through their line and send enough fighters through to roll them up?

"Get ready, Moose-Boy," growled Kraki. "That is the best of knives. Don't let me regret handing it over."

"Old man," thrummed Frothi's voice, "this had better be a good blade because I intend to test it on every entitled cuntling here."

Alfhild's bitter voice screamed something behind us and was the only discernible voice in the chaos. Not the chant of a spell or a call to negotiate this time. She was giving commands.

And the main command was: Get the skald.

For about a second, part of me thought she might mean Bjorn. But no, it was me. Or, more specifically, it was what I carried.

Two warriors, a man and a woman, rushed me. I held my spear out, hoping one of them would run into it, but they never got that close. One of our crewmen thrust out to ward them off but over-committed and took a spear to his armpit. He fell backward. I thought, belatedly, that I should probably move forward and fill his space in the line.

I was too slow. Thorir stepped in and made a counter-thrust across the face of the man to skewer the woman through her cheek. Blocked that way, the man ducked as he tried to press on. By that point, I thrust at him with my own spear. I did not draw blood, but it was enough to send both warriors back to their line.

"Look for him later," said Thorir when I chanced a look back at the man with the wound to his armpit. "Hold this line and let my brother through, and maybe he'll live."

Confusion was the order of the day for Alfhild's people. They could have swarmed me right away without regard for losses, but too many didn't know who "the skald" was. Powerful sorcerer as she was, Alfhild was shit at providing clear directions on a battlefield. Some trying to command on the ground were pushing to encircle our little boar's snout, while others were sure they had to hold that middle before anyone got through.

That confusion was to our advantage, but the fight was still taking too long. The longer we fought, the less likely we were to win through.

I thought our last moments might be upon us. With a final effort, the difference between winning and losing was down to the child of a god under-estimating Nanthild's strength.

Maybe he thought to be the hero who would break our line and win himself some fame or at least some favor with his master. He held back his mates for a moment and locked shields with Nanthild, ready to shove her back and strike at the middle of the snout.

Nanthild threw him back with some force, making room to swing. The first such swing took the leg off one of the three warriors engaging Styrgrim.

Down to a mere two against one, Styrgrim broke the jaw of the first with an uppercut from his sword pommel. On the downstroke, he took off the arm of the other.

In four quick movements, the line of god-children was broken. Moose-Frothi and Kraki dove through the opening.

I think you know what it would be like for Kraki to bring down that bone club on the back of your head, but let me be clear about Moose-Frothi: He was *big*. If you've ever had a moose charge you, then you might have an idea what it was like, even though he had two legs rather than four. Those massive haunches launched him against our enemies trying to reform, knocking them away as he bellowed.

Soon, there were foemen on the ground and backing away. Frothi caught the arm of one and lopped off her hand at the wrist. She fell back with the others, and Frothi took her short sword, both hands now holding blades. No one wanted any part of that fight; the ones hoping to be the heroes of their lot were nowhere to be found.

Kraki, no unpracticed hand at this, was through and crushing enemies beneath every thunderous strike. Blades turned on his body, finding little purchase on his bare skin.

One warrior leaped forward to stab with his spear and struck true, but to little effect. Kraki pulled the spear forward and crushed the man's skull, and then no one wanted any part of that fight either.

We moved forward and blocked Alfhild's people from the exit on one side, the other line doing the same opposite us. Some of the enemy made awkward attempts at edging around our flanks, but they did not have the coordination to do it well.

Styrgrim's commands, contrasting Alfhild's, were short, clear, and obeyed at once. He sent Kraki and Frothi down the tunnel as shock troops in case any foemen were left down that passage. The rest re-formed.

"Reverse the wedge!" Styrgrim shouted, grabbing Nanthild by the shoulder. Now we were facing away from the tunnel, the tip of the snout pointing in the opposite direction and intended for defense. "Give the injured time to move!" He and Nanthild took new positions just behind the tip of the snout, the 'Steins holding the foremost point.

If there was anyone blocking the exit or arrayed outside on those steps, Kraki and Frothi would clear the way. The prisoners who could not fight much but could walk helped the injured. I saw the man who'd taken a spear to the armpit holding one arm to his bloody side as he hobbled through the tunnel behind us. That wound was a deep one, and at a glance, I wasn't sure he would make it to the ship. Another man caught him as he stumbled and helped him continue: The man who had run, who Styrgrim had brought back. Our exit had begun.

We would hold there. I would hold there. It would probably be fine until we needed to break formation to retreat. And that struck me as the kind of idea that sounded good until you got to the end. The first steps might be difficult, but not nearly as much as the last ones when all the others had fled down the passageway and every spear was focused on the last warrior to leave.

Above us, Alfhild chanted a spell. I braced for the unknown. Would it be another demon boar? Would Grimhild rise and attack us? No, it would be something unforeseen. When nothing seemed to happen, that was even worse. Soon, I saw her intent. If she could not reorder the chaos below, she would embrace it by conjuring a *berserksgangr* upon her warriors.

The first major onslaught of *berserkir* hit the side of our wedge opposite me. Nine of them hit us and broke through. Over my shoulder, I saw the milky white eyes of a drooling warrior lock on me as he rose, having been knocked down from the impact. Fear and indecision hit me. I did not want to leave a gap in my side of the line, but our other side was broken and we had to repel that attack first.

Ingolf was on the side with me. In one fluid motion and with only a single initial glance, he spun his spear overhead and buried it in the man's back. His eyes hardly leaving those foemen ahead of him, he spun the spear back over to continue his defense of the line before those facing us realized it had been a good time to attack.

That took care of one problem without leaving a gap in our line, but there were other problems to deal with. One of the prisoners holding our other line had been knocked down in the charge. She could not reach her spear in time as another *berserkr* towered over her.

In the next moment, the downed woman locked eyes with that frenzied god-child, and he froze. His mouth twitched, but no other part of him moved.

Magnus came on like a blur, his feet never stopping as he struck at that frozen god-child and the other temporary *berserkir* who had broken through. Axe and seax flashed against one, two, and then a third. Not much for holding a shield, the melee played to Magnus' strength.

Two more *berserkir* thought to mob Nanthild, to their detriment. She slew them both. Styrgrim threw back the last one with his shield, following it with a feinted overhead slash that turned into a thrust to the throat. The charge repelled, more of us fled down the tunnel, and we shortened the wedge.

I took up position where Nanthild had left a gap in the line, right next to Innstein. At the very front was spear work, and plenty of it. The points of enemy spears always seemed to be aimed right at one of my eyes, and I flinched and shook, my counter-thrusts never finding anything but soft linden or hard shield bosses.

"You just have to—" Innstein thrust forward with one smooth motion to pierce an enemy through his helmet's eye socket. Not a fatal thrust, but enough to end his participation in the back and forth. Innstein recovered as fast as he had attacked, leaving no opening. "Like that," he said.

"Spear work is so boring," said Utstein.

"Brother, you are just jealous my spear is longer than yours."

"Ha! It was I who killed the eagle, and you are jealous you didn't think of the weighted hook first."

"The eagle survived the fall. It was I who killed it with a rock and a concentrated effort."

"Which would have never worked if not for my idea in the first place."

"Back, move back!" Styrgrim called again.

We had survived so far, but we would not hold much longer. We stepped over bodies, mostly theirs but some of them ours, as we retreated to a smaller and smaller wedge protecting the tunnel entrance. Again, Alfhild chanted, this time faster and more feverishly. The enemy's front line pulled back, waiting for those in a frenzied state to punch through. I was not sure we could stand many more such assaults. And I was not sure we could outrun her warriors.

The 'Steins were looking at me, and I could tell they were thinking the same thing.

Then they looked at each other and hatched a plan, as only those two could do.

"If you die after we pre-avenged you," said Innstein, not finishing his sentence other than shaking his head.

"That would be a big insult," said Utstein. "And we wouldn't get our poem, either. You had better go as soon as we do this."

Innstein ducked across me and fiddled with my bag. "We know how to ruin this witch's day!" he shouted.

"We'll send that torc right down their rancid poop chute and into the sea!" Utstein continued.

Which is exactly what I thought they were about to do—only not at all. Innstein was only making as if to take the torc from me when he took a few wooden discs instead. His own bag stuffed, and the view of what was happening blocked by his brother, the 'Steins lit out sideways across the floor to go around the main host and draw the *berserkir* away from us.

"Stop those two, whatever it costs!" yelled Alfhild, confirming for us all that the two brothers had just executed a most brilliant battlefield deception.

And confirming they would spend their lives to do it.

"Come on!" Styrgrim shouted at the 'Steins. "Get behind me!"

My stomach twisted itself in knots. Again, my friends would die to save me, and again I would do nothing to save them. Even my father didn't want them spending their lives to secure our retreat.

Sacrifice required to sail on. The cost of loyalty lays many low, one way or another.

Few remained still outside the small entryway. Styrgrim continued to slash his way through the enemies that came near. "Move!" he shouted, and I knew he intended to be the last one to retreat.

"Don't forget that poem you owe us," shouted Utstein.

"It needs to be a good one!" finished Innstein.

Styrgrim cursed but moved the rest of us into the tunnel. I was ahead of him but slipped on a patch of wet rock as he ran by, egging me on. I stumbled, and Magnus caught me. *If only I had kept my crampons on*, I thought.

And in that instant I realized I could do better than a poem before I left.

"We are going," said Magnus, lifting and dragging me at the same time.

"There is one more thing I can do," I said, pulling back. "Just hold that opening for a moment!"

"Get yourself and that jewelry of Alfhild's, whatever it is, out of here!"

"I need you to trust me," I said, "I must do this."

Magnus cursed but stopped with the dragging and held the entrance of the tunnel.

Slipping just into the shadows, I pulled a disc from my pouch. I didn't much care which one it was. It would be the carving that determined all. Ketill's words from a year ago rang in my ears.

"Fire in concentrated form? You should have inverted isaz."

But I didn't want fire. I wanted *isaz* just as it was. That and *fehu* would do it. Ice, and plenty of it.

I sliced my palm crossways against the scar from last summer to make an X on my hand. Recalling the icy cold of being caught out in the blizzard when I first saw Svipul, I felt the energy flow through me and into the disc as I bled into the runes. It was taking a lot out of me, and even so, I poured more of my will into it.

It would not save the 'Steins, but it would give them a last laugh, a laugh to die for.

I threw the disc out as far as I could into the open area. The effect began as soon as it struck the waterlogged floor and shattered as if it had been made of ice.

Blueish mist spread out in all directions where the pieces shattered and then billowed out from there, quickly covering the entire floor. It was as if the runes channeled cold directly from the chilliest parts of Niflheim. The mist evaporated and ice formed in its wake as if it were a living thing. And it grew, not just freezing the wetness that had been there but overtaking the rock to become a lake of ice.

That was a slippery thing for anyone not wearing crampons.

Frenzied as they were, Alfhild's warriors slipped and slid and went everywhere but where they intended. Meanwhile, the 'Steins fought with sure footing, spearing and hacking down foemen as they drew all attention to themselves and to their declared destination.

The sounds of weapons clashing and men and women screaming echoed down the hall as I turned and ran, but nothing was as loud as the sound of two men laughing.

It was a long corridor, and eventually, there were no more sounds of battle glee. It was an even longer set of stone steps on the outside. I knew I had to continue on, but it was with heavy feet and a heavy heart that I reached the *Sea Squirrel*. Magnus threw me in, and I hit the deck with the most colossal fatigue I had ever felt.

But I had made a promise. I had failed enough of my friends; I would at least give them what they asked for. So I spoke a verse, though it came to me in an unfamiliar form, the words coming not to tell a story or speak wisdom or cast a spell but to honor a memory.

> "Spear sailors, not sparing
> spies of strolling troll-kin,
> crushed throngs of the cat's plaything,
> crying out at trifles.
> Many a troll mangled,

Might and Wrath kept fighting.
Settled others' safety;
  second lives as legends."

Magnus told me later I pitched forward face-first and that he saved me from a bad fall. All I remember after the verse is the dream.

Chapter 50

Limited Hospitality

I came to as I rolled off a bench and fell face-first onto the floor.

Not really, because I was on the *Sea Squirrel*. This was just some uncomfortable dream. Hopefully not involving any more trolls.

I pushed myself up from the floor and looked down the length of a seemingly endless longhouse. About to rise with one hand on the bench, I drew it back as I felt the chill of cold metal instead of wood. The bench, as all the benches in that hall, was lined with mail.

The other side of the longhouse boasted an ornate chair set on a pedestal as the high seat. Torches and generous hearth fires lit the place, illuminating the brightly painted shields hung on the walls. It was not Hrolf's hall, as that felt warmer and more familiar. Not Silfast's hall, as that felt safer. Familiar, though. All the designs on the shields were animals of different sorts: A falcon, a salmon, a ram, a boar—two different boar designs, actually.

I had seen this hall once before on a trip to deliver a sword, about a year before I met Magnus and the 'Steins. Out in the mist of a forest so deep it seemed like a place in-between realms.

I wheeled around purely on instinct, and there was the lord of the hall. He looked different, but I had met him before. Twice, now, though he'd used a different name each time. He had been Hrani when I met him for the first

404

time in that unnamed forest. He had been Redbeard when he courted Arrow-Odd and advised him in the war against Ogmund.

And both times, he'd had both his eyes. Not this time, though.

One eye full of malice and mirth stared back at me. A long, silver beard and hair glowed in the firelight. The spear at his side was not hidden to look like a staff by any glamour as when I first met him. 'Hrani the farmer' he'd called himself, disguising his identity.

Here was the Gallows Lord, the Father of Magic Songs, the Terrible One, stripped of pretense.

"Odin," I named him, truly this time. "What is your business here?"

"Ha!" he shouted, the mocking laugh piercing my ears. "Valholl is my house, the benches lined with mail, roof lined with shields, the abode of the chosen slain. And you ask *my* business here!"

"The roof is lined with shields," I repeated, looking up. "That must be shitty when it rains."

Odin did not acknowledge the jibe. "It seems to me you should be more thoughtful about *your* business in such a place."

"I have not come by choice. It is you who brought me. If you'd speak to me, why not wait until I returned to see you as Redbeard?"

"You make many assumptions, skald. As for Redbeard, I believe he's run his course. You're unlikely to see him again." He strode forward and around me, not with the gait of an old man but one of a spry warrior. He snapped his fingers on his way to the high seat and, as if anticipating the command, two valkyries appeared.

They were mail-clad and girt with fine ring swords. Each valkyrie offered a large drinking horn. Sitting in his high seat, Odin took one horn for himself and fixed me with his one eye. "Have you forgotten who gave you good advice regarding how to deal with a *draugr*? It was not so long ago, not even by your standards."

"I recall that delivery," I said. "I recall you baiting me into a contest of wits—"

"Challenge, skald. It was a challenge for you to rise to or not," he interrupted, then drank deep from his horn, some of the wine spilling into his beard. "Had it been a contest, I would have pitted my wisdom against yours. And you would not have succeeded so easily, in that case."

"Challenge or contest, you tried to take my sword!" I said.

The valkyrie offered me a horn in turn. It was a rich red wine the thing was filled with. I could smell it even before I saw it, that rarest of drinks in the north. But I was not about to accept anything from the likes of Odin, and I waved off the valkyrie.

She grinned without mirth, showing the ruts filed into her front teeth. I cringed at that, and her mood seemed to brighten. I was glad to see her go.

"Why bother trying to take the sword?" I continued. "Your spear is dwarf-made. The sword my grandfather made could not have been of any value to you unless you enjoyed taking it from me."

"Here you are with more assumptions," said Odin. "Disappointing. I expected you to see a bit further."

"To Hel with your expectations and to Hel with you!" I said. "Maybe Ketill is right to hate the gods so. What have you done for us other than disappear when looked for, when most needed?"

"Done for *you*?" he repeated, low and slow, his voice rumbling through the hall like an earthquake. "I tried to take that sword from you is what I did for you. You rose to the challenge and won out against a sorcerer, changing your outlook utterly. Done for you? I gave you the exact advice you would need to survive the next night. Done for you?!" he bellowed, standing from his high seat. "Do you think me some gust of wind to be called upon whenever you feel uncomfortable? I am *Odin!*"

The force of his voice blasted through me and rattled my insides. Had I taken that drink, I would have surely dropped it. I kept my footing, somehow, though not with any comfort, and snarled back at the sorcerer god. If he wished to kill me, he certainly could, so there was no point in facing him with anything but defiance.

"And why am I so important to Odin as to be summoned by him?"

"Did I summon you?" he asked, his wrath abated. "Maybe you're just dead!"

Oh shit, maybe I was. He sounded serious. But then, isn't that how a good liar sounds? And Odin was no god of truth-telling.

He grinned at me with a smug expression as if he'd heard all my thoughts in succession.

"I think it might be that you have questions," he said, his words sweet as honey.

Truly, this was a crafty god. He knew what to say and how to say it to keep me guessing or to raise my hackles. This last comment certainly raised my hackles. Whatever his plan to get something out of me, I had the urge to deny it. So I crossed my arms, straightened my back, and said nothing.

"Come now," said Odin, his manner apologetic with open arms. "You asked Heimdall your question and got nowhere. Why not ask it here and now?"

"Is that what you offer me? Truth?"

He chuckled at that. "You have so many questions, skald, and so few get at the heart of a thing. Has it not occurred to you that I've appeared twice now, and both times you needed good advice? Oh—I see it now. It is fear that holds you back. You explored the deep lore, and it frightened you, and that is why you ask no good questions."

If anything, I am yet unable to convey the extent of Odin's manipulation. There is no one better at it. I crossed my arms, determined not to let him win and yet having no idea what that meant.

"What is the Spear of the Gods?" I asked.

"A prophecy. And a plan. And perhaps something else, but that remains to be seen."

"That is no answer. Did you call me here to trade riddles?"

"I do love the riddling, as you well know. Perhaps I will give you one after all. Here is a riddle, though not in verse: Why would the gods sire so many damned children all at once?"

A memory flashed through my mind. Conversation amongst Thor, Frey, and Heimdall. I was injured, near death even, after the battle of Lejre. But in my semi-conscious state, I had found myself in a hall with them again.

"A single acorn is just a hope. It is many seeds that make for a good harvest," Frey had said.

"Harvests come and go. An oak is unconcerned with passing storms," Heimdall had replied.

"Tell me why you find me so interesting first," I said. "Then I will consider your riddle."

"What a greedy little wisdom hoarder you are!" said Odin.

"Says the king of wisdom hoarding!" I shot back. "Tell the people of Midgard how to cast the spells you learned while hanging nine nights on that windswept tree, and share your knowledge before you call others greedy."

"Ah," he said, tilting his head back. "No. It is enough to know such spells are there for the learning. I sought no hand to hold when I hung on that tree, spear-pierced and alone. And alone you must be to travel that road." He drank deep from his horn and stroked his beard, eyeing me as if trying to decide something. A lone finger reached out to point at me. "Your wizard said as much, though with different words. What if such lore was written down? There would be no threshold to cross for it, and it would be mis-learned. It is the crossing of the threshold that teaches the lesson. I won't cheapen such wisdom by offering it to those unwilling to learn. But you? You are interesting. An undaunted crosser of such thresholds. Well, mostly undaunted. You are a bit fearful concerning your own history as of late, though you keep seeking lore about everyone and everything else."

I never felt very courageous for seeking out the lonely paths. Most of the time, it was to avoid danger. Then again, the curiosity that drove my explo-ration had almost gotten me killed on several occasions. And I couldn't honestly deny my fear.

"I have answered your question," said Odin. "Now, answer mine. Why have so many children? I think you've had a hint of it already."

I started to respond that I had not, but then I recalled my most recent trip to Heimdall's hall. I mostly remembered meeting Skadi and Njord, but that was only the second part of that trip. During the first, Heimdall had indeed given me a hint.

"New stories . . . you want what—new gods to arise from these children to create those stories?"

"Hardly!" Odin guffawed. "You are a skald. What is your magic if not to hear what is unsaid? Or do you have no such magic? Come now, try again."

I shook my head, anger rising in my gorge. Cold fear spread in my guts as I sensed the reason was worse than I could conceive. "You wanted sons and daughters. Most of them are quite keen on lording their heritage over others. Why you would sire so many is truly a mystery to me, as I can't imagine you wishing to share word-fame any more than you would share your wisdom."

Doors of the hall were thrown wide all of a sudden. I don't mean 'the doors,' as in one set of doors at a main entrance. I mean all the doors, of which there seemed to suddenly be hundreds. Battle-clad men and women poured in from every entrance, down the hall farther than I could see.

One of them close by took off his helmet. A reasonable thing, as his helmet had been split. And then I saw: So had his head. The gaping wound in his skull showed down to his brain, yet even in the brief moments I saw him, the wound closed and he was whole again.

Wounds of the others were all different, yet healed much the same.

Blood disappeared. Wounds closed. Severed limbs reattached. Rent armor found its shape again. Here were the *einherjar*, Odin's picked warriors. Every day, they fought, and every night, they feasted until the doom of the gods.

But hadn't Ketill made that doom up?

"Of course, you're right about all that," shouted Odin over the din. "It's only that you can't see your own assumptions keeping you from the rest! Who says we would *share* word-fame with such children?"

Straight to the benches went the *einherjar*, sitting and speaking among one another, many of them laughing. Dozens of valkyries appeared, bringing ale to the tired warriors and joining them in the drinking.

I stared at the last of the wounds closing up as the *einherjar* drank. Wisdom closed in on me like a shroud, like it had in the deep places. Only I was not seeing something new, just changing my understanding.

"The *einherjar* don't have word-fame despite being your picked warriors. Neither will these god-children. They all serve only to be folded into stories." My eyes were wide. Could this really have been their intent? "Stories about you gods."

"Ah!" said Odin as he smacked his lips. "So many competing stories. So many stories forgotten over the centuries! I heard a prophecy from a dead *vǫlva* about the doom of the gods. No, not the story you know. About a slow, sad fading unless we were to find our Spear. And so it is a hope. A wager, even," he added, his grin growing wider.

"So it was never your spear that was the Spear of the Gods." I pointed at his dwarf-made weapon, Gungnir. The spear that never missed its mark.

"This old thing? It is a fine spear, but not the one the prophecy speaks of. I am confident of that."

Einherjar bumped me one way and then another as many more piled into the hall, all looking for empty benches and ale. Valkyries shoved me just as hard as they ran about, refilling cups.

"You—all of you—you wanted to fill Midgard full of your children to keep your memories alive?"

"Did you forget the rest of the prophecy you heard? *Ancient lore is likened as useless. Inspired fables are fully forgotten.* Is that the outcome you would have for Midgard, no more tales of great deeds, no more stories of confronting the impossible?" He pitched his tone and his chin lower. "No more memories put to verse for fallen heroes?"

I shook my head. "You haven't made any heroes! You've only made a rabble for heroes to rise up against."

"Perfect!" he said and sipped his wine like a dainty.

That cold feeling in my stomach expanded. Heimdall had warned that seeing the whole picture would do me no good. Now, I began to see.

"You don't care who wins," I said. "You only care for the conflict."

"The mere fact of children means nothing," nodded Odin. "It is what they do! And they will strive for word-fame, to be much like their fathers. The stories they will make in their striving will rekindle all those old tales and make some new ones. As will the striving of their enemies! And those tales will put our names to the lips of skalds such that there is no more forgetting!"

"Is that why my friends are dead?!" I shouted. "There wasn't enough battle in the world already that you had to contrive a greater conflict, whoever might benefit? Why you helped Arrow-Odd as Redbeard, but now you're done with him? Is that how the name of Odin lives in Midgard, by making more of us die?"

"What a sensitive skald you are! There is value in the struggle. What heroes does Midgard have other than the ones willing to strive against the impossible? Would you rather give word-fame to those who kept to easy victories? I think not."

I had always known Odin was a tricksy one to be avoided. I had never guessed I would dislike him as much as this, however. Again, I was wiser, and again less glad.

"You miserable old drunk!" I shouted. "Of all the plans I've ever heard, that is the stupidest one. What foolishness did you consult to make such a conclusion? Outhouse Lord I name you because your advice is such shit!"

Loud as the hall had become, my insult got the attention of a few of the *einherjar* nearby. They pointed and commented, grinning, though I couldn't hear what they said.

Odin raised an eyebrow. "I might have expected a bit more understanding from someone such as you. It's unlike either of us to remain exactly as we are, as we're always looking for something new. There's a similarity there, even if you'd deny it. More disappointing is that you've failed to see the great opportunities my plan has given you. What is a skald without great battles to put to verse? And worse, what is it you have in your bag, little skald? Is that torc not worth a story itself?"

I reached down to my bag only to see it was not there. Belt and clothes, yes. Bag, carving knife, and Need, no.

"Think I will make a new legend for you rotten shits with that torc to aid me? Ha! I'll throw it into the White Sea as soon as I can and let your legends sink along with it."

The valkyrie who had offered me a horn before exchanged a look with Odin. She was headed for me, if slowly.

"You could do that," mused Odin as he stroked his long beard. "And yet, it is no ordinary torc to stay where it's been put. Washing up on King Harek's shore would certainly be interesting! Then again, I doubt it would come to that. Ogmund has more sea monsters than Lyngbakr to aid him. I think he's likely to retrieve it himself if cast into the sea. Unless it becomes a powerful thing in your own hands, I mean."

Goat's breath and cat piss! It was all playing into his hands, whatever I did. I could call him names all I wanted. He was still winning.

The valkyrie headed my way drew closer. I did not like her expression.

"I'll send the thing back to Freya, then!"

"Do you think it would have come to Midgard if she still desired it?"

"I'll destroy it!"

"Haha! And how will you do that?" Odin shook his snowy head at me. "Well," he mused, even more pleased with himself, "I suppose you could destroy it after all! Not with that blade of yours, of course. You would need a more hateful weapon to cleave that torc." He raised his eye to the ceiling in thought and tapped at his chin as if the next thought was only now occurring to him. "There is one that might do it—you know of Tyrfing, don't you?"

The evilest sword ever made? I was certain that evil-working god would be most satisfied if we unearthed it and set it loose in Midgard once again.

"I won't do your work," I said, hoping more than believing that was true. "Frey thinks all the acorns you idiots dropped will result in many stories, but it won't. Those fools follow Ogmund and Alfhild. Heimdall might be right if one rises to be a mighty oak, but you've set them up not to be. Not one! You needed a spear and planted a bunch of blades of grass!"

Odin shrugged in mock thoughtfulness. "An interesting thought, ANS-GAR, if that is your name. This is a game played on a board so big you cannot see it all. But I? I see." He winked at me with his one eye. "You will move as a *tafl* piece, one way or another. Love and loyalty will see to that."

The valkyrie caught me up by the belt in one hand and the collar in the other. I struggled to no avail. With uncanny strength, she lifted me off the ground as if I were a small dog that had overstayed its welcome.

"It's a pity we don't have more time for discussion," Odin crooned as I was dragged away. "Now is the hour for feasting. But only for those who earned it."

The valkyrie tossed me out of Valholl ass-first.

Out the doors I flew, and then down from there, and down, and down into a thick white mist until I could no longer tell whether I was falling or not. Eventually, I forgot where I was or how I had gotten there. I closed my eyes and thought this was what I faced, dreaming or awake.

Perhaps there would be no more striving against fate than there would be against a fall from the sky and the certain thud at the end of it.

CHAPTER 51

THE WHITE SEA, STAINED RED

I OPENED MY EYES TO WHAT PASSED FOR DAWN ON THE WHITE Sea in summer. The wind was up and pushing us steadily on. If we'd had no wind, I'm not sure I could have summoned the strength for rowing—mental or physical. Haldor Skullsplitter had died for all of us. The 'Steins had died for me to get away with that damnable torc. The bone-deep pain in my shin and the hot throbbing at my ear were almost welcome distractions from how I felt otherwise.

Most lay asleep on the deck or huddled against the gunwale like Ketill. Not Kraki. He held the rudder steady and his chin high. Even gave the hint of an impression of the possibility of a smile as he looked out across the ship at the piles of people on it. Twice as many as we had come with, and that was despite our losses. They lay out on the deck where they could. I was close to the aft and, therefore, to Kraki.

"How are you still awake?" I asked in a low voice, trying not to disturb too many others. "I've never been so tired and miserable in my life."

"I have stayed awake much longer than this and still fought," said Kraki. "You've slept longer before, though I think maybe you were dying the last time. Go back to sleep and recover."

My hand throbbed, hot with pain. It was hardly anything compared to my head or leg. Someone had washed and wrapped my injuries, at least. The soreness would keep me wide awake. "Sleep won't undo what's done."

I considered the last of Odin's words and wondered what he had meant by that. Was I in love with Steinvor? Maybe. I was quite taken with her, though I'd just met her. We would return soon, in any case, and we hadn't been away very long.

Here were the cold, airy waters of the Far North, our situation as bleak as the landscape in winter. The crew of the *Sea Squirrel* had come to be as close to me as family in my time with them. Three betrayals and three deaths in that family would have been unthinkable even a day ago. Styrgrim had led us back to the ship, but he was not our Brother. Now, we were leaderless on land. And who knew what happened next when we reached Arrow-Odd? Would he laugh at our attempt, the one he had warned us about?

"There is no undoing what's done," said Kraki. "No undoing anything at all. Only what to do next."

If only I knew what that was.

At that moment, I gave no shits for gods or their trinkets. We did not even have the bodies of our friends to burn. How to move on to what was next without processing what had just happened?

"Ha, damn!" laughed Kraki. "Should've seen it. Right in front of me."

"What was right in front of you?" I asked. "The prophecy?"

"Curse the prophecy," said Kraki. "My dream! Last year, the strange one with the wolf pleasuring itself. Couldn't have been more obvious!"

"The one you asked me to interpret," I said. "Because I knew all the myths. But it wasn't referring to a myth. The wolf pleasuring itself was Ulf rubbing himself raw in the woods. Only that hadn't happened yet. And you didn't even know about it until later."

Kraki nodded. "Not until you made a verse about him doing it. I should have known it then, but I'd forgotten all about the dream. Ha! Shit."

"We have to kill him," I said.

"Aye," said Kraki. "That's what you should tell the crew when they wake up."

"Me? I don't think I will be telling them anything. You have the ship, and Magnus is more likely to command. Or Styrgrim, since he was giving orders already."

From under a pile of woolen blankets at the aft, the wizard stirred. Though he'd not had to fight his way out, he'd had no more sleep during that abortive raid than I had, and he must have been tired. His voice sounded every bit of it.

"You really are one to play the fool," said Ketill. One eye beneath his long hood was open, fixed on me, his arms held tight to his chest for warmth. "And after that verse you spoke! That was not *galdralag*, that was a different meter. A new meter. What was it?"

What verse had that been? I could barely remember speaking it. It had been more than speaking, though. It had been like pouring my will into a spell on one of my discs. I shook my head and shrugged. "The words just came," I said.

The wizard considered me for a long time. "No doubt," he finally said, and that was all we spoke for a long time.

My thoughts plagued me in a thousand ways. Snatching the Brisingamen had seemed like a necessity once I learned of it. But now that I had it, what would I do with it? I could not get rid of it. Could not destroy it. Could not use it. The only certain thing was that having the torc put the rest of the crew in danger, and that was what I least wanted.

Should I leave and take the torc elsewhere to keep it hidden? How would I get anywhere if I left? See if one of the jarls would take me on, maybe. Not Sirnir, I hoped. Perhaps Vignir could see his way into this kind of crazy quest.

Many questions and problems occurred to me as we sailed on, but the answers and solutions were not equal to them. If only Haldor still led, he would know what to do.

"You have the look of a man with a burden," said Svipul.

She held herself halfway up the mast with one hand, the other grasping her spear. The same wind filling the sail lifted her raven-black hair in long, streaming waves behind her.

It was rather a contrast to the rest of her warlike figure, armor, helmet, and spear. Most fighting men and women either kept their hair shorter than that or tucked it into the helmet. But I suppose the spirit of a dead woman coming to give unasked-for criticism at random times doesn't have practical concerns like having her hair pulled in a fight.

Some *fylgja*. She somehow made me want to dismiss her out of hand while, at the same time, my attention hung on her every word. Another thing I could not explain. She hopped down from the mast, boots hitting the deck near Magnus' sleeping head. He stirred and turned over as if someone in his dream was making too much noise.

"I know that look. It is moody-broody nonsense. As if you are put upon by others when you are just isolating yourself."

I looked out at the sky and then the sea. We were headed southwest, and the outline of land was just visible. Perhaps if I spoke to myself in the right way, even someone hearing me would not think it strange.

"I hope those who made it to the ship will heal," I said, supposedly to myself. "It would be a pity to lose more of our Brothers after so much loss already."

"Family dies for you if necessary," Svipul said. "They are not delicate flowers you must protect while you take on all burdens. They would not treat you as such, either."

No one had seemed to hear my previous statement. Kraki was distracted and most others were asleep, so I decided to chance a more direct question.

"Is that how you died?" I whispered.

Playfulness fled her face, and she aged ten years in a few seconds. "I did," she said, deadly serious. "I would do it again."

Her words made sense, but as soon as I tried to accept them, I thought of Fanya. I did not want others to die for me, regardless of blood or oath-ties.

"Why do you think Kraki smiles?" she asked. "Do you think it is because he is glad to be rid of Haldor?"

I laughed at the absurdity of the suggestion.

"Ask him then. I dare you."

I couldn't say no to that.

"Kraki," I croaked, "this is no great day for us. We will not celebrate when we reach Odd's camp, nor will we be celebrated. I know you cannot be happy that Haldor is dead."

"You talk a lot, skald," growled the old cook.

"So how, by the burning balls of Surt, are you so damned cheery?"

"How are you not?" he answered in a voice loud enough that it woke some of the others. "And you forget to mention the 'Steins. What an end they had, as good as Haldor's! And a good poem after. How many men get even one of those?"

"Yes, but," I shook my head. Any time I thought I understood the old man, something popped up to show me I did not. "But they are no longer with us. The 'Steins will not repair the ship again or make those improvements they hinted at learning from the codex. We won't hear them argue or bet anymore. Haldor is not here to lead us."

"On land."

"On land. Hel's dragon, you crazy old man!"

And then he laughed. Head back, full-throated laughter. "Never thought I would lecture a skald on poetry!" he gasped. "Did you fail to hear Haldor's verse?"

"It was not bad. Alfhild did not even respond."

"'Not bad?' Few of *your* verses have had such an effect! He left every warrior Alfhild had wondering who would be her next sacrifice. He made Svein out to be a coward in front of all. That verse will have Ulf watching his own back until the end of his days. They will not be so comfortable in their new home after that. And he reminded all of his name in a way they will not forget.

"And boy, he did all that knowing he was bound to die in that place. That dead man accomplished much, I think, and his enemies heard him die laughing. Ah, they won't forget that, not when they speak in low voices around their fires at night, not when they bed down and dream!

"And the 'Steins, Magnus told us what spell you cast for them. They wouldn't want an ending any different. You know we weren't sure they could be trusted because they didn't seem to trust anyone else? Never had any family to rely on other than each other. But they were ours and we were theirs by the end. Not too many can say the same."

More of the crew woke and nodded at Kraki's words. Bjorn and Styrgrim, Moose Frothi and Thorir Houndsfoot. Some voiced their assent or even cheered. That woke others and soon most of the ship had awakened, our crew and Alfhild's former prisoners, both. Svipul had disappeared by then, but she had done her part.

Only Ketill sat unmoving, his hood covering his eyes. He had his grim look about him as if the cheering grated on his ears. He kept to himself but made an inadvertent snarl for a fraction of a second. Perhaps if I explained, I thought, then he, too, would be less miserable.

I got up from my seat and worked my way to the aft. "Wake up, wizard," I said. "I have secrets to tell you and questions to ask. I need your wisdom."

I poured out a lot of what I'd been holding back in that conversation. Principally, the conversations with the gods. I had to do less explaining than I expected. Vilgrip had done much explaining after I had passed out. The use of the Brisingamen and the nature of the prisoners freed, or at least most of them, explained much of Alfhild's intent.

He nodded heavily at each explanation. "It is well that you've told me. Especially the conversation with Odin."

"You said you recognized him when we first met him. Why not tell us when we first saw him?"

Ketill shook his head. "That's not quite how it was. I knew the face, the expression, the way about him. I could not recall from where exactly, and it was a long time ago. I knew he was more than he claimed, could see he was more than he seemed. It gave me an ill feeling, but that was all."

"He said the game was played on a board too big for me to see, and that I would be a *tafl* piece moving regardless of my inclination."

Ketill snorted. "That god is more important now than he was in my youth. It seems he fancies himself such as well." The wizard shook his head. "It always seemed whatever choice I made, it played into the hands of the gods, one way or another."

"That was my impression as well," I said, feeling no better for being right. "What's to be done in a case like that?"

He shrugged. "The last time I was faced with the situation, I made myself drunk and did not stop for . . . I still don't know how long. I will not take that path again."

"What will you do?"

"What will *you* do?" he shot back. "Give up and admit nothing matters or struggle against fate and impossible odds only to see those pampered gods get their way again?"

I hated the question, shook my head at it. It seemed like one of his early lessons, where I was given an impossible task and expected to make one bad choice or another. The first of which was to avoid dying as he shot arrows at my head. But that was a lesson, not an impossibility. The test had been for me to subvert the narrative and create my own solution.

"Neither," I said. "I will calculate the desires of those gods not at all. Only our own. We need to destroy this necklace, and we need to kill our enemies. And we may be able to do both with the help of Arrow-Odd's army."

"That may be less of a possibility than you think," he said with a deep sigh. "What I see ahead of us is not good."

"You see the future?"

"Not at all. But I have the sight, and sometimes I see more than others. And what I see on the White Sea looks bad for Odd."

I stood up and looked out across the sea. It was still mostly calm and with a clear sky. I saw nothing amiss. More people stirred on the *Sea Squirrel,* crew and freed prisoners alike. A few looked back at me, their interest in the conversation with Ketill clear.

"I have no such sight," I said. "But in some of the sagas, they tell of granting the sight to others. Can you share the sight with me in such a way?"

Ketill nodded. "To look through the hands of a sorcerer or through arms akimbo you may see more than you would have otherwise. Whether that is advisable or not is another matter."

"I would see."

The wizard rose, and I followed him to the ship's fore. "See for yourself if you like," he said and made a triangle with his thumbs and forefingers. "Look through this."

It was just two hands with an opening between them. I started to feel foolish as I positioned my face behind it, craning my neck to push my head forward. Nothing was changed. The sea and sky were still there. A few clouds dotted the sky on an otherwise bright day. The breakers were low despite the wind.

Then I blinked, and the world, as visible through Ketill's hand, changed.

Gray storm clouds blotted out the sun. Lightning lit an angry sky, crackling from cloud to cloud. The clash of arms and screams of men and women filled my ears. I could smell the iron of weapons and blood. The waves frothed a deep, viscous red. And for a moment, I felt a most awful pain of loss.

I blinked again, and that world disappeared. I shuddered as if released from a hold and fell on my ass.

And Odin's words about love and loyalty came back to me. Had I survived again only to find out Steinvor had died like Fanya had?

"You saw," said Ketill.

I swallowed hard and nodded. I took my time getting back on my feet.

"What did you see?" asked Bjorn.

"It's the meaning that's the thing," said Ketill. "That's never clear."

"How far are we from Odd's camp?" I asked.

Bjorn looked out to starboard at what coastline he could see. "Hard to say, but I suspect we're about halfway there. It is morning now. I think we will be there before evening."

"But what did you see?" growled Moose-Frothi. "Damn the meaning, I can decide that for myself!"

"I heard the sounds of battle, I saw an ocean of blood," I said. "I hope Arrow-Odd's army is still there when we return."

CHAPTER 52

NOT AGAIN

WE SPOTTED THE SMOKE SOMETIME IN THE AFTERNOON. IT HUNG in the air, not in high plumes reaching up to the sky but rather in a dirty, indistinct cloud covering Arrow-Odd's camp.

We sailed past broken and burning ships as we approached the shore. Odd's or otherwise, there was no way to tell. It seemed more likely from what we could see that the majority of the battle had been on land. And, a bad sign, that it had centered on the camp itself rather than an outlying region. Fighting inside the camp meant they had been taken by surprise.

No one on the ship spoke as we took this all in. There was no point in voicing concern or regret, though I read both on Styrgrim's face. He was no less loyal to his crew than Haldor had been to us, and he had not been with them to do battle. How many survived? Did he even have a ship anymore?

We disembarked and pulled the *Sea Squirrel* up onto the shore, all armed and armored as well as we could. What we all would have given to hear Haldor's voice then. Instead, Styrgrim took charge and had us form up, though not to the liking of all.

"Why don't we keep sailing?" said one of the former prisoners. "Who knows what's happened here? We would do better to leave it alone."

"And if this lot had said that about us?" barked Thorir.

"To escape that place just to die here?"

Moose Frothi cuffed the man so hard it knocked him down. "You'll die here or elsewhere. But not in those cells. If you've got no thanks for that, then shut your mouth."

"Everyone is free to choose," said Kraki. "Let him go if he wishes to go. This ship will not go anywhere until we know what's happened here."

"I follow the skald," said Vilgrip. "He saved my life and stole the necklace."

"Did you not notice who led us out of that place?" demanded Bjorn. "Only a bunch of fools would take Styrgrim the Bear with them and then ignore him."

"The skald follows me," said Styrgrim. "If he has any sense."

"Kraki leads by sea," said Magnus. "We no longer have a leader by land. Not one we've chosen, at least. And there is no other kind."

"We do not have time for this!" said Styrgrim.

"I agree," I said, to the surprise of many. "We do not have time. Not for argument or voting or oaths. There may yet be fighting to do. If there is, we should direct it at those deserving and not ourselves."

I didn't wait for anyone to react, just strode off on my own so fast that even Styrgrim had to catch up. It was not the tight formation he would have ordered, but I did not care. I cared about very little, in fact, and for all the times you know my stomach was tied in knots, this was the worst. Whatever there was in that camp, be it foemen or worse, wounded allies or their corpses, I had to know.

I had to know if Steinvor still lived.

We didn't get very far before meeting the same coast guard we had come upon the first time. His face was bandaged and blackened with soot this time. His raven shield was in tatters, and one of the fingers holding his spear was visibly broken.

When he saw Styrgrim and Bjorn, no man could have had a bigger grin.

"Hjalti!" said Styrgrim. "Good to see you alive. We were not sure what to expect as we approached."

"Likewise, we had given you up for dead," said Hjalti. "Things went badly after you left."

"How badly?" demanded Styrgrim. "What of our men? How many are left? What of Pike-Tooth?"

"Most are left," said Hjalti, "but none whole. It was a hard fight." The man cut himself short, his difficulty in speaking clear. "Pike-Tooth lives, though many others do not. Come with me, and I will show you."

Bjorn's chest rose and fell with a sad sigh. Styrgrim nodded.

"And the skalds?" I asked as we moved off again.

Hjalti shook his head. "Some still live," he said. "Horsefly, for certain. He has been counseling Odd since the battle. Of the others, I know nothing."

We made our way past the camp's outlying tents and got no curious looks. People busied themselves with practical things: Carrying bodies, bandaging wounds, and repairing armor and weapons. Many were still snuffing out the fires that smoldered among tents and supplies. All were dressed for battle.

It was clear further in that the attacks had come from the camp's other sides and that the attackers had penetrated deep into the camp before being expelled. Odd's army had not been ready for this. They had expected Ogmund and his few remaining people to be their last threat, holed up in the cliffs on the sea. Somehow, Ogmund had called up an army to attack from the other side.

"To Hel with this," I muttered to myself. Things were taking too long, and we had no foe to face here. "I will meet you at the council tent. I have something to do first."

And then I was sprinting, running like my life depended on it, heading for the circle of skalds. Would she be there? What if she was not? Someone must know something!

The rowan branches of the skalds' little enclave lay just as I remembered them. The circle was undamaged but empty of people. It looked like the fighting had not reached this far into the camp. I wanted to take that as a good sign but knew it did not matter. No skald would have hidden here while there was fighting to do. Not then, and not now when there was work to do in the aftermath of the battle.

Of course, she wasn't there. Why would she be? She was probably near her tent or somewhere else near Gardar's people. I could find my way there, surely. Again I was sprinting, heading towards that area, but it was difficult to remember. We had been here a day and a night, and Steinvor had led me back to her tent when I had more important things on my mind than its exact position within the camp.

Even finding Gardar's people in a general sense soon proved more difficult than I expected. Some tents had burned, been trampled, or taken down in the fighting. More of the camp was open air and being reorganized.

Soon, I was completely lost and had to consider asking for directions. I swallowed hard and steeled myself.

"Are you lost?"

A woman sat with her left leg stuck straight out while a fat man tended to it. A small river of pink-tinted water ran down from her foot. Her eyes distracted me, or rather the black makeup set around them that reached back and over her ears. Both sides of her head were shaved, and the top of her hair she wore short. She had a calm tone to ask me such a thing while having a wound dressed.

As I drew closer, I saw her wound was more severe than I had realized. Something, probably a broad axe, had split the webbing between her big toe and the others. Split it so deep I wondered if it would heal.

The man working on her foot seemed to think so as he washed it and prepared bandages. He had a bowl of steaming water and a few vials at hand. His other tools lay within reach—a sewing kit and tweezers. He looked familiar. One of the skalds I had seen but not been introduced to. One of Gardar's 'fat ones,' Steinvor had mentioned.

"I will pick out what I can see," he said. "I need to separate the parts of your foot to do that. Then, I need to—"

The woman cupped his bearded chin with one hand and grinned, revealing her filed teeth. In a voice sweet and smooth, she addressed him despite the pain beading into a sweat on her face. "You sweet, fat man. I need no coddling. But charging into battle will be difficult if I lose the foot! So clean this one as you must." A gentle caress of her foreknuckles brushed the side of his beard, and she leaned back again. She looked at me, her expression as serene as her visage was maniacal. "If you're looking for the pleasure tent, I think it is closed for the time being."

"I am looking for someone," I said. "One of the skalds."

The man opened up her foot and picked out a bit of what I supposed might be leather.

"You have found someone!" she said with great cheer.

"And found one of the skalds," said the man, not looking away from his work. "No poetry right now, and I am busy until I finish Hrafn's foot; may she stomp our enemies evermore."

"No poetry," I said. "I am Ansgar, skald of the *Sea Squirrel*. That is quite an injury."

"Oh, Skullsplitter's man," he said, still not looking up from his work.

"Yes, quite the injury. You should see what happened to the man who caused it, but I doubt his face is recognizable anymore. I am Gizur. This is Hrafn."

"Hello!" she said with a wave.

"Isn't that a man's name?" I asked. It meant "raven," but Hrafn was the male form. The female form would be Hrefna.

"I don't know this 'a man,'" she said. Her voice never once wavered or lost its casual pleasantness despite the tweezers picking bits of leather out of her foot. "But I know Hrafn is my name."

It didn't make much sense to me, but neither did filing one's teeth, and that was no rare thing to see. Besides, I'd already met the *jǫtunn* Skadi herself, and she had a man's name. "As you like, Hrafn," I said, then turned my attention to Gizur and asked, "Do you know where I can find Steinvor?"

"Injury tents," said Gizur.

"Is she," I said, "I mean, do you know . . ."

"She lives," said Gizur, meeting my gaze this time. "Turn to your left. Walk straight about a hundred yards. You'll see them."

I ran rather than walked, Hrafn's call of "Good luck!" fading behind me.

The injury tents were not difficult to find. Broad canopies open to the air were spread three abreast across a wide field, dozens of them. Three large but closed tents lay beyond where those who were unlikely to rise again would have been treated in. Two crude trenches had been dug out, running between the tents and away from the camp toward a slope down to the sea.

Healers, red to the elbows, dumped waste and buckets full of bloodied water into the trenches. Runners took the empty buckets without so much as a signal and scrambled between the tents and a half dozen cauldrons of boiling water.

My heart leaped when I saw Steinvor emptying a bucket. A cut ran down her face from above her right eye to her cheek. She was alive. Not only alive, but she was there to help render aid, not because she had been wounded.

I didn't stop running until I was mere feet from her.

"It is good you are here," said Steinvor with a grin. "We need help tending the injured and could use a lucky man like you." She threw me a bucket. "Fill that with water and bring it back here."

That was a far cry from a warm embrace and the most welcome words I'd ever heard.

Without thinking, I rushed away to get the water. About ten seconds later, I realized running had suddenly become difficult. The stinging sensation in my leg where the bone had been pierced reasserted its existence. My ear burned, or what was left of it after Ulf's teeth got a hold of it burned. Every stone stair I'd hit on the way down reminded me exactly where it had collided with my body. The world spun as if Ulf had punched me in the head again. The leg wound was more than reasserting itself—I could not run, and then even walking seemed too much.

My chest compressed, my eyes watered—I could hardly breathe. I ducked into an empty tent to hide and fell to one knee. I leaned on the bucket for support but fell over sideways.

It hadn't happened again. She was alive. And every worry, every emotion I'd denied burst forth inside me while every recent injury howled for attention.

I imagined Fanya smiling, then felt guilty that I felt so relieved, then felt hemmed in from all sides not knowing how to feel. I wasn't supposed to cry because that's not a thing men did then. But I couldn't stop the flood of emotions, couldn't stop crying once I'd started, and that made it all the worse.

I emerged from the tent minutes later with fatigue and pain hounding every inch of my body. How had I just sprinted? I could hardly walk. But I did walk and made my way toward the cauldrons. I returned to the injury tents with a filled bucket and an apologetic look for taking so long, but not a word of anything else on my lips.

Steinvor had no time to talk. There was much work to do, and even those tending the wounds had their own injuries to work through. I helped in silence, quickly understanding the area's organization.

Huld was in charge of those caring for the injured. Healthy men and women hung on her every word. When she said she needed something, they rushed to bring it to her. A strange thing for a *vǫlva* to have such respect in Arrow-Odd's camp.

It was a time for many strange things to happen. She didn't see me approach, so I thought I would try to sneak up behind and surprise her.

"So!" I said, accusation in my voice. "This is the something that comes after, if I remember your words right."

Huld turned to me with her sweetest grandmotherly smile. "How brave you've grown!" she said. "Assuming you recall the last time you tried sneaking up on an old woman. It seems you are injured already, so I won't add to that. I have henbane to dull the pain if you like."

"I'll take no henbane, thanks," I snapped. Effective or not, it also dulled my mind, and I didn't want that. "How forgetful you've grown if you think to change the subject. You stayed here because you knew an attack was imminent, didn't you?"

Huld shrugged. "That seems no great wisdom," she said. "I predicted warfare would occur where an army sat. Even you could have done that much."

"Back to avoiding direct answers," I said. "Well, do what you will. Haldor is dead. You will have to swear loyalty to someone else if you wish to travel with the *Sea Squirrel* again."

"Is that someone you?"

"Ha!" I thought it was a joke, but it was a simple question with a complicated answer. Ultimately, I did not know who would lead on land.

"I hope he made it a good death."

"He died laughing," I said. "With his enemies insulted and made to look small. Buried his axe into the skull of Ogmund's mother just before he died. After Ulf and Svein betrayed him."

"Ulf and Svein?" she replied. "Not Hemming?"

"Killed by Ulf. I think Hemming tried to undo his treachery, but it was too late."

Huld shook her head. "The wolf lying in wait was not the one who shared his home with the wolves, then. I thought the tracker might be the one. That was much of why I kept to myself."

"Haldor called Svein a *tafl* piece on Alfhild's board. What a good description, don't you think?" I leaned in close to Huld's face. "But I wonder if he is not the only one being played as a piece."

"Those brothers are good players, I think," said Huld.

I had tussled with Huld for foolish reasons before. This time, I spoke with real anger. "Those brothers are dead," I snapped. "They gave their lives to cover the escape of the rest of us."

"Who are the rest—"

"No more questions from you," I said. "You owe answers and more after all your secrecy, I think. If you want to know what happened with us, go and ask the crew. They are at the council."

"Pity," said Huld as she turned away. "There was nothing in the prophecy to foretell the end of those two."

I let her go. I was in no mood for riddles or redirects or for anyone who might be using us as *tafl* pieces on a board.

She was plenty busy without more news from me. There is no substitute experience for hearing the groans of the dying. Some made more sound than that. Delirious with pain or loss of blood or both, they called out to their loved ones or to comrades-in-arms. Dying stoically is an easier thing to talk about than to do.

The worst of it, at least for me, was the quieter sounds of thin, labored breathing that told of a chest wound. Blood would pool inside the body, maybe the lungs. If not relieved, that internal bleeding would kill a person, and sometimes, there was no way to relieve the pressure without doing fatal damage in the healing process. In and out, they wheezed, each breath a testament to suffering. Most of those would not last the day.

I decided to make myself useful as well as I could. The rest of the crew could wait. My wounds had been seen to, much as my leg and ear still hurt. I was in good shape compared to the dying. I could help carry supplies and set bones. Steinvor knew healing arts better than I, and it was she I wished to be near, so I took her directions.

"I heard you talking to Huld," said Steinvor. "I know you dislike her, but you should know she saved us."

I blinked. "Saved you? You mean the skalds?"

"I mean the entire army!"

"I know she is a powerful *vǫlva*," I said, "but that seems overstated."

Steinvor shook her head. "Odd and Vignir fought Ogmund and his eight followers. They expected this would be the only fight, just as we did. Every eye in the camp was on them rather than on anything behind us. The Rus surprised us from behind and were in our camp before we even knew it."

"But you're still here," I said. "You repelled the attack before they got too far in."

"We outnumbered them," she said. "It was never meant to be the only attack. We would have been hit in the back when the Bjarmians beached their ships. By the time we saw them coming, we knew there would be no good way to fight on both fronts.

"Vignir was dead by then. Odd was at a loss to give commands. Redbeard had disappeared. Then the dragon came, soaring out of the sky and spitting poison. Arrows of fire rained down on us. This great army was nearly destroyed.

"And hardly anyone paid attention to Huld. She had already tried to warn Odd and failed. Nobody wanted anything to do with her. Only Horsefly listened. Got her a chair, rallied who he could to protect her while she sat *seiðr*.

"She turned the wind, Ansgar. Turned it hard against the Bjarmians and pushed their ships back out to sea. I thought we were done for, another army of Arrow-Odd's sent to the grinder for his grudge against Ogmund. She stopped the landing, and we fought the Rus until they had enough and retreated. I've never seen a *vǫlva* call on power like that. Never heard a voice like that. That's why I was surprised when you sounded angry at her."

"Huld is many things, but straightforward is not one of them," I said. "I still don't understand her motivations. I believe every word you've said. She has done everything she could to get here and fight in a war she has no stake in. Why? All I have heard are cryptic answers and questions to my questions." I shook my head. "I have just seen a man who used many a skill to get here turn around and betray us. I don't wish to be surprised again."

"Life is a surprise," said Steinvor, her voice dropping as if I had spoken out of turn. "Not all of it is so bad."

Her gaze stilled my voice, and in that pause, I took a deep breath. For the first time in my life, I heard what a woman wasn't saying.

"You are right," I said. "Some surprises are what make life worth living."

CHAPTER 53

THE RAVEN-HAIRED VALKYRIE

THE SUN WAS HIGH WHEN CLOUDS DREW ACROSS THE SKY LIKE A thick white blanket. Soft wind blew in from the east with a cool air that belied the camp's sadness. Some stayed by their fires and simply stared into them, as close to relaxation as any of us might get. Others set up tents and tried to sleep. Most of our crew had rested enough on the ship and looked for something to occupy themselves with.

Ketill was one of those looking to busy himself. Which was good for me, because I needed to speak with him. Waking up an irate wizard is generally a bad idea. I caught up as he shuffled away from our camp area. I didn't know where he intended to go, but he appeared unsurprised when I approached him as if he had been expecting me.

"The sight," I said. "I want to hear more about it. Some of those we've come across, trolls and sorcerers, were they likely to have it?"

"Very," he answered without stopping.

"And more than sight, would they be able to sense the heritage of the *Æsir?*"

He shrugged. "Perhaps."

I leaped forward and stood in his way, locking eyes with the wizard. "Jormungand, for example. If the Midgard Serpent were to chase a ship, could it be because he sensed something among the ship's crew?"

He stopped. "I have never been a giant sea serpent, so this is not something I can answer with confidence." Then he gestured for me to continue moving.

I did so. "Then out with it," I whispered. "What did you see when you first saw me? What did your sight tell you?"

"Ah," he said. "Why do you want to know? Will this answer all your questions?"

"Not whatsoever. But I wish to know my own history and the truth or lies of it."

Ketill took his time in responding, and then asked a question. "In all the stories of the gods you know, do you find them characters to emulate?"

"Of course not," I said. "They are gods, not people. The lessons in how to be or not to be is in aspects of them, in the extremities of their features and stories. That makes them interesting and instructive, but none are models to be followed on the whole."

"You have the idea right," said Ketill. "They are extremes in many aspects. The great might and wrath of Thor, matched with his great mirth. Odin's fanatical pursuit of wisdom. And only the most extreme crosser of thresholds would have been able to approach my home in that forest."

I hung my head. He would not give me a direct answer, but he had answered me close enough.

"I think you understand, even if you don't understand," he continued.

"But I don't. Do you? Is Styrgrim who he says he is? Am I who he claims? I can't tell what's been a truth or lie or what's been left out."

"You must speak with Styrgrim about it directly."

"I wanted to speak with you about it first."

"That's understandable. As is the anger I can hear boiling in your belly. Now you've spoken with me, and I can guess how your next conversation will go. I will give you some unasked-for advice: Seek understanding only, even though your frustration is justified."

"Hmmph! I should shout his lies for the entire camp to hear."

"The why of a lie is more important than the what. You should know that by now. And you were not with us when we heard what happened from Gardar and Sirnir. Odd keeps to his tent. Redbeard is gone. Styrgrim's friend, Vignir, is dead. And now there is a council without his best allies."

"He has had far worse defeats."

He shook his head. "Consider how things might be worse than defeat. I told of your dream, and confirmed for him that Redbeard was Odin in disguise. Styrgrim pledged his life to the god of fury, and the god of fury fled the field. The thing Styrgrim held strongest to is gone, and gone with it is meaning for all he's done before. Now he has no sense of the world or of himself in it. Don't underestimate what such an upheaval can do to a person. The treachery of a friend is worse than that of an enemy, as you must now know from Ulf."

I snarled but said nothing for many more steps. Still, it was hard to believe that would take such a toll on the old warrior. Hard to believe until Haldor Skullsplitter's words came back to me.

There is nothing worse than betrayal. And what if the betrayer is a god?

"Maybe it can drive a man to crawl into a barrel of ale and keep him from coming out again," I said, looking to Ketill for a reaction.

He met my gaze with characteristic intensity. "That's *exactly* what it can do."

It was still a hard idea to accept that I would lay no blame on Styrgrim. I almost told Ketill a flat "no." But as much resentment as I had building in me, I had not sought him out just to dismiss his advice. I nodded, and I left to find Styrgrim.

Defeat hung in the air of Arrow-Odd's war camp like a heavy mist. None of those I passed by despaired outwardly. I could see it in their heavy movements, though. Hear it in their voices. Many here would not go home again, and many going home would not reach it. Even if they did, it was months away and without much hope of victory or reward between now and then.

I found Styrgrim past the edge of the camp, on a craggy slope shooting upward toward the sea cliffs. He was sitting on a rock overlooking the gentle waves. Up a ways from the camp but not so far as where Odd and Vignir had fought Ogmund and his followers, I reckoned. The ravens were clustered nearby in what I guessed to be their normal gathering place. A few took tentative steps toward the man, but I shook my head and they hopped away.

He was alone and looking content, as far as Styrgrim ever looked content, which would look more like a sour mood on any other face.

"There is something I want to ask you," I said, setting my jaw against my own emotions. "And I ask so that I might have understanding rather than judgment."

Styrgrim looked at me, appraising my tone and manner. Nothing escaped those eyes. "I have no fear of judgment," he spat.

That nearly broke me of my desire to heed Ketill's advice, but I stammered on after a few breaths and sat down. "Perhaps you fear my understanding then, or you would have done differently."

"Done what differently?"

"You would have told a different story," I said. "Let me first tell *you* a story. Last year, I saw Lejre's troll injured beyond healing. Haldor had ripped his arm off at the shoulder. Here is what I never told: He asked me to end his life."

Styrgrim screwed up his eyes. "So Haldor did not kill it after all, it was you? Why did you say nothing?"

"I never fought him, and I was not about to take credit. His name was Olgram. I think he was as much a victim as anyone, raised by Alfhild in such a way as to be a piece on a *tafl* board. But by the gods, he was hard to kill. I brought a sharp rock down on his head, and it took three tries to break his skull."

"Interesting," he said, shrugging. "But why tell me this?"

"Before I bore down for the deathblow, he called me 'cousin.'"

"Again, why—"

"Wait, and I'll explain. I thought this might be delirium on his part, but now I think I understand. Alfhild claimed one of the gods was the father of her child. A big claim, not surprising for her. Yet what we found in that ruin of hers . . . there were so many children of gods that her claim now seems to have been one among many. So, I do think Olgram was the son of such a god. I do not think he was delirious when he called me his cousin or that it is a chance all those children of gods are more or less the same age as me."

Styrgrim stared down rather than straight ahead, his shoulders slumping, his back slouching.

"I seek only understanding."

He snapped his head up. "You knew about the arrow," he said, spreading his hands. "I supposed then that you had pieced it together. I thought you were goading me about it in the camp, that you would not let it lie."

Goading him? I had been angry he lied about my mother. But he thought I knew more than I did. Gudbrand's story came back to me.

He had taken an arrow through his balls. I know—I am the one who cut the fletching and removed it.

My gods, it had been right in front of me for so long.

"You could not have children after that injury?" I asked.

Styrgrim shook his head. "Every healer who saw to me after the battle made it plain: I would never sire children."

"Perhaps another would say different."

"Have you ever known Taika to be mistaken when it came to healing arts?"

My foster mother was never mistaken about such things. I shook my head, and he continued.

"I returned from Arrow-Odd's war on three different nights," he continued. "Or so Bodda told me on the third night. On the first night, she welcomed me back, overjoyed to see me, but she said I left before she woke the next morning. Then, I returned for a second night as if it was my first. And again, I left before she woke the next morning."

"You never did that."

"Oh, I came back. The *third* of those nights, I came back. But the other two nights—that was someone with my shape. Someone good enough to fool even my wife, and that would have been no small thing."

"Whose son am I then?"

Styrgrim fixed me with a miserable look. "Who else?" he said. "You are Bodda's son, and that's all I know."

"So you were not lying at all then," I said, my heart heavy as if I had lost another love. A wise man's heart is seldom glad, and the more I learned, the less glad I felt I might ever be again. Still, I pressed on because there is no use in doing things halfway. "You meant what you said about my mother. She died of illness when I was too young to remember. She died in childbirth. The illness was me, a foreign thing that killed her."

He stared out at the sea. "I was Odin's man. Sacrificed to him. Gave him glory and praised him, even after defeats. After I survived that battle against Ogmund, I asked him for a son who would continue my line, in whose memory I would live on. Perhaps he granted it in his own way. It may be Odin who is your father."

"It seems that Odin has set things up so he will get something he wants," I spat. "One way, or another."

"That's what I believed before," he said, shaking his head. "I always thought I liked the story of *Ragnarøk*."

"Liked it?" I asked, incredulous. "It's the doom of the gods, the end of everything!"

He shrugged. "If you want to fool your enemies, it could work well to spread tales of your imminent defeat. How better to gather them all in one place than by making them think they are fated to win? Good idea for a god of fury with a deeper plan." He shook his head. "Foolish, for me. It seems his deeper plan was to let others do the fighting after all."

"I hope I am not Odin's son. I have had enough of faithless friends."

"I as well," he said, his voice low.

Neither of us spoke for a long time. I felt foolish to have pursued the question of my parentage. I had been happier with my understanding of my place in the world before I had learned about its origins, just like he had been happier never knowing the real Odin. That my father had wanted little to do with me was not so difficult a burden as the wisdom of knowing why he wanted little to do with me: He was not my father at all.

The why is always more important than the what.

"You did not suspect until recently?" he asked eventually.

"Of course not," I said. "How would I have known? I only got the first clue last year. And Gudbrand made no comment on your virility. He spoke of your injury only as a testament to you as a warrior and a leader."

"Gudbrand," he said, grinning. "A good man. He never knew your mother, though. I suppose you can't have any memories of her, but did you never question why your hair is so fair when mine is entirely black?"

I stared at him blankly. He met my gaze and winced.

"All right, *was* entirely black." He ran a hand through the thick, graying mane. "I am getting older."

"I imagined her with very fair hair like mine," I said. "Light blond, or so I thought when I tried to picture her. Dressed in an apron and telling me stories. A younger version of Taika. A different version of the mothers in town. Something wholesome and nurturing, in my imagination. Foolish ideas, I suppose, but that is what my mind conjured absent anything else."

I gazed out onto the small waves breaking on the shore. Svipul walked there, spear in hand, atop the water as only a spirit could. She faced away from us and toward the open sea and took off her helmet, shaking out her long, black hair. The light caught it just right to bring out its blueish sheen.

Styrgrim shook his head. "No, you got fair hair from your real father. I suppose you never know what you will inherit from a parent. Let me tell you, your mother's hair was black. So black it shone blue in the right light, like a raven's wings."

My eyes became the size of shield bosses. I had not been prepared for the implication of that statement.

In the distance, Svipul danced along the waves. She grinned sadly at me, then turned, spear resting on her shoulder, and walked toward an isolated part of the beach.

"And wholesome? She was not! I found her on the battlefield giving the Gallows Lord no less glory than I. Her spear licked out fast as an adder's strike, strong as a bear's swipe. She chose her victims one at a time, and one at a time they fell. No shield or armor could stop her. Blood smeared her face and painted her mail as the entrails of dying men spilled from her strikes.

"And I thought, here is no shield-maiden. Here is a valkyrie, one of Odin's own.

"I thought to test my mettle with her. None on that battlefield were more deadly, and I had not come to fight the weak. I gave a good accounting of myself. But when that challenge was at an end, my axe was broken and I stared down the shaft of her spear."

"But she did not kill you," I said.

"No," said Styrgrim. "I asked her about this later, about deciding my fate. She did not like that idea. She said people should not make fate their master any more than a fickle god. Fate was strong, but there was always luck. Luck might not change fate, but it might change fate's meaning, and that was more important."

Svipul. 'Changeable' was the meaning of her name. Not her real name, only what she had told me to call her. She had been hiding in plain sight, the raven-haired valkyrie turned mother turned *fylgja*.

Styrgrim's voice took on a bitter tone. "In the end, her life was just as changeable as Odin's moods."

Ketill had told me to seek understanding rather than judgment. In finding that understanding, I could no longer judge Styrgrim harshly. Maybe he deserved criticism, but the truth of the man's life, the whole truth, would have to include more than that. He was so full of complication and contradiction that any judgment would either be immediately tempered or else be a half-truth at best.

The whole truth left me not knowing what to think of him. I knew what to think of some, though.

"I don't give a shit what those stupid gods want," I growled, rising to leave.

Out of the corner of my eye, Styrgrim raised his head. If he had meant to say anything more, he thought better of it and let me go.

A year before, I decided to walk back into the world and make more of my story rather than despair of what I had lost. I had been knocked down, but with Kraki's help, I stood back up. This time, standing up was not sufficient. I would need to follow where my story led, even if it led across the world from one end to the other and back.

It would come close to doing just that. For the time being, I had a shorter, harder trip to make.

I found Svipul down on the beach, far from people and ships and ravens. It was a quiet spot where the water lapped lazily onto the rocks.

"Why did you not tell me?" I asked. It hurt to feel deceived. Especially then. Especially by her.

She drew in a deep breath and told me her story. It took a long time, even though I did not interrupt. She spent the longest part of it describing the battle in which she'd found Styrgrim. By the end of her story, I understood what a good match they had been. But I still did not understand why she had kept her identity a secret.

"Perhaps you will understand in time. Right now, you can only think about why I did not tell you everything then that you know now, but you forget how difficult it was to learn big things all at once. Bit by bit is usually better, though even the wisest don't always know the best way for certain."

I was sad and happy, close and disconnected all at once. She was right, though. Despite the deception, she was with me when I needed her, not too unlike us deceiving King Hrolf. We stood on the beach gazing out at the White Sea, saying nothing for a long time.

"I am not certain of anything anymore. I've learned Midgard is a plaything for the gods. If misery for people makes the gods more famous in stories, they are all for it. I am no happier for knowing that."

"Not certain of anything?" she asked with a smirk.

Haldor's armring was hot on my arm as if calling to me. I put a hand to it and thought I could feel the silver pulsing, as if my own blood flowed through the thing. It made me think of the man's story, the one few people knew. The story that drove his every decision, from his rules to his last laugh.

"I'm certain of the dead," I said bitterly. "But the gods? And Ulf! He wore the same armring! Swore the same oaths!"

Svipul paced across the water, her feet leaving shadowy ripples along the surface of the water. "Will you take that as your lesson then? Go back and suspect Magnus? Ignore Ketill? Accuse Kraki of being a liar?"

"No, but—"

"Don't allow Ulf's story to poison your well of wisdom," she said, rounding on me. "Draw your wisdom from Haldor's story."

I hung my head, frustrated at myself. I had spoken of myths and legends for most of my life, drawing lessons from them as I went. In less than two years, I had walked among many of those myths and legends. Despite my experience, I had almost fallen into a pit of my own making, focusing on exactly the wrong story before Svipul brought me back to my senses.

Once I had my senses back, I realized all that wisdom of unhappiness was a choice. Not an easy one, but still a choice.

"Vengeance against Alfhild and Ogmund together? Now Ulf as well. And I want to destroy the torc, somehow." I shook my head. "I won't despair, but they're difficult burdens to manage. And the gods are no help."

"You've learned more wisdom than to make rash decisions," she said. "Ketill taught you that no plan survives the first arrow's flight. Haldor taught you luck often finds a person whose courage holds. Kraki taught you the virtue of revenge, and that even dead men can get it. It seems to me you have help from the wise, if not the gods. And the courage to look, despite knowing what you may see. It will take all of that to make a different story of Midgard than the gods would."

Thinking about Ulf, knowing the real Ulf, I was reminded again that a wise man's heart is seldom glad. But for the first time, how an unglad heart might find hope in that same wisdom.

If you enjoyed this story

Please help other people find this book.

Rate it on Goodreads and Amazon or wherever you purchased it. Review it on Instagram and Bookbub. Write about it wherever you Internet. Tell your friends—even the old-fashioned way!

It means a lot to me. It's how independent authors like me keep writing. There is no advertising more important than your ratings and reviews.

I like to keep in touch with people who like to read my work. Check out my website at AmatoAuthor.com and sign up to receive my newsletter. You'll get project updates, cool Norse-related content, and free fiction!

Coming Next in Spear of the Gods, Book Three: Fallen to Fury

- The evilest sword ever made
- State-of-the-art interrogation techniques of the early 8th century
- Conversing with the insane dead
- The most metal viking longship of all time
- Sorcerers, giants, more dwarves than you can count, and a dragon
- Huld vs Alfhild: The crazy screaming *seiðr* showdown

. . . as the *Sea Squirrel* sails to the conclusion of the saga!

About the Author

Gregory Amato made a career of selling his quill as a mercenary writer for many years. He wrote true and important things for newspapers, magazines, academia, and, for over a decade, intelligence analysis for the FBI.

Now, he writes fantasy stories based on the myths and sagas of the vikings. His fiction is often influenced by tales lost to time, usually full of high adventure, and always the sort that makes readers late to dinner.

Outside his time spent spinning yarns about vikings and wizards, he teaches Judo, brews beer, and plays DnD when he gets the chance.

Gregory lives happily with his family in the Pacific Northwest.

Sign up for updates, free fiction, and fascinating musings at **AmatoAuthor.com**!

Acknowledgments

Like the skald in my story, I did not get where I was going by myself.

A huge thank you to the many friends and family who supported me along the way. To my wonderful wife CJ. Without your love and encouragement, this series would not have gotten started, much less come this far. "This is good" means more coming from you than from anyone else. Thank you also to author Michael J. Sullivan and Robin Sullivan for your friendship and mentoring, especially around our little writer's group. Little but mighty!

Thanks to my advance readers Michael Klaas, Angela Howe, CJ Grimes, and Brandon Claycomb. All of whom saw a slightly different version of this text, and all of whom provided critical feedback to help make this story read as well as it could. And to John Petrila, also of my little-but-mighty writing group, as my source for Latin translations.

Dr. Carolyne Larrington and Dr. Tom Shippey: You deserve special thanks for your amazing scholarship, making so much more of Norse history, language, and culture accessible and understandable over many decades. Also, thank you for giving *Burden to Bear* a shot, and for your subsequent kind words. I can't overstate the importance I place on positive reviews from such titans of the scholarly world.

Thanks to Dr. William Short for your applied research on many viking-related topics, including (but definitely not limited to) authoring *Men of Terror: A Comprehensive Analysis of Viking Combat*. And for your correspondence!

Rowdy Geirsson, thank you for being an early and consistent supporter, as well as a friend I could talk to about metal, excellent beer, and Norse everything. For the record, Kraki says he is against leprechaun enslavement, which is no surprise. But he's also prone to punting them into the next realm when they mouth off, so it's a complicated relationship.

Thanks to Jessie Kwak for organizing a community of authors in the Portland area and for putting together the Author Alchemy Summit. Writing can be a lonely profession, so creating that community space where many of us can come together fills a huge need. And as a fellow introvert, I know how much work "I'll set everything up so people can be social" can be. It's much appreciated.

I owe a debt to purveyors of my local mead and beer halls for their generous hospitality: Travis Sigler at Wyrd Leather and Mead, Jeffrey Farrar at Ridgewalker Brewing, and Elliott Kaplan at TPK Brewing. You all run such excellent establishments, and you've been gracious to host me for readings and book sales. I even got to help launch a Nordic Cascadian Dark Ale. How many authors can say that?!

Three early supporters online gave me airtime when I was practically nobody. Liam Hall, Gabriel Garcia, and Merrick NH Ulrik - you shared your forums to help promote my work when there were plenty of other authors you could have chosen to highlight. With much gratitude, I wish you all continuing success. And I hope to revisit your channels soon!

To all those who supported the *Rune to Ruin* Kickstarter campaign, which exceeded even my most optimistic projections: You are awesome. That includes, but is not limited to:

The love of my life, Dussstyyy, Bob Amato, Cathy McLoughlin, C.Saulter, Rae Steward, William Robbins, The Grinch, RyanLeduc, Ian T, Christopher Brooks, Stu Brown, Sylvia L. Foil, Seamus Sands, Chris Mahers, Ben Kaeder, Jennifer Katsch, Tyler Binz, Stephanie Fischer, Mary Jones, Annarose Willhite, Adam Maynard Myers, Alex Taylor, Phil Wallace, Jared Crowley, Joi Tribble, Stephen Linden, Alison Tierney Mahdak, Justin Muncy, Gerald P. McDaniel, Michael Johnson, Billye Herndon, Brad Bolt, Matthew Rosengren, Robert Brown, Spyrako, Nicholas Paynter, Steven

Mitchell, Irinel Finco, Jason Emmons, Jeremy Griffin, Eric Vilbert, Ike G, Quinn Giguiere, Mason Rensch, David Holzborn, Alexander Edwards, Kendra T., Kylee Doyle, Terry M Hulett, Adriana Loughridge, Michael, Faye Quinn, David DeHaan, Richard Nimmons, Duncan Wilcox, Jerome P. ANELLO, SnapDragon Esq, Jeffrey M. Johnson, Franchesca Caram, Michael H. Sugarman, Justise Briones, Danae, Jenn Fedele, Jim Schwetz, Russell J. Handelman, Cortney Babcock, Reginald Von Duke, Mark Geier, Bryan Fletcher, Marge pepe, Josie Straka, Phillip H, J.Billington, Justin Wearing, Andrew Cobble, Diff, Kyle Woodcock, Marvin Langenberg, Greg Blaney, Jason & Nisa Martinko, Michael J. Sullivan, Blaine, Tommy, Dr. Charles E. Norton III, Stephen Hill, Uncle Ralph, C.K. Sorens, Cody L. Allen, Mark D, Ernie Ridley, MK, Jessie Kwak, Scott Frederick, SarLitten, Amy Meskill, Karen Matic, Ian, Angela Marie Howe, John Muir, Jennifer Hilmoe, Jon Sorenson, Rowdy Geirsson, Ashley Hagood, John Petrila, Douglas Boettcher, Samantha Ghormley, Gianna C., Tatiana Johnson, Francesco Tehrani, Heiko Koenig, Aaron Granofsky, Alexandra Corrsin, Tim Hardie, Leslie Claire Walker, Amanda Balter, RichardNovak, CMT, Darlene N. Böcek, Rowan, Gavin & Lyra Ridenour, Steffen Nyeland, Autumn Engdahl, Sarah Birchard, John Idlor, Mistril Merendras, Saleh M. Abdullah, Michael Brooker, Andy99000, Elizabeth Kiefer, Colin S, René Schultze, Brian Grimes, J Mills, Regina D., Christa Niehot, Monogurui, Ben Jacobson, Jason Halley, Justin Reinschmidt, Craig Esser, OriginPlays, Jackson Fulmer, Jan Berkman, Stacy S., Nathan Turner, ALB, Wendy Martinez, Felicitas Odemer, Yashtruna, April Ayton, Richard O'Shea, Ian Brown, Thomas Legg, Ivaylo Lyubenov (Ивайло Любенов), Tassilo, Jamie Dockendorff, Kurt Boulianne, Kate Sheeran Swed, Sarah L. Stevenson, Thorn Coyle, Ty Rowdon, pj, Jonathan Korman, Max Moyer, Kaitykat, Justin Greer, LordTBR_FFA, Carrie Eidsness, Tracy Popey, J Goode, Sam Cunningham, and Arthur Fortune Jr.

The soundtrack this book was written to was produced primarily by Amon Amarth, Korpiklaani, Bolt Thrower, Iron Maiden, and Alestorm. Some days it's not easy to think, let alone sit down and write. Your music provided a lot of inspiration and energy when I needed it.

Finally, the biggest thanks of all goes to you, the reader. Without you, there would be no Ansgar, no skalds, no need for stories. Thank you for reading!

MAJOR CHARACTERS

x next to name: This character died in book one.

Aldis – Alfhild's handmaiden. Last seen after being bashed over the head by Fanya in order to help Ansgar escape.

Alfhild Smooth-Cheek – Powerful sorceress who married King Ragnvald of the Danes. Alfhild groomed her trollish son, Olgram, in secret in a plan to take power. When the plan failed, she attacked the city of Lejre and was barely defeated by Haldor's Heroes, a drunk wizard, a turncoat witch, and a mysterious cat. The cat left her mark on Alfhild's face, hence "Smooth-Cheek."

Ansgar Styrgrimsson – The narrator and protagonist of the saga. A skald by trade, he joined Haldor and crew to prove himself to his father, Styrgrim the Bear.

Arrow-Odd – The legendary saga hero and seemingly ageless enemy of Ogmund Tussock.

Beigadh the Bold – One of two Danish champions loyal to Ragnvald and Hrolf during Alfhild's attempted coup.

Bjorn the Skald – Styrgrim the Bear's skald and advisor. A particularly strong and tough skald, with more battle experience than most.

Efraim – A monk on Gotland who knows many languages.

xFanya – Ansgar's previous love interest. Formerly a handmaiden to Alfhild, Fanya chose to help save the city of Lejre. Her final spell, as she was dying from a belly wound, lit the sky to show Ansgar where Alfhild was hiding.

Finnr – A dwarf and master weaponsmith. Forger of a sword that was meant to kill Lejre's troll. A close friend of Huld. Closer still with Kraki Bentleg, who he helped raise.

Gardar – A Danish jarl who has partnered with Arrow-Odd to pursue Ogmund Tussock.

Glumra – A trollwife/ogress.

Grimhild – Ogmund's troll of a mother.

Gudbrand Shirtless – The Danish king's staller. Ostensibly the keeper of the king's horses, he is more like the king's general problem-solver. Said to wear a chain shirt even when he's bathing. Prefers to fight from horseback—unlike most others—and uses an atgeir (heavy hewing spear). Fought alongside Ansgar's father for Arrow-Odd twenty years ago.

Haldor Skullsplitter – Leader of the Brotherhood, his sworn men and women, and commander of the *Sea Squirrel* crew when it comes to leading on land. A huge warrior, he and his Brothers seek out bounties no one else will take, supposedly all in the pursuit of their everlasting word-fame.

Hallfred Horsefly – Arrow-Odd's skald. Also the organizer of the Council of Skalds.

Halstein the Smith – Ansgar's grandfather and foster father. A smith of great renown in Midgard.

Harbard – A small troll (goblin) and wizard in the Down-Below.

Heimdall – The watchman of the gods. Incredible vision and hearing. Has appeared in Ansgar's dreams before.

Helgi Pike-Tooth – Styrgrim the Bear's second in command. He filed his teeth to be sharp and savage-looking, hence "Pike-Tooth."

Hemming – The Brotherhood's tracker, trapper, and forward scout. Incredible woodsman, but poor as a warrior. Ill at ease in cities. Doesn't even like to sleep in a longhouse when he can avoid it.

Hrolf – King Ragnvald's nephew, now King Hrolf since Ragnvald's death. Alfhild's main target in the past, who she failed to kill.

Hromund the Hard – One of two Danish champions loyal to Ragnvald and Hrolf during Alfhild's attempted coup.

Huld – A mysterious *vǫlva* (wise woman) who befriended Finnr and chose to come with the crew after helping them free the dwarf. Disappears often and without warning.

Humor – A raven who frequents Ketill's company.

Inga – Lejre's main brewer after her husband Lambi was killed by Lejre's troll. Distrusted all associated with Ragnvald and Alfhild before but may have had a change of heart.

Ingolf – Joined the *Sea Squirrel* crew with his sworn brother, Leif, shortly after Ansgar. Serious, stoic, dependable.

Innstein – One of the two shipwrights who keep the *Sea Squirrel* seaworthy. Brother of Utstein. The inside 'Stein. A bit shorter than his brother, but faster. Prefers to bet on long odds.

Jorun – A very pretty skald with Arrow-Odd's army. Prefers a hornbow as her weapon.

xKari Swifthand – Haldor's closest advisor. Tall and agile, always tense before battle. Saved Ansgar once by catching a spear thrown at him, a second time by shielding him from a goblin javelin, and a third time by distracting the lindworm that was crushing him. Killed in battle by the lindworm.

Ketill – A *galdramaðr* (wizard) known for his knowledge of runic magic and intensity. Expert archer. Former (very recent) alcoholic.

Kraki Bentleg – The elderly captain of the *Sea Squirrel*. Carries a bone club. Never wears armor and usually doesn't even wear a shirt. Despite his advanced age, he is still strong and is hard against steel.

xLeif – Joined the *Sea Squirrel* crew with his sworn brother, Ingolf, shortly after Ansgar. Silly, awkward, fun. Killed by Alfhild to power her spells.

Lyngbakr – Sea monster. When his back sticks out of the water, it looks like he is an island full of heather, and he uses this to lure sailors close and eat them.

Magnus the Red – Ansgar's first heckler and closest friend. Short with bright red hair and arms like iron. Not a great fighter in a shield wall but almost without a peer in a melee.

Moose-Frothi – Moose from the waist down (but with two legs), man from the waist up. Strong like a moose and sometimes sounds like one when he's angry, which is almost always. Brother of Thorir Houndsfoot.

Nanthild the Silent – Young Frankish woman who was kept as a thrall at the Danish court with her brother Ulfberht. Avoided ritual sacrifice by Alfhild when the crew of the *Sea Squirrel* intervened. Fought bravely in the Battle of Lejre but stopped speaking when her brother was killed in the same battle. Spends most of her time helping at the forge. Stronger than she looks.

Njord – God of the sea. Supposedly has very pretty feet. Husband to Skadi.

Odin – A god strongly associated with war, sorcery, death, and wisdom. Hung on a tree as a sacrifice to himself in order to gain knowledge. Capricious and fickle, yet charming and wise.

Ogmund (Eythjof's Killer / Tussock) - The son of Grimhild and a sorcerous king, Ogmund was birthed and raised to be a weapon for the Bjarmians to use against Arrow-Odd. A powerful sorcerer himself, Ogmund has feuded with Odd for generations.

xOlgram – Lejre's troll and principal thief of fermented beverages until Haldor and company arrived. Actually Alfhild's secret love child she planned to put on the Danish throne as her puppet. Killed by Ansgar as a mercy after having his arm ripped off by Haldor. Called Ansgar "cousin" at the last moment, which has confused him ever since.

xRagnvald – The previous Danish king and Alfhild's husband. Killed after being run down by Alfhild's demon boar in the Battle of Lejre.

Redbeard – Mysterious but charismatic advisor who introduced Arrow-Odd to Gardar and Sirnir and encouraged them all to become sworn brothers. Gives a lot of advice but is not likely to participate in battle himself.

Silfast – Owner of the mead hall where Ansgar first met Magnus and swore to join the crew of the *Sea Squirrel*.

Sirnir – A Danish jarl who has partnered with Arrow-Odd to pursue Ogmund Tussock. Also, Haldor's brother.

Skadi – Beautiful *jǫtunn* who married Njord. Good to call on if you're skiing or hunting. She prefers the mountains to his seaside home.

Steinvor the Slim One – One of two female skalds in Arrow-Odd's camp. Has been in many fights and has the scars to prove it. Interested in Ansgar.

Styrgrim the Bear – Ansgar's father and a man with a reputation for fighting. Mostly absent during Ansgar's youth and someone he wants to prove himself to.

Svein Helgisson – The biggest man on the crew of the *Sea Squirrel*. Bigger than Haldor and younger, but also fatter and slower. Knows Ansgar from growing up in the same village, where they both hated each other. Good fighter. Dumb as a rock.

Svipul – Ansgar's *fylgja* (follower). A spirit only he can see or hear. Outfitted like a valkyrie with armor and a spear. Hair so black it has a blueish sheen like raven feathers in the right light.

Tafi – Older Swede, now a Christian. He took over a monastery on Gotland when his teacher, Candidus, died.

Taika – Ansgar's Sami foster mother and grandmother. Wife of Halstein the Smith. Taught Ansgar some woodcraft and gave him a lot of good advice he ignored.

Thorir Houndsfoot – Mostly man unlike his brother, Moose-Frothi, only with a dog's feet. Less temperamental than his brother. Can run very fast.

Ulf – The *Sea Squirrel's þulr* (chief negotiator and diplomat). Formerly chief translator as well, but less so since Ansgar's arrival. Charming when he needs to be. Creepy voyeur at other times.

xUlfberht – Young Frankish man who was kept as a thrall at the Danish court with his sister, Nanthild. Avoided ritual sacrifice by Alfhild when the crew of the *Sea Squirrel* intervened. Fought bravely in the Battle of Lejre and was killed while protecting Ketill.

Utstein – One of the two shipwrights who keep the *Sea Squirrel* seaworthy. Brother of Innstein. The outside 'Stein. A bit bigger and stronger than his brother but not quite as fast. Prefers creative ways of getting people to make stupid bets.

xValborg – Alfhild's handmaiden. Trapped our heroes in Ragnvald's hall and set it on fire as the Battle of Lejre began. Crushed to death by a giant polar bear soon after.

Varg (Tiorvi / the Charmer) – Powerful jarl on Gotland, whose magic battle cow makes armies turn on themselves. Valborg's abusive father.

Vignir – Arrow-Odd's half-giant son. Though very young, he is much bigger than his father and wants to make a name for himself. Easier going than his father. Likes to joke with his men. A popular man.

Vilgrip Tyrsson – One-handed prisoner of Alfhild.

GLOSSARY OF OLD NORSE WORDS

Æsir – Group of gods living in Asgard, including but not limited to Odin and Thor.

argr – Cowardly, weak, unmanly.

berserkr – Literally 'bear-shirt' or 'bare-shirt.' Usually a bully who is overrated in martial ability but howls a lot and wears too many animal skins. Occasionally, a dangerous warrior who is hard against steel. Plural: **berserkir**

dísir – Supernatural female being with its own cult. This is a general term that may refer to a local spirit or spirits, or may refer to valkyries or the goddess Freya. Singular: **dís**

dísablót – Sacrificial ceremony for *dísir*.

draugr – A dead person who returns to harass the living. Usually this person was not well-liked in life. A ghost, but not in the sense of being a spirit, as they are fully corporeal; more like a ghost/zombie/vampire. Plural: **draugar**

drengr – A person of integrity and honor; a stalwart, courageous/brave person; a badass.

fornyrðislag – The meter of stories. A simple but effective poetic format consisting of eight half lines, each with two stresses, where one of the even numbered half lines contain a stress alliterating with the above half line. Example of two half-lines (stresses underlined):
This writer's blood
  blackens the page.

fylgja – A female guardian spirit. Not subject to worship like *dísir*, this kind of spirit usually follows families. Plural: **fylgjur**

galdr – Sorcerous incantation, spell, sorcery, magic, song (with magical connotation), charm.

galdralag – The meter of magic. Poetic format with the intent of casting or describing spells. Structure is *ljóðaháttr* with one to two additional long (three stresses, sometimes just two) lines. Example:
This writer's blood
  blackens the page;
Summoning the ink elves.
Crushing the keyboard warriors.
Whispering the unheard words.

galdramaðr – Sorcerer whose chief magical practice involves *galdr* and *galdralag*, focusing on linguistic aspects to cast spells. A wizard.

hamr – Shape, form, or skin.

holmganga – Ritualized duel for settling disputes.

hákarl – Fermented greenland shark. The worst food in the world.

Hávamál – 'Words of the High One.' Wisdom on how to live well delivered in verse, supposedly from Odin himself.

hnefatafl – Board game pre-dating chess, where one player tries to move his king from the center of the board to one of the edges, while the other player tries to capture the king.

hugr – Mind. Related to Odin's raven Huginn.

jǫtunn – Member of a tribe equivalent to the *Æsir*, but antagonistic to them. Frequently translated as 'giant' despite *jǫtnar* being of the same size as *Æsir* most of the time. Some are giant in size, but not all. Plural: **jǫtnar**

landvættir – Land-spirits.

ljóðaháttr – The meter of wisdom. Poetic format consisting of a full line of *fornyrðislag* followed by a third line, where the third line has three stresses (two of which alliterate). Example:

This writer's blood
　blackens the page;
　I hope it had an effect.

níð – Scorn or libel so strong, it could lead to the speaker's outlawry.

níðingr – Villain, traitor, truce-breaker; a person worthy of scorn.

níðstǫng – A pole carved detailing a curse against someone.

Ragnarǫk – Series of events involving the doom of the gods and the end of the world.

seiðr – Sorcery involving spirits used to work spells or for divination. Generally performed by women. Considered 'unmanly' despite Odin being its foremost practitioner. Possibly a victim of post viking–age sources' dislike for such magic.

útiseta – Sitting out in the open air for the sake of sorcery or prophecy, especially at night.

vættir – Spirits or supernatural beings, including but not limited to land-spirits, *dísir*, dwarves, and *jǫtnar*. Singular: **vættr**

vǫlva – A female practitioner of *seiðr*. Prophetess, wise woman, or witch, depending on the intent of the speaker. Plural: **vǫlur**

þulr (thulr) – Member of a court considered as a main speaker. Identical to Old English *thyle*.

þurs (thurs) – Giant, ogre, monster. Carries connotation of malevolence, but not necessarily large size.